# HOOLIGAN

By the same author

**THE LANDSBIRD**
**RETRIEVAL**
**RATCATCHER**
**BLACK ICE**

# HOOLIGAN

## A Novel

## Colin Dunne

W·W·NORTON & COMPANY
*New York    London*

Library of Congress Cataloging-in-Publication Data

Dunne, Colin.
Hooligan: a novel/Colin Dunne.—1st American ed.
p.   cm.
I. Title.
PR6054.U554H6    1988
823'.914—dc19                            88–12413

ISBN 0-393-02627-2

W. W. Norton & Company, Inc., 500 Fifth Avenue, New York, N. Y. 10110
W. W. Norton & Company Ltd., 37 Great Rusell Street, London WC1B 3NU

1 2 3 4 5 6 7 8 9 0

*For*
*The Boy*

# 1

It's not everyone who wants to have a hedgehog named after him. All in all, Charles Noble took it pretty well.

'What's your name?' I asked him, as the two of us leaned over the shoebox and peered down on it. There wasn't much to see. It looked like a tennis ball dressed to repel boarders.

'Noble,' he said, mistaking this for matiness. 'Charles Noble. And you're Joe Hussy, I gather.'

I ignored his outheld hand, and gazed down at the bundle of spikes. 'In that case, we'll call him Charlie.'

'The hedgehog?' He looked at his namesake, then at me.

'People give their names to battleships. Why not hedgehogs?'

'Do you know,' he began, his face softening with pleasure, 'I do believe I'm rather flattered. Might I ask why I am so honoured?'

'Because when you talk your nose twitches at the end, like his.'

His slim fingers briefly touched the end of his nose as a slight frown shadowed his face. 'I'm still flattered,' he said. 'Although by your reasoning, I should have thought that perhaps Joe would be a more appropriate name.'

This time it was my turn to look puzzled.

'You're something of a prickly little customer yourself,' he said.

I liked that. I wouldn't want to think I'd gone to all that

1

trouble to be awkward without anyone having noticed it. Prickly but proud, that's me. So this time I did take his hand.

Although, if I'd known the trouble both Charlies were going to cause me, I'd have evicted the pair of them there and then.

They both came into my life at the same time. I'd been for my evening run. Okay, so it's more of a lurch and a gasp these days, but it's my atonement for all the pints of bitter and plates of chips that I've stuffed down my throat during the day. It doesn't do a lot for the waistline but it helps keep the conscience in trim.

Most nights I vary my route, just to show that all that taxpayers' money wasn't wasted on my training. I came back through the allotments at the back of the garage and, as usual, when I got to within twenty or so yards of the road, I stopped, dropped to one knee, and had a look and a listen. Also – although, of course, this was quite incidental – it did give me a chance to try to get my heart and lungs from a gallop down to a nice manageable trot.

So there I was, half-kneeling in the scrubby grass beside the hedge which marks the boundary of the Hussy estates, waiting for my night vision to come in, and taking in the scene. It was the end of October, a clear night, silvered with moonlight and frost and crackling like tinfoil.

Through the bare hedgerow, I could see where the light from my room over the MoT bay shone dully on the tar-coated shack where Jamie lived. That, together with the four petrol pumps, was our mighty commercial empire. In Muswell Hill, we like to leave the flashier aspects of the oil trade to the Arabs.

I'd just got the drumming out of my ears and red mist out of my eyes when I saw an old Saab turn off the road and come crunching slowly over the cinders. I felt a certain grim sense of anticipation. Since it was a couple of hours past our seven o'clock closing, this was probably one of our quieter customers. They come in quietly during the night and empty everything from their ashtrays to their bladders all over the forecourt. Or if it was any of the noisier night-callers – the ones whose girlfriends shriek like bald tyres on tight bends – then they weren't any more welcome either. I've got all the memories I

2

need without any aural aids, thank you. What I really wanted to see was what Jamie did to them. She packs a fair old punch does Jamie, and I'd seen her curtain flicker at the sound of his engine.

Just as I saw a man, tallish and thinnish, unfold himself from the car, I heard this shrill piping noise not a yard from my face. My nerves jumped, but I stayed still. Bipeds apart, north London is relatively free of dangerous animals.

I didn't need to refocus my eyes. Through the leafless twigs, the car's headlights lit up the bottom of the hedgerow and I caught a glimpse of a bright black eye. Then the lights dimmed and it was gone.

'Put those bloody lights on,' I shouted, rising, so I could see over the hedge.

The man only hesitated for a moment before bending back into his car, and in that second I heard a scuffling among the grass. When the lights came on again, the hedgehog had gone.

'Lost something?' The driver's head and shoulders came over the hedge.

'You'll lose something if you tip any of your old rubbish on my forecourt.' That was Jamie, arms folded, in her doorway.

'I can assure you. . .,' he began, but her cold-chisel voice chipped in again.

'And we don't want none of your old johnnies neither.'

This time he could only manage a splutter.

'It's all right Jamie,' I called out. 'I'm here.'

'Aye.' She sounded less than reassured. 'Give us a shout if he's any bother.'

'Not exactly welcoming,' he said.

'For Jamie, that's gushing affection.'

'In that case, I'm glad that I'm looking for a Mr Hussy.'

'Shhh.' I waved him down. I could hear the piping noise again. Stooping, ears and eyes tuned, I inched my way along the bottom of the hedgerow. Three or four yards along, tucked into a nest of leaves in the bottom of a smelly compost heap, was the hedgehog. Dead.

I'd never seen a dead hedgehog before but most animals – us among them – go under a basic change of structure when the last breath departs. This one was flattened out. Its front paws were stretched out before, its back paws behind. Even so, drawn out like that, it would still barely cover a cigarette packet.

'Found something?'

'Only a corpse.'

I heard his whistle of amazement as I touched the dead creature's head with my finger. Cold. Stiff. If that was the one I'd seen up and running a moment ago, it had certainly faded fast. I reached over the flopped out body to where I could see the pale leaves were pressed into a dip. It was warm to my chilled fingers. By this time I was down on both knees and when I heard a movement behind me I knew that the car driver had come through the gap in the hedge.

'Ah, that sort of corpse. . .'

'Ouch,' I whipped back my stinging fingers just in time to see what I'd taken for another bundle of leaves quiver and shuffle into a new position. This time it was my runaway, balled up at the back of the nest.

'Is that one alive?'

'Alive and pricking, as they say.'

'I should be careful, if I were you.'

'Should you now. And I should be quiet if I was you.'

'I was about to say,' he went on, sounding only slightly wounded, 'that these might be of some use.' He was removing a pair of heavy driving gloves.

He was right. They did take the pain out of the operation. With him holding doors open for me, I was able to get the ball of spikes up the stairs to my room. He watched the hedgehog while I emptied a box of car shampoos.

He came up with items of folk memory about hedgehogs liking bread and milk. Even my larder can run to that, so we lowered it into the box with him and watched. That was when I noticed his nose twitched when he spoke. My visitor, that is, not the hedgehog. His twitched all the time. Which was how he came to be christened and we got introduced.

'And apart from hedgehog mercy missions, what brings you here?' I'd decided some time ago that a furtive night-time urinator wouldn't lend his gloves to save God's little creatures.

'You are Joe Hussy?'

'I am, may the Lord forgive me.'

'Excellent. I'm hoping you will help me to find my brother.'

'Your brother?'

'Yes.' I could feel his eyes on my face, searching. 'Richard. Richard Noble.'

I didn't react. 'And why do you need my help to find your brother Richard Noble?'

He sucked in a deep breath and I saw his face go pink with emotion. 'Because he has become a traitor to his country, Mr Hussy. He must be caught, and then I shall have to see what I can do to help him.'

# 2

He had sideways hair. Once I'd got him sat down with a glass in his hand, that was the first thing I noticed.

Sideways hair is just about the last visible insignia of upperclass rank. The governed – we, the shirtless ones – usually run our hair from front to back. If we bother to train it at all. Those who do the governing – the shirted ones, I suppose – don't. They have sideways hair. It goes from ear to ear. And Charles Noble's sandy hair, running from a parting that appeared to have been placed with an axe, fell down to the ear below, and higher up charged straight over the top to the far ear.

Even with that clue, he wasn't easy to categorise. More tall than short, more thin than fat, a spare figure with the clear eyes and skin that betoken a blameless life and a dull conversationalist. His clothes yelled a message I couldn't quite interpret.

You could've got the whole lot – soft tweed sports jacket in a grey herringbone, grey flannels, cotton shirt, club tie – for two hundred quid, but I've seen thousand-guinea suits that weren't as beautifully pressed and cared for. His shoes, brown brogues, glowed like a port drinker's nose.

But behind his air of eager innocence, I thought I detected a bedrock of authority.

When he did tell me what he was, I could've kicked myself for not guessing. He was a housemaster at a public school in Surrey; it wasn't in the Eton-and-Harrow belt, but even so it was somewhere around the top of the second division.

I got the gasfire sizzling and sat him down in the best – or, since he was a schoolmaster, better – of the two fat old prewar armchairs I'd picked up for ten quid in a junk shop. He had a scotch and water in which he insisted the scotch was outvoted about a hundred to one. So I had one with the ratio reversed so that, between us at any rate, we achieved some sort of moderation. You've got to think globally these days, I believe.

'Your brother?' I prompted him, as soon as we got comfortable. 'The traitor.'

'Well.' He wriggled and swallowed noisily. 'It could be that there's some perfectly innocent explanation. Perhaps I'm jumping the gun.'

'Could be.'

'I mean, Caroline insists there's nothing to worry about.'

'She'd know, I expect.'

'Who? Caroline?'

'Who else?'

'Do you know her?'

'No, but since she – along with the rest of the world – knows a hell of a sight more about this business than I do, I'm inclined to take her word for it.'

His nose twitched again. 'I take your point, Hussy. You really must forgive me. The whole thing's so . . . well, embarrassing. I do think you could be a little more helpful.'

I looked at my watch. 'It's an unhelpful sort of time.'

'I know, I know.' With both his hands, he massaged his eyes and face. A sudden weariness had hit him.

6

'What does he do?' I thought that might help him to get cranked up.

'Richard? He has a stable and riding school. Down on the south coast near Ditchling.'

'Is that right? Now I wouldn't have thought that a riding school would give a lot of scope to an ambitious traitor, but that just goes to show how little I know about these things.'

He managed a smile that came out more as a wince. 'Perhaps traitor is too strong a word, Hussy. Perhaps he's merely gone mad.'

'I know how he must feel.'

He made an apologetic gesture with his thin well-tended hands. 'Have you seen any of the rioting on the television news programmes over the past few weeks?'

I nodded. You could hardly miss it. It had died down in the last two weeks but before then, it had run like fire through the city slums. Like fire too, it had blazed up without warning, raged for a few hours or days, then died away. A day or two later, again following no pattern, it had burst out once more. First, Liverpool. Then Deptford in South London, and Stoke Newington in the north-east of the city. They'd had one bad night in Birmingham, and then it had switched back to Liverpool with even greater savagery.

Young males, West Indians on one side and coppers on the other, had fought desperate battles with all the sophisticated armour of street warfare: shields and snatch squads and CS gas against petrol bombs and broken paving stones, knives, and axes. And fire. Whole streets were gutted by flames; houses, shops, cars.

Charles Noble drew in his breath and let it go in one long whoosh. 'I'm afraid that my brother was mixed up in all that.'

'Not, I take it, while wearing a blue uniform.'

He shook his head. 'No. I very much regret to say that my brother was one of the rioters. One of the ringleaders, I suspect.'

'How do you know?'

'Television.' He was beginning to talk freely now. 'I was watching the early evening news while the boys were in prep and I thought I caught a glimpse of him. You can imagine how I felt.'

His jaw clenched as he faced up to the unhappiness of that moment, even in memory. 'I simply couldn't believe it. I mean, Richard. My brother. Not possible.'

He locked his hands together and leaned forward. I put him in his mid-thirties: because of the job he'd kept a sort of first-form freshness.

'Naturally, my first thought was that I was mistaken. I was able to video the later news, however, and I was obliged to accept that there was no mistake. It was Richard. Beyond all doubt, I fear. After that, as you can imagine, I watched every single news bulletin. I saw him on two subsequent occasions. I managed to video both those too. On one of them' – at this he shook his head and kept his eyes down on his twinkling toecaps – 'he was throwing a petrol bomb. A Molotov cocktail the newspapers call them. He threw it at some policemen.'

I got up and went over to the cardboard box. Charlie had wriggled down into one corner and was asleep. But the bread and milk had gone.

'Is he all right?' Noble called over.

'I think so.' I went to the window and stood looking out. A car followed its own lake of yellow light along the road and up the slope until it went out of sight around the corner. Jamie's light was still on.

'It happens.' I turned to face him. 'Young feller, new ideas, doesn't like the way all the BOF's run the world, decides to move things round a bit. Nothing wrong with a bit of revolution. Clears the air something wonderful, I always think. Can't say as I blame the lads who do it either.'

'BOF's? Can you clarify please?'

'Boring Old Farts.'

'That's exactly the sort of thinking I am constantly trying to root out in my boys.' Poor old Noble was aghast. 'Substitute crude abuse for any attempt at a real rational process, and then employ it as justification for killing policemen. Can you seriously endorse that sort of behaviour?'

'Not your man who goes out to kill a policeman for the

pleasure of it, so to speak. But it is the sort of accident that's apt to happen when some of these young enthusiasts set about changing the ground rules.'

He was upright and uptight by that point. 'I'm afraid I can't be as philosophical as you evidently are about these things.'

'I dare say not. Do you know, I often feel that public opinion wouldn't be half so inflamed if it was only the odd traffic warden who got knocked off the twig.'

I looked down at the indignation burning in his face. 'What I'm trying to say, in my somewhat informal way, is that young men who get seized by ideals do get mixed up in the most godawful messes.'

He gave me a long steady look. 'Hussy. My brother is 32. He was an officer in the Gurkhas before he had his own business. He rides to hounds. He's a useful club cricketer. Caroline's father is a highly respected surgeon.' He leaned forward and his eyebrows came down hard over his pale blue eyes. 'He's simply not the sort of chap to be involved in that disgraceful nonsense. Do you follow me?'

When he put it like that, I suppose I did. The Pony Club, as a rule, keep well clear of insurrection.

'You have a point,' I said.

'Thank you,' he said.

'Now, will you be having another glass of the coloured water while you tell me all about it?'

If I'd been a schoolmaster and Charles Noble had been one of my pupils, he'd've got none out of ten for doing his homework. The only thing he seemed able to remember about his brother with any clarity was his name.

He wasn't sure of the date when he'd vanished. He couldn't quite remember when he'd last seen Richard himself, and he wasn't sure who had seen him last. When I suggested talking to Caroline to fill in the details, he advised me against it: 'she's under a lot of stress, as you can imagine.'

About all he could give me was a reasonable description. Richard was five-ten, thirteen stone, fit, sandy hair, fair complexion, grey-green eyes, and – you should've seen Charles' lips purse as he said it – a sloppy dresser. A sloppy ex-officer? His lips tightened up another notch but he didn't respond beyond that. Again, he wasn't absolutely sure how long Richard had been in the Army, or even when he'd left.

'You're sure he is your brother?'

'We lost touch for a while,' he said, almost stammering on his own explanation. Then, as though to prove he knew, he suddenly slapped his leg in a self-conscious gesture of self-reproach. 'His moustache. Gosh yes, he has a moustache. Fancy forgetting old Richard's moustache.'

Then there was the minor technical difficulty of how I was supposed to find Richard Noble if he didn't want me to approach his wife. Where did he think I should start?

'Chap like you shouldn't have any problems.' He gave me a knowing smile.

'Chap like me's got hundreds of bloody problems. Where'd you get my name?'

'I think I saw it in an old magazine ad.'

As he was going, he shook my hand enthusiastically on the doorstep. 'I have every faith in you, Mr Hussy. I will, however, be doubly grateful if you can find him quickly. I want to get to my brother. . .' he paused, as fat tears rose in his eyes, and took a deep breath before carrying on. '. . .before it is too late.'

After he'd gone, I shoved some baked beans into a pan with an onion studded – now there's a gourmet word for you – with cloves. Shoes off, feet above gas stove, bowl in hand, thinking about Mr Charles Noble and his missing brother. An urban guerrilla. Would he want to give it all up because his big brother was cross with him? Seemed a bit unlikely. Still, I could try.

For one thing, I could try because looking at rusty exhausts is low on artistic fulfilment: believe me, you can't see the world in a blob of Castrol. But more than that, I wanted to try because of this gawky housemaster.

And that ad. It must've been an old one, before I packed in my security business. I'd put it in a magazine that only goes out to a restricted circle of interested parties. I wouldn't have thought housemasters were on the list, not unless they're getting a very rough class of pupil these days.

# 3

That's the trouble with being a single-parent family, you've got no one to turn to. The next morning Charlie was looking pale. Well, his spikes were looking pale, and he could hardly raise them when I put my hand in the box. Hedgehog droop – a serious condition.

A pal in a newspaper library in Fleet Street put me on to a hedgehog hospital in Aylesbury. I didn't believe it either until I rang through and spoke to a Sue Stocker; and yes, it was true, they did run a home for battered hedgehogs.

'Is it weaned?' she asked. She sounded a merry sort of woman, which was perhaps as well in that line of work.

'He won't say.'

With that sort of good-natured impatience that you develop if you deal with half-wits three times an hour, she said: 'Look in his box for green droppings and a damp patch.'

That had me looking a bit pale. I've got up to some funny stuff in my time but checking hedgehog droppings hasn't been among them.

A minute later, in a small voice, I reported that I'd found both.

He was weaned.

Then she told me what I had to do. Like get rid of the bread and milk which, despite popular legend, isn't good for them at all. I cleaned the box out, filled it with torn-up paper, and nipped out to the shops to get some puppy food. I put that on the old ashtray in the corner, water in another, and gently lowered Charlie back into his new home.

'What you doing with that damn fleabag indoors?'

It was Jamie. Gruff voice, pug-ugly face, five-foot nothing of Yorkshire grumpiness. Her birth certificate said she was female but with those oily baggy mechanics' overalls you'd never have known. Or without them, for that matter. That didn't bother me though. To me, she was a combination of sister, brother, best-friend, and sergeant major: she didn't have to be a sex-bomb too.

'Ignorance, Charlie, blind ignorance.' To Jamie, I repeated what Sue Stocker had told me: 'Hedgehog fleas aren't interested in people. Can't say I blame them, personally.'

'Couldn't make this place any muckier anyway,' Jamie said. She could be awful hard on her mates, could Jamie, but she still had the old twenty-two carat heart. She knelt down next to me and when she saw the way I was vaguely stirring the paper about she bashed my arm to one side. 'Hellfire Joe, you're that cack-handed. Get out of the road, I'll do it. Who was your visitor then?'

'Another dumb friend. Wants someone to find his brother.'

Her eyes, tucked deep into their creases, flicked up at me, then back down again. 'Does this mean you're off again?'

Between jobs, women and other assorted disasters, Jamie's garage – or garridge, as she called it – was my home. She didn't like it when I moved on.

'No chance. I might take a look at it though. You know, ring around, talk to a few people.'

'Aye. Like last time. Well don't think you're coming back here all shot up again. Bloody daft mick.'

Because my father was a Dublin man and I was raised in the stout-dark streets of Kilburn, Jamie was apt to blame my bloodline for any shortcomings in reasoning power.

'No no, it's just a couple of inquiries, that's all.'

'So you say. What's that for?'

12

I was filling a hot-water bottle from the kettle. 'Charlie. Got to keep him warm, he's only four or five weeks old.'

'I'll do that.' She almost snatched the bottle off me and, after a quick glance around, pulled my second-best shirt off the radiator and wrapped it round the bottle. From her overall pocket, she pulled one of the thick gloves she used for working on the pumps on cold days and pulled it on. She'd come fully equipped for hedgehog handling. Gently she raised him and slipped the covered bottle beneath him. 'Do they like that?'

'Love it, my expert tells me. The warmth persuades them to unroll. Like women.'

'Fat lot you'd know about either,' she said, and there wasn't much I could say to that: she knew my record.

Half an hour later I heard a car sounding its horn somewhere downstairs. At first I didn't bother, but after ten minutes, when it was still bleep-bleeping away, I went down to have a look.

By the pumps, a small crowd of half a dozen or so had assembled to watch the detergents take over the world. It was an astonishing sight. A wall of foam, ten-foot high, was slowly being squeezed out of the entrance to the car-wash bay. Invisible, somewhere in that vast bank of bubbles, was the man sounding his car horn.

'The old trick, eh Jamie?'

'Aye. Never fails.' She was standing in front of the main group with her arms folded, and as close to smiling as she ever gets, which isn't all that much like the real thing but quite moving in its way. 'In he comes, smart bugger, accuses me of turning down the soap to make more money. So I gave him a free go and turned it up. Right up.'

Inside, the horn was still going. 'I'd say he's had his money's worth now, Jamie?'

'Aye, I dare say.' She went in the office and switched it off. Then she turned a hose on the foam and washed it down. The cleanest blue Rover in Britain rushed out and sped away up the road, and all we saw was a glimpse of purple-faced embarrassment and rage. The spectators managed a small cheer.

'Rather juvenile, don't you think, Hussy?'

I knew the voice without turning. 'I like to think so, Cringle,' I said. 'I try to keep myself young.'

# 4

KOCH, KLAUS

Born Munich, 2 January 1951. Father Ernst Koch, lecturer in economics; mother, Adelheid, housewife.

Recruited to Red Army Faction while a law student in home town in 1972, possibly by Inge Viett, leader of 2nd June Movement. In revolutionary legend, Koch is credited as author of Faction slogan: 'Don't Argue – Destroy.'

Throughout seventies, involved in bombings, bank raids, assassinations in campaign to break 'the imperialist feudal system'. Worked in five-man groups scattered throughout Germany. In 1976, led armed raid on Moabit prison, West Berlin, to free Inge Viett. At various times in early career, attended training camps run by Cuban Direccion de Inteligencia and Popular Front for the Liberation of Palestine.

Helped set up Revolutionare Zellen (Red Cells) to exploit social conditions: unemployment, strikes et cetera. Activity in this area undocumented, but significant. Believed to be instructor in incendiary bomb attacks expressing revolutionary support for striking British miners, 1984.

After arrest of Christian Klar, October 1982, Koch established as senior terrorist leader. In early eighties, moved to Paris to revive Action Directe. Worked with Cellules Communistes Combattantes in Belgium in attempts to weld single European front for all terrorist groups, as outlined by Renato Curcio (Italian Red Brigades); limited success. Worked with Jean-Marc Rouillan.

Arab connections stem from early training with PFLP, later action with Lebanese Armed Revolutionary Factions. Koch has been link man between FARL, RAF and Action Directe. In mid-eighties, worked as adviser/instructor/mercenary with new men of Islamic Jihad, Beirut-based Shi'ite groups, and the Shia Muslim fundamentalists of the Hezbollah movement. Later, Cuba as training advisor: sinecure.

*Personal notes.* Koch has charisma, intelligence and ebullient charm. Has great authority among the Arabs. Middle-class in tastes and lifestyle. Enjoys expensive hotels and restaurants. Prides himself on gourmet tastes.

Koch enjoys glamour status and privileges. Now avoids messy mass actions. Prefers solo operations, top-level assassinations, et cetera, calling for analytical planning and expertise.

Hires out.

Uses Dragunov sniper rifle.

May be disenchanted.


When I finished reading it, I looked up to say something, but Cringle was standing by the window, looking down on to the forecourt.

'Do you enjoy this life?' he asked.

'It's the only one I've got.' He gave one blink, which on the Cringle scale of emotional reaction was pretty high: it meant irritation.

One of my few talents – and even he wouldn't dispute it – is that I can, in moments of inspiration, really annoy Cringle. And, as the Bible tells us, it is criminal to neglect a talent. I joined him at the window. Jamie was sweeping the empty forecourt. Since the shampoo cabaret, it had quietened down. 'You know what I mean,' he said. He made a gesture to the scene below. 'Not very busy. Not very exciting.'

'Oh I don't know. It can be fun when Jamie gets her teeth into a customer's leg, as you've just seen.'

'Good for business too, I see.' He turned away and picked up the report from the table. 'Well?'

'Well what?'

'Fair summary?'

15

'It ought to be. I wrote it.' It wasn't a computer print-out, which meant that Cringle must've edited it and then had it typed up, so I would only see what he wanted me to see. Even so, I recognised some of my own golden phrases.

'Anything to add?'

'Like what?'

'Anything. What's that "May be disenchanted" supposed to mean, for one thing? Bit opaque for an official report, isn't it?'

'Bit of an opaque impression really.' I perched on the edge of the table and thought about that. It was just under a year since I'd written it, and there was a lot more detail Cringle hadn't bothered to bring.

'Like I say, he's getting on. He's not a kid any more. All that youthful fervour that drove him out on the streets in Munich, that's all gone.'

'Motivation now?'

'Money.'

He raised his eyebrows. 'Over-simplification, surely?'

'Well. Money, and maybe professionalism. What you've got to remember with these lads is that although they're just pictures on the wanted posters here, in some large chunks of the world they're heroes. Free drinks, lots of girls. But he's well clear of thirty and that's geriatric in his business.'

'And yours, Hussy.'

'So maybe he's had enough too.'

I saw Cringle run his eyes over me and the room then, in the same way he had over the garage. I knew what he was thinking. Serves him right. Perverse little sod, always wanted to paddle his own canoe, look what's happened to him. Same old Cringle. Same young Cringle, more like. He was a good five years younger than me but he was so rigid with self-control and self-discipline that if he'd tried to laugh he would've snapped in two. So would I: out of shock. Also, he had this sawn-off way of speaking to me like a dog-handler talking to an untrainable mongrel, so I was tempted now and again to score a point or two for the mongrels.

Not too many, mind. What I always had to remind myself was that he was a section head of that Unit in Whitehall that I

16

used to work for. Anything that was too criminal for the coppers, too dangerous for the Army, and too disreputable for even the politicians, that was what we got. He'd put his name to operations that would get you socially shunned in Dartmoor, and people like me had gone out and done them. It didn't bother him because he was convinced he was going in first wicket down for God's eleven. He'd never forgiven me for leaving and he still tried to re-recruit me now and again. Occasionally I even let him: but not for long.

And here he was again, spotless in suede jacket, fawn roll-neck sweater, whipcord trousers and desert boots. Sunday. If he was wearing that lot, it had to be Sunday. And if he came out on a Sunday, asking me questions about a carefully doctored report I'd done months ago, it had to be something important.

He folded the extract from the report and put it into his pocket. 'Did you have any conversation with him?'

'Quite a lot. He's a chatty sort of bloke. Don't you remember that business about the pies?'

'Of course.' He was still trying to imagine what that meeting had been like, so he could see if there was anything in it for him. 'Rather odd, wasn't it, Shi'ite house in Zikak Blat, informal chats with one of their best men?'

'Got to pass the time somehow.' It was no use telling him that we were like a couple of boxers: we might go at it like hell in the ring, but outside we could quite happily gas away about the price of gloves and the lousy gym conditions. Bank clerks, boxers, assassins – they're all jobs.

'What exactly did you talk about?'

I cast my mind back to that stinking cellar, the unbelievably black night outside, and the gunfire. 'Pensions. We talked about pensions and retirement.'

'I expect you did,' he said, and suddenly I realised he thought it was another of my pointless jokes. If he didn't want to believe it, that was up to him. In any case, he was on to his next question.

'How'd you rate him?'

'Koch? Good. Very, very good.'

'If you were hiring, would you go for him? In preference to

Ramirez Sanchez and Sabri al Bann, for instance?' Only Cringle would insist on giving terrorists their proper names.

'Carlos isn't playing at the moment, not since he got married and set up home in Damascus, I think he's lost his taste for it. They say he's stuffing himself with grub again. Abu Nidal's technically pretty useful, got all the right connections, but that Hindawi business set him back. Also, he's a nutter. Yes, I think I'd go for Koch. He knows what he's about. He can set up an operation himself. Logistics, documentation, research, the lot. He could move into the Savoy tonight and pass as a business-man. He's a first-class shot, too. Course, it would depend where.'

He ignored that one. 'Ever see that chap you pulled out of West Beirut?'

'Clarky? No, not lately. Jesus though, the last time I saw him he was going great guns with the one hand there. He reckoned he could do everything except take the top off an egg. I think he's got an artificial one now.'

'Good, good.' He was a chilly swine, was Cringle, but I think he did care in a refrigerated sort of way. 'That Finch woman you took up with – what happened to her?'

That was the last job I'd done for him. A grisly business up in the north, and I'd come out with a lovely lady called Victoria Finch. I'd spent six months helping her run a wine-bar in South Ken until one morning I looked at her and wondered what I was doing there.

'I left.'

'And this Jamie woman?' He moved to look out of the window again. 'You're cohabiting, I take it.'

'If you think that, Cringle, your intelligence is as bad as ever.'

He turned back to me, his thumbs locked behind his back. 'If we located your old friend Herr Koch, would you want to help him find that early retirement?'

I shook my head. 'Not me. Why are you so interested in him suddenly?'

His square serious face gazed into mine. It was only then I saw it filled with anxiety. 'Why? Because he's here, that's why,

18

Hussy. Not the Savoy, but you weren't far off. He spent the last four nights at Claridges and we only missed him by an hour.'

'He'll be out by now.' I found myself trying to console him.

'Doubt it, sad to say. We hear he's over for a job. What sort of job would bring a man like that here, Hussy?'

There was only one answer. 'A bloody big one. Bloke like that, moving him around, protecting him, you've got to bung a lot of people. It's expensive stuff. And these days he'll be very pricey himself. It's not just that he's good at his job, which he is, but someone like Koch gives credibility to his employers. You have him on your books, people'll take you seriously. The top half-dozen of these boys transfer like footballers, everyone wants them, there's a lot of cash involved.'

Cringle's face was marked with distaste. He refused to think of them as real heroes. 'Like?'

I could only guess at that. In the trade you hear talk, but it's mostly wild. 'You want him to leave Cuba where he'll be the king of the midden, lots of booze and dark ladies and it's nice and safe, that'll cost. Crossing borders, very exposed stuff, that'll cost. And to come here, where security's not bad, that'll cost more. And if they want him to get out that fancy Dragunov and start popping off, it'll cost again. Think of a figure and double it. You're talking about a superstar really.'

'Superstar?' he repeated, with contempt. 'He's just another thug.' I felt quite sorry for Cringle when I saw how gravely his face was set. Having someone like Koch dropped on your manor was enough to alarm anyone. But he was wrong if he thought he wasn't a superstar.

He was. He'd told me so himself.

# 5

The deal was that we could have Chris Clark in exchange for seven Shi'ites the Israelis were holding, and a selection of Fortnum's excellent pies.

Admittedly the pies came as a late addition to the package that had been worked out between an Amal lawyer in Beirut, who was the standard go-between in these things, and London and Tel Aviv. After a week of whispering in corners, the deal was stitched up, and they asked me to take delivery of Clark. Two hours before take-off I was asked to take the Fortnum's pies. Cringle couldn't even manage a smile as he handed the bag over to me. Then I was pretty certain I was going to see Koch. His appetite for good living, yachts and five-star hotels was known to include the Queen's grocery store.

Clark hadn't been with the Unit long and his Beirut trip wasn't much more than a real-life training exercise: sort of on-the-ground analysis with gunfire sound effects. Anyway, he got picked up. It was a bad time. It was in that summer when all young enthusiasts from Islamic Jihad took to making videos of themselves to say how proud they were to be giving up their lives for the liberation of their lands and people, and then driving a truckload of explosives up to the nearest Israeli or American. 'We are soldiers and we crave death' was one of their slogans. I remember telling Clarky: 'I'm a soldier and I crave death, but only other people's.'

Then they all started joining in, putting on their berets and trimming their moustaches before announcing that they were slaves of God and would see that the enemies and collaborators had their hands chopped off.

Poor old Clark more or less walked into it all, and it wasn't even his fault. He got a taxi-driver who took a wrong turning, panicked, and decided to ingratiate himself by denouncing his passenger as a spy. It was just Clark's bad luck that he was so near the truth – although that's an accusation that could apply to half Beirut. Anyway, that's how these things happen: courage and skill aren't worth a damn if luck's agin you.

He'd been picked up by a bunch of Shi'ites who, because of all this heady suicide stuff, were hysterical even by Lebanese standards. They were attached to the Hezbollah movement, the pro-Iranian lot, and by and large they weren't very amenable to reason, Western-style. The suit-and-tie boys got on to it quickly of course. Since we had nothing to trade other than the secrets of the doner kebab business in West Kensington, the Shi'ites decided to use him as a lever to retrieve seven of their men who were prisoners of the Israelis. Arms were twisted in embassies around the world, and Israel, none too willingly, agreed to cough up. The Amal lawyer, who was about the only Shi'ite who was halfway reliable, promised he'd deliver. But there was no hint of Koch until I had to load up with Fortnum's best.

That also explained why a deal had been possible. At that time, the Shi'ites were carving up anybody who passed and, frankly, we didn't give Clarky a chance once they'd got him. But the German had a reputation for being . . . well, not exactly merciful, but at least straight. Or as straight as you could be if assassination is your business. Anyway, we reckoned he wasn't particularly drawn to wanton slaughter.

I sat in a pool of sweat that was half terror, half humidity, while a silent young man who looked about fourteen drove me into Zikak Blat in West Beirut. That's Shia Muslim country, and no place for a lapsed Catholic. The transport didn't inspire confidence either. No one mentioned the previous owner of the rattling Toyota estate, but judging by the position of the bullet-holes he wouldn't be wanting it back.

In a deserted street of bombed-out houses, I was toppled out and rushed down crumbling concrete steps into a hot black stinking cellar and left with one instruction: Wait. I did. For two hours, sitting on a canvas chair, beside a wooden box which was presumably some sort of table. Even there, underground, I felt the night drop like a portcullis, and I fastened my cuffs and neck against the insects. Everything's bloodthirsty in the Lebanon.

The heat washed around me in the dark and the stench was appalling. And all I had to do was to listen to a little Beirut night music.

The crack and rattle of small arms fire. The clatter of machine guns. The steady bump-bump-bump of the mortars, and the double thump of the RPG's. From time to time the thunder of artillery would shake the building I was in so that I could hear the loosened plasterwork falling to the floor. But at least the artillery wasn't whistling: when it's whistling, it's coming your way.

Then I heard the sound of motors roaring up the dust road. Brakes, doors, and voices outside, and the door to my cellar opened slowly to let in a powerful torchbeam. It pryed into every corner, a stiff accusing finger of light, before finally settling on me, or – more accurately – my Fortnum's bag on the box beside me.

'Ah, excellent,' a voice said, and, to my surprise, he turned the light around so that it shone on himself. 'Koch,' he said. 'Now we both see. That is fair.' He moved across and put the light on the box-table so that it threw its light more evenly around the room.

He was all the things I knew about him: mid-thirties, light to medium build, dark, balding early, thin features. Our records had him down as a snappy dresser and from what I could see, even in that dungeon, he looked as though he'd just strolled in from a round of golf. His jeans looked tailored and the short-sleeved shirt was the sort you see around the classier club bars. To complete the image, over his shoulder he was carrying a beautiful and very expensive Ram golf bag.

It was the sort the pro's use, leather, green with a white trim, and the one club protruding from the top was wearing one of those comical little woollen socks, also in green and white, with a matching pom-pom on top. Only of course it wouldn't be a club.

He set the bag down carefully, so that it was propped against the table, and then picked up the Fortnum's bag and took out one of the pies. After brushing the box with the side of his hand, he laid the pie down as though it was a sacrifice. In a way it was. In a second, he had an open-bladed knife in his hand and with two quick movements he cut a wedge. He held it up in the light to look at it.

'Chicken and ham. Very very good.' And he bit into it.

I sat there quietly, watching this man who, in our trade if not among the headline-writers, was probably the world's top terrorist, as he munched his way through a chicken-and-ham pie, while guns grumbled and chattered in the city.

He finished off the last piece, brushed his finger and thumb together, and gave a murmur of appreciation. 'I could not tell you how long I have been thinking about a Fortnum's pie.' He moved his dark eyes to me. 'When I heard you were coming in. . .'

There was a knock on the door and some more shouting outside. Three strides took him there; he flung it open, shouted some Arabic, and then slammed the door and came back to the table.

'These bloody people,' he said, shaking his head. He opened the bag and looked inside it. 'Pork. Is there a pork pie?'

'I think so.'

'It does not matter. One at a time we will eat them. You?'

At times like that you don't turn down gestures of friendship. I stood up and, facing each other in the heavy gloom, we ate our slices of pie together. A pie of peace, I thought, suddenly wanting to laugh.

'These people are crazies,' he said, after a minute or two. 'What am I doing here? I should be in Europe where you can live a civilised life. This place. Bloody flies. Bloody filth. Bloody madmen. I am mad too to be here.'

'Oh, I dunno. Some of my best friends are Druse.'

'What is that?'

Instead of trying to explain, I asked him about Chris Clark, and he waved it aside as though it was an incidental. Clark would be here soon. He was all right, he was unharmed. Then he said one of those things that sprang from his own life and so accurately touched the same point in mine that for a moment it was like a bridge between us. 'Clark is lucky,' he said. 'He still has the passion. What happened to our passion, eh Hussy? Where did it go?'

When he saw my face he knew he'd hit the button. But what really mattered to Koch was the pie, and, oddly enough, this contact with me: somehow it soothed his homesickness and aggravated it at the same time.

'I am right – you are Hussy?' he said, after his second slice.

'I am.'

'High-risk? That is what they say.'

'That's a joke . . .'

'No no, no joke. I hear things. You are good. What do they pay you?'

'About the same as your father.'

'Paid like a teacher! You!'

'Come and see the boss for me when I'm after another wage rise.'

He laughed. 'I will go with you. I will.' He touched me on the sleeve. 'That is bad. Men like us, we are like the best footballers or the best pop-singers. We are the superstars.'

As I smiled, he gave me a gentle punch in the chest. 'It is true, it is true. We are the best at this job. We are the best in the world and so we must be paid like the best in the world. Not like schoolteachers. I tell you, you come here, here with me, and I will see you get very good pay. Lots of money.'

'And no Fortnum's pies.' I flicked my eyes towards the noise outside to get him back to business. 'And the crazies.'

That was enough to get him going again. 'Ah, those people.' He banged the side of his head, and suddenly I realised that he trusted me. To him we were two professional men discussing the conditions of our trade under difficult circumstances. Like a couple of French chefs in a motorway cafe. In a funny way, I felt quite privileged.

From outside, some distance away, there was a burst of automatic fire. He cocked his head towards the sound. 'They fire guns like spraying paint. No aim. No skill. Feu de joie.' He ducked his head and closed his eyes, while miming firing an automatic weapon all around. He stopped and opened his eyes and added: 'And I am supposed to train them. How can I? These people are not true craftsmen. We are the craftsmen and the superstars. With us, every bullet has its job. Yes? More pie?'

'The Dragunov?' I gestured towards the pom-poms sticking out of the golf-bag. That didn't surprise me. What he was saying was true, certainly about himself. Snipers are craftsmen, artists almost. You won't catch them using weapons that fold or come apart. Once it's zeroed they leave it alone, which was why a golf bag was perfect for a long, heavy rifle like that.

A white smile flashed over his thin dark face. 'You like it?' I didn't need to reply. He could see from the look on my face that, along with a lot of other people, I rate the Dragunov as the best sniper rifle in the world. He lifted it almost entirely out of the bag, so I could see the wooden stock and the curved magazine, and then lowered it gently back.

'Ten rounds?'

'That is right. But not the Kalashnikov 7.62 calibre bullet. No no.' He made an impatient cancelling motion with his hand.

'Not enough power?'

'You understand. I use old rimmed cartridge from Mosin-Nagant. Bigger bullet, bigger charge, more power, more accurate. You understand. Now, more pie.'

Watching him cut it again, I could see what our records didn't show. He was encased in a steel shell of calmness and confidence. He had been there and back many times, had Koch, and he knew there was nothing around the next bend that was going to bother him. That's a knowledge that gives you great power, but you have to pay for it with innocence and idealism. It's more expensive than it might sound.

'So, you come and work with me. We both get rich.' He lowered his voice a fraction and enunciated his words with exaggerated lip movements. 'They are crazies, but very rich crazies. People like us, they pay . . . huge. Huge pay, is that right?'

'I'm with you. The problem is, Koch, that I might have to shoot the wrong people.'

He gave a sharp, bitter little laugh. 'Wrong people, right people. They all think they are the right people.' He did the

25

chest tapping again, to underline that we were both in the same game. 'Sometimes I think they are all the wrong people. Maybe we are the only ones who are right.'

'The superstars,' I said.

'Yes yes.' He licked his fingers, before going on: 'Tell me, what do people like us do in England when they . . . er, stop?'

'Retire?'

'Retire. What job then?'

'I know one who runs a pub near Hereford. Another runs the tuck-shop and teaches the cadets at a public school. Another's a doorman.'

'Doorman? You will be a doorman?' He really was aghast.

'If I pass the exams.'

He ignored that. 'A doorman, a pub man, it is mad also. I make lots of money, go and live in the sunshine. South America maybe.'

'But no pies.'

Quite seriously, he replied: 'Hussy, you will bring the pies. Right? You will be the pieman?'

'I'll be the . . .'

If we hadn't been so busy talking, we would have noticed the silence outside. But it didn't strike me until I heard the scream. More of a scream-sob really, a gulp of noise that sounded pure animal in the quiet and dangerous night. Koch was out before me but not by much.

Chris Clark was on his knees where he'd dropped, facing a flat-topped rock. Around him, the terrorist band – a dozen or so, beards, bandanas, jeans – had stepped back, and even in the dark I could see the wildness that brightened their keen young faces.

All the light seemed to gather on the shining silver blade of a knife in the hand of an older man, one in the traditional headdress. It looked a parang-style weapon with about a twelve-inch blade. The light gleamed on that blade, but all the eyes were on Chris Clark. He was on his knees, swaying and still trying to keep his balance. It wasn't easy, with his left hand around his right forearm as he held the stump aloft to try to stop the blood pumping out.

On the white rock in front of him, his hand crouched, fingers still bent. If it hadn't been for his signet ring, it would've looked like a well-fed spider.

After a lot of shouting, Koch and I got Clark, his stump dressed after a fashion, in the back of the Toyota. He stayed stretched out where we'd put him. He couldn't talk properly and his breathing sounded ragged, from the shock. So did mine, come to that.

The Shi'ites had backed off into the buildings when Koch began to tell them what he'd like to do to them, in several languages. That showed how sure he was of himself and of his authority. Whatever the strength of their religious convictions they weren't going to argue it with him. To me, all the time we were sorting out Clarky, he kept apologising. It was the crazies. The mad people.

I had to drive back through Beirut. When I started up the engine, Koch put his face almost through the open window. 'You know how I feel. This is not professional.'

'Certainly isn't.'

'I am sorry. I can do nothing.' I switched on the lights and caught a last glimpse of his lean face. It was full of genuine concern. He'd been doing it so long that he even believed in an etiquette of terrorism.

'It happens,' I said.

'Thank you for the pies.'

That was the last time I saw him. Until that mayhem in the Rockies.

# 6

The best I could get out of Jamie was a Ford Capri which belonged to a fizzy-drink rep who'd left it for an MoT. If he noticed the extra one hundred and fifty miles on the clock, I could always say I got lost on the road test.

I liked our slice of North London. I liked our fifty-yard strip of black cinders, the tarred shed that was the office and Jamie's home, and two rooms over the MoT where I lived. I liked the way the shopkeepers turned the pavements into open-air bazaars with their rows of secondhand chairs and heaps of discarded washing-machines, and the churches that had been converted into bingo-halls for those who didn't want to wait until the hereafter for their rewards. It was the sort of area that helped a man to keep his ego under control.

Still, just for a change I was quite glad to drive across London and out into the country. That journey's like peeling a sociological onion. In South London, you pass the layers of the dark and dispossessed. Then the terraces and semi's of the honest toilers. Next you're among the two-dustbin homes where salesmen and dentists wear sleeveless jackets and buy retrievers in the hope they can pass as gentry. Finally you're down into Sussex where the politicians and the pop-stars go when they've plucked their fortunes off the punters.

The downland is the most feminine stretch of country in Britain. Soft, mysterious, shaped by sweeping curves and sweetly secret hollows. It was in one of those that I found The Wheatstones, a long, low, brick-and-flint farmhouse, partly shaded by the leafless trees and sheltered by the long flank of a hill at the back. The house looked as though it had been built about twenty minutes after they'd finished the hill.

Instead of driving in, I stopped by the peeling white-painted gate which hung open. What Charles Noble had said was fair enough. Richard's wife Caroline would be distraught if he'd upped and away like that. How long ago did he say? Weeks, maybe months? It was one thing deciding to ignore his advice and hop in the car; it was another going up to the door and knocking on it. Like most men, I'm not at my best confronted with women's tears.

In the mirror I could see the sun shining in the sky like a misty brass ball. I could see it again in the diamond panes of the

28

house windows ahead. All around the countryside was dank and silent.

I heard her before I saw her. The unhurried clop of heavy hoof after heavy hoof on the road, then the same hollow noise muffled by the soft ground of the verge. I got out of the car to wait. The horse rocked slowly into sight, her figure moving to the rhythm of its slow progress.

She passed me, with the horse blowing plumes of breath into the late October air, and went through the gate with only a movement of the hand to acknowledge me. I followed. At the same easy gait, she crossed the gravel drive to the yard at the side of the house where, without a word, she dismounted and handed the reins to a man with a thin cigarette nipped between his lips.

As I sauntered over, she turned to face me.

'You don't like horses?'

'Does it show?'

'You stayed well back. Are you actually afraid of them?'

'I like them well enough in their place.'

'Which is?'

'On the screen at my bookies, well in front with a bundle of my dough on its back.'

Her laugh wasn't the laugh of someone practising for widowhood, and she didn't look ready for the role either. With one hand, she ripped off her riding hat and with a startling show of colour, a gleaming metal sheaf of fair hair fell suddenly to her shoulders. Her face was square, her eyes wide and grey, and her skin had been polished by the country air. Genetically she was a Saxon milkmaid, but she was a milkmaid who'd been to finishing school.

'Caroline Noble.' She peeled off a thin riding glove and I held her cool muscular hand. 'And you?'

'Joe Hussy. I've got to be honest with you – I'm making a few inquiries about your husband's disappearance.'

'In that case, Mr Hussy, I really must ask you to leave.'

That did shake me. Not so much being turfed out, which isn't such an unfamiliar sensation as all that, but the way she did it. On her lovely face there wasn't a sign of distress or despair, only a slight frown. I was a passing irritation, no more. But at least that gave me the nerve to push on with it.

'You don't seem to be terribly upset about your husband vanishing like that?'

I thought perhaps I'd put the question a bit too strong, until I heard her cool reply.

'Don't be so silly, Mr Hussy. Richard hasn't disappeared, and the only thing that I find remotely upsetting at the moment is someone like yourself being a nuisance.'

'Can we talk about it?'

'I don't wish to appear rude but there really is nothing to talk about.' Whatever she saw in my face almost made her smile. 'Honestly,' she added.

Behind her, an older woman appeared in the doorway of the house. She was wearing a broad-brimmed hat which nearly touched her shoulders and a soiled coat which trailed around her ankles. In New York she'd have been a bag lady but in the English countryside she had to be lady of the manor. The rich, like the other lot, are always with us and it's amazing how alike they look.

'Caroline, don't keep your visitor standing out there, it's so terribly damp this morning. And if you're not quick, the tea will be cold.'

'Thanks mummy.' As she looked at me, she gnawed her bottom lip and took a deep breath.

'Come on,' I said, starting towards the house. 'Tea's getting cold. You don't want mummy wrecking the furniture in rage, do you?'

Head back, she gave that laugh again. 'You obviously know mummy. Tea, but that's all.'

As I followed her in, I thought I might have to revise my opinion about riding. Anything that could persuade her into those tight ivory trousers had to be regarded as in the public interest.

From what I've seen of country-house life, the horses get the best of the deal. At least the stables are warm.

The drawing room was like a half-furnished aircraft hangar.

Around the room, which was about one-third carpeted with patternless rugs, slumped a few spavinned chairs and sofas waiting for a kindly furniture doctor to put them down. In chipped gilt frames on the wall, and through a fog created by centuries of smoke and grime, faded huntsmen chased an invisible fox. Logs smoked sullenly in a pile of ash. Caroline gave them a kick, without much success, before taking off her jacket and tossing it over one of the maimed sofas.

At a table by a long window, she poured two cups of tea and brought them over to me. 'We have Ceylon in the morning.'

'What, all of it?'

She grinned. My jokes didn't bother her. There wasn't much about me that did.

'So who sent you? Or aren't you going to tell me?'

'I thought I wouldn't. Not just yet, anyway.'

'I thought you wouldn't either.'

She drank from her cup with a good healthy slurp and her intelligent grey eyes watched me over the rim of the big blue-and-white breakfast cup.

'And you're not going to tell me about him?'

She shook her head. Her hair moved like a solid sheet. 'Tell you what,' she said, mischief all over her face. 'You tell me about Richard. Let's see how much you know.'

That wasn't exactly how I'd planned my pitiless interrogation, but as an alternative to silence it was something.

'He's thirty-two, five-ten, weighs around thirteen stone. He was with the Gurkhas and now he runs this place as a riding establishment. Bit of a cricketer, country gent, rides to hounds . . .'

I had to stop then. I couldn't hear my voice above her laughter. It made her shake so much she had to put her tea down. 'That's awfully funny, that really is. Richard will howl when I tell him.'

She looked up at me. 'Oh, this must seem terribly rude, but you've no idea. Riding to hounds! Richard! And what was it you called him – a country gent? That's too funny for words, it really is.'

'He doesn't ride to hounds?'

31

She sobered herself down to reply. 'No. Richard hates all that. He doesn't have anything to do with the riding and he's not in the least social. As mummy is frequently reminding us.'

'So what does he do?'

She gave me a steady look and thought for a moment before replying. When she did she chose her words carefully. 'If you really don't know, there can't be any harm in telling you. We run this place as an outdoor centre. I do all the horsey things, Richard teaches survival and adventure courses. Shouldn't you have found that out before you came?'

'It's beginning to look that way, I must agree. Was I right with the rest?'

She gave me another old-fashioned look. 'You could have guessed his height and weight from that picture.'

It was on the table by the tea tray. It was a home snap blown up to a five-by-ten, black and white, in a broken silver frame. He was standing on a pebble beach in swimming trunks, holding aloft a surfboard. She was right. You could've guessed his height and weight from the picture. You wouldn't have guessed much else, it was so blurred.

'Does he have his moustache here?' I held it up to the light but still couldn't see.

'He shaved that off years ago!' Now she was beginning to sound puzzled as well as amused.

'Looks like I've been given a bad steer.'

'A very bad steer.' Her face was hard now, her voice cold. 'I think you should tell me who you are.'

'I'm a private detective and I've been engaged to make inquiries about your husband who has gone missing. But you tell me he hasn't, so can I see him perhaps?'

'He isn't here.' She saw my face and her square jaw went even squarer. 'He frequently isn't here. He has to go off on a lot of courses and things.'

'For weeks?'

'Quite often for months.' She gave an exasperated blink. 'I know where he is, I know what he's doing, he isn't missing and I don't need any private detectives to find him. I do hope that is quite clear.'

She walked back to the fireplace and kicked the logs again, this time with some venom. They hissed and spat, then subsided once more into the ash. She wiped the toe of her boot on the rug.

'I think you ought to go.' I could see her face in the mirror above the fire.

'I was beginning to have that feeling myself. Thanks for Ceylon. By the way, I was thinking about that . . . isn't it Sri Lanka now though, or am I thinking of Taiwan? Do you have trouble with that? Jesus, geography's got like musical chairs. Every six months they move round and take a new name. If you go on a long bus journey these days, they've changed the destination before you even get there . . .'

I kept this stream of rubbish up all the way back to my car. I turned in front of the house and as I drove out she stood watching me, without waving. That was a right cock-up and no mistake. Not only did brother Charles know sod-all but what he did know was wrong, and if she was a bereft wife unable to face the world, then I was a vestal bloody virgin, and there were a few explanations due: all from Mr Charles Noble, and all due to me.

Just then I had to slow and pull partly on to the verge to let a car travelling towards me get past. It was a white rust-scabbed Ford Escort, and as it went past I saw the driver's face in profile. There was something about it that made me slow, then stop. He'd gone by quickly, I hadn't seen much, but it still made me stop. I recapped. The driver – I couldn't see the passenger – was youngish, male, dark, foreign-looking, with a hooked blade of a nose. Somehow it wasn't a face you'd expect to see down a Sussex country lane. I drove up the road to a farm gate and swung round.

By the time I got back, the Escort was outside the front door. The front door wasn't quite closed. As I moved softly up the steps I could hear the voices from inside.

'No, I adamantly refuse to look at any photographs.'

'It will only take a second, madam.' Whoever he was, he was a Scouser. That's one accent you never mistake.

'I've already had one man here saying he was a detective . . .'

'What, today?' He was on to that quick.

'One minute ago.'

'What you make of that, Cracker?'

A new man's voice, also Liverpool, only this time as thick as the Mersey, replied: 'The Capri. Passed us coming in. A detective did you say, miss?'

'That's what he said. A private detective.'

The first man cut in there. He was the one who was setting the pace. 'I wouldn't bother about that, love. Like I said we're from the Merseyside Police and all we need is for you to take a quick shufti at these pictures just to make sure it's your old man like . . .'

He stopped dead as I pushed the door open and stepped inside. What I saw made me spread my feet to get evenly balanced. He was some sort of odd race mix: you could see Africa in his thick pad of hair and his lips, but his thin curved nose and accentuated cheekbones were pure Arab: his skin colour was a beautiful pale black that was almost an iridescent blue where it caught the light.

He was wearing a scuffed brown leather jacket, blue jeans, and a collar and tie. He was two or three inches taller than my five-foot-six, and from the way he dropped his shoulders when I came, I wasn't the only one weighing up the talent.

The other one, standing one step behind the boss, looked as though he'd been chipped from cement with a blunt chisel. Short, solid, cropped hair, bushy sideboards, with a neck twice as thick as his head. Even in his denim jacket you could see his arms were so muscled that he couldn't keep them in to his sides. To get like that takes about a century in the gym.

'Who's this?' It was the black, the one who spoke mild Mersey, who snapped the question out to Caroline without taking his eyes off me.

'A friend. Don't stand in the doorway, Joe, come in.' She said it with such warmth that for a moment I felt like an old friend. She'd obviously decided that, out of her present spate of callers, I was the least undesirable.

'So you don't feel as though you can help us?' He paused with some photographic prints in his hand. He was having one last try before he pulled out.

'No, I don't think so.' She moved round to face me. 'These chaps say they're from Merseyside Police.'

'I expect they'll have shown you their ID.' I smiled cheerfully at one, then at the other. They weren't any sort of cops. No one's invented disguises that good.

The black Arab sighed and began to slide the photos into a large brown envelope. 'We don't show our cards to any berk who happens to ask, pal. Still, since the lady can't help us . . .'

'Perhaps I can.' I held out my hand. Two things were worrying me. First, if he went out of the door I didn't fancy my chances of stopping him. Secondly, if he did, I wouldn't get to see these photographs.

'Do you know Noble?'

'Ask Caroline.'

'Does he?'

I saw a good-humoured smile move his mouth. I thought I'd put him on the spot: instead, he was enjoying the guessing game.

'Yes, of course he does,' she replied, abruptly enough to sound genuine.

This time his whole face softened into a friendly smile. He relaxed. 'In that case, sir, I'm sure we can sort this business out in a jiffy. I do apologise for being a bit offhand a moment ago, I didn't quite realise who you were, walking in like that. Now here we are . . .'

As he spoke he slid the prints out of the envelope again. Instead of holding them out towards me, he kept them close to his body, about waist height. That meant I had to lean forward and down a little to get a look at them, and even as I did it I thought perhaps I was being out-manoeuvred.

That was what I thought. I knew it for sure when I saw his sky-blue jean-clad knee come rocketing up towards me and felt the steel grip of his fingers on the back of my neck. Mistake, I thought. Bad bad mistake, as I studied every thread in the denim which was on its way to iron out my nose. Moved nose to one side, which regrettably meant offering ear for high-speed knee. Knee seemed unworried by this change of plan, as did shoe which drove twice into my stomach as I lay on the floor. Kicking, quite pointless. Pain allocation was totally filled by exploding head. Stomach pains secondary and distant. As was female screaming, rush of cold air, glimpse of sky, car engine starting and howling away into the distance. Cold tiles. On cheek.

'He may have a fractured skull, of course.' Mother's voice. May have? Only may? Skull has been sliced into quarters and taken away in a wheelbarrow, madam.

'The poor man. Help me get him in here, mummy.'

The first whisky didn't do a thing. The second located an ember of life. The third fanned it into feeble flame.

'Don't you have any Irish whiskey?'

'You're feeling better, I take it,' Caroline said.

'And in a well-run establishment like this, I'm disappointed, I've got to say it.' There was a cushion or something under my neck and as I went to sit up properly, thunder and lightning filled my head. 'Christ, what the hell happened?'

'He sort of smashed your head down on his knee, then he kicked you up and down the hall.' Caroline was kneeling beside me holding the whisky.

'I'll call the police.' Mummy, standing behind her daughter, sounded quite firm. Dazed as I was, I couldn't think how to stop her. The last thing I wanted was a visit from the local expert on hen-rustling or whatever crime they had round there.

I was relieved when Caroline glanced up quickly and said: 'No, don't do that, mummy.' When she turned back to me, her hair fell forward like a gold fan. 'I don't think you're very dangerous, are you?'

She laughed. She was entitled to. I must've looked about as dangerous as a maimed mouse. That was how I felt too.

'Not unless his knee hurts as much as my ear, no.'

'Was it Richard on the photograph?' She put the question almost too guilelessly.

'I didn't see.' That was enough. I didn't particularly want to say that I had caught a glimpse of the picture, and that it showed a broad-faced young man sitting at a table with what

36

looked like a thick stick in one hand and a packet in the other.

I didn't want to say because I couldn't be sure the man at the table was Richard Noble. I couldn't be sure that the stick was a length of copper piping either, or that the packet was weed-killer. But I was dead certain that the two together can make a very nifty home-made bomb.

'You do look awfully groggy,' Caroline said, as I clambered back to my feet. 'Why don't you stay here a little longer?'

I steadied myself by holding on to her shoulders. For a moment the dizziness was so bad that I thought of suggesting that the two of us should lie down until it passed.

'I've got to go, I'm expected.'

'I'm sure you could ring your wife.'

'It isn't a wife.'

'Or whoever then.'

'That's the problem. It's a hedgehog.'

# 7

When I got back to Muswell Hill, Jamie was on her hands and knees in my bathroom. She was rummaging around in the bottom of the airing cupboard.

'This is what they like best,' she said, turning her beetroot face up towards me.

'But is it what I like best?' She'd shovelled my clothes out of the way to make room for Charlie, whose box was pushed against the cistern, on the floor.

After worrying about him all day, she'd dug out the number of that woman in Aylesbury, Sue Stocker, and telephoned her. I bent to look down into the box. Nothing was happening in there that I could see. Charlie had burrowed down into the torn-up paper and wasn't stirring. It didn't look good.

'He could be all right yet, that woman said,' Jamie went on. 'She reckons they're right hardy little creatures and she says they've got a very fierce will to live.'

'Let's hope so.' But there was no sign of it then. To my surprise, I found myself worrying about him.

Jamie sat up and rubbed her face with the back of her hand. Oil smeared across her brow. She squatted there for a full minute looking down at the box, concern all over her funny, mucky, pushed-in face. She caught my eye and immediately scowled.

'Well. Don't stand there like cheese at fourpence. I've done four MoT's this morning while you were out gallivanting. Get yourself down to that garridge and I'll go on the pumps for a change.'

That's what I loved most about Jamie: the way she said 'garridge'.

Since the security work fell off, I'd been working more or less full-time for her as a mechanic. Unqualified, of course. I always tried not to do any serious harm to any car I took on, which is more than most garages can say, but I could only do the basics. Jamie was a real mechanic. She could tell what was wrong with an engine by listening. She loved it too, but when her lumbago played her up – and I could see by the way she straightened that she was having a bad day – then she was glad to get on the pumps for a rest. And also to have a chance to give the customers a bit of a savaging.

While I was down the workshop, I had a think about those two Scousers. With its history as a port, you did get some weird mixtures of race in Liverpool. Many of them had been there for generations, so they ended up with the same thick accent and the same quick wits and fists as the natives. Smoked Irishmen, they used to call them. When I'd walked in, it was the pale black who'd handled it. What impressed me was the way he'd done it. I know that my five-foot-six of leprechaun charm isn't all that terrifying at first sight, but when I walked through the door he didn't even break his stride. There he was impersonating police officers and God knows what else he had in mind and my arrival hadn't even given his nerves a flutter. The heavy – Cracker, was it? – had been riding on his ticket.

When I got back inside, I rang up Jim Cassidy, a crusty old mate who's been stuck on the lower twigs of the Special Branch for years. He explained to me that the computerised police records must never, under any circumstances, be used for personal inquiries. I said that I went along with that. What's more, I said that I wouldn't ever embarrass him by asking him to do that. He said that was just as well, because he couldn't and wouldn't do it. We both said we realised how important it was to observe the individual's right to privacy in a society where there was a constant danger of information being centralised and put to improper use. Then we both had a good laugh and he asked me what I wanted.

Once I'd told him it was about this bloke who was hanging round my daughter, he said fair enough. 'She fancies him and you don't, eh? That it?'

'Bit of a waster, I reckon.'

'You should bloody talk.'

I'd only just put the phone down when it rang again. It was Charles.

'What an elusive fellow you are to be sure, Hussy. I've been trying to get you all day.'

'I went to see Caroline.'

His voice hardened. 'Caroline? Look now, Hussy, you know perfectly well that I asked you not to . . .'

'She was fine. In great form.'

He sounded guarded. 'In what way, exactly?'

'Well, she says Richard isn't missing, that he's away on either business or pleasure, she didn't say which, and she's quite happy about it.'

There was a pause, and when he did speak it was in a clear and decisive tone.

'Jolly good for her. As you know, I asked you to leave her alone because she was so distressed about the whole business. Obviously she's made up her mind to put on a brave face for the world, and good luck to her. Bags of character, that girl.'

'She doesn't want him found, Noble. And I must say she looked a pretty serene young woman to me.'

He spoke slowly and with patience. 'These ladies of ours can be wonderful actresses when the occasion demands it, you know. She says she doesn't want him found. Of course she says that. She is very much in love with my brother, you don't really expect her to admit what he's up to.'

'It was a very convincing performance.'

'And that's why I say good for old Caroline. I admire loyalty, however misplaced. Actually, now you mention it, in some ways I think she's perhaps persuaded herself it hasn't happened. You know, simply refused to face the facts.'

I thought about that. It was a common enough reaction from someone faced with an unpleasant truth.

'Anyway,' he went on, 'you can make your own mind up about Richard and his assorted nefarious activities. I found an interesting paragraph in the *Telegraph* this morning that I'd like you to see. We've got these videos of the news programmes too. Veronica and I thought perhaps you might take a bite with us. Tomorrow any use?'

It would have to be at the school house, he said, because he was combating a fierce outbreak of smoking among the boys. He said it with a sort of cheerful zeal that made me shiver a bit. Puritans always make me nervous.

'Before you go, your brother hasn't got a moustache.'

'What do you mean, he hasn't a moustache?'

'You said he has, and he hasn't. Or so his wife says.'

'Hasn't he really?'

'He shaved it off.'

'How extraordinary, I never noticed.'

'He shaved it off years ago.'

His laugh crackled in the earpiece. 'Good Lord, my own brother too. Even by my abysmal standards of observation, that is distressingly remiss. As I recall, it was a singularly unpleasant growth, and I suspect I have been avoiding looking at it. I can only say thank goodness.'

That was the first time I felt it – the invisible wires that connected the two brothers. That was the time to get out, before

40

I got tangled up between the two of them. But I didn't know that then, and when I did it was too late.

One thing about all that training, it does last. At ten minutes past five that night – or next morning, I should say – I moved from sleep to waking as quick and clean as a snapped match. I held my breathing steady and undisturbed. That was the first giveaway of waking. So I lay quietly, breathing steadily, half-opening my eyes to adjust to the light, and listening for whatever it was that had triggered all my alarm systems.

The bedside clock told me the time. Ten past five. All over the world that's the time they come for you. When the heart's slowed to a limp and the human soul itself is in limbo. When night is cold and dead and day hasn't begun to move, and your metabolism is stuck somewhere between last night's pint and the next day's bacon sandwich.

And the funny thing was that the same face kept slotting up into my mind: hook nose, half-smile, the pale black I'd met at Caroline's. I don't know why. God knows there are enough people left alive who'd like to see me otherwise, but his was the face that kept clocking up.

Then I heard the noise and I knew why my personal burglar alarm had rung bells. It wasn't one of the standard night noises, like an off-course juggernaut shaking the pans on the shelf or the baby shriek of one of the foxes that live on London's dustbins. It was a careful, furtive, determined sound, and it made me shiver and my scalp tighten. What was it? Someone picking putty off a window frame. Someone working a knife under a catch. Someone persuading a mortice lock to turn back into its housing. It could be any of them.

Whichever it was, it was coming from the kitchen, on the other side of my living room. By this time I had my eyes open and could see enough by the street lamp through the window to know that my bedroom was clear.

So quietly I hardly heard myself, I slipped the duvet aside and moved to the door. Again I heard the noise. It was in the kitchen. Crouching in the half-light to keep below the usual line of vision, I slipped through the door and into the living room. It

41

was clear. Tiptoeing across the room, I froze as a small crash came from the kitchen. I even recognised it as the plastic rubbish bin going over – I'd kicked it over so often myself. Dear God, either I was being turned over by the worst burglar in the world, or it was someone who was so confident he didn't care who woke up. Again, I saw the same face.

Now that annoyed me. I smacked into the door with my shoulder and did three fast steps, crouching again, to get behind the front door. There was light enough through the glass panes for me to take the room in at one glance.

Empty.

The only furniture was a spindly table and two chairs that wouldn't hide anyone. Then my spine crawled as I heard the urgent scraping again, only feet away from where I huddled.

The plastic bin was on its side. Cans and bags and kitchen rubbish were spilling out on to the floor. As I watched, fascinated, a dark round shape which was at first still, suddenly began to move.

It was Charlie, with his head dipped into an empty tin of puppy food. Around his back legs trailed the paper I'd shredded so carefully for his nest. Good old Charlie. He'd obviously picked up on the advice they gave to that bloke in the Bible: he'd taken up his bed and walked – and frightened the bleeding life out of me for one.

I slumped down against the door on the cold tiles and laughed out loud. Charlie was going to make it after all.

# 8

Cassidy rang back the next morning. I heard the phone as I was dragging my body up the stairs after taking it out for a morning stumble around the block. That's about the only way I can do this health stuff: if I think of my body as an old dog that's had a few bad handlers, I feel better disposed towards it. Anyway, I heard the phone but that was all. At that moment I was halfway up the stairs with my lungs about to explode and my head swimming with the red mist, so I wasn't rushing anywhere.

I dragged the body up the last few steps, sat it down, tipped some fruit juice into it and tried to stop thinking with yearning of the days when breakfast was three fags and a coffee. I was about to convince myself that a three-mile run meant I was morally entitled to a bacon sandwich when he rang back.

'Joe?'

'Yeah. S'me.'

'Gawd you sound terrible, cock.'

'I've been keeping fit.'

'Seriously? Don't sound like it's working. You're breathing like you got miner's lung. 'Ere – you don't wear them stripey leg-warmers, do you?'

'The leg-warmers, the tights in a sort of eggshell colour with navy satin shorts to tone and headband . . .'

'You having me on?'

'Did you turn anything up?'

'Tell your girl to stay well clear, Joe. Bit of a waster? He's one of the fucking bomb boys with Rich Pickings, that's all.'

I gave a whistle of surprise down the mouthpiece. 'Maybe he's one of the weekenders.'

'Don't kid yourself, he's a star is this boy. You know what Rich Pickings are all about? Crime, strikes, riots, they're into

43

the bloody lot. And I 'ate to tell you this, Joe, but your girl's little darlin' has been up at the sharp end slinging petrol bombs. The lads've only managed to lift him a couple of times – obstructing, threatening behaviour – but the off-the-record stuff has him as one of their top boys.'

'Got an address?'

'Here somewhere, 'ang about. Yeah, squat in Liverpool. Toxteth, you know, coonsville. Highly bloody salubrious round there.'

He'd pulled the file of parking tickets too, as I'd asked him, but he plainly regarded that as small change after what he'd told me. Under protest, he read it out to me, then quickly went back to what he'd been saying before.

'You know about Rich Pickings, do you?' He thought I hadn't got the message.

'Kick-the-fuzz brigade, aren't they?'

'No they bloody ain't. They're one hundred per cent trade-tested bloody shitehawks, and serious with it. This last lot of riots, it's all down to Rich Pickings. Birmingham, Brixton, you name it, cock, and they're in there at it. Cut their fucking teeth on street crime, they're pushing hard to get into the industrial end, and word is they've got international connections so they can go for the full terrorist bit. Take my word for it, they're not joking, this lot. Tell your girl she's gotta stay home and make her dad's dinner.'

'I'll do that, so I will. One thing, Cassidy, who's that bloke who's the boss of Rich Pickings?'

'That darkie?'

'Half-darkie, isn't he?'

'Winston. No surname. Just Winston. After Winston fucking Churchill, I expect. He's a Scouser, bright boy they reckon, the one that holds it all together. Why they don't give his name to one of your old mates with instructions to give 'im a heart attack, I don't know.'

'Trouble with this country, Cassidy.'

'Let 'em all piss on us, don't we, me old cock.'

Afterwards, I went and stuck the kettle on and waited for it to boil. Noble's little brother was big in Rich Pickings, and

Winston was down in Sussex calling on his wife. One thing was for sure: if Cassidy was right, and if it was on the computer it had to be right, then Richard Noble was well beyond amateur-night-out status.

I splashed the kettle on to my extra-strong teabag and took my mug over to the window. A big Renault swept up to the pumps and after about ten seconds the driver gave two impatient bleeps on the horn. Promising.

Rich Pickings wasn't just trouble: it had a philosophy of sorts. They claimed that the millionaire had no more right to his mansion and his Rolls than the pauper. That was the theory. In practice, they urged the paupers to grab their share. Burgle the mansion, and if you couldn't nick the Rolls then at least make sure to run a rusty nail along its nice shiny coachwork. They enthusiastically advocated mugging old ladies, so long as they were middle-class and upwards old ladies.

Those who participated in the social order, which seemed to cover anyone from the cops who protected it to the old chap who got an OBE for running a sub post office, were dubbed 'system paupers' and marked down as targets. At first, everyone said they were too extreme to take hold in Britain, and a few years ago they would've been. But they'd keyed into a generation of city youngsters, mainly the blacks and the unemployed, who only caught glimpses of the good life in telly commercials. To them, it made sense. No doubt about it, if you had revolution in your heart, Rich Pickings was the team to be on.

The Renault horn beeped again. The window came down and I could see a middle-aged face with purple jowls that had seen a lot of lunches. Tailor-made for Jamie. As she came rocking over the forecourt, I opened the window so I could hear.

'I'm in rather a rush and . . .'

'Excuse me, sir,' she said, in her posh voice, which was always a danger sign, 'but are you a Frenchman by any chance?'

'No, matter of fact, I'm not . . .'

'In that case,' she said, her voice suddenly switching to a bellow, 'get your hand off that fucking horn.'

Dinner with the Nobles wasn't unlike the night I spent waiting for Clarky in West Beirut. You could hear all this metalware going off and you knew the night sky was full of it, and you couldn't help but wonder if any of it was going to come your way. They lived in a sort of domestic Lebanon, and several times during the evening I thought I'd got in the line of fire.

Veronica – his wife, that is – was cast as the militia, and poor old Charles was the nervous citizenry. She kept up a steady bombardment of shot and shell while he sat twitching, wondering what was going to hit him next.

Two things I learned very quickly about Mrs Noble. One was that she wasn't very happy, and the second that someone was going to pay for it. At a guess, I'd say it was going to be Charles; for a moment, when I arrived, I feared it was going to be me.

'Charles,' she called over her shoulder as she saw me on the step. 'Your little friend is here.'

'Don't bother opening the door any more,' I said. 'I'll just slip underneath it.'

Charles, looking about as relaxed as a rabbit in a greyhound stadium, appeared in one of those striped aprons that men put on when they're playing at chefs. 'Giving Veronica a bit of a rest,' he whispered. 'She's been somewhat tense lately.'

If she was tense, she was certainly prepared to share it. 'You will realise, of course, that I am older than Charles.' That was one of her earlier remarks and it had layers of meaning that I could only guess at. 'Only two years, in fact, but of course he looks much younger.'

With his boyish manner and sideways hair, he looked ten years younger. In a way she looked more masculine than he did. Her black hair was piled in a clumsy bun on top of her head and her meaty face was marked by channels of disappointment.

In a gown of floor-length velvet, she looked out of place in her own home. It was one wing of the school building, a cheerful place of sagging chairs and worn rugs and books that actually

46

showed signs of having been read. Two table lamps warmed the place up with a soft yellow light that made the amateur watercolours of the North Downs glow like Renoirs. From upstairs and through the thick walls, I could hear the occasional sound of the young savages tearing each other to pieces in preparation for life in government and the city.

'I don't suppose you have experience of boarding schools, Mr Hussy?' she said. That was to let me know that she'd detected my lack of a classical education.

'They were very popular round our way,' I said. 'Only we called them Borstals.'

Charles attempted a brave chuckle. 'From what I hear, the two institutions have a considerable amount in common.'

After dinner, she sat quietly while Charles ran through his videos of rioting from television newsreels. Sadly, it was nothing new. Dark streets suddenly ablaze with the frightening light of fire. Police drumming truncheons on shields. Harsh voices echoing in cold streets. Rush, scatter, re-group. When it happened in the States in the sixties, we smugly said it couldn't happen here: we were wrong.

'That's him!' Charles stopped the tape and ran it back. We both leaned forward to see more clearly. From the shifting mob facing the police and the camera, one man ran forward. You couldn't see his face because he was wearing a Palestinian-style headdress. His arm went back and a blazing bomb looped through the black sky. Just then his headdress unwrapped and Charles froze the picture there.

'Richard, that's him.' In that light, at that distance, all I could swear to was that in a mob that was mostly black he was white. But Charles was adamant. 'That's Richard, isn't it darling?' he said, turning to Veronica.

She was sitting behind us, smoking one cigarette after another. 'Oh yes, that's your delightful little brother.'

There was more. Each time he'd freeze a picture of the street rioting and point out one man who he was sure was his Richard. As Cassidy had said, he certainly was one of the star performers. Finally, he showed me a cutting from yesterday's *Telegraph*. It was a report of some cases which had been left over from the last set-to in Bristol. Noble was listed among those given a suspended sentence.

'So why don't you nip up to Liverpool and see him?'

Charles was nodding in anticipation before I finished the question.

'I wouldn't have the foggiest idea where to find him or, for that matter, how. And I would like to know what he's up to before I go poking my nose in. Wouldn't you say that's a reasonable precaution?'

That sounded fair enough.

Then his wife spoke. What she said was addressed to me but aimed at her husband. It made us both sit up.

'Sooner or later Charles really will have to face the facts about his beloved brother. He knows as well as I do where he's gone.'

Noble said nothing. It was left to me to put the question. 'And where would that be, Mrs Noble?' It would've taken more nerve than I've got to call her Veronica.

'Off with one of his women, of course. Ask Charles.'

As I turned to him, he pushed himself up to his feet. 'I do think that's most unfair, Veronica. I quite realise you don't particularly care for Richard, and I can see there are aspects of his character that you find disagreeable, as indeed I do myself; but I really don't think you should make accusations of that nature.'

He'd backed up to the fire to warm his calves, and he stood there looking down at her, with his thumbs locked behind him. Through a haze of cigarette smoke, she looked mildly amused by his display of sincere indignation.

'Do try not to be so naive, darling.' Then she moved her head slightly so she was looking at me. 'Richard Noble is a womaniser. He's one of those wretched specimens who simply can't keep his hands off women. Charles insisted that he would settle down once he'd married but of course he didn't. Men like that never do, do they?'

'What about all that?' I indicated the screen where a blurred and darkened picture of street fighting was still frozen.

'Typical Richard. What perplexes me is why Charles finds it so surprising.'

48

'Oh darling, do be fair . . .'

She ignored his interruption. 'I mean, how can I explain it to you other than to say that's Richard. He's a ne'er-do-well. He always has been and I don't doubt he will always stay so. He simply drifts from one scrape to the next, and from one woman to another. Once you realise that Richard is totally irresponsible, all immediately becomes clear.'

While she was saying this, Charles was watching her. His eyes were filled with anxiety and he seemed on the verge of interrupting her without quite having the nerve to do it.

'Don't you agree, dear?' The tone and the final word were a mockery. She was goading him.

He shuffled and took his hands from behind his back and slipped them into his pockets. 'It's a matter of interpretation, I believe,' he said, adopting a classroom manner. 'Richard is a very physical man, no doubt about that at all. You could argue that he is a man who is attracted to danger, which is no doubt how he's got himself mixed up in this sort of nonsense.' He jabbed a polished toe towards the screen. 'But I wouldn't call him a womaniser, not in the real sense of the word, and I don't think for a moment he would go off and leave Caroline. He is awfully fond of her.'

In a voice of icy amusement, Veronica replied: 'Then we must all hope that Caroline is awfully grateful.'

To me, in a calmer tone, she said: 'He used to vanish for days, weeks, at a time. Poor Caroline never had the faintest idea where he was or what he was doing. Now he's gone off with one of his cheap tarts and she's surprised.'

Still trying to stay affable, Charles forced a weak chuckle. 'If only life were quite that simple, eh, Hussy?'

She rose and tossed her cigarette past him on to the fire. She looked over his shoulder into a gilt-framed mirror above the fireplace, and with one finger touched the lines that ran from the corners of her eyes and mouth.

'If only it weren't quite so wretchedly simple, Mr Hussy. As you have doubtless realised by now, my husband even chooses to glamorise him as some sort of ghastly revolutionary figure.'

The reason I'd given up my security business was that I'd got

49

sick of other people's maimed marriages. I'd seen too many people like this, who'd rather heat their homes with hatred than face the coldness of being alone.

'Why would he do that, Mrs Noble?'

'Because he won't admit the truth. Which is that his brother is a . . .' she lit another cigarette then, in a calculated piece of theatre: 'his brother is a See You Next Tuesday.'

It must've taken me a minute to work out what she meant. By then she'd switched her eyes to Charles' face. 'Exactly why Charles is so reluctant to face that is something I feel would come better from him. Isn't that so, dear?'

She was facing him, but she was gazing over his shoulder into her own face in the mirror. With her right hand, she collected stray hairs which had fallen from her half-collapsed bun, and lifted her chin to give herself a tight, clean jawline. Ten years fell from her face in that moment, and I saw what a lovely woman she had been before the sourness ate into her.

I rose. 'If you two want to pass the time away throwing pots and pans at each other that's your privilege, and I dare say it's more fun than television. But don't bounce them off me, if you don't mind.'

She continued to stare at herself in the mirror. Charles shot her a glance, then looked back at me. In the silence, the rumble of young feet and the scratchy voices of adolescent males swelled into a stormy chorus. For a musical about marriage, it wouldn't have been a bad score.

'Yes, you are absolutely right, Hussy.' Charles' eyes flicked towards his wife then came back to mine when he found no support there. 'I do think we have not behaved too well. Please accept our apologies.'

His nose was twitching so much it had almost taken on a life of its own.

I held up my hands. 'It happens.'

'I'm afraid we're under stress, isn't that so, darling?' In the mirror, her eyes found mine. All I could see in them was derision. I still felt sorry for her. We all bang up whatever barricades we can when we're under attack. Still looking into the mirror, she spoke.

50

'I really can't think why we're making all this fuss anyway. Charles and Richard haven't seen each other for years. The truth is they don't much care for each other. Isn't that so?'

Taking my arm, Charles steered me quickly towards the door. 'Time for the evening round of the house, Hussy. Come with me, there's a good chap. Now, let me see, where did I put my flashlight? Let's see if we can catch the smokers red-handed.'

It was a relief to leave the leaden atmosphere of that room and the woman looking for her youth in the mirror, and follow Noble on his night hunt of the illicit smokers. From black tragedy, we went to farce: not that Noble was aware of either, so far as I could see.

From the moment we stepped out of the cosy warmth of their quarters into the wide corridors and the high-ceilinged rooms of the school house, I knew we were one move behind the game. No matter how quietly we went through the darkened and silent building, vaguely scented with sweat and stale food, I had the feeling that word had gone ahead. Tiptoes on hard linoleum, we sneaked up and down stairs, bursting suddenly through doors where his accusing pencil of light found only sleeping angels. Like cartoon cats, wherever we pounced the mouse had gone.

'All in bed, boys?'

'Yessir.'

'Where's Stephens?'

'Bog, sir.'

'I think that might stand a little investigation. Would you like to wait downstairs, Hussy?'

I went down the stairs in the dark. At the bottom, in a room off to my right, I saw a sudden small flare of fire.

'Stephens?'

'Yessir, oh hell, hey you're not . . .'

'He's coming, quick, move!' As I hissed out my command, from the foot of the stairs I heard Noble's feet and saw his torch pierce the dark.

'Ah, there you are, Hussy. You've found our stray, I see. What are you doing in the games room at this time, Stephens?'

'Putting the table tennis ball back, sir.'

Noble sniffed the air. 'Hands out, let's see them. All right, Stephens, I'm prepared to believe you this once, although I can't think why in view of your previous record. Get back to bed.'

'Yessir. Thank you, sir.'

We walked outside. The five-storey building loomed big and black above us.

'As I said,' he began, carefully, 'I do apologise if we caused you any embarrassment, Hussy. Veronica has been under a lot of strain lately and I'm afraid she's taking this business rather badly.'

'Is it true that you hardly saw your brother?' If he didn't, that might explain the moustache and description of him as a country gent.

'We had rather grown apart, I suppose. I say, Hussy, I didn't know you smoked?'

I flicked the fag-end off into the night, trailing sparks. 'Just the odd one after meals,' I said. Well, I could hardly say I was looking after it for someone else, could I?

He gave a little neigh of laughter. 'Do you know, I thought I could smell smoke in there, and I was half-convinced it was Stephens.'

'Just shows, it doesn't do to jump to conclusions. You'd grown apart, you say – so when did you last see him?'

'I don't remember exactly . . .' He blustered away for a couple of minutes, not answering the question, and I thought what a funny bloke he was. Innocent as a lamb one minute, lying away like mad the next.

In the great dormitory of life, Noble was the swot with clean knees and good marks, and I was the grubby little sod grabbing a sneaky drag on a fag round the corner. Cringle? Oh, Cringle was the headmaster.

# 9

Gray's Inn Road runs from the lawyers' offices of Holborn down to the massage parlours of King's Cross, thus linking the traditional professions of the rip-off and the strip-off. It's a good area because it hasn't yet been turned into a ghetto exclusive to any particular one of London's tribes. You get 'em all, round there. Little old ladies creep out of hot, cat-flavoured basements to watch clean young families taking off in their estate cars to Cotswold cottages. Career girls with tawny hair walk leggy Afghans watched by unshaven and undiscovered rock stars. Asian shopkeepers lament the collapse of morality with shuffling pensioners who smell of peppermints. It's a good mix.

I had a pint of nutty beer in a boozer and tuned in to the conversation. A red-faced man with thin hair and crooked teeth turned from the bar to see his wife pushing a slot-machine button. 'I have often wondered who the morons were who played those things,' he intoned. 'Thank you for answering my question, Eleanor.'

He was listening to a freckle-faced photographer who must have strayed up from the *Mirror* offices. He was moaning about a prize-winning reader who'd been taken ill in his car. 'I says to the Desk afterwards, I says what a bleedin' liberty. I bin all over the world, I snapped all the big Hollywood stars, I even snapped Royalty, and here I am wiv this disgusting old bird shouting Ralph in the back of me Jag.'

It was good stuff all right, but it wasn't telling me why Richard Noble came here so often that he picked up parking tickets. I stepped out into the street to find that a rare city wind was frightening hell out of some paper bags. The sky was that very hard pale blue that you find in the eyes of girls who marry rich men.

Whatever I'd hoped to see in Doughty Mews wasn't there. It

was a short street of converted mews houses, many with the double garage doors still in place, and they'd been dolled up in jaunty nursery colours and decked out with window boxes and plump flower tubs by the doors. The only people around were a pale man panting as he stooped to clean his car wheels, and a Greek-looking woman with wrestlers' arms lashing a rug. Otherwise those who go to work had gone, and those who stayed at home were doing just that.

I strolled up the right-hand side, sauntered over, and strolled back down the other side. I was halfway down when I heard a voice that stopped me mid-stride. Five words, five half-whispered words, but it was enough.

' 'Bye, sweetest.' I heard first. Then: 'Ring you tomorrow.'

Instinct told me to spin round to see who it was, but I managed to resist that. Instead I dropped to one knee to fiddle with my shoelace.

He was stepping out so briskly that Charles Noble didn't notice me as he swept past. I watched his slim erect figure, wearing a light waterproof jacket and carrying a scarred briefcase, long-legging it towards the main road, and I was just beginning to move in the same direction when the second thunderbolt hit me. Coming towards both Charles and myself was the pale black with the Liverpool accent who'd snapped me in two at Caroline's house. Winston. Beside him, the bunch of muscles in denim.

For some reason, I was expecting them to recognise each other. They didn't. Even though they brushed shoulders, Winston ignored Charles as they passed. He said something to his mate and he waved and broke into a trot to get to me. You'd have thought he'd spotted an old pal.

'Fancy seeing you in the Smoke then.' He was standing in front of me, his hands tucked into a faded brown leather jacket and a happy grin all over his face.

'Fancy.' Over his shoulder I saw Charles turn the corner and go out of sight. I made a brief effort to make the connection between the schoolmaster and these two, then abandoned it.

'Remember matey here, Cracker?'

'I remember him all right. Got hisself 'airt, dinnee?'

Again, it was clear that for all his muscles, Cracker was only slipstreaming the other man.

I took another look at Cracker's neck and shoulders. To get like that, he must've started with lead pram beads. Still, what was it I always said about weight-trainers? If you have to look for it in a gym, you'll never find it.

'He did, didn't he?' Winston said. The wind didn't touch the tight mass of his hair, and I saw again how his skin had a blueish tinge. 'Might again too.'

'Reckon?' Cracker began rubbing his hands on the front of his stiff denim jacket as though cleaning them for a delicate task.

'Unless he tells us what he's doing here like. Are you going to tell us then?'

'Sorry gents, must rush.' I tried to push through them, thinking maybe they wouldn't have the nerve to try too much on in a public street. I was wrong. Cracker caught my hand in his and didn't give it back. It wasn't particularly painful. It was just that I thought I might never see it again.

Between them and someone's front door immediately behind me, I was neatly imprisoned. The three of us so close we could have been standing on the same manhole cover. Down the street the woman still thrashed her carpet with slow heavy blows, and the car-cleaner straightened, rubbed his back, and bent to his task again. To them we were probably three old buddies.

Cracker's hammered features smirked into mine. 'You gonna tell Winston then?'

Winston smiled and slowly rubbed the side of his curved nose. 'Go on. Do yourself a favour – don't give blood.'

'Like I was saying, I'm in a terrible rush. . . .' I'd raised my voice in the hope that it would catch someone's attention.

'Show him how much we want him to stay.'

With his right hand still gripping mine, Cracker slid his left around me and I felt his fingers go into my ribs. Jesus! They were like iron moles. Mentally I re-wrote my rules: he'd looked for it in a gym, and found it. Until then I didn't even know I could whistle through my teeth. So much for my theory about body-builders. Before, at Caroline's house, it had been the other one who'd chopped me down. Now he was watching, a smile not of malice but of bland contentment on his face. In a way that frightened me more than the mole fingers.

'Ever see those Filipinos on the telly?' Winston was going on, in the same affable tone. 'Those fellers that can do magic operations just using their fingers, no knives, nothing like that. Cracker's the same. Show him again, Crack. He can pull your kidneys out and stamp on 'em on the pavement. Can't you, Cracker?'

The younger man's face wrinkled up in a brief effort of concentration, and through the red blaze that filled my head, I only just heard Winston tell him: 'It must be warmer than I thought. He's sweatin' – look at his face.'

I sucked in a couple of deep breaths to shift the pain and a few long blinks to clear my head. Then down the street, skipping and singing out loud, came my salvation: a little girl, around ten or so, heading for all three of us. 'Forty-three, forty-four, forty-five.' As she counted, she bit briefly on her bottom lip in determination.

'This,' I said, 'is where I start shouting.'

'Please yourself.' He half-turned to face the girl. 'Hey you, scufter. Man 'ere wants to talk to you.'

Cracker's faced creased up with fun: 'He reckons he's scurred.'

Lifting her chin higher, keeping her eyes fixed straight ahead, counting in a steady voice, the girl pranced past us. She couldn't see the bright glare of menace that bound us all together. We were just another collection of London loonies like the ones she'd been ignoring all her life.

'See?' He was facing me again. On his smooth brown eyes, there was a sheen that made them impossible to read. 'See? Nobody gives a toss if we mince you right here. Go on, call up the reserves. I think that woman'll be more use than that bloody cripple cleaning his car, mind, but they won't even cross the road. Talk about Samaritans. Typical bloody Londoners, let you die in the street, this lot would.'

He was right and I knew it. Cracker could tear my liver and lights out and fill me up with chestnut stuffing right there and then if he wanted. Sweating or not, a chill slithered down my veins.

'Okay, let's talk.' Even as I said it, I heard a sound behind me that set my mind racing.

'No. You talk, we listen. Right?'

'Right.' I heard the noise again, only closer. I swivelled my head to show them how I was boxed in and lifted the hand that was still firmly encased by Cracker's. 'Do you think I could have this one back? You might've noticed, I'm not going anywhere.'

'Put the gentleman down, Cracker, he's being helpful now. So. Tell us all about yourself. You wouldn't be a friend of Mr Noble's now, by any chance, would you?'

He stopped then as the noises I'd heard behind me – footsteps on stairs and along a hallway – turned into the rattle of a door opening. I moved a couple of inches round and saw a black mass of curls. A woman was stooping to pick up a bottle of milk. She wasn't even aware of us until she straightened up. When she saw us, she gave a little hop of alarm and stood there, the door half open.

'What on earth are you doing here?'

'Just chattin' miss,' Winston said, with a reassuring nod.

She opened the door another foot or so. A frown of annoyance set up camp on her face. She leaned out towards us.

'I'd appreciate it if you would go and chat somewhere else.'

She began to close the door, and I knew I had to make my move then. In one short, fast, explosive burst, I swung my arm, snatched the bottle out of her hand and brought it round in the same fast arc, smashing it into Cracker's face. A fountain of milk flew up and a yelp of pain broke the morning calm. Over he went, reeling backwards, one hand out to break his fall, the other trying to clear his face. As he hit the floor, his head and shoulders were white with the milk but gaudy scarlet buds were flowering in his face. All the time he was snuffling and snorting with fury. That was all I had time to take in. Then I was through the doorway rolling the woman back before me, and I slammed the door in Winston's dumbstruck face.

The astonishing thing was that she wasn't terrified. She was angry. 'I don't know who the hell you think . . .'

I grabbed her shoulders and rammed her against the wall. I snapped one word at her. 'Phone.'

'Let go of me, this really is . . .'

I grabbed her chin so that she had to look into my eyes and when I spoke again it was a blast of authority. 'Telephone! Now! This is urgent!'

That quietened her. With one steady hand, she pointed to the first door on the left.

'Wait.'

Luckily, the table was in the bay window. I picked it up and moved in to the centre of the bay. I dialled. Outside, Cracker was dabbing at his face with a rag of some sort, and Winston was examining the front door as though he was going to kick it off its hinges at any minute. It only took him a second to see me. Even so, all he did was to give me a formal nod as he took his pal by the arm and marched down the mews and out of sight.

From behind his car where he must have dived when it all happened, the man with the bad back emerged with caution. The woman, her beating arm by her side, began shouting in a Mediterranean flood of noise. People appeared at doors and windows and a babble of chatter began.

'Are you calling the police?' She had followed me into the room.

'They thought so.' I looked down the mews again to make sure they'd gone. 'I dare say that's enough.'

It'd have to be life or death before I'd phone Cringle. It looked like life, so I put the phone back on the table.

'If you don't call them, I will.'

That was the first time I really got to look at her.

She was too small to be beautiful in the classical sense, and she had too much presence ever to be called pretty. Five foot, seven and a half stone, trim enough to be a dancer maybe. She was wearing designer jeans, pale brown cashmere sweater, and pearls that had been mummy's. No one told me, but with women like that they always are designer, cashmere, and mummy's.

58

'Don't let's do that.'

'Why not?'

'Well, I'll tell you why. The lads'll be passing around the *Mirror* in the canteen at the station and doing the crossword while they're getting stuck into the pints of tea, and we call them out – what for? To tell them about a couple of fellers who've gone away anyway, and who just happened to have a quiet disagreement with me. Now maybe disagreeing with me ought to be a criminal offence, I'll grant you that, but so far it's not, so I think perhaps we'll let the peelers get on with their crossword, don't you think?'

She was examining me as I spoke. 'You do go on, don't you?'

'I'm highly strung.'

She pointed out of the window at the splashed stain on the pavement. 'And what about my milk that you stole?'

'There's a saying about spilt milk, so I've heard.'

Her hand went to the pearls and she ran them through her fingers as she thought. 'Perhaps it isn't those men I'm worried about. Perhaps it's you.'

'Me?' I did my best to sound aghast.

'Yes.' She dabbed an American cigarette from a soft packet on the glass table, inserted it neatly between her lips, and lit it with a plastic lighter in the shape of a strawberry. 'Little old highly-strung you.'

'Ah. But I'm a friend of a friend.'

The high arches of her eyebrows flicked even higher. 'I rather doubt that, but please prove me wrong. Who is our mutual friend?'

'Your last visitor. Charles Noble.'

'Charles?' She really did sound astonished. 'I don't believe you. Prove it.'

Solemnly I moved my forefinger up to the side of my nose and pushed it three times so that it twitched. She gave a short, wild laugh.

'So you are,' she said. 'So you are.'

59

# 10

That got me through to the kitchen for a drink. I would've settled for coffee, but she said we needed something to give us a lift. A minute later, to my surprise, I found myself unbuckling a bottle of champagne, while she tumbled oranges into the juice extractor.

'Do you know,' she called over her shoulder, 'I've heard that people sometimes make Bucks' Fizz with canned orange juice. Do you think that could be true?'

'You never know. Now meself, I make it with Algerian white, orange squash and a handful of Alka Seltzer.'

She gave me a doubtful frown, a look which I have studied closely on a variety of faces over the years. She emptied the machine into a large glass jug. 'You realise that I do not believe your absurd story.'

'Why not? What's wrong with it?' The cork came out with a gasp.

'Everything. You say you are doing a security job for Charles and that is why you follow him up here, where those two men suddenly grab you. What security job is this? What does a schoolmaster have to do with security? How do those men know you, and what are they to do with Charles? I tell you, it is absurd.'

'So what am I then?'

'That is what I hope you are going to tell me. Follow me, please. We will be more comfortable in the rumpus room.'

Rumpus room. I liked the sound of that. I didn't know people had rooms specially designed for it. On the way through, I paused to look at a picture on the wall. Immediately she stopped and turned. 'You know about oils?'

'Oh yeah. They're the ones with lumps in. Like porridge.'

I looked at it and thought I'd chance it. 'Vermeer?'

She stretched her eyes. 'Not bad. A fake actually.'

'Ah.' I bent forward to squint at it, not that it made me much wiser. 'In that case it's a Han Van Meegeren.'

'Even better. A liar who knows about art – that could be an interesting combination.'

'It takes a fake to know a fake.' I squinted at it again. 'Tell me something, if you gave that to me, as recompense for sexual favours say, and I flogged it down the Portobello this afternoon, what would be the sort of figure I ought to ask for it?'

'For sexual favours, you say?' She repeated it without any emphasis and without much interest either, which was a bit disconcerting.

'Well, cutting the grass then.'

Her mouth gave a tiny twist of amusement. She wasn't accustomed to having her desirability put on the same level as lawn-mowing. 'I would advise you not to take less than a hundred thousand.'

'You're on. Not a penny less will I take. But I thought you said all the family cash had gone down the tube.'

While we'd been loading up the juice machine in the kitchen, she'd reeled off a potted biog without any hesitation. It had all been printed so often in the gossip columns that I suppose she regarded it as public property by now. When she told me her name, even I knew some of it. Anna Mauch, which she pronounced to rhyme with torch because the German pronunciation sounded like a cat being sick.

Father, Swiss. Mother, English. Brought up in France, which accounted for the slight accent. Parents split, divorced, regrouped elsewhere, which had knocked a hole in the family fortunes. Then for a little while there had been a Liechtenstein husband, who'd vanished with large chunks of the family cash and left her with a title, Baroness Tinpot or something.

Well, if she had no money then she was getting a hell of a good deal off the Social Security. You'd think that house had been vandalised by a gang with limitless time, taste and money. The heavy furniture was only Victorian stuff, which meant it was probably let furnished, but through a series of small rooms, I saw exquisite paintings, porcelain, and silver. On the floor

61

were beautiful Chinese rugs as pale as I would've been if I'd had to pay for them.

Anna had the same touch of quality. Beneath that head of black curls, her skin was that finger-smooth ivory colour that doesn't need a tan. It looked pale until she laughed, and then it darkened against her bright flashing smile. Someone who had Vermeer's touch with light had done her eyes. They were brown-almost-black, and swimming with amusement. Black, brown, cream, ivory, white. She was colour-coded all the way through. And it was all underlined by her air of perfect serenity. Brawling men burst through her door, and she served Bucks' Fizz. She had so much cool style you could've siphoned it off and sold it by the bucketful.

'I am serious,' she said, as we emerged into the rumpus room. I took it all in. The walls were all windows and the floor was nothing but huge cushions in all shades of blue. Somewhere a man was crooning in croaky French. Perhaps it was a room for rumpussing after all.

She sank into a cushion and passed me the jug, while she reached for glasses from a small corner cupboard. 'Once, I promise you, if I dropped my napkin it would be caught before it hit the ground. Now I have only one cleaning woman.'

'Yeah, but you've managed to keep up the payments on the old paintings and bits of china and everything.'

'Ah, yes, things. I still have plenty of things. Alas, I do not have any money and that is what we all need to live. But you are not a money man, are you?'

'Does it show?' I glanced down at my old cords and jacket. 'No, I don't think money's very interesting myself.'

'Not in itself. But it is a measure of success, of power.'

'In that case I must've been born overdrawn.' I took a long swig of the fizz. Already I could feel the orange juice putting back in what the champagne knocked out. I decided to let the two of them fight for possession of my veins.

My nerves must've been a bit more strung out than I thought, because as I leaned backwards on the cushion, I felt a movement beneath me, and sprang to my feet.

'It's only Harrod.' From beneath me, a slim Burmese cat

stepped out like a chocolate-coloured duchess. It moved over to Anna and pressed an upcurved back against her arm.

'So why name a cat after an Old Testament king who's only remembered for murdering the first-born?'

'He's not, he's named after the department . . .' She stopped herself and treated me to a long lowering of her eyelashes. 'You never say anything you mean?'

'Only when offered a drink.'

She leaned forward, concern suddenly taking over her face. 'What on earth have you done?'

'The milk bottle . . .' She'd seen the red slit across the base of my thumb where I'd been cut. I'd kept it under control by discreet licking. A bit like a mother hedgehog, I suppose. I was going to give it some more treatment when she knelt in front of the cushion where I was sprawling and took my hand in hers.

'That's rather nasty. Deep. It might need stitches.'

When she raised her eyes to mine, she saw something that had nothing to do with first-aid. From somewhere inside, a light rose up in her eyes and face. That was the first time I saw it – that surge of vivid life that was never far away. Then she sat back on her haunches, her eyes twinkling and her face aglow with pleasure. She knew what I had seen in her face. She reached out and put her hand to the side of my face in what might've been a gentle slap or a muscular caress. 'Don't even think about it.'

'No?'

'No.' She shook her head so that the black curls bounced. 'You couldn't afford it.'

'There's a price?'

'Everything has a price.'

'And what's the price for an Anna Mauch, one-owner, as new?'

She wriggled her face around as though she was working out a difficult problem. 'Does a million pounds sound reasonable?'

'What does that buy?'

'Me.' She cocked her head sideways and watched my reaction. 'At least a million, I think. These days you could not begin to live on any less than that. I need beautiful houses, I

63

need to travel. There are times when I must be ski-ing, there are other times when I must be in the Caribbean. You understand these things.'

I looked down at the patches where the ribbing was rubbed off my cords. 'Yeah, yeah, I know about all that.'

'The best tables at the best restaurants . . . I must dress suitably, of course. A jewel . . .' hastily she pressed one elegant hand against her breast, 'even a dull little jewel, needs the correct setting.' She dropped one hand to stroke Harrod's arched back, and with the other raised the glass to her lips. Her eyes were laughing at me over the rim. 'A million might be enough. Just.'

'How'd you feel about hire purchase?'

She shrugged. 'I said you couldn't afford it.'

'And schoolmasters can? Or has Charles won a scholarship?'

That was a bit on the cheeky side but it didn't seem to annoy her. She hopped up to her feet and said: 'Put your thumb back in your mouth to stop yourself talking such rubbish. I like you, Joe. You're different. Don't become like everyone else. Don't disappoint me, not so soon. I'll be back in a moment.'

The million-pound lady swept out of the room leaving me feeling like an old quid note: limp, crumpled and almost worthless. The cat took one look at me and followed her; even if he'd been called Woolworths he would probably have done the same. When she came back she had bandages, dressing, antiseptic and cotton wool. She knelt again in front of me.

'Give me your hand. There. What did those two men want?'

'Dunno. Maybe they're planning a bit of blackmail.'

'On you?' She glanced up again. 'Oh, I see what you mean. No, that doesn't frighten me. I am not vulnerable to blackmail. I never do anything of which I am ashamed.'

'Perhaps Veronica Noble doesn't see it that way.'

Whatever I was hoping for didn't happen. She worked away, putting the dressing on the cut and tightening the bandage around my thumb and wrist. 'There, see a doctor if you can. I think it should have some stitches.' She sat back again. 'I believe she knows all about me. Anyway, whether she does or not, that is not my problem. I don't care.'

64

'Perhaps Charles does.'

'That is possible.'

'So, if they say cough up the cash or we tell the little woman at home, what happens then?'

'Let them tell her.'

Whatever she saw in my face made her laugh. She picked up the jug again and filled my glass. 'Here, have another drink. You don't really take me for a quiet little mistress, do you, Joe? Tucked away in a love-nest awaiting my lover's call? That is such nonsense. You should know about my life. I do many things. I read. I write a little. As I was saying before, I travel. I have friends in politics and business all over the world. I visit them, they visit me. These are influential people. In the middle of all this, there is a schoolmaster of whom I am very fond. But he is not my life. Oh, not at all.'

That made me feel stupid. She'd got style and brains and there I was talking to her like an escapee from a flower-arranging class. Well, she'd given me a quick poke in the eye for misjudging her, and I had to admit I deserved it.

'What is it about Charles, tell me that? I'd like to know why you're so . . . fond of him.'

'You men are such hypocrites.' She was laughing again and all the lights had come up in her eyes again. 'They way you say that – fond.' She repeated it in the loaded tone that I'd used. 'Yes, of course I go to bed with him, which is what you have been wondering since you came through the door. Why? Well, he is physically attractive, I think. He is slim and fit, certainly, but of course it is much more than that. He is the perfect English gentleman, and that is a type of man you cannot find anywhere else in the world.'

That nettled me. 'You mean a wimp.'

'No, I do not mean that. The English gentleman is kind and courteous, naturally, but without being weak or ineffectual in any way. Charles can talk about honour without feeling pretentious. He believes in a set of rules and he tries always to observe those rules.'

'They must be fairly elastic if you're allowed.'

She only gave me a small frown for that. 'Do not talk about

things you do not understand. As I was saying, all these things, all these qualities, make a woman feel safe.'

'It's funny you should say that.' I topped my glass up from the jug. 'Because I'm famous for my safeness.'

Her shiny dark eyes were watching me over her glass. 'Oh no, you are not. You are a dangerous man, and that is something quite different.'

She rose and went and stood by the window. She pressed her finger tips against the glass and looked absently out at the garden. 'Charles did not mention me at all? No, of course, he wouldn't do that. So what do you do now? Tell him you've discovered his wicked secret?'

I hadn't really thought that far ahead. 'I don't know. Maybe not. It would only embarrass him.'

She laughed and her breath misted on the glass. 'Yes, I am afraid that Charles does have problems fitting me into his concept of honour.'

'He's probably got you on the school timetable between physical education and biology.'

'Poor Charles. It is so difficult being a gentleman. You still haven't told me why he hired you.'

'He wants me to find his brother. Richard.'

She half turned so that her eyes fixed on mine, and I saw the elegant curve of her eyebrows rise in mild surprise. 'A brother? He never mentioned his brother. But then, Charles does not include me in his intimate family circle.'

# 11

'Is she one of your daft lasses?'

'No, she isn't. She's not a lass, she's far from daft and I'm sorry to say she isn't mine.'

'Aye. So you say.'

Jamie was being at her most difficult. I'd only mentioned Anna Mauch's name because Jamie read all that gossip column rubbish and knew quite a bit about it. She'd reeled off a couple of snippets about her Liechtenstein ex-husband and a racing driver who'd been hanging around before she'd sensed a personal interest at work. That did it. We got me, my past, my lousy taste in women, how they always ripped me off, and finally a terminal warning to the effect that her doorstep would remain undarkened if I did it again. She would've made a great Victorian father, would Jamie.

'They're welcome to it,' she snapped.

'To what?'

'That,' she said, which covered the whole territory from puppy love to one-night lust, hay-rolls and lifelong fidelity. A grimace of annoyance wrinkled up her flat pug face. 'Folk making damn silly fools of themselves, that's all it gets you.'

'You're right, Jamie.' I let her have it because I understood her. She was a soppy old romantic at heart, and I'd seen the pile of Mills and Boon books under her bed. She dreamed of tall men with cleft chins and forceful personalities who would wrench her away from the MoT bay.

As it was she'd got me, which wasn't much of a substitute. So she'd settled for some friendship, a couple of laughs, and left her secret dreams under the bed.

'You're right as usual,' I added, 'but don't drop those bloody flies' eggs on my poppadum.'

It was a week after I'd met Anna and we were getting the flies' eggs out of Charlie's eyes. I'd noticed them first, little flakes of white like bits of pastry. I'd phoned Sue Stocker and she'd told us what they were. But Jamie reckoned to be more adept at the nursing than I was, so here we were, the two of us, Charlie, and a couple of vindaloos from the takeaway for supper.

'Keep still, baby, that's another one,' said Jamie. I'd got Charlie on my knee and she was sitting on the floor with the tweezers. Apparently if hedgehogs get crocked, flies like to move in and use their eyes as maternity wards. Apart from that, he was in good form. He was a two-bottle-a-day man now – hot-water bottles, that is. He was eating his puppy food: well, he was eating it as soon as he'd trampled, peed and crapped all over it, which is how your gourmet hedgehog likes his grub. Sue Stocker had said not to let him hibernate because he was too young, but he didn't seem inclined to at all. In the evenings he liked to come out for a little social life – you know, a chat, bit of telly, gentle stroll around over his grub.

'Hang on to 'im,' Jamie shouted, as Charlie leapt about four-foot in the air. He didn't like the telephone.

'Hussy?' It was Cringle.

'It is.'

'Schoolteacher. Think you know him. Is he trying to engage your services?'

'Yes.'

'No.'

'What you mean, no?'

'I mean no, don't.'

'Just like that.'

'You know how it works.'

'I dare say, but just to ring up like that and . . .'

'Drop it, and get on with the oil changes. It would cause some annoyance if you didn't.'

Some annoyance: in Cringle's language, that meant I'd have my intestines removed inch by inch.

'Good man,' he said, without waiting for my reply. He rang off.

'Who was that?' Jamie asked.

'A well-wisher.'

I waited until she'd gone before I rang Charles. I was expecting him to be upset, or even a little annoyed, but the man was almost distraught. At first he didn't seem able to take it in at all. 'You must,' he kept on saying, and I had to repeat time and again that I was backing out. I knew he wanted to find his brother, and I knew it meant a lot to him; even so, I wasn't sure what to make of it. When I told him to have a look in the papers for a real private detective – who'd probably do a damn sight better job than me – he wouldn't hear of it. 'You're the only one who can find him,' he said again, 'the only one.'

I didn't want to walk out on him. For one thing, I didn't like being pushed around by Cringle. That was one of the reasons I left: I *never* liked being pushed around by Cringle, sometimes I declined to be pushed around, which made me feel very spirited for a while, then very nervous. But most of all, Charles had got me interested in the whole Richard Noble mystery. I wanted to know what sort of man could come from the same background as Charles, a Gurkha officer for God's sake, and end up throwing bombs at bobbies.

So, in a way, perhaps I wasn't all that upset when he called again three days later. Even so, I wasn't ready for what he had to say.

'If you want me to find your brother, the answer's no.'

'It isn't that.' He was speaking in a voice that was well out of character for him. 'You'll have to help me now. Someone is trying to kill me.'

If you want to get attention, that's not a bad way to do it. I asked him all the obvious questions – who, where, when, and so on – without getting much back. He'd had two telephone calls, he said. Each time a male voice, English, uneducated, had said: 'We're going to kill you, Noble.' No, he didn't recognise the voice at all. Yes, he was sure it wasn't Stephens or one of his endangered smokers having him on.

'He meant it, Hussy, whoever it was. There's no doubt about that.'

Then I realised what was so odd about the way he was speaking. He sounded thrilled. Anxiety, agitation, certainly; but there was a lot of excitement in the way he spoke too, and again I found myself wondering about the schoolmaster. You can't devote your life to catching schoolboy smokers without learning something about being devious.

'There's two chances of someone trying to kill you, Noble.'

'Two chances?' Now he sounded baffled.

'That's right. Fat chance, and no chance. Forget it.'

'It is true, I promise you.' He didn't like the sound of himself saying that, so he gave an embarrassed cough. 'Sorry to sound so melodramatic.'

'It's probably just some headbanger, don't worry about it.'

'No.' He spoke more quietly now, and with more authority. 'It wasn't. I'm quite sure of that.'

'Why? Why would anyone want to kill you?'

'It's obvious, surely. To stop the hunt for Richard.'

I didn't need to think about that for long before Cringle popped up. He didn't want Richard Noble found, and Cringle and his masters wrote their own rules. But were they reduced to threatening to knock off schoolmasters with trembly noses? I found that hard to believe.

The more I thought about it the more it sounded like some scheme that his fevered mind had cooked up during a particularly dull Latin lesson. He was a prewar model all right, was our Charles, with a lot of prewar ideas. But when I repeated that I wasn't going back on my decision, he said he knew that. There was just one job he wanted me to do. He was going down to Church Crookham to see some sort of Gurkha festival for his school's CCF and he wanted me to go as bodyguard. Bodyguard: he spluttered on the word, but he managed to say it.

'You really believe you're in danger.'

'I imagine I'm fairly safe around the school, but I think I may be vulnerable in strange surroundings.'

'What? Even when you're surrounded by tough little Gurkhas?'

'Yes.'

It was the next night. He'd been invited down for the festival of Dashera, whatever that was. He emphasised that he wasn't

70

asking me to get involved; all I had to do was to keep an eye on him, for which I would be paid the proper fee.

There was a silence. In it, he could sense my hesitation. 'If it's any help to you in reaching a decision,' he said, a little frostily, 'we shall be accompanied by Anna Mauch.'

'Ah. Anna. You heard then.'

'I did.'

'Okay. You're on.'

From the floor by the gasfire, Jamie gave me a look soggy with disgust.

'Some folk never bloody learn,' she said.

'Some folk never even try.'

I'd had my eye on a Granada but once she knew Anna was going, Jamie wouldn't go above a crummy little Fiesta, with rust trim, and she was fairly grudging about that. At Charles' suggestion, I picked him up outside the school at six the following evening, and we went down to Aldershot to meet Anna off the London train. It was already dark.

From the minute he got into the car, I could sense the tension in him. I didn't believe his murder threat story for a minute. On the other hand, I did feel bad about letting him down, and this seemed an easy way to make it up to him. And even Cringle couldn't object to that.

In the car, he wasn't able to add much to what he'd told me. Two telephone calls, definitely not schoolboys, and the message the same each time: 'We're going to kill you, Noble.' He didn't know who, he didn't know why.

Oddly, he didn't seem too worried that I'd found out about Anna.

'Followed me, I suppose? Neat bit of sleuthing, Hussy,' he said, as we settled in a pub near the station. 'Cheers.'

'Trained bloodhound, me. Yes, bit of a surprise really. I wouldn't have taken you for the class of man who'd have a side-bit.'

'Side-bit?'

'Bit on the side, you know the sort of thing.'

He fairly snorted at that, and drew himself up so he loomed like a large angry bird over the plastic-topped table. 'Anna is not a bit on the side, as you so offensively put it. I love her. I propose to marry her.'

'Hadn't you better get rid of the last one first?'

'Might I remind you that you're my bodyguard, not my confessor,' he snapped, his boyish face lighting up with unexpected anger. It faded as quickly. 'Forgive me, that was uncalled for.'

He sipped his pint of shandy. 'I can quite see that it must appear to be an irregular arrangement to you.'

'If it works, it works.'

Once he'd set his dignity on one side, he wanted to talk about it. 'I meant what I said about Anna. I shall marry her.'

'Good.'

'Veronica knows.'

'Not so good. She sleuthed you too?'

'No. I told her.'

At least that explained her edgy performance the other evening. I looked at his face across the table. The parting looked like a white wound cleaved through his hair. His eyes were blue. A bright baby blue. Behind him, a fruit machine flashed, buzzed and shuddered with pleasure.

I nodded towards it. 'I used to know how to get women to do that, but I could never find where the tokens came out. You told Veronica yourself then? Shrewd move.'

He ignored the irony. 'You might find this hard to believe, but I could not be dishonest. I'm not saying it was an easy decision. It wasn't. Moral decisions never are easy, a point I have frequently made to my boys. But I am happy that, in difficult circumstances, I was able to find the courage to do the right thing.'

I whistled in admiration. 'Whew. Like your footwork there. How to knock off a bit on the side and still stay in the right. You want to sell the recipe – thousands of men would go for that.'

His face hardened and his voice rose a notch. 'I am not saying for one moment that I am in the right,' he said, hitting each word singly and with firmness. 'All I am saying is that I am seeking to behave honourably when faced with an apparently insoluble dilemma.'

'It's not insoluble. Give one of them up.'

'I shall.'

'And if it's Veronica, then give me plenty of notice so I can get out of the country. That day, whenever it is, I'm not your bodyguard.'

He frowned, then nodded. 'She does have a volatile streak. For that reason, I thought it best not to reveal Anna's identity, or at least not at this stage.'

At the station, in a clatter of heels and rush of cold air, Anna Mauch burst upon us. She was wearing a short white fur of the sort that doesn't melt when you put it next to the radiator. She opened it when she got in the car and the aroma was like an opened oven door. When she shook her dark curls, I could feel the spray of the night mist. From the back, Charles hung over her seat, like a proud parent on open evening. That's the trouble with having a classy mistress. It must be like having a stolen Renoir – you can gloat over it in the attic but you hardly ever get the pleasure of public ownership.

'I must be mad to do this,' she said, knocking down the passenger visor to look in the mirror. 'Is this your idea, Joe?'

'Mea culpa, darling,' Charles crooned, delightedly. 'School work, really. The CCF want me to find out all about this Dashera festival to see if I can bring them next year, if it's fit for my young scoundrels. I gather that it's rather like their version of Christmas.'

Then we swept up the drive of the Queen Elizabeth barracks. Through the rain-smeared window, peering in, I saw a brown-berry face under a wide-brimmed hat that wouldn't have been out of place on a duchess. As he turned to lift the white rail of the barrier, I saw the curved kukri on his belt at the back and remembered the story: one blow from the kukri could behead a goat. We were in Gurkha country.

# 12

I never did much with the Gurkhas myself, because British governments don't have the nerve these days to use what they call mercenaries. That's a shame because they've got a pragmatic approach to soldiering that ought to go down well in these unsentimental times. In Malaya, for instance, they used to bring back terrorists' ears in a matchbox, just so no one could tell whoppers about how many they'd killed. I'm not saying it would work in South Armagh, but it might be worth a try – for the earrings alone.

It's a funny place to find those cheerful warriors from the Himalayas, tucked into a corner of the Surrey–Hampshire border, yet it's amazing how easily they slip into the English countryside. When they came back from the Falklands, they had to post guards to fend off young females who wished to demonstrate a nation's gratitude. Apparently they got a lot more fight from them than they did off the Argies.

So all in all I was looking forward to a pleasant night out, plus the advantage of another sighting of Anna Mauch. That's how it was looking two hours later when we were cooling down a scalding curry with glasses of beer and watching what looked like an end-of-term concert.

Along with the other guests, councillors and local bigshots, we'd been put in the guest seats, old armchairs nicked from some mess, beside the yard-high stage. Down the length of the hall, in the half light, we could see the soldiers' scrubbed and eager faces looking like so many freshly fallen leaves.

Officers were scattered among us. Dress was informal, which for them meant well-cut but worn tweed jackets, and for the Gurkhas, dark off-the-peg suits, still shop-stiff, with white shirts and tight ties. Dotted among their dark ranks was the odd soldier in the cool, white, loose cotton shirt and trousers of his homeland.

74

I say end-of-term, and it did have that feel about it. It's a custom their officers must have brought from their public schools over the years, and the Gurkhas have moulded it into their once-a-year festival of booze, religion, and fun. Here, against a backcloth of a Himalayan scene – silver mountains, blue sky, both painted with dazzling hard-edged clarity – they put on a series of sketches and songs that was an unlikely mix of Nepalese life and regimental in-jokes. The costumes too were a comical combination of native dress and uniform, saris and Sam Brownes, rags and medals. So were the jokes.

In one sketch a pregnant girl lined up all the men of the village to identify the father of her baby. By the way the lads laughed, it wasn't altogether fantasy. In another, a doctor who was examining a pretty female patient was looking in some very odd places for a headache.

They were exactly the same jokes you find on seaside postcards – or on the ones I send, anyway. From the men's guffaws and the self-conscious chuckles from the officers, I gathered there was some high-class mimicry involved. That's what I mean by the atmosphere: you know, that giddiness that you get from licensed insubordination.

'I say, that's the MO,' said the young captain who'd been allocated to us, as a Gurkha wearing a white cotton shirt and stethoscope affected a hoarse bellow of a voice that identified him to everyone on the camp. 'Lord, that's old Toby to a tee.' He had to raise his voice to be heard over the band's snake-charmer music.

The captain was a dark young man called Ben Adams who somehow managed to make his herringbone jacket and open check shirt look like just another uniform. He probably did the same for his pyjamas. While we'd been eating our curry, Charles had subjected him to an interrogation. He got more information than he could ever need for the CCF, but when he got around to asking about his brother – as I knew he would – the flow of information dried up.

'Richard Noble, you say. He'd be before my time. Excuse me, sir,' Adams called to an older man in half-glasses, two rows behind us. 'Do you remember Richard Noble? This is his brother.'

'Say again?' Half-specs was doing a rapid assessment of our trio.

'Noble. Richard Noble, sir. I gather he was with us four or five years ago.'

'Ah yes. I think I can place him. You're his brother, you say?'

'Yes, I was just . . .'

'Noble left us. He went elsewhere, as I recall. So what's he up to now?'

'Actually I've lost touch with him myself . . '

'What?' he said, with a fruity laugh. 'A chap who can't keep tabs on his own brother. Still, I imagine your information will be much more up to date than ours.'

'Sorry,' Adams said, as the older man turned away.

I can't say I was all that amazed. If Charles couldn't crack the fifth-form smoking ring, he wasn't going to get far against Army security. And he wasn't going to get me involved in that again.

That left him gazing into Anna's eyes, and me talking to the young captain about his beloved Gurkhas. He was a third-generation officer with the regiment. Like most of them, he'd joined partly out of tradition, partly out of regard for what they call the best infantry in the world, and partly because he wanted to live in a museum of social manners where the values of the boys' comics still prevailed.

'They're honest, they're proud, and they're thrifty.' He leaned towards me and cupped his mouth to be heard over the wailing band. 'The worse the conditions, the more they like it. About the only thing they won't take is abuse.'

Behind us, I heard Half-specs' voice again. 'Lean and keen. Hillsmen, that's what they are. Not fat, idle, work-shy, bloody slobs like we have in this country.'

I looked down the hall at them. With their baby-round faces, they looked like so many suntanned choristers. To look at them, you'd never believe how much trade they put the way of Swan Vestas by way of ear packaging. When you think about it, it's a weird combination: posh young Englishmen and peasants from the other side of the world. If it was sexual, you'd call it rough trade. But it worked, and in that long hall you could sense something of the respect and affection that bonded them.

'Are they interested in ladies?'

Adams leaned forward to get a better look at Anna, who was on the far side of Charles. 'Very much so,' he said. 'They're rather enthusiastic about that side of life. How appropriate, I think we're going to get the *maruni*.' He craned his neck forward to see Anna again. 'You may find this interesting.'

We did. From the moment she came on stage.

She was all hips, wrists and eyes, and she'd somehow trained all three to operate in independent synchronisation. A slight figure, scarcely five foot tall, when she swayed into view all conversation died. She was swathed in a sari of ice-blue silk, with shawls and scarves, soft velvet and floating chiffon, and a dozen different shades of blue. Her arms, ringed with shimmering silver bangles, tinkled as she moved. Earrings the size of medieval shields glittered in the lights. There were two male dancers with her, but she was the one we were all watching as she advanced, hip by hip, twirling those angled wrists, dark eyes watchful in their blue-painted pools. Teasing, amusing, wicked.

Someone began to clap and laugh. Someone else shushed him into silence. Laughter was for later, maybe, but not for now.

The two male dancers, who were dressed in jodhpurs and waistcoats, paraded around to show her off. Suddenly she seemed to see our group, and, without breaking the rhythm of the music, she somehow managed to slink down the three wooden steps and moved towards us.

I was thinking that this would make a pleasant change from polishing boots for the school cadets, when I saw who she was heading for. It was Charles.

He realised too, and pulled one of those faces that was half pain, half pleasure. Over his shoulder, Anna directed a questioning look at me.

By the time she got to him, the Gurkhas were howling encouragement. First of all, the dancer circled his low-backed armchair, with melting movements. From the back, she reached over and stroked his head, so swiftly that by the time he'd begun to turn she'd moved again. Then she was in front of him, her feet still, but snake ripples running up and down her body, arms writhing like cobras, eyes like dark lamps.

Anna, I saw, was lighting a cigarette. Charles still wasn't sure whether to die of embarrassment or delight. But when he saw the look on Anna's face, which was no more than detached amusement, he made his move. In that instant I saw how it was: with her, he would always have to be proving himself.

The dancer had circled him. Fleetingly she rested on the arm of the chair, leaning backwards so that her face looked up into his, and the heavy drapes of her oiled black hair brushed his face. In the same movement, she somehow rose, turning, and touched his cheeks and brow with her silver claws. As she turned the next time, with the whoops of the soldiers in his ears and his eyes looking for Anna's, he swung his hand to give her a cheeky crack on the rump.

The dancer nearly ripped his arm off.

While we were still smirking over the scene, she had caught him by the wrist and wrenched him round into a fierce arm lock. It flung him forward in his seat so that his face was rammed into his knees and his thumb was touching the back of his neck. Somewhere out in the audience some of the soldiers were cheering, but it wasn't anything to cheer about. They couldn't see how his body had been contorted and they couldn't hear the strangled chokes as he fought for air. If it was a joke, it had gone way beyond the limit.

And I was supposed to be his bodyguard.

As Captain Adams called out sharply in the native language, I moved in. I grabbed the dancer firmly by the shoulder – and almost jumped back in surprise at what I felt. Muscle. Hard, young, trained, tough muscle.

She turned.

He turned.

One look into those eyes, and right through all the paint, all the snake-like beauty and the silk and chiffon, it showed. This was a man. And in his eyes I saw hatred.

We stood there for a second, the two of us. Captain Adams was calling out again and rising to his feet and I heard Charles moan: 'Oh, heavens!' Quite suddenly, the dancer let go of his wrist, spun round, and on flat masculine feet he walked up and across the stage, and through a heavy beaded curtain, out of sight.

From the roar of laughter that went up, it was obvious that it was a routine trick to play on guests. It was just as clear, from the general merriment, that no one realised how close Charles was to having his arm broken. Just as quickly, the audience were cheering four more dancers who leapt on to the stage spinning plates.

Charles slowly sat up, massaging his wrist and working his neck.

'Jasus, I thought you were a little goner then, for sure,' I said.

'I really am most terribly sorry,' Adams was saying, bending over Charles in his concern. 'I can't understand it. It's not like our chaps to do a stupid bloody trick like that.'

'What the hell was he playing at?' Half-specs had risen in his seat to see what was wrong.

'Damned if I know, sir. All I can think is that Bhimi must have had a drop too much of the rum.'

'Bhimi?' I asked.

'Rifleman Bhimbahadur. A bit of a rascal, and our finest *maruni* dancer, but not an unpleasant sort of chap at all. I simply don't know what to say. Shall I get the MO to take a look at your shoulder?'

'No, no, it's all right now. He probably got a little over-excited.'

'Yes, probably. Still, you can take it from me that I shall be having a word with Rifleman Bhimbahadur tomorrow morning.'

'Are you really all right?' Anna was bending over him too. From the look on his face, he would've sacrificed every limb he'd got to win her sympathy. She looked up at the captain. 'Was that really a man?'

With the crisis fading, he was delighted to explain. 'Yes, that's right. He's what they call a *maruni* dancer. Nepal's rather

79

like Elizabethan England in that it isn't at all proper for respectable women to go on the stage. So men take women's roles, as I believe they did in Shakespeare's plays.'

'Isn't it unusual for a soldier?'

He laughed. 'I know what you mean. On the contrary, it's regarded as a social accomplishment. Sometimes our chaps have even used them as women terrorists on exercises – that shakes up the opposition, I can tell you.'

'You don't have a gay Gurkha problem then?' Adams could see I was joking. Half-specs, from a couple of rows away, couldn't, and he rose to his feet. 'Gay Gurkhas? Don't be bloody stupid, man. Johnny Gurkha'd get his leg across anything . . . Oh. Awfully sorry. Excuse me, madam.'

Anna gave him a friendly smile. 'I'm delighted to hear it,' she said. 'If the men look like that, we wouldn't stand a chance.'

# 13

When we came out, it had been raining. The night dripped unseen all around, but there was still enough light in the sky to see the bare trees clawing for the clouded moon. Fine layers of metal lay on the sloping roofs of the single-storey buildings.

We were leaving early. I assumed it was because Charles had been roughed up, although he denied it. He jerked back his cuff, looked at the time, and said he wasn't getting anywhere so we might as well be going. From all I'd seen, there hadn't been much point in coming at all. He'd got nowhere with his questions about Richard, and – unless he'd had a premonition about over-enthusiastic *maruni* dancers – I still didn't know why he'd wanted a bodyguard along.

We drove out of the camp and turned right up a road flanked

by trees. We hadn't gone two hundred yards when Charles, who'd insisted on taking the front passenger seat this time, yelled out to me to stop. I hopped on the brakes and the little Fiesta lurched, then skidded to an angled halt.

'What the hell is it?' I snapped, beginning to open the door and trying to search the night around us. I don't like sudden stops. I don't like sudden anythings.

'Thought I saw something in the road, old man.' Charles was already heaving himself out of the car. 'Stay there, I'll have a look.'

I watched him pick his way along the side of the car and stand in the near-side headlight. He shuffled around, looking at the road.

'What on earth is he doing?' Anna, back in her coat, shivered. The heater had hardly got going and already he was letting the night air in again.

'Don't bother if it's another hedgehog. I can't cope with any more.'

He strolled two or three yards ahead of the car, brightly lit in the car's beam. When he spoke, he almost shouted, as though we were halfway down the road. 'I really don't know what it was.' Slowly, his face clear in the light, he walked back. 'I was sure I'd seen something, but obviously I was mistaken. However. . . '

'Oh do come along, Charles,' Anna said.

'Righto, darling.' But he didn't move. The only sound then was the buzzing of the engine and the drip and drizzle of the night outside.

The shot swept the night of every other sound. Unmistakeable, unexpected, the wicked and familiar crack-thump echoed around the skies. There was a clang as it hit the car bonnet and fizzed away into the night.

'Hit the deck!' I shouted. All I could see was the figure of Charles lit up like a public monument by the full glare of our headlamps. I slapped my hand into the back seat and felt it hit some unidentified part of Anna. 'Get down,' I hissed, and at the same time I was fumbling for the lights. I was almost too late. The second shot ricocheted off the bonnet again just as I came out of the car low and fast. I hit Charles at thigh-height and carried him with me into the ditch, with my hand over his mouth before he could even squeak. Once he did try to move, so I squeezed his face with my hand. After that, he didn't move.

I put it together as quickly as I could. We'd dropped down a couple of feet into a ditch. The water was soaking up through my trousers and elbow. The car, maybe eight feet away, with both doors open and the interior light on, looked deserted. Good old Anna. She'd be down on the floor.

The shots had come from this side of the road – I'd seen the muzzle flash in the dark – and I didn't think the marksman could've been all that far away. From the sound? High velocity. Heavy calibre. SLR? Possibly.

'He was trying to shoot me,' Charles managed to whisper between my fingers.

'Shuddup.' I calculated where Charles had been standing and looked at the two silver streaks left by the bullets on the car bonnet. A thought struck me. I knelt up, nerves tingling. A soft wet wind fussed my hair. No shot. I was right. I didn't think there would be. 'Stay there. I'm going after him.'

'No,' he said, without attempting to whisper. I was straight up and into the woods and going like hell up the bank, but I still knew that Charles had stood up behind me. He was standing and almost shouting. 'No, Hussy, don't go after him. Don't.'

Even in the dark, I must've presented the sort of target assassins dream about as I pounded up that slope. If I was right, I'd be okay. If I wasn't, it would save one government pension. All I wanted now was to get to the top of the slope as quickly as possible: that was where the gunman would be.

Halfway up, I slammed myself into a tree, stopped and listened. Night noises. Then, up and over to the left, the sound of someone passing through the bushes. I set off again, turning a little to the left, swerving and crashing through the undergrowth. Quiet? I didn't want to be quiet. This man wasn't going to shoot me. And I had to run him, to push him, into making noises, making mistakes. He had the gun, but I was the hunter now.

I stopped again. Nothing this time. I swore hard to myself.

The moon had got itself muffled behind a heavy cloud. I couldn't see the car lights any more, or the road, or even the top of the slope against the moonlight, so there was nothing to do but drop and wait for my night vision to improve.

Damn, damn. If only I'd taken off straight away instead of hanging on to Charles in the ditch. Then I heard the gunman in the bushes: he was only yards ahead. How many? Forty. Maybe only twenty. The bark of the tree was hard and damp against my cheek.

I forced my sight out into the night. Bushes, branches, tree trunks, mixed and mingled in what little light there was. It was no good. I'd lost him. As I rose to backtrack, I heard another noise, this time a crashing sound of someone falling. Again, I took off, this time the bushes and branches whipping me as I rushed on; speed, not silence, mattered now. Without bearings, I couldn't fix a direction, so I aimed uphill, then cut back down again. I only just managed to grab a sapling in time to save myself from going over the same drop. Instead, I clambered down. It was only about thirty feet down, a steep valley cut by a stream, but it was far enough if you went over it flat out at night. There was no one there. Whoever it was had got up and gone. I hauled myself up the other bank but now I knew I'd really lost him.

The moon was out again. The road was fifty yards down to the left, and a little further down the road I could see the entrance to the camp.

In the distance, I heard Charles call out my name. I slid down the muddy bank again, over the stream, and up the other side. As I pulled myself up on a branch, the moon came out again and doused the whole place in light. The dark stream was now as bright as chrome. All the trees and branches took on a sharp-edged clarity.

A bunch of roots, hanging down below the opposite bank, wet from the rain, looked like a nest of vipers, frozen mid-writhe.

Except one. It was as straight as a rifle barrel. Which is exactly what it was.

The rest of the night belonged to men in uniform. First a couple of coppers in a patrol car who managed to whistle up a DCI, and he got on to the Senior Assistant Provost Marshal – a major at Aldershot – who in turn appointed a corporal from the Army's Special Investigations Branch as liaison officer with the police. By then the cops had turned out a detective superintendent and opened an incident room at Fleet police station, a few miles down the road from the Church Crookham barracks. It's a modern building on the edge of the town and we sat in the waiting room, drinking tea made by the duty sergeant. One by one, we trooped in to give our statements. As the night dragged slowly away, they announced we'd been booked into a pub in the town.

My Save Hussy's Health campaign collapsed the next morning. Without my trainers, I couldn't go for a run. And, since it was one of those country boozers where they still think bran is something you give to horses, I had to reconcile myself to an old-fashioned bad-health breakfast. Well, I couldn't disappoint the Hampshire Constabulary, could I? It's not often they get to treat me. So I was ploughing steadily through the fruits of hen and pig, successfully disguising my distress as gluttony, when Captain Adams came in.

He chucked his cap on the windowsill and flopped down beside Charles. He looked tired. So did Anna, who was sitting on my side of the table, but Charles looked like death. A grey pallor had pushed the pink innocence out of his face.

'Looks like he's got clear.' Adams helped himself from the coffee pot.

I waited for Charles' reaction, but he said nothing and he listened to the captain with a sort of grim concentration.

'Keshar- whatsit?' I'm not too good on those complicated eastern names.

'Rifleman Kesharsing. Keshar for short. He's our man, no doubt about that.'

'Never heard of the chap.' Charles obviously felt obliged to respond to all the eyes that were upon him. After such a frenetic night, this was the first chance we'd had to reflect on what had happened. 'As I explained to the police last night, I don't know a thing about any of them. I only came down to get some info for the CCF.'

'Then why should he shoot at you?' That was about the first thing Anna had said all morning.

'That's it exactly, darling.' He aimed for his customary boyish enthusiasm but fell a mile short. 'He can't possibly have been shooting at me. I'm sure it must've been someone else who fired' – he gave me a quick glance at that point – 'and this fellow's vanishing act is simply a coincidence.'

I knew the answer to that, but I let Captain Adams spell it out. He frowned with irritation at Charles' theory. 'That won't wash, I'm afraid. That was Keshar's SLR in the woods, which he'd clearly dropped when Hussy was after him. Which reminds me, Hussy, that was a rather foolhardy thing to do, to chase him. Brave, perhaps, but foolhardy.'

It wasn't either, of course, but since I wasn't sure if he'd worked that out, I dipped my head in apology.

'What was this Keshar character doing romping around in the woods with one of Her Majesty's rifles at that time?'

Young Adams gave a sigh to indicate it wasn't his favourite question, but he didn't try to duck it. 'Keshar was one of a shooting team which had been down at Warminster for a school of infantry demo. They got back about twenty-one-thirty hours and the armourer opened up for the return of weapons. The storeman says he signed in fourteen weapons. Unfortunately there were fifteen men on the detail.'

'Didn't they do a complete arms check?' The conversation was between the two of us now.

He shook his head and screwed up his face in shame and annoyance. 'Apparently they'd done a complete check at fifteen hundred hours and they were only waiting for these weapons. So, they didn't bother counting them in one by one because they were keen to go on to the party. Our old friend human error, I'm afraid.'

'Ammo?'

He gave me a funny look. 'You ask all the right questions, don't you, Hussy? Oh yes, of course, you're some sort of inquiry agent, aren't you? Or so our liaison chap was saying.'

'Something like that.' I'd had to declare myself – well, partly – and now it was all round the cop-shop, the barracks and very likely the old people's home. Great security. 'But even if I was a milkmaid I'd take a keen interest in someone firing rifles in my earhole.'

He hummed a point-taken sort of noise. 'I'm afraid it's all too easy to pocket a few rounds if you're shooting all day. So, Noble, unless there were two men running around the woods with SLR's last night, which seems unlikely, then Keshar is your man, like it or lump it.'

'I still don't see . . .' Charles' protest was drowned by the sound of a helicopter thrumming slowly overhead. For all their failure, Adams was impressed with the police response. They'd called in manpower from the division to set up a cordon to try to anchor the fugitive and restrict his movements. Then they'd called in support and dog units to sweep the area. But the cordon had had problems staying in line of sight of each other at night, and in such a heavily wooded area, and by daylight they were beginning to think he'd got through. The helicopter over the top, with heat-seeking camera, was their last chance to pick him up before he cleared the area.

'What sort of a man is this Keshar?'

Adams looked grateful for Anna's question. 'First-class soldier, jolly nice chap. What else can I say?'

'He's not usually in . . .?' she gave an apologetic laugh. 'I was going to say trouble, but that makes him sound like one of your naughty schoolboys, Charles.'

Adams smiled. 'I know what you mean. The answer's no. He's quite a feisty little character, which is why these chaps make such good soldiers. He likes a jar and a bet, and he's not totally averse to the ladies, but that applies to almost all our men.'

He looked around the table. 'But if I had to put my life in someone's hands, he'd be okay for me.'

'Apparently Charles did,' I said.

That set the schoolmaster off again, and left me free to shovel butter on to a fifth slice of toast, while trying not to think how many marathons it would take to clear a cholesterol overload like that. I was just taking my first bite when I saw him.

The window gave out on to a narrow street. At that moment, a juggernaut came grunting through, so near that it closed off the outside world. It was only when it passed that I realised that the darkened window of a supermarket across the street was a near-perfect mirror. In it, I could see the front of the coaching inn where we were eating, and I could also see the passageway next to it. Originally it must've been constructed for coaches, I suppose, but now it led through to the car park.

The man in the blue padded anorak sheltering in the passageway plunged his hands deeper into his pockets and shook his feet to keep off the cold. You'd think they'd be used to that, coming from the Himalayas, wouldn't you?

'I'm hitting the boys' room.' I chucked my napkin on to the table.

'On the left at the end of the corridor,' the waiter whispered discreetly as I passed. It was, too. But I went straight out into the yard at the back, looped back up the passageway from the rear, and up behind the shivering man huddled against the wall.

With his hood up he never heard a thing. The first he knew was that my arm was locked round his throat and I was in sole charge of his oxygen supply. You'd think that would be enough to guarantee some sort of co-operation, but I could feel him tense his muscles, brace his legs and his fingers feel for my arm. Suddenly he snapped his head back at my face and tried to twist his body into a throw, just like he'd been taught.

'Do that again and I'll break your neck and you'll be back in Nepal before you're out of traction.'

It wasn't so much the idea of a broken neck as the thought of being sent home in disgrace. That really does hurt those lads. I loosened my grip, and in my most paternal voice, I said: 'Now, hadn't you best be telling me just what the hell . . .'

Once he saw me, his face broke into a smile of relief. 'You detective?'

'Sort of. Hang on a minute though, aren't you . . .'

'*Maruni*, sahib. Rifleman Bhimbahadur.'

87

I'd seen the remains of his blue eye-shadow and the black stuff on his lashes. Without his sari and his wig, he was as boyishly plump-faced as the rest of them.

'And what's a *maruni* dancer doing lurking in alleyways?'

His cherubic features tightened up into a look of intense emotion. 'Keshar is not murderer.' He hissed the words up into my face.

'He had a fair try at it.'

He shook his head vigorously. 'No no no, sahib. Keshar good man. My friend. Good soldier.'

'So why does he go around popping off at passing motorists?'

Again he shook his head and I saw in his eyes something close to despair. 'My friend Keshar, he is in trouble.'

'I could've told you that.'

'No, no. Before this. Before last night.'

'What sort of trouble?'

He hesitated. I could feel his dark eyes searching mine for enough hope to carry on. 'You will help him?'

'If he's worth it. What was all this trouble about then?'

'A woman.'

'It's always a woman. But what's that got to do with him running amok in the woods? And where is he now?'

I was looking down into his face, willing him to spill all the words that were still locked inside him, when Adams' voice echoed in the main street.

'I don't know where Hussy has got to, but I really must be making a move myself. My driver should be here any minute.'

Then Noble's voice cut in. 'He's probably had to go to his room or something. You have our numbers, I think?'

The Gurkha's eyes moved quickly and he tilted his head to hear what was being said. He pulled a black packet from inside his jacket and held it between us, as though uncertain who should have it. When he spoke, it was a rushed whisper.

'Please help him, sahib. I am worried. I do not know what Keshar will do next, and I am frightened.'

'You're not the only one, but what do you want me to do?'

Just then a car passed the end of the passageway and we

could hear Adams' and Charles' voices join in a duet of goodbye, thanks, and sorry.

'The Gurkha Rose.' All the intensity had surged back into the little soldier's face again.

'The Gurkha Rose?' I repeated. But he'd gone.

As the car door slammed and the engine revved up, he turned and sprinted down the passage. I watched him as he vanished behind the rows of parked cars and I caught a last glimpse as he rolled over a four-foot wall at the far side of the car park.

Then I looked down at the black packet in my hand. Whatever it was, it was mine now.

I didn't bother mentioning either the packet or the *maruni* to the other two as we drove back to town. I doubt if I'd have had the chance anyway. All the way, Charles kept telling me how this proved that someone was trying to stop him finding his brother.

'Now you've got to help me,' he said triumphantly.

'That's the way it looks,' I said. 'That's the way it looks.'

We drove back to London through the faded winter greenery. On a village green I saw a circle of rain-blackened ash that was the remains of some kids' Guy Fawkes bonfire. When I was a kid in Kilburn, I used to read those old boys' comics about boarding-school life. It fascinated me, although God knows why, since it might as well have been science fiction for all it had in common with the vandalism and petty larceny that were the features of my schooldays.

Catching sight of Noble in the mirror, I thought that's him. Smith of the Lower Third. He'd never left school, physically or emotionally. The problem was, was he school hero, school sneak, or school bully?

# 14

The minute I got home I shot upstairs to get the packet opened, and what did I find? Jamie playing coochie-coo with Charlie. He was loving it too: needles in, legs out, and snuffling away at her fingers. Traitor.

'Don't do that. He's a one-man hog.';

'You're not fit to have him, going off like that. Come on, who's a lubberley little baby then?' She was down on all fours, and all I could see was the back of her lumberjack's tartan jacket and her bum in some oil-stained overalls.

'Don't spoil him. He'll grow up a homosexual hedgehog.'

'Aye, then 'appen he won't allus be in trouble like you. That reminds me, one of your bloody fancy women were on for you while you was out. Right snotty-nosed bitch by the sound of her.' She looked up so her grey-mix mop of hair swung back and screwed her mouth up to the size of a shirt-button. 'Kaindly tell him thet Veronica Noble was wishing to speak with him – daft tart. Oh aye, and a man called Cassidy. He sounded a bad 'un an' all.'

'He's a policeman, Jamie.'

'Well, I were right then, weren't I?'

As she clambered to her feet dusting herself down, I took her by the arms. 'Tell you what, Jamie. Let's get married and adopt Charlie, shall we?'

She stared at me, the crimson rising in her face like a flooded river. 'No thank you very much. I've enough problems without marrying a bloody waster like you.'

That was always a sure way to put her to flight. I dumped the packet on the table and I was tempted to open it there and then, but the thought of those phone calls was nagging me.

'School House.'

'Mrs Noble. Hussy here.'

90

'Ah yes, Mr Hussy, I'm so glad you called. I thought you might be interested to learn that I was quite correct about Charles' brother.'

'Richard? Correct?'

'Yes. As I believe I suggested the other night, Richard has taken himself off with another woman. No doubt you think that's admirable.'

'Since I don't know him and I don't know her, I don't have a very strong opinion either way. Who is she and how do you know about it?'

In tones marinated in venom, she replied: 'Alas, we do not know the name of the lucky lady so far. Perhaps we shall have to wait for the banns to be read – do you think? And it was Caroline herself who told me, the poor dear. Apparently he devoted all of two minutes on the telephone to informing her that her life was ruined. Isn't he a little charmer?'

I didn't want to get sucked down into her black emotional whirlpool so I stuck to straightforward factual questions. 'What does Charles have to say?'

She gave a ladylike whoop of amazement. 'Most strange, Mr Hussy. He went quite pale when I told him, then insisted there must be some mistake, even after he'd spoken to Caroline himself. He really is being too ridiculous for words.'

'Fraternal loyalty, I think it's called, Mrs Noble.'

She laughed. It sounded like broken glass. 'What a quaint notion. No, it isn't fraternal loyalty at all, as I'm sure you understand only too well. It's the mysterious trade union of males at work. In these matters, you're all boys together, aren't you? Although I must say I believe it has less to do with comradeship than it has to do with shared guilt. What do you think?'

'I'm sure I hope they'll all be very happy, whoever they are. Would you ever ask Charles to give me a ring when he has a minute?'

'Of course I will, but do you know, I told him I was going to let you know this . . . what shall I say?. . . this snippet of news, and he said he didn't have time to speak to you. I was astonished because I know what good chums you two have

91

become lately. So you may judge from that how shaken he is, the poor lamb. I was right after all, wasn't I?'

'Right? About what?'

'About Richard.'

'You don't like men much, do you?'

'Possibly I have been unfortunate in the ones I have chanced to meet.'

'Even your honourable husband?'

'Is Charles an honourable man, do you suppose?'

'I wouldn't know. It's funny stuff, honour. It's a bit like a sense of humour. Everyone has his own version and no two are quite the same. And everyone thinks his is best.'

'All boys together again, are we?'

As I put the phone down, I gave a long deep breath. Escaping from Veronica was taking off thumb-screws. In the way she talked you could hear an unholy mix of malice and glee. Even so, I still felt sorry for her. Men fear failure and women fear being unloved: her wicked witch act was only camouflage.

But what she'd said was enough to re-start my curiosity. Immediately I rang Caroline and got her mother. Caroline, she said, had gone up to town but if I was the dog-meat man I was to deliver as usual. I said I wasn't but if I saw him I'd be sure to tell him.

That left Cassidy. He was on day-off so I got him at home. He gave me another number and I went up the road to a payphone. When he answered I could hear someone shaking half-a-dozen broken harps in the background.

'Where the hell are you?'

'What? Oh, local chinky takeaway. That's the bloody Shanghai top ten you can hear.'

'Why are we being careful all of a sudden?' All these outside telephones were sound security practice but it didn't seem necessary.

'Funny feeling in me water. You wouldn't be pissing on my shoes this time, would you, cock?'

'Leave off, Cassidy. What d'you pick up?' I wasn't going to tell him he'd been wasting his time because I'd dropped the

Noble business. Anyway, after that shooting at Church Crookham, I thought I might keep my options open on that.

'The word is that matey has been playing the tables and picking up a lot of extra housekeeping.'

'Has he now? Lots?'

'Enough to get the gossip going.'

'Lucky lad then?'

'Maybe, and maybe not.'

'Well he won't get away with any funny stuff in the casinos, you know that. They're as tight as a nun's crutch since the Seventy Gaming Act. You couldn't cheat at snap in those places, not nowadays.'

'No one's complaining. Smiles all round. Love and friendship.'

'So what's funny about it then?'

'What's funny is that he goes in, sits down, pushes a few pennies around, wins and loses, then he begins to win, ups the dough to the big zeroes, and then just goes on winning. Five nights. Handshakes all round, do come again, take it in cash round the back, leaves with his guv'nor.'

'Who's his guv'nor?' I could tell from his voice that this was the juicy bit.

'You're gonna like this, Joe. A Scouser darkie who's a bit useful at the old street rioting himself.'

'That bloke.'

'Spot on. Funny that, innit?'

'Yeah. That's funny all right. What's Noble playing to pick up all these readies?'

'Do you know much about gaming?'

'No.'

'Right. It's called Punto Banco. Big wog game. The Ay-rabs lap it up, so do the lads with the compulsory sun-tans, because the old doubloons don't half change hands fast. You can lose a hundred grand on the turn of a card. That's how those boys like their thrills. Me, I'm still into WPC's – you ever see one with her epaulettes unfastened, Joe? Don't half give you a pain in the privates, take my word for it.'

'But your man just goes on winning?'

'And winning. Now the club ain't complaining, so strictly speaking we've no interest in it. I'd put the word out on matey and I got a whisper from a West End Central DS who'd heard something from a friendly croupier. Davina's – that's the name of a club. Posh. Bloody pricey too. He's due back for another session, they reckon, so do you fancy a squint at him?'

'How do we rig it?'

'The sort of stakes he's playing, he's got to get clearance from Central Credit in the US. That should give my tame croupier a chance to give us the tip-off.'

'Are your boys going to pull him in?'

'Strictly not. Far as I can make it out, he can burn London to the bleedin' ground and we stand by and applaud. Not that the buggers would tell me anyway – this one's down to the politicos. So you're not going to do anything that would make my life difficult are you, little Joe? Know wharra mean?'

'Don't worry about it. We'll watch from the ringside seats, eh?'

'Just so long as you don't get over-excited and join in.'

'What, me, Jim?'

'You, Joe.'

We left it at that, and I went back to the flat. I put the kettle on, while I decanted a vintage Heinz. Then I took my bowl of oxtail broth down to floor level, in front of the gasfire, and got out the black packet the *maruni* had pushed into my hands. Charlie ambled over for a sniff, then did some modest steeplechasing over my ankles. Sue Stocker had been right: once he'd got my scent, he'd become quite tame.

At first I'd taken it for black plastic, but now I looked closer I could see it was an old leather wallet, brown that had been aged into near-black, and wrapped around with a rubber band. Pouch was a better description because when I took the band off I saw it had only two large pockets, with two smaller compartments stitched on the front. I sat looking at it as I finished my soup and Charlie came sniffing over.

'What can it all mean then, young hog? Your namesake nearly gets his arm broken by a Gurkha in drag, then someone wings off a couple of shots in his direction. Just like he said they would. Whatever has our schoolmaster pal been up to, Charlie? Then his little brother Richard buggers off, just like Veronica said he would, and the next thing I hear is that he's breaking the bank with my Winston, the off-white black of blessed memory. I don't like it, Charlie. I don't like any part of it. I can't see the connections. There's a young soldier running amok in the south with the law snapping at his heels, and the little brother playing cards in London and revolutionaries up in Liverpool. And the only link is Charles. Then up pops the Gurkha's best mate and gives me this. One mysterious package. Well, if I remember my Robert Louis Stevenson, we open this up and find the map which leads us to the buried treasure. Am I right?'

I finished off my soup with a slurp and a burp that are the perks of living alone.

'So, Charlie, shall we have a look at Billy Bones' old map? And them as dies'll be the lucky ones, I dare say. They usually are.'

Naturally enough, that was when the doorbell rang. I did think of ignoring it, but on second thoughts I wrapped the wallet up, pushed it under the chair, and clattered down the stairs.

'You've got a very cheeky colleague, Mr Hussy.'

'Have I, Caroline?'

'Yes. She says I am to tell you that there are some cars that need servicing too. By the way she emphasised the last word, I imagine she was being ironic.'

'That's possible. I only wish I shared her sense of optimism.'

Later, Caroline said: 'You know Richard has gone?'

'I nodded.

'Veronica? I thought so.' She looked around. 'Gosh, it's six or seven years since I was in The Flask. Three of us used to share a flat in Parliament Hill and we always came up on Sunday mornings.' She deepened her voice to underline the self-mockery. 'The in-place for in-people.'

I'd taken her up to Highgate because in my local boozers she would've looked like a jewel in a dungheap. Not that she was a dressy young woman. As far as I could see she was wearing one of those baggy outfits that come in half a dozen layers – shirts, tops, jacket and flapping trousers – all held together in the middle with a heavy leather belt. A sombre look took some of her girlish quality away, but it didn't diminish the beauty in her square pert face and cloud-grey eyes.

'Are you still looking for Richard?'

'I should tell you right off I don't do matrimonial cases. I don't bring back runaways.'

'I wasn't going to ask you to.'

I glanced up. To my surprise, she had her head on one side and she was giving me a hard, determined smile. There was no anger or bitterness in her face: only a soft sheen of regret. That cheered me up. After Veronica, I'd had all the marriage misery I needed.

'You're taking it pretty well.'

'Well, I always knew it couldn't last.'

'Always?' That surprised me. Women usually like love on a long lease.

'Yes. If you knew Richard you'd know what I mean.'

'Tell me about Richard then?'

She sipped at her Perrier. I bit a piece out of my pint.

'He's an adventurer really. Excitement, change, fun, those are the things that attract Richard. Danger too. Danger more than anything. That's why I laughed when I heard how Charles had described him as a country gent. That's how Charles would've liked him to be, I'm sure. But Charles was the sensible one of the two, and Richard was the wild one. That's why they didn't get on.'

'Not at all?'

'Not really. In the past they'd had one or two blow-ups when Charles tried to tell him off for being reckless and Richard just laughed in his face, which made him even more pompous. They haven't seen each other for years. I suppose that was why Veronica found it so hard to ask for Richard's help.'

'What was that over?'

A brace of young advertising men, all matching spots and

stripes, raised braying voices to try to catch Caroline's attention. Her grey eyes never moved from mine.

'She came to him with some story about Charles being in some sort of trouble. Apparently he took to going to town rather a lot.'

'And the trouble?'

'Oh, it was only a girl-friend.' Quickly she added: 'It was ages ago and I'm sure it all came to nothing. Anyway, I think that only counts as a misdemeanour these days, doesn't it?'

The ad-men were getting shriller by the minute. They couldn't take their eyes off her. Without looking at them, she said quietly: 'A few years ago I would've been quite flattered by those types.'

'Not now?'

A pale smile moved over her face. 'That's what makes me really sad. When you've been married to Superman, everything else is bound to be such a let-down. I must say, the next few years look awfully grey from where I'm sitting.'

'Did Superman commit many misdemeanours?'

She drew a menthol cigarette from a packet, lit it, and blew a blue tube of smoke away into a sunbeam. She wasn't embarrassed by my question; she was giving it thought, that was all. 'I should imagine so. I mean, he kept it well away from me. He wasn't a hurtful person. And I certainly never went looking for clues, searching pockets or all that ghastly furtive business.'

She knew what my next question would be and answered it unspoken. 'He was an adorable, reckless man who didn't give a damn about what the world thought. He probably had ladies by the score. I didn't mind as long as he came back to me. He always did. Until now.' She blinked her eyes quickly and turned to look out of the window at the cold skies. 'He tried to be kind about it when he phoned. He did his best to . . . to make it acceptable.' Again she anticipated my question. 'He didn't say who the new woman is, and I didn't ask.'

To occupy herself, she undid the wide leather belt around her waist and fastened it again. 'So, I knew this day would come and I always tried to be ready for it, but it's still a bit of a knock when it arrives. It's a case of grit the teeth, Caroline, old girl, and soldier on.'

That's what she did then. Opened her lips to show me her gritted teeth as she tried to make a joke out of it. Just for a moment, she was teetering on the edge and I was relieved when she swept into the ladies. As she passed, one of the ad-men rolled his eyes and said to his friend: 'Class-ee.'

'Gosh, you are a good listener, you know.' She plonked herself down opposite me again, her face glistening pink.

'I'm not much good at handing out advice.'

'Thank goodness. I don't want advice. When I went with Richard, this was the risk I took.' She held her hands up, fingers splayed out.

'What – sort of like a firework display? Short-lived but bloody spectacular?'

She gave me a moist-eyed look and reached over and touched my hand. 'That's exactly it, Joe. And now the fireworks are over.'

I asked her why she'd come to see me as we were walking back to the cars.

'To give him a message.'

'What message?'

'Thanks. Thanks for everything. That's all. I forgot to tell him when he phoned.'

She'd got in her car and was winding down the window to say goodbye when I asked her the last question, the one I'd been nursing all the time.

'Was he a Marxist?'

She frowned and pursed up her lips. 'He was an individualist, even anarchist. But no, I wouldn't say he was a Marxist.'

Then her face lit up. 'Oh I know, you're thinking of the riots and Richard being fined. I did say he liked danger. He called it "fighting the good fight". You will remember if you find him, won't you?'

'Just thanks, is that it?'

'That's right – thanks for everything.'

Off she drove. And I did find myself thinking that if Richard

Noble had traded that woman in for a better one, I'd like to see the replacement.

As soon as I got back, I pulled the wallet out from under the chair. I cleared some of the old pots and crumbs off the table, opened it up, and began to empty the pockets.

Letters. What do soldiers always carry? And I don't suppose the ones from Nepal are any different. They were written in Gurkish or whatever it is they speak, pages and pages of swoopy swirly patterns. A purple colour against pale blue paper, and scented too, so that from the pile there arose a secret stored perfume that made you think of yashmaks and harems.

When the indecipherable letters slid away like scree, they revealed a small stack of happy snaps from home. Gurkha and Mrs Gurkha with two mini-Gurkhas. In uniform. In native cottons. Mrs G. in sari. In front of white-washed hillside houses. Arm in arm. Very proper. Very proprietorial. Very Mr and Mrs. I didn't recognise the man in the snaps. He was taller than the average, and not quite so round-faced. In the background, looking as garish as the Dashera backdrop, were more icing-sugar mountains and Hollywood blue skies: only these were the originals.

Valuable as his family mementos undoubtedly were, I didn't see why I'd been given them.

I shovelled that lot to one side and picked up the wallet again. It was as soft as silk. I opened both pockets with two hands and shook them, and all that came out was some Himalayan dust and the smell of tired donkeys. So then I started on the two smaller pockets. Knotted toggles held them fast and it was a struggle to undo them. I could only get one finger in the first one. Empty. In the second pocket, I had to twist my finger around to get them out.

One newspaper cutting. One more happy snap.

I skip-read the cutting. It was an article about Beachy Head. Once I saw the photograph, I lost interest in articles about tragic scenes at Britain's chalk cliffs. This one definitely wasn't from the family album. Someone else thought the same because they'd scrawled on the back, in ballpoint: 'I don't think the wife would like to see this, do you? Or your CO.'

99

Certainly, unless his dainty little wife had put on four stone and lost her tan, all her clothes and most of her inhibitions, it was someone else. And there was Mr Gurkha clambering around on what looked like Himalayas of white flesh, and – by the look on his face – not expecting someone to hop out with an Instamatic at exactly that moment.

Then I remembered what the shivering little Gurkha had said to me when he gave me the package at the hotel that morning. Perhaps it did make some sense after all.

Not much. But some.

## 15

I got the news about the Gurkha Rose the day we had the panic over Charlie's ticks.

I spotted them first. It was six days after Caroline's visit. Jamie had chucked everything at me, from blowing up kids' footballs to mending punctures on invalid chairs: she said it was to make up for all the time-off I'd taken, but I suspected it was more of a punishment for having visits from pretty ladies. Still, I did owe her a bit of spanner-work.

I'd sneaked upstairs to try to snatch a mug of mid-morning tea while Jamie was giving a full character assessment to a county lady who'd been foolish enough to try to empty her ashtray on the forecourt. As I put the kettle on, I could hear Jamie weigh in with a polite inquiry about the woman's home address. Next came the deafening blast: 'Right – now tonight I'm coming to tip my rubbish all over your 'ome.' Still chuckling, I had a quick look at Charlie, who was kipping away in his self-filthed bed, and I saw this grey-blue balloon down among his spikes. I hauled him out and examined him. There must've been eight or nine of them clinging to his skin.

Sue Stocker was out saving a damaged badger, so I phoned a local vet. He declined the case because he didn't treat wild animals. Apparently they think it's unethical to interfere in the universal plan of the Almighty, possibly because of talk to the effect that the Lord can be a bit slow in meeting His bills. By the time I'd got Jamie upstairs and well into a dour Yorkshire panic, Sue Stocker rang back and told us what to do.

'I 'ope you're not going to eat off this table,' Jamie said. She was holding Charlie on the table while I plucked the first tick out with a pair of eyebrow tweezers. I dropped it on the table and squashed it with my thumb. It made a deeply satisfying plop and left a small pool of blood on the table. Someone else's blood, I suppose, since that's what ticks live on.

'It's the only protein I get. Hang on to him.' You'd be amazed how hard you have to tug to get a determined tick away from its loved one. They dig their teeth right down into the flesh. I was just prising away the last one when the phone went. It was Adams.

'Hussy? I believe I can help you after all.' I'd rung the young captain to ask if he could find out about the Gurkha Rose. Was it a pub? An Indian takeaway? Or – as I thought – a woman. He'd admitted that, under great strain and the influence of drink, without the flawless example of their officers in mind, it was just possible that small Himalayan legs might be got over. Once we'd got that established, he relaxed and said he'd ask around.

'You were right, she's a whore in Aldershot and I gather the name Gurkha Rose is something of an ironic title.'

It would be, wouldn't it? In the body-buying business, it's the wealthy Arabs in Knightsbridge who get the brand-new models straight out of the showroom. Defenders of the realm, and particularly darkish defenders of the realm, get the clapped-out bomb-site wrecks.

'She's an old slag?'

'I think that's the expression. The story is that in her younger days she tended to the Welsh Guards, and, as her commercial value declined, she worked her way down through the Paras and then our chaps.'

'Don't knock it – that's the free enterprise culture you've sworn to protect. She'll probably end up delivering ecstasy to the first battalion of traffic wardens. Where do I find her?'

He'd done his stuff all right. She worked from a pub in Aldershot, where she picked up most of her clients, and then took them back to a ninth-floor flat – 'hardly ideal-homes, I gather' – in a tower block. He'd also heard talk of a ponce who kept an eye on things.

There was still no sign of Kesharsing. That wasn't so surprising. If he wanted to, he could probably live off the country. And even in small country towns these days, an oriental face is commonplace. Picking him up could prove a problem.

'I'm worried about him, Hussy.' Young Adams was anxious to talk about it so I just kept my ear plugged in. 'All the stories you hear about the Gurkhas are quite true. They are very courageous fellows. In general, the worse conditions are, the better they respond. But they do have a strong fatalistic streak. I don't doubt there's a perfectly good explanation for this mess Keshar's in, but he's obviously ashamed to come back and face the music. It doesn't happen often, but once they start to think they're beaten, they give up totally. I can't help thinking of poor old Keshar beginning to believe he's doomed and getting into a downward spiral.'

'What would he do then, d'you reckon?'

'I simply don't know.'

I stayed late in the workshop to keep Jamie happy. In any case, I didn't want to risk my life with the early evening commuters racing down the A3 with four large gins under their waistcoats: they really were fatalists. And it did occur to me that someone in Rose's profession wouldn't do a very heavy teatime trade.

At least it got me back in Jamie's good books – she let me take a snazzy little Honda CRX that was in for a suspension check. I got down to Aldershot just after nine and I found the pub Adams had told me about almost immediately. In the saloon bar, half a dozen blokes were playing a listless game of darts, and round the side in the snug a pair of pensioners were nursing their precious glasses of stout. The only female in the place was stark naked, with breasts that had been dangerously over-inflated unless she was thinking of carrying heavy loads at high speeds. She was on the calendar on the wall to help those people who can't tell the date without the assistance of an agitated nipple.

That meant I had to ask the barman, who looked about fourteen and whose skin area was being contested by acne and a tattooist. Suffering Jesus, I'm not such a sensitive little flower but even I winced when his pasty face broke into a leer: 'Gurkha Rose? You wanna bunk-up?'

Before I could formulate an answer to that, he was off into an apology for her. Rose was out of commission. She'd got a dodgy leg acquired in pursuit of her professional duties, when a customer had got over-excited. She'd phoned to say she wouldn't be in for a couple of nights at least.

'Tell you what though, mate, why doncha go round anyway? She'll be chuffed to get a white bloke again.'

A bit prim, I marched out beneath the incredulous gaze of the darts players. At least, I hoped it was incredulous.

She lived ten minutes away in a tall glass-and-plastic modern slum that had been built to replace the short brick out-of-date slums. The designers had placed it in a traditionally land-scaped parkland of litter, broken glass, rubble, half a pram and a maimed supermarket trolley. All the graffiti artists agreed on what should be done to the Government, the Social Security, the National Front, the blacks and the police. By happy coincidence, it was exactly what Rose did for a living.

The lift button was dead. So were the lights. Cautiously, feeling my way up the handrail in the near total dark, I climbed the nine flights of stone stairs, cold with the stench of old vomit and defeat. I was standing in the dark, blinking around me, when at the end of the corridor a door flung open and a torrent of pink light and mushy noise poured out.

'Come on in, darlin'. Little Terry phoned to say you was on

your way. So I says to him, the least I can do is to get meself glammed up. There, sit yerself down.'

I stepped into a room crammed with cheap and shiny furniture, which in turn was decorated with cheap and shiny ornaments, plates, chrome teapots and bright trays. With heavy curtains at the window, a carpet as long and tangled as dreadlocks, and a scattering of tasselled lamps, it looked in need of a good lawnmower. After the cold, sour smell outside, the sweet heat was heavy on the stomach.

In the midst of this, the Gurkha Rose stood, a smiling marshmallow of pink flesh in a black mini-dress she must've put on when she was about nine, which was the last time it would've fitted her, and kept on ever since. Judging by her sagging face, that was about fifty years ago. She was bending in front of a gilt-edged mirror straightening up a bubbly blonde wig without removing a king-size cigarette from her mouth.

'There, that's better, in't it darlin'? Little drinkies first?' She limped over to a selection of bottles on a gold-coloured trolley. 'That'll be twenty quid, now if you don't mind love.'

Twenty quid. By the year, it was daylight robbery. By the ounce, it was probably good value.

Before I went in I should've made up my mind whether I was going to buy or bully. I knew what I should do: give her a touch of the terrors to make her sphincter twitch, then she'd tell me. But I'm a terrible old-fashioned thing about women; that's why I stood there, wavering, and that's why I tried to take the easy route, and buy it. Mistake.

'Tell me something and you can have the twenty quid.'

She froze. When she spoke her voice was harsh and wary.

'Oh yes, and what would that be?'

'I want to know about that.' I crossed the room and put the photograph on the sideboard.

She looked at it without moving. I watched.

'Don't know nuthin' about that.' She did straighten then and faced me. 'No, it don't mean a thing to me, that.'

'Twenty quid. Maybe a bit more if you tell a good tale.'

First Neville Chamberlain, then me. It's always the same. Try to be reasonable and someone will take it for weakness. The

Gurkha Rose did just that. Her stony eyes ran over my face, and she produced her cigarette from somewhere and stuck it back in her pink-painted face.

'Out.' She angled her man-made hair towards the door. 'Piss off, you little creep. We don't like fuckin' peepers round here.'

I sighed. One last try. 'A chat, that's all. Thirty quid. Save us both a lot of trouble.'

'I told you, out, fuck off, you dirty little bleeder.'

'That's a shame.'

Three strides took me to the window. I pulled aside the curtain. It was one of those wide metal-framed windows that pivot in the centre. I opened it so the bottom half moved outwards.

'What you doin'?' She spoke in a hushed voice now. The bluster had gone. Suddenly she shrieked. ' 'Ere, don't you bloody touch me . . .'

She slammed out with an arm like an oak. It lashed over my ducked head and shot straight up her back as I spun her round and rushed her at the window. With her free hand, she pushed at the window to halt the charge, so with my left hand I grabbed the back of her neck and forced her head down and through the gap. Before she knew what had happened, I rammed my knee up her backside to drive her further out, and then seized the huge haunches of her thighs on either side of my own legs and lifted them wheelbarrow-style.

I shunted her another foot forward. Now her crutch rested on the thin metal window frame. Her great fat bum – naked where her skirt had pushed up – see-sawed in the middle, and the rest of her body jutted out into the night sky like a ship's figurehead.

I looked at myself. Holy Mother! Standing between the fat monster's thighs gripping her hips. It's an approved sex position, I know, but will you find it in the murder manuals?

At first the top half of her reared upwards, screaming and waving her arms. Then the physical effort was too much and after a minute or so she flopped down against the side of the building. Like shed plumage, her bright wig fell from her head and swung slowly downwards, turning until it sank into the blackness below. Two other blocks of flats, separated by a few hundred yards, were patchworks of light and dark. Beyond them the lights of the town centre were a civilised glow. But at this ninth floor window, there was only my grip on her thighs to stop her following her wig into the deep darkness below.

Fear of falling is a powerful persuader. It's the oldest fear, the only one babies are born with and it still haunts our dreams.

After five minutes she was draped over the sill like half a ton of uncooked sausage meat. Will, resistance, dignity, anger, hope . . . all gone. All that was left was a blubbering lump of badly-kept flesh.

With my left hand still round her thigh, I gripped the back of her flashy little frock with my right, and edged her back into the room. I couldn't hear what she was saying through the terror and tears. I held her with her waist over the sill, her feet on the ground, and only the top half of her body out in the night. That way I could hear her talk. That way I could easily push her out again if I didn't like what she said.

'Ooooooo.' She wailed like a spook. 'I'll tell you about him, I'll talk.'

'Talk.'

'He's one of them Gurkhas from up at Church Crookham. Keshar I think he's called. 'Ere, can I come in now, mister?'

'Talk.'

'Well, it warnt my idea, none of it. Warnt Gary's neither, so don't blame 'im.'

'What wasn't?'

'That photo. The shootin'. Everythin'. Please can I come in now? I never bin so scared.'

I hesitated for a moment, because I didn't want to have to go through the whole performance again, and – like I say – I'm sentimental about women. Then I dragged her in and dumped her in one of her long-haired armchairs. She crashed into it, panting. When I'd arrived she wasn't exactly a finalist for Queen of the May, but now she looked a real sight. Her face was translucent with fear and her mouth hung open as she sucked in the air. The skimpy dress had ridden both up and down so that now it covered only the area between her pelvis and her breasts.

The rest hung out, and it wasn't womankind in all her glory, I can tell you.

'Whose idea was it?'

'This bloke.'

'Who?'

'She turned up her pudding face. 'I don't know, honest mister. It was all 'is plan. He got Gary to take that snap, the one you've got, then he had to show it to Keshar and get him to do what he wanted.'

'Blackmail.'

Slowly, she nodded.

'And what did he want?'

'All he wanted Keshar to do was to frighten a feller.'

'How? How did he frighten him?'

She was breathing better now, and she sat up and brushed back the pathetic clumps of thin hair the wig had concealed. 'He had to hide up in the woods and shoot near this feller. Not at him. Gary'd never muck around with anythin' like that. No, he just had to shoot somewhere near him to give him a scare. Like a joke he was playing on one of his mates.'

'How did he know who to shoot at? Or near.'

'This bloke – the one who'd planned it all – said the car would stop and this geezer would get out and walk round near the headlights. All Keshar had to do was to fire off his rifle.'

'You don't know the man who fixed it up and you don't know the man who was shot at? Does Gary?'

'He's not 'ere.'

'Where is he?'

'Isle of Wight.'

'Visiting?'

She nodded. At this level of the social strata, he wouldn't be sailing, that was for sure.

'But Gary must've met the fixer, the man who set it all up?'

Again, she nodded.

'Well? What did he tell you about him?'

'He said he was posh, smart clothes and fancy accent and all that.'

'How did he know that Keshar could get his hands on a rifle?'

'Gary had to work it all out with Keshar. There was one day when he could do it.'

'Just like that.'

She shook her head. 'No, no, we had an 'ell of a job gettin' him to do it. He swore he wouldn't, said he'd rather be court-marshalled, but Gary sent him a copy of the photo and kept going on about sending it to his missus in India and to the high-ups at the camp. And we had to keep tellin' 'im it was only acting, nobody was going to get 'urt, and that way we got him to do it. He wasn't to tell anyone either but the daft little bugger did.'

'Who did he tell?'

'One of his mates. Another Gurkha. He musta told him 'cos he came round to the pub the other night. That was after the cock-up.'

'What cock-up?'

She was beginning to recover her composure. I had to keep her shaken and running. 'Look mister, I don't know who the 'ell you are or what . . .'

I sighed. 'Looks like we'd better try the window again, Rose.'

She watched the curtain moving in the wind and gave a little shiver. 'Gary says some geezer took off after Keshar, he lost his bloody gun and the whole place was swarming with coppers and MPs and God knows what. Now Keshar's done a runner.' She gave me a narrow-eyed look. 'You'll know all that, it was in the papers.'

'What'd he give you for it?'

'For what?'

'Twisting Keshar's arm.'

She came half out of her seat and reached past me to grab her cigarettes. 'Not bleedin' enough, I can tell you. All this fuckin' trouble. What're you then? SIB?' She started oozing her breasts back into the dress.

Her confidence started coming back with the nicotine. I let her have it. She'd told the truth, or the bit that mattered anyway. I'd finished with her now.

I took out one of Jamie's garage cards and wrote my name on the back, and put it on the arm of the chair. 'Give Gary that. Tell him I want to see him.'

From inside a huge cloud of smoke, she muttered: 'Yeah, an' he'll want to see you, mate.'

Driving back to town, I decided that at least I now had one less puzzle. The shooting had bothered me. The Gurkhas regularly walk away with all the prizes at Bisley. What they don't do is miss a target like a full-grown man, standing in the headlamps of a car, at one hundred yards. Which was why I'd felt confident enough to take off in the darkness after the gunman. It wasn't foolhardy at all. I knew he'd been shooting to miss.

But if it cleared up one problem, it created another. There are plenty of good reasons for shooting at someone to hit him. Shooting to miss – now that calls for a very strange set of motives.

It was all either much trickier than I thought. Or much simpler. What bothered me most of all was that the target had been the innocent schoolmaster.

Back in the flat, Charlie, now he wasn't sharing his blood supply, was truffling round looking very perky. I got on the phone.

'Caroline?'

'Yes. Oh, it's you. Have you . . .'

'Sorry, no. But I'm hoping to. Soon. Look, a question. Was Richard a big gambler?'

'A gambler? Do you mean backing horses and things?'

'No. The serious stuff. Casino gambling. I mean big money, big games.'

She laughed. 'Never. Indoor games weren't his thing at all.'

'Never?'

'Never. It would be far too dull for Richard.'

'He'd rather fight the good fight?'

'Any day.'

I thought about that picture of him making weedkiller bombs. You could classify that as fighting the fight, okay, but whether it was a good one or not was veering towards the subjective. Dull? No, it certainly wasn't dull.

'One more thing. Someone said he was away a lot on business. Was he really on business?'

'Yes, I'm quite sure he was. I don't have any doubts about that.'

I rang off and gave her last answer some thought. If your husband's just scarpered with another woman, surely you wouldn't be all that confident about his movements. What should she have said? 'I'm beginning to wonder.' Or: 'I don't know what to think.' Something like that. Not that unquestioning certainty. I'd thrown the question at her straight enough and it had come back at a funny angle.

The phone rang again before I had time to move.

'Charles Noble. Any news for me?' Ever since the shooting, he regarded me as back on his books again. I thought I'd go along with it. After all, it hadn't been one of Cringle's five-star warnings.

'No. But I'm hoping for something soonish. Hey, look Charles, if I do turn him up, what exactly do you want me to do with him? I don't think he'll want to come back for tea somehow.'

'I realise that. I suggest you simply turn the information over to me and I'll take it from there.'

'If he's starting the brave new life with some young girl he might not be delighted to see his past walk through the door.'

'I'm perfectly aware of that possibility also.'

'You sound a mite peevish tonight.'

'Do I? Yes, I suppose I am rather feeling the strain. I'm sorry if I sound . . . disagreeable.'

'Don't you worry about that now. Something's been bothering me. You know when we were leaving the Gurkha party and we stopped by the side of the road?'

'Yes.'

'Can you remember why we stopped? You know, why you got out at that particular point?'

'I'm not sure now but I seem to recall that I thought I saw something in the road. Yes, that was it. I remember now. I thought I saw something.'

'I remember.'

'Oh, Hussy, as you know I am most grateful that you agreed to address yourself to this problem once again, but I hoped you wouldn't be offended if I mentioned that there seems to be a degree of urgency about it now. If there is any way of speeding things up a trifle . . .'

'Why is it more urgent now?'

'Let's say it's more a general sense of hastening events. So if you can turn up that wretched brother of mine, I would like to see him sooner rather than later.'

# 16

'Joe, old cock, what the fuck've you pulled me into?'

'Howd' you mean?'

'Don't you give me that old cobblers, you know bloody well. Oh yeah, this is Rob Thaw, inspector at Davina's. Rob, Joe's the crooked little mick I was telling you about. Give us a couple of minutes to sort this out.'

Thaw, thirtyish, grave face over a spade-shaped beard, trenchcoat and gleaming black shoes, collected his alcohol- free lager and found an empty table in the corner. Two days after I'd last spoken to him I'd got the call from Cassidy. A game was on tonight. To my surprise, the only suit I owned still fitted me: also to my surprise there wasn't any confetti in the pockets from the last time I'd worn it. One way and another, that was the most expensive suit in the history of men's tailoring.

We'd fixed to meet in this Hooray's boozer round the corner from Chelsea barracks. It was so quiet, I thought the Bun-throwing Olympics must be on somewhere.

Then in burst Jim Cassidy, pale, skinny, like six foot of

uncooked spaghetti with his bony wrists sticking out of an orange anorak. Dressed like that, he wasn't going to any casino. And as soon as he'd shunted Thaw off into a corner, he grabbed me by the elbow and started giving me a going over.

'So what's the game then? I told you, don't piss on my shoes, I'm supposed to be your mate . . .'

'What's the problem?'

He took a deep breath and rubbed his long sheep face with his raw-boned hands. 'I ran a check on you, Joe.'

'Me? You know me, Cassidy.'

'Nobody fucking knows you, cock. I knew you'd been wed but I didn't know nuthin' about your family and that . . .'

'I get you. No daughter.'

'No daughter.' He leaned back on the bar and glared at me with red sore eyes. 'You been telling me porkies. Naughty. Very naughty.'

'Jim, I had to dress it up a bit for you. I knew you wouldn't dip into the computer unless you thought it was worth it. That's all. On the grave of my sainted mother, God bless her.'

'Yeah, and we know what she did for a living, don't we?' Jim's suspicious eyes watched me over the top of his pint of stout. 'Straight up?'

'As I live and breathe.'

'Cod me again like that and you won't be doing either much longer. I'm out.'

'Hey, come on, don't start getting all bloody dainty. . .'

He moved his long rough-skinned face nearer to mine. 'You're playing, Joe. I can tell. You got something on and you're not saying. I'm out. You wanta stay with it?'

'Ach, you know me. I'd fight a monkey in a dustbin for a few laughs.'

He stood upright and drained his glass. He beckoned to Thaw who was reading the *Standard* in the corner.

'I tried. This Rob, he's a good bloke. Mate of a mate. Used to work at the Ritz and that means perfection in this business. He don't know nothing about the background. Far as he's concerned, he just saw some fishy stuff at the club and

112

mentioned it to this mate of mine. Keep him in the clear. Keep me in the fuckin' clear too. I don't know you, cock. Right?'

'Right. And thanks for the favour.'

'Some fuckin' favour.'

'Jim had to go?' Thaw arrived as Cassidy's stooping figure swung through the door.

'He couldn't stay. So, have a drink and tell me all about it.'

'Do you know much about casino games?'

'Hopscotch was the last game I played with serious intent.'

The next half-hour we spent back at the corner table while he tried to explain to me all about Punto Banco. The way Rob explained – with great patience in the face of my ignorance – it was like pontoon: one of those games where you add up the value of your cards to get as near as you can to a set number. With pontoon, it's twenty-one. With Punto Banco, it's nine.

'What I don't get is why it was so remarkable.'

'Well,' he said, again with great patience, 'it's just so unusual for someone to win continually like that.'

'Bent?'

He screwed his face up in a way that meant he wasn't sure but he certainly didn't like it. 'Casinos are very clean these days, but wherever you get money in millions someone's going to try to bend the rules. If there is something funny going on, why no complaints?'

'Maybe all the other punters haven't noticed.'

He stared at me. 'Oh, didn't I explain that?'

'What?'

'There's only one.'

'What d'you mean, only one?'

'Only one man beside your friend. Noble, is it? Noble bets one way, the other guy bets the opposite, and they both bet the same stake.'

'Just the two of them?'

'That's right. So every time Noble wins, the other man loses the same amount. At Punto you play the house, but it's just as though these two are playing each other. But since the man who's losing seems quite cheerful about it, then who am I to complain? If you see what I mean.'

'Any idea who he is?'

'A Brazilian. Businessman. I believe he's called Santos.'

'You'd think he might get a bit sick of losing to the same guy every time, particularly if it looks a bit of a dodgy game.'

'That's what I think.'

'But he doesn't.'

'Apparently not.'

I tried to think what that might mean. 'Just the two of them?'

Once again, he began to explain, and slowly I began to see it. They played in a *salle privée*, a section of the club which was roped-off for a special game for high rollers. It was the same every time. They started playing for modest stakes, both winning and losing a few. Then the stakes would shoot up, Noble would begin to win, and go on winning.

'How many hands does he win?'

'Fourteen, one night.'

'Is that unusual?'

His earnest face nodded in front of me. 'You could say that. Six or seven banks in a row is unusual. Eleven or twelve is exceptional. I did hear of a woman once who won seventeen banks in a row.'

'So it's possible.'

He gave a small sigh. 'It's possible, in the same way that lightning in the same place twice is possible. Odds are something I understand. It's my profession. Whatever the punters tell you, in the end the statistics win, like the house keeps twenty per cent of all the money that comes through the door. So, yes, of course it's possible. Once. Twice even. Very unlikely but possible. But he's cleaned Santos out five times, and each time with a run of ten or more banks.'

'But Mr Santos isn't worried?'

'If he is, it doesn't show. That's what makes me wonder why I'm bothering.' He combed his beard with his fingers and I saw he was chewing his bottom lip. For the first time I saw the fear in his face. 'The truth is that if it is fixed, it's very big money. That could be dangerous, couldn't it?'

I nodded. 'Could it be fixed?' I banged the side of my head. 'Now there's a stupid question. Anything can be fixed.'

'It would be difficult, and I think it would cost a lot. The way to do it would be a rigged shoe.' He gave me an uncertain look. 'You remember I told you the shoe is a sort of box that holds all the cards – six packs in each one. In Davina's, to save time, they have the shoe made up beforehand. That could be set up to give the cards out in a certain sequence.'

I could follow most of that. What nobody had mentioned so far was how much Richard Noble – who never gambled, according to this wife – was picking up at his shady games of cards. I asked. Rob told me. It took me a full minute to take it in. Then I saw why everyone was getting nervous.

'Over a million quid? Playing cards?'

He gave an apologetic smile. 'Well over. I know what you mean. It all gets rather unreal, doesn't it?' He looked at his watch. 'We'd better leave. They will have started by now.'

# 17

I dropped Thaw at the club and then went for a stroll around Mayfair. One thing Cassidy had done for me was to fix up a membership card to get me in, to get around the forty-eight-hour wait, but it wouldn't do for the two of us to be seen together. I was glad. It gave me fifteen minutes' calm to sort out my own thoughts. There was plenty to sort. First there was the amount of money Richard was winning. Thaw had been amused at my amazement – millions really do get lost and won in casinos and those who work there soon cease to marvel at it. Even so, it was dangerously big money.

Then there was the whole idea of Richard Noble himself. I found myself getting fascinated by him. I'd been given three versions of the man. The country gent turned traitor, from

Charles; the slimy womaniser, from Veronica; and Caroline's Superman. I had a few ideas of my own about him too. That was one reason why I wouldn't take up Cassidy's tip to back out. After all this, I wasn't going to leave without seeing Richard Noble.

Why they call them games of chance, I'll never know. There's one stone-cold certainty and that is that although plenty of casinos have been closed down for being bad boys, not one has ever closed for lack of money. Casinos don't go bankrupt. You may be clever, you may be skilful, you may even be lucky; you may have a system, you may have an inspiration, you may have prophetic dreams; but of all the money taken by all the punters into all the clubs in Britain, a thick slice of it stays right there. In the clubs.

That's why they like to dress the whole business up to give it a spurious respectability. From the first Mississippi riverboat dealer who put on a frilly shirt, to the tails and toppers of Ascot, they cloak the process in elegant finery, so that they bolster the confidence of those whose wallets are about to be lightened. Davina's was no exception.

Discreet swing doors, panelled hall, marble and gilt bar and restaurant, wide curving mahogany staircase to the gaming area, where dinner jackets and dark silk suits and ladies in Parisian sheaths drifted between crystal chandeliers and hushed carpets. Emotions, voices, reflexes all heavily suppressed. Losing money is a civilised business.

I could have found Richard Noble without Thaw's directions. Even I could see how the composure of the room was – in the most discreet fashion, of course – disturbed in some invisible but volcanic manner. From the musical tick-tock of the roulette wheels and the subdued calls of the croupiers, there was a drift towards the far end of the room where a bunch of people had gathered.

As I crossed the floor, I sensed more than heard the hum of excitement. Two wine-coloured velvet curtains were parted to reveal the *salle privée* Rob Thaw had mentioned. All that stopped anyone going in was a yard of crimson rope on two brass stands, but it was enough. They stood there at the entrance looking in, like kids round a toy-shop at Christmas.

Inside, Richard Noble was quietly piling up another fortune.

I recognised him immediately. He looked like Charles and he looked unlike Charles, both at the same time. He was shorter, more leathery, more used. Where Charles looked like a puzzled visitor on a day trip to Earth, Richard was a bona fide inhabitant, and a shop-soiled one at that. He didn't look like a man who would puzzle easily. But he did have the light skin and fair colouring, and there was something else there too that I couldn't quite identify: perhaps the way he sat or held his head. He and his brother shared the same ingredients but they'd been cooked to a different recipe.

He didn't have his brother's sideways hair. His was a mousey scrub that had been finger-combed by the look of it, and he wore a shabby dinner jacket that might as well have had the Return by Tomorrow ticket pinned on the lapel.

He was facing me, sitting at the table Thaw had described – a long round-ended affair, with two dealers at the centre on one side, another opposite them, and a dozen or more chairs around either end. They were all empty, apart from Richard, and Santos. That's who I took it to be from what little I could see of him. With his back to me, he was at the seat at the table which was at the farthest point from Richard's. All I could see was that he was short, dark and wearing a cream silk suit.

For the next few minutes I tried to pick up the play from what I'd been told.

If they'd started with small stakes, as they had before, then tonight they must've been playing for quite a while, judging by the pile of plaques and chips in front of Richard. I tried to remember what Thaw had said about their value, but the only ones I could recall were the blues which were worth five thousand, the greens which were worth ten, and the biggest in the house, the twenty-five-thousand-pound gold ones. In front of Richard there was plenty of green and brown, and at least four golds. He was doing it again.

Then the dealer spoke.

'The first coup of the new shoe will be on eight.'

Richard was holding the polished wooden box containing the

117

cards they call the shoe. That meant he was holding the bank, and would deal the cards. First, he picked up one of his plaques and slid it carelessly into the segment of the table marked eight. He was betting on the bank, so he put his stake in his own numbered section.

From the people around me, there was a tiny hiss of breath. The plaque was gold. He was backing the maximum. Twenty-five thousand pounds.

Rising slightly in his seat, Santos leaned over and dropped his plaque in the centre of the table. He was backing punto. Against the bank. Against Richard Noble. And also in gold.

'Any more bets?'

Santos was lighting a cigarette. Richard was inspecting his thumbs.

'No more bets.'

The dealer looked down at Richard beside him. 'Cards, please.'

From the wooden shoe, Noble drew one card and slid it across to the punto. He dealt another to himself. Then he repeated the process, and the dealer sang out the cards. Two two's for the punto giving a total of four. Two and a ten for the bank, which – since tens and picture cards count nothing – gave a total of two.

'Card each.'

Again the dealer sang it out. The punto had got another two, giving a total of six. The bank had drawn a seven, leaving him with a total of nine. Noble had won. You couldn't get much closer to nine than nine.

The seated dealer scooped up the two plaques and paid Richard out with one gold and a pile of greens and browns. What was it Thaw had said? A twenty-quid win on the bank got you nineteen back. In about a minute, he'd made a profit of nearly twenty-four thousand pounds.

When the dealer called it, I could sense the softening of tensed up muscles all around me. Then came the gulp for oxygen. For gamblers, this was a classic: two men, high stakes, the only skill the intuition that all chancers swear they've got, all over in seconds.

'That's a run of how many?' I tuned in to the conversation behind me.

'Eight? Nine? Not sure.'

They were whispering. The atmosphere was closer to a cathedral than a betting shop.

'Eight or nine? Phenomenal! That must be one for the record books, mustn't it?'

'Apparently the same chap did it the other night too.'

'The same man? I doubt that.'

'That's the rumour.'

The whispering died. Richard was dealing again. And again the doleful voice of the dealer announced the cards. A seven and a picture card for Richard – adding up to a total of seven. For the punto, a three and a valueless picture card – total, three. That allowed the punto one more card. Richard slid it out and turned it over. Another picture card.

'Seven, three. Bank wins,' drones the croupier. Richard had done it again.

Once again they paid him out. As before, his own gold plaque back, plus another £23,750 in greens and browns.

As they began again, I watched the two players. They were as far apart as the table allowed them. They never exchanged a glance, let alone a word. For all that passed between them, each man could've been playing patience. Richard Noble sat up at the table, a raffish figure. Almost anxious to have it done, the way he flicked the cards out quickly; but, if he had to wait mere seconds, his eyes roved the room in what looked like boredom. The Brazilian slumped in his seat, a frog-shaped figure who moved only to place his bet. Neither the sums of money, nor the repetition of the winning and losing, none of it was reflected in their faces. Even for a business that prides itself on stoicism, that was quite something.

Watching them, I had to keep reminding myself that they weren't men who'd happened to hop on the same bus together. They chose to be here. They chose to play together. They both chose to place the maximum bet. There was no mistaking it: it was a gladiatorial contest.

Yet even though they were bound together by the power of

the drama they created, they did everything they could to pull away from each other. No word, no glance, nothing passed between them, except the cards and the money. They reminded me of something: suddenly I remembered what it was. They were like illicit lovers, caught in the act.

Six more times they played. Six times Richard dealt in that let's-get-it-over style. Six times, the silken frog rocked up out of his seat to place his plaque. Six times the dealer's deadpan voice called out another win for Richard. The spectators thickened and bunched. The murmuring and the breathing sank and rose like a tide.

Then, incredibly, it ended. Just when it seemed that the pattern was unalterable, that one man was born to win and the other doomed to lose, it all changed. Santos won.

Because the dealer announced it in the same flat voice, I missed it, but the sudden craning of necks and movement around me tipped me off to it. The flat wooden scoop pulled in Richard Noble's gold plaque. Two golds – punto gets odds of two to one – were passed over to the South American.

Immediately Richard rose to his feet and made a movement with his finger to tell the casino staff to collect his chips. He came quickly towards us with an athlete's walk that was out of place here, and he had to brush past me to get through.

I couldn't resist it.

'Caroline sends a message.'

He halted. Quite slowly he turned to face me. The expression on his face was one of pleasant inquiry. 'She does?'

'She says thanks for everything.'

For only a second or two he examined my face. 'That's nice,' he said, and walked away.

That was my signal to go. According to Thaw he would now go downstairs to the manager's office, collect his winnings in cash, and leave through the back door. I wanted to see that. I had half an idea about trying to follow him. Maybe I could do something with the registration number. But more than either of those, I simply wanted to witness the last act of a high drama.

I got out quickly and brought my car up and left it almost outside the front door. It was worth a go.

120

I was just getting out when the swing doors turned and ushered Santos on to the pavement. He was fastening a dark-blue heavy overcoat and tying a rag of silk into a flop-over knot. He raised his face uncertainly against the soft drizzle which was drifting in the air before taking an umbrella off his arm, opening it and setting off down the street. He'd just lost a quarter of a million pounds. I've seen more reaction from men when they've got a parking ticket. I left the Honda unlocked for quick lift-off and went looking for the back door to the club.

I walked thirty yards to the end of the block which, apart from one small gown shop, seemed to house only offices. There I turned right down a narrow alleyway which gave out into a long rectangular yard, walled in by the tall backs of the buildings. With the exception of the club, whose four storeys were bright with lights, they were all in darkness.

At that moment I heard a car outside in the street begin to slow down, and then engage low gear as it turned into the alley. From where I was standing I saw one of the brick walls light up in the headlamps. I scuttled deeper into the dark of the yard and began to look around for somewhere to hide. There were doors and there were windows but even in that light I could see they weren't the sort you opened with a plastic pocket comb.

In the street, the car stopped, re-engaged gear and I could tell from the line of the headlights that he was backing out again. He'd missed the turn. Then I saw the van.

It was parked at the bottom of the yard, hard against the far wall. It was dirty grey where it wasn't rust which was presumably why they made them leave it round the back. It wasn't a Mayfair sort of vehicle at all. I got down there fast. It was so snug against the wall that I couldn't get in that side. I could always slide underneath, but – without much hope – I tried the driver's door. Miraculously, it glided open. One second was all it took me to swing up behind the wheel and close the door behind me. Nice timing. Just then, the car swung into the yard and threw long fingers of light at the walls and doors and windows, and at the same time an outside light came on at the back of the club and the door began to open. In the driving seat, pressed up against the side of the van and leaning well back in the seat, I could see it all in safety. A ringside seat.

The trouble with a ringside seat is that sometimes you get splashed by the blood. The arm round my neck and the metal nose rammed into my ear came as a complete surprise.

'Stay there, Hussy.' No more than a rough whisper behind me, but I knew the voice. Whose? I couldn't think. What I did think, with a lot of self-kicking, was that a mucky old van was just about everybody's favourite for a stake-out. Why hadn't I thought of that? I hadn't thought of that because I was so damn glad to find somewhere to hide before the car drove up, that's why.

'Watch the show.'

Locked together, my head jammed into the crook of his arm, the gun in my ear, his breathing hot and steady on my neck, that was how we watched the show. The car, a shabby Merc, bounced down the yard and pulled up facing the back door to Davina's. By that time the door had opened, and out came Richard Noble. He still wasn't wearing a coat or hat, but in his hand, hanging casually down by his knee, was a nylon tote-bag. He was taking home a quarter of a million in the sort of bag school kids use for their sports kit. As he stood in the doorway, shaking hands with a man in a dinner jacket, the Merc door opened and the driver got out. Even before he'd walked round into the headlights I'd recognised him.

It was Winston. He was wearing the same leather jacket and his face was almost silver in that light.

I must've moved because I felt the arm harden around my neck and the gun twist in my ear.

By the way he brought the car up, you'd've thought Winston was the leg-man. As soon as he got out of the car, you could see he wasn't. He was the gov'nor. With a swift glance behind him, that skated right over our van, he moved quickly round to the illuminated scene in the doorway. He ignored the club man.

'I'll take that. You're driving.' He whipped the bag out of Richard's hand and went round to the passenger side. Richard was beginning to move, holding up one hand in farewell.

When Winston spoke again, it was more of a snarl. 'Move!'

He threw the bag into the back seat, climbed in, and slammed the door.

Richard Noble got in behind the wheel, the door closed, and he performed a careful three-point turn before bumping slowly up the yard, and out into the streets of London.

They were gone. The door to Davina's was closed. The yard was dark, empty, silent.

'Now it's your turn, Hussy. The keys are in the ignition. You drive.'

'Where?'

'Fellowes Road. Think you can remember where it is?'

'I remember.'

'Cringle's going to be really pleased to see you. Really pleased.'

'No more pleased,' I said, 'than I shall be to see him.'

A little civility, I've always said, seldom goes amiss.

# 18

'Why you?'

'Well, though I says it as shouldn't – as the saying goes – I imagine it's because he was looking for someone with that all too rare combination of responsibility, experience, and discretion.'

Even though I was trying the much-acclaimed Hussy charm, I didn't care for the look on Cringle's face. It looked charm-proof.

From beneath his colourless eyebrows and eyelashes, his pale eyes washed over me. Long ago he'd stopped being fooled by my fake humility and enthusiasms. But that didn't mean they didn't annoy him.

I hadn't been in the Fellowes Road house since Tiger Tomkins brought that girl in from Poland. It hadn't changed. It had been furnished from one of the auction rooms by a civil servant with three luncheon vouchers and half an hour to spare. The furniture – sideboard, dining-table, four chairs, dresser and corner cupboard – was made out of a stiffish cardboard that was the colour of egg-yolk. Whoever had done the buying must've got a job lot of ornaments: every shelf and crevice held a cherry-seller or a shepherd boy or some other highly-glossed entrepreneur that was inscribed in memory of someone's coastal holiday. Sometimes I wondered if it was an ingenious test of defectors' sincerity. There must've been a few second thoughts in that room.

'Why did you chose to ignore my instruction to steer off Noble?'

'Charles Noble, as I recall, sir?'

'And you didn't realise he had a brother called Richard – is that what you're asking me to believe?'

'All I'm saying is, sir, that if you'd intended the ban to cover the entire family you should have made that plain at the time.'

'You know what I mean now and what I meant then. And for Christ's sake stop calling me sir. You've always been a perverse little swine, Hussy.'

'I wouldn't say perverse, sir, I'd say it's more a question of how you look at things, and with me having the old Celtic blood flowing . . .'

'The old Celtic blood will be flowing all over the floor if you give me that Irish rubbish again.' He picked up a pink cup and saucer and drained it. He was in a winged armchair, behind a badly holed card-table. I was in a canvas chair, facing him. I hadn't been offered any tea.

For a moment I'd nettled him, but now he'd iced over again. 'You're in a difficult position. The fact is that you ignored an order. Correct?'

'More or less.'

'You don't take advice, do you, Hussy?'

'Some I do and some I don't, sir, you can't always say. Why, I've had advice I've heeded all my life, and then there's been advice I've forgotten the minute I heard it. I get over-exuberant. It's a character failing.'

That burst of nonsense did nothing to him. Inside my stomach felt hollow. I was in a hell of a hole, and I couldn't see a way out.

'So something a little sterner may be indicated. Is that it?'

'I do hope not, I really do.'

The phone rang. As he picked it up and listened, his eyes fixed on the starburst light fitting. He picked up a ballpoint pen and drummed it on the table. 'I see. Forty-one, no family, nothing known, her business, bank loan. Gotcha.'

He put both the phone and pen down. I didn't like what I'd heard, which was why he'd let me hear it. What was more, I wasn't at all cheered by the hard look in his eye. I teased him because he was humourless; all the same, I knew damn fine that in the name of duty he was quite capable of removing your eyeballs and juggling with them. He was a heartless bastard, Cringle – it usually goes with being humourless.

'Your partner, Miss Ada Jameson?'

I didn't say a word.

'She's never had any trouble with the police, has she?'

'No. Never.'

'Let's hope she doesn't.'

'Let's hope that.' The bastard wasn't going to draw me so easily.

'Those big petrol companies, they don't like to deal with unreliable people.'

I sat looking at him. He picked up the pen and tapped it on the edge of the table this time.

'If she was in any sort of legal trouble, they probably wouldn't want to deal with her. I think a business like that could only end in the bankruptcy courts, don't you?'

'She's not in trouble with the law and she's not likely to be.'

'As I understand it, she's forty-one. A spinster. That's the sort of age when women do become a little unstable. It's not uncommon. A hormone problem, I seem to recall.'

'Jamie's as sound as a bell.'

'Emotionally, I mean. Mentally, perhaps. Now if she was

125

involved in anything like shop-lifting, say, which happens more than you might think to women in that age group, I dare say that would represent a black mark against her.'

I looked at him: pale, upright, principled. Would he do that to a great lass like Jamie? Would cats catch mice?

'What you want is me out, right?'

'I want you out, and I want to know that you're going to stay out.'

'I could give you my word.'

'You could, Hussy, if I wanted it.'

'You wouldn't believe me?'

'You have a credibility problem round here.'

I thought for a moment. 'Trade?'

'You've nothing I want.'

'You don't know that.'

'Tempt me.'

'Tonight, your man's on the outside in the back of a van. I'm on the inside where all the fun is.'

'You don't know where my men are.'

'I know. And I can get places they can't. I can turn up stuff they can't.'

'Example.'

'Example? Let's see. Background, okay. Would you like to know that Richard Noble has left his wife, Caroline, and does not intend to return?'

Silence slowly filled up the room. Although his eyes never left mine, his face remained immobile. Had he got that already? Did he want it anyway? Did it matter as much as I thought it mattered?

'I'll take that off you, Hussy,' he said eventually. He spoke in an agreeable tone now. 'Another woman? I believe he is susceptible in that area.'

'Maybe. Either way, he's packed in his marriage.'

'That's worth something. Of course, that could merely be a bit of gossip you've picked up and you don't have anything else at all.'

'Like what?'

126

'Something of a more substantial nature. Something more seminal.'

'As in fluid?'

'No, not as in fluid. Nothing else? No?'

'Well, sir, you've got me a bit early in my investigations, as we chaps like to dignify our trade, but I don't doubt that if you gave me more elbow room and a little more time, I could come up with something better.'

There could only be two reactions. One would be a sneer. The other would be nothing. I watched. Nothing. The pen drummed. I'd hooked him.

He stood up and walked over to the sideboard. He picked up a squirrel which was frozen in the act of eating a hazel-nut, in memory of the New Forest. He read it, then replaced it. 'You're not telling us anything we don't know.'

'Perhaps augmenting would be a better word.'

'Why would I want to do that?'

'Because you're not happy about Noble.'

His face registered about as much emotion as a paving slab. I didn't expect to see anything there, but when I heard his reply I knew I was edging through the door. Then I knew I had to chance it and go all the way.

'Why am I unhappy about him?'

'You think he's cracking.'

'Anyone can crack under that sort of long-term pressure. You know that, Hussy. We build that into our calculations.'

'So now you have some reason to suspect it might really be happening.'

'How did you get there?' He unfastened the fat brown leather button on his hound's-tooth jacket so it fell open. His belly was as flat as an ironing board. He lowered himself back into the winged armchair again.

'You wouldn't be listening to me otherwise. And you wouldn't be checking up on him every chance you get.'

He didn't confirm it, but then Cringle wouldn't tell you the time by the Town Hall clock.

'Augmenting, you say. Perhaps.' He put his hands in his pocket to indicate that he was relaxed. 'All right, you've convinced me. Pursue your line. Keep from under our feet. Keep me informed.'

'Fair enough. And there'll be no nonsense about Jamie?'

'That's my decision.'

'They're all your decisions, aren't they, Cringle?'

He did smile then: it was like splitting ice. 'Mostly.'

I got up and went to the door. 'And what if Noble is cracking? Do I do anything or do I just report in?'

He studied his fingers locked in front of him. 'Report in, of course. If he's folding, I want him out of there. If you have to, lift him.'

'Regardless.'

'Regardless.'

I got up and gave him the widest grin my face could accommodate. 'Well, sir, I'd just like to say what a pleasure it is to be working for the old firm once again. Cringle and Hussy, eh? The dream ticket, you might say. Don't you worry, sir, I've never let you down yet and you can rely . . .'

He raised his eyes to mine. 'Leave.'

I left.


# 19


Jamie hauled me out of the MoT bay for Adams' phone-call. 'And don't think that means you're goin' off gallivanting about again neither,' she said.

I wiped my hands and took the call in the pay booth.

'Hussy? Glad I caught you, how's things?'

'I'd put it no higher than average.'

'Splendid.' Like most people, when he asked a rhetorical

question he didn't listen to the answer. 'Tell me now, were you able to see our friend, the Gurkha Rose?'

'I was.'

'Was she . . . er, was she much as we had speculated?'

'I'd say she's had enough cock to put a handrail round the Isle of Man.'

Silence. Audible gasp. Then: 'Really? Well, I suppose that is . . . I mean, well, pretty much par for the course, yes?'

'Possibly Anglesey too.'

'Jolly good. I know your inquiries are confidential, but since I was able to help you with that, I wonder if there's any chance of your helping me out.'

'No problem, if I can.'

I pulled a face at Jamie who was looking at where her watch would be if she had one and pointing to the workshop. God, the woman was merciless.

'I wondered if you'd come across any connection with Hastings.' I could hear him shuffle some papers, and then, hitting the word like a Chinese gong, he added: 'Wrong.'

I love that military self-correcting style. 'Not Hastings at all,' he added. 'One moment, please. Ah yes, here we are. East-bourne. Any tie-up with Eastbourne, I wonder.'

'What? Connection between Kesharsing and Eastbourne?'

'Just so.'

'I thought Eastbourne was one of those towns where they won't let you in unless you have a pension book. Being under sixty-five's an indictable offence there.'

'It doesn't ring a bell?'

I ran that through the brain, with no result. Mind you, there are those who say that to get any sort of result out of my brain you have to kick it a couple of times first. Without removing it from its container.

When I told him, he hummed around for a while. 'We got those television chaps to put it on the Southern news and we've had quite a few calls from people who think they might have seen our man. The police followed up some of them and I'm afraid they came to naught. Our friends from the ethnic restaurants, I don't doubt.'

'I suppose. So why Eastbourne?'

'We've got a report in, just now as a matter of fact, from a supposed sighting at Lewes railway station. If it was him, and I do stress the *if*, he asked for a ticket to Eastbourne. Rather than have the police whistling around all over the countryside, I thought I'd check with you to see if there was anything to suggest it might be true. He'd hardly go there for a stroll along the beach, and . . . what's the matter, Hussy?'

I must've gasped or something down the phone. 'Isn't Eastbourne near Beachy Head?'

'Right next to it. We take our chaps up there hang-gliding as a matter of . . .'

'Don't go, back in a minute.'

I raced upstairs and got out the missing Gurkha's wallet. I had it unrolled in a second and from among the letters I found the newspaper cutting I was looking for. Beachy Head. Jesus Joseph and Bloody Mary.

'This is it, Adams. Get there as fast as you can. Forget the town. Straight up to Beachy Head. I'll see you there.'

Three words into her big-stick routine, Jamie took one look at my face and stopped. 'Take that Jag, it'll get you there faster, wherever it is the 'ell you're going.'

'He's collecting it this afternoon, isn't he?'

'He was.'

It was two days after the visit to Davina's. I'd done nothing since then. There were reasons for that. For a start, I wasn't quite sure how to interpret Cringle's last conversation. Was I back on the first team again? And, much more important, did I want to be? I'd been thinking about trying to see Richard Noble in Liverpool, but Cassidy was my best address man and I didn't like to try him again so soon after that daughter business. I'd also been expecting someone to call on me, which hadn't yet materialised. Plenty of reasons, but as I whipped down the A22 they were beginning to sound like excuses.

This Jag owner – like all Jag owners, I suspect – had more Neil Sedaka tapes than one man may need in his lifetime, and surprisingly few by Blind Lemon Jefferson. None, in fact. But what he did have was a fully-furnished map book. I always used to wonder who it was who bought those special offers: you know, bound in elk-hide, with the margin filled with illustrations of Birmingham's birds of prey and what fossils to look for in motorway restaurants, every page complete with its own compass and pencil-beam torch.

I could almost forgive him the Neil Sedaka for that. It meant I was able to navigate as I drove. I was able to swing off at Polegate and drive west to Beachy Head without going through the town.

After that there was no problem. I could see the rescue team from a quarter of a mile away. And the small crowd.

They'd had to rope off their Land Rover which was backed up to the edge of the cliff. They'd rigged up a winch and dropped a man over the edge on a wire. At a guess, the cliff was about four hundred feet. It was grim, it was also dangerous, but to the dozen or so people who gathered round, it was entertainment. God knows where they'd come from at that time of year. Perhaps they cruise round listening on short-wave radios for a good disaster to home in on. Even when the wind sawed in off the sea and whipped at their coats and scarves they wouldn't be driven back.

'You can see better from here, Valerie.' A man who was shivering in a sports-coat waved to his wife. 'They've got a stretcher down there.'

Adams was beside the rescue vehicle and he called me over. Beside him stood a hefty lady in a sheepskin coat and man's deerstalker hat. She had a spaniel on a short lead.

'Mrs Wood here saw it.'

She pulled a large hankie out of her pocket and mopped her stricken face. She didn't need any prompting. Shock silences some people and unbuttons others.

'I was taking Amos here out for a run and I'd stopped just over there, not for any special reason, just to get my breath and have a look at the view, just the usual things, when I saw this gentleman approach. I did wonder for a moment, I must say, because there wasn't anyone else around, and he was rather roughly dressed and he appeared to be foreign too, although goodness knows there's nothing wrong with foreigners. Who'd

131

run our hospitals if it wasn't for foreigners, that's what I always say. But he wasn't really looking at me at all. He was looking down at his feet and I believe he was talking to himself as he came past. Not English. He wasn't talking in English, or certainly not so far as I could make out. He did look up and his face had the most terrible expression on it. I couldn't say what it was. Anger. Fear. Both maybe.'

She stopped and ducked her face into the hankie again.

'Then?' Adams spoke gently.

She lifted her face. 'Then? He ran past me and jumped off.' With a howl of anguish, she hid in the linen folds again. 'The poor man, he must've been so desperately unhappy to end his life like that.'

'That's it,' Adams said to me. 'How did you know?'

I told him. Turning his back to keep the wind off, he read the cutting. It was a newspaper story about the increasing number of people who were committing suicide by leaping off Beachy Head, with a statistical breakdown showing how it had increased each year, and a neat little graph. There were theories too: unemployment, divorce, drugs. The usual things.

While he was reading it, I looked around at the eager faces. For people like them, television has destroyed reality. To them it was just another stunt. If you'd said it was time for the adverts they would all have gone for a cup of tea. Then, in among them, I saw a plump brown berry of a face and my heart hit the roof of my mouth. His black eyes fixed on mine. Then I realised. It was the *maruni* dancer, Bhimibahadur.

'He was Keshar's best pal. He desperately wanted to come along. Poor chap's been very unhappy since Keshar took off.' Adams had seen me start. He folded the cutting up and began to put it in his pocket. 'Mind if I keep this? For the inquest and all that business.'

'Sure.'

I stood there looking out to sea with the wind pulling at my hair and the downland springy beneath my feet. I felt disgustingly alive. He guessed my mood.

'Even if you had read it, you would never have guessed this was what he planned.' He touched my sleeve.

'How far down is it?' The cropped turf of the clifftop dipped into a slope before crumbling at the edge. From where we were, we couldn't see where it fell away into a sheer drop.

'About five hundred feet. The Devil's Chimney it's called, apparently. It's a favourite place for jumpers.' He nibbled his lower lip in distress. 'There was no need for this, you know. I wonder why he did it?'

'He was being blackmailed.'

At that moment, there was a series of clumping noises.

'Here they come, Valerie.' It was the man who'd spoken earlier. 'He'll be dead, mark my words. They never bring them up from there alive.'

The woman in the deerstalker began sobbing and walked round the back of the rescue vehicle so she didn't have to watch.

With a grunt of effort, the coastguard bobbed into view. He was wearing a crash helmet and padded boiler-suit. He braced his feet against the top of the cliff as he guided up a stretcher. The body was covered and strapped in.

'You said blackmail?'

I gave him a quick outline of how they'd worked it.

'It's preposterous. Quite honestly, all he would have got would've been a slap on the wrist, if that, and these people had no means of getting copies of the picture to his wife.'

'We know that, but he didn't.' I pointed to the stretcher now being hurried into an ambulance. A seagull, busking for food, swooped low and filled the air with mourner's cries.

'And you say it was someone who wanted to stage an apparent assassination attempt on your schoolmaster friend? I don't see the sense of that at all, I'm afraid. But you've no idea who it was or why?'

As they lifted the stretcher into the back of the vehicle, Bhimi pushed through. I saw him move the cover so he could see his friend's face, and he touched it and whispered something, as though passing on a secret. As the rescue team began to pack up, I moved him to one side. The whites of his eyes were yellow and his face was full of quick nervous movement.

'Beachy Head. It was in newspaper I give you.'

'I know.' We'd both failed to make the connection. If we had, they might not have hauled a dead body up the cliff.

'Find him.' He grabbed my hand and squeezed it in both his. 'Who?'

His eyes shot to the stretcher and back to mine. 'The man who make him do it.'

'I'm working on it.' That was all I could offer him. The truth was that I wasn't working hard enough. I'd waited for one of them to come looking for me, and I'd waited too long.

But he came. That night he came.

# 20

But Cassidy came first. I found his note pinned on the door when I got back. 'In the Junk,' it said. Since it wasn't signed and I didn't know his writing, I was half-expecting someone else when I went round the corner to the Junction. But there was Cassidy, long scrawny figure in his orange anorak, bending over the bar billiards table so that his hair hung down like a silver fish. When he straightened up, it went back in one piece. He must've used more oil than a pre-war Alvis.

'Watch this, little Joe. Straight back up the middle for the ton. Can't miss. You could bet your wedding tackle on it. You any good at this lark?'

'Only brilliant.' I rolled a cue on the table to see if it was straight. By the way it wobbled they must've cut it straight from the tree and stuck a tip on it. Cassidy brought us two pints and I reduced mine by fifty per cent at the first mouthful. Sea air makes you thirsty. Sea air, and suicide. It was six-thirty. The saloon bar which would be solid by ten was empty: they don't do much early evening trade in North London back-street boozers.

'You gentlemen all right?' The landlord settled his elbows on the bar for a chat.

'Kill that fuckin' row, eh, cock?' Cassidy's red-speckled eyes shot a look at the loudspeaker on the wall. The landlord was just about to argue when he saw something he'd missed in his scruffy customer. Without a word, he reached under the bar and the music died.

'Then some fuckin' privacy.' Again the landlord thought about saying something. Again he looked. Then he left.

'Helpful geezer,' said Cassidy.

He was an awkward bloke, Cassidy, which was probably why he'd never get very far with the Branch; these days they only seemed to use him for routine jobs like vetting. It was a hell of a waste, because, as anyone who knew the business would tell you, he had the best contacts in London, and he had a good nose too. I rated him.

He broke. The red rattled in the bottom corner and then dropped down the thirty.

'Sixty,' he said. Red scores double.

'You interested again?' I watched him settle over the cue. He was one of those blokes who had to close one eye to sight it. No score. He stood up and put the butt of the cue on the floor. He looked like Davy Crockett at the Alamo.

'Thaw was right.'

'Rigged game?'

'Yeah. You jammy bugger.'

'I told you I was brilliant.' I'd put both balls down the thirty and now got to cue off again. 'It had to be, didn't it? Was it the way Thaw reckoned?'

'Just like he said. A fixed shoe. Dead simple. Cards in a certain sequence. They'd monkey about playing for matchsticks until the sequence began to run, then they'd bet big till it ran out.'

'How'd you know for sure?'

'The croupier coughed to Thaw. He belled me last night.'

'So what was all that about the clubs being run by saints and virgins?'

'Well.' He dropped the red in the thirty again, waited for it to roll through, then picked it up as the cue-ball. He did it again. 'The way the croupier tells it, no one was getting hurt. Your mate Noble wasn't complaining 'cos he was winning. The South American gent was losing, but wasn't complaining either. All the club had to do was turn a blind eye – and pocket the pay-off.'

'So what's the point?' He did the same shot again, and again waited for the red. 'This is getting very boring.'

'Typical mick, can't stand an 'ammering. The point, me old cock, is that the man who's supposed to be fancying your non-fucking-existent daughter is up to his oxters in Rich Pickings, innee? And they are not nice. Least, that's what I'd say.'

That's what I'd've said too, but I was glad to hear he had the same idea.

'I reckon you knew he was best mates with Winston. I reckon you just forgot to tell me, didn't you, Joe?'

He gave me a hard look. He didn't really mind. It was a difficult balance to bring off at the best of times, for both of us. Our masters liked to keep us all working in blinkers. That's good for tight all-round security. But it isn't always good for personal peace of mind, so what we did, those of us who were of a timid disposition, was to tell our masters a little less than we should, and each other a little more. That way, you got to get a peep around the blinkers. The problem was how far to go.

'I wasn't sure. Are they serious people?'

'Very serious people.'

'They ran the riots, didn't they?'

'Choreographed every last bleedin' step, I reckon. And they run half the street crime. Word is that they're moving up a division too.'

'What does that mean?'

'That means we wait and fucking see, that's what that means.' I'd hit the limit now. If he knew, which was possible, he wasn't telling me. It was fair enough.

'So who's this Brazilian?' It was my turn again. I brought the red up off the bottom cush so it dropped through the one-hundred pocket like a dead man. I heard his grunt of exasperation.

'Christ, you're a bloody chancer you are, Joe.'

This time I ran the red down so it shaved the inside of the white and came back off the cush to the same pocket. He whistled his disbelief. 'Think big, Cassidy. Remember – there is a tide in the affairs of men which, if taken at the flood . . .'

'Will drown the bloody lot of us. Problems with the Brazilian. Can't raise anything on him.'

'Nothing at all?'

He shook his head so his hair flopped down again, and pushed it back with his thumb.

'Perhaps he's led a quiet life.'

'So quiet, you wouldn't know he'd been alive.'

I realised what he meant. If Cassidy couldn't turn up anything on him, then maybe there wasn't anything to turn. Maybe Mr Santos wasn't Mr Santos. He answered my next question before I'd even phrased it.

'Old mate of mine on security at his hotel. Had a look over his room. Clean.'

He missed on the fifty and stood up. 'He's got one of those poofter handbags that the oilies carry and he don't seem to like to put it down too much. My mate thinks it might be worth a look.'

'You mean I ought to have a look?'

'Bit illegal for me, in't it? Apparently he gets up early for a night-rake, breakfast around eight, takes the paper back up to his room for an hour or so. Three five two. Quietish around then.'

'Thanks.'

'This Noble. He's one of your lot, innee?'

'My lot?'

'Hooligan.'

'Hooligan?'

He sighed. 'Don't be a pain in the arse all your life, Joe. The hooligans from Hereford. Well, is he?'

'Who can say, who can say?' Any sort of security work these days and everyone assumes you've done the SAS courses.

He stopped, cue resting on his fingers, and turned his face up towards me. 'So he's having a look at Rich Pickings from the inside, that it?'

'I wouldn't know.'

'He wouldn't get that close to Winston without the darkie knowing his track record, so he must've sold himself there all right. Must've. Otherwise, you'd never get a shrewdie like Winston using him as a front man.'

He was thinking out loud. He didn't really expect me to comment on that. He played the shot quickly and a white dropped down the ten. 'Noble'd make a good front man for a money operation. Particularly in a flash 'ole like that Davina's.' He flicked me a glance.

No score. Sweet as you like, I cannoned the red off a white at the bottom and it just made the hundred pocket. This time Cassidy was thinking so hard he forgot to complain.

Behind my back, he asked: 'But if he is one of your lot, this Noble bleeder, how come I got hold of the file on him, no problem.'

'They're not my lot any more.'

He gave me a jeering look. 'That's a club you never leave, you know that, Joe.'

Concentrating, I brought the red up to the fifty and began to play in-offs with the white. One, two, three. That brought him round. 'Are you sure there ain't a limit on how many of those you can do?'

'You got hold of his file because someone wanted you to. They want you, me and everyone to know what a bad lad Richard Noble is.'

I did one more in-off. Now he wasn't even looking. He leaned his cue in the corner and picked up the remains of his pint. 'Know what I think, Joe?'

'Yes. You think someone's letting him run, that's what you think.'

He wiped his mouth with the back of his big bony hand. 'Yeah. Matter of fact, I do, cock.' He gave me his gaunt grin. 'Now where's that bloody landlord? That's the trouble with this country, no bleedin' service when you want it.'

I dropped my cue next to his and pointed at the scoreboard. 'Another historic day for Ireland. This business. You said you wouldn't want to know if it was a hands-off job. Now you're all interested.'

'Yeah, I am, aren't I? But this is as far as I go. All a bit clever for me, this is. I wanted you to know about the Brazilian, that's all.'

'Why?'

'Why? You're a mate, and if you're playing with the big boys you'll need all the help you can get. Anyway, I'd like to see you crack it.'

'Why?' There was something else behind the leery grin on his face.

'There was something I forgot to mention too. Thaw was knocked off the perch last night. Surprised some break-in artist who stabbed him. They reckon the burglar was probably panicked into it. Didn't really mean to do it, you know. Shame, that, in't it?'

'And this was after he got the croupier to talk, and after he phoned you to tell you?'

'Yeah.' He gave his mirthless smile again. 'Tragic, in't it? I worry about your playmates, Joe, I really do.'

# 21

I was still thinking about poor young Thaw when I drove back to the garage. Jamie had locked up, and I was walking past the pumps when I saw a little Fiat parked down the side. Just as I saw there was someone in it, he called through the window. 'Here, can you help me, guv'nor?'

I strolled over and bent down.

When the instructor used to tell us about that one, we always laughed. I mean, no one would ever be so stupid. Bending down by car doors, along with strangers asking you for a light so you have to put your hands in your pockets, is banana-skin standard. So what did I do? I bent down, of course.

Or I began to bend down. As my face descended, the car door cracked open. The next few minutes were a roaring cascade of noise and fury and pain. When it all subsided, I was lying on the gravel at the front of Jamie's house. She was standing over me holding a two-foot monkey-wrench. At her feet, in even worse shape than me, was the driver. It took me a minute to put it all together.

He'd been waiting for me, and did the old car-door-face routine. Instead of breaking my nose all over my face, which is the objective, it had caught me over one eyebrow – at least I'd attempted to turn away at the last minute. Then he'd followed me, kicking and reaching down to get me.

What they do in films, in these situations, is to grab the man's foot and throw him over the nearest tall building. What you do in life is to try to keep moving so the little bugger can't hurt you any more. That was what I did. In my pain and confusion, I rolled, crawled and scrambled away from him, desperately trying to get my head and tender bits out of the way of his boots. At the same time I'd tried to aim for Jamie's door in the hope that she'd hear the row.

He got me in the kidneys with a vicious kick that spun me over and when I saw him coming again, I scrambled up on to my knees to try to do something before he got me with a head kick. I saw him grinning as he came in at me and I tried to focus my eyes as he pulled his boot back. It set off, but it never arrived. A look of intense surprise lit up his face and he sank, like me, to his knees, and then keeled over sideways.

For a minute, I collapsed myself.

'Ista alright?'

I could've laughed. Jamie always went into dialect when she was really upset.

'Think so.'

'I saw 'im waiting. I wondered what he were up to so I took

140

the wrench in the house just in case. 'Appen it were as well.'

' 'Appen it were, Jamie. You're a little Yorkshire angel, you are. Come on now, help me get his trousers off.'

And we did – once she realised what I was doing. He was spark out, and lucky to be alive judging from the split and bleeding lump at the back of his almost hairless head. When I came to look at him, I realised it wasn't my most famous victory. He couldn't be a day under fifty, and he was only average height and build. On the other hand, he'd done his homework: he hadn't got a scarred forehead like that reading poetry. When he came round a few minutes later he was on the floor of the kiosk, Jamie was sitting behind the desk about three yards away, and I was perched on the edge. I also had the monkey-wrench. And I had the portable radio tuned in to LBC. That's the rolling-news station.

'Wharra the blurry ell . .' He stopped talking as he realised where he was and his eyes squinted up at the two of us.

His hand went down. His gaze followed. From the bottom of his stained sweater, blue shirt tails sprouted. Between there and his socks, there was nothing other than short, bowed, knobbly legs. 'What you done with my trousers? C'mon, don't piss me around – gimme me bloody trousers.'

'Good evening, Mr McKenzie.'

'You what? How you know my name?'

'We know your name, Mr McKenzie. Or do you prefer Gary?'

He didn't like that one bit. He chewed inside his cheeks and his eyes jumped around. An announcer was reading out traffic conditions on the radio. We said nothing.

He climbed up to his feet, holding on to the wall with one hand and his shirt tails with the other, and as he did so he saw the open door one yard to his right. Glance at us, glance at the door, quick lick of the lips.

'You're free to go, Mr McKenzie. The door's open as you can see.'

He leaned out so he could see his car. 'Keys?'

'No keys. Walk, Mr McKenzie. It'll help clear your head.' I held my hand up then and said 'Shhhh'.

He was getting really nervous now. Without knowing why, he knew that people were reacting wrongly. He was dizzy. And he had no trousers.

His screwed-up face switched between the two of us. 'Gimme me bloody trousers.'

'Shhhh.' I held my finger to my lips like you would to a child. 'This is it.'

I turned the radio up. He stared at the two of us in stark disbelief, until he realised what the newsreader was saying. He was reading a story about the missing Gurkha soldier from Church Crookham camp who was wanted in connection with a shooting incident being found at the foot of Beachy Head cliffs today. He had fallen to his death. No one else was involved and the police believed he had taken his own life.

He watched the flat black radio. I watched him. Slowly his mouth began to gape, and, as the news item ended, he moved his gaze up to me.

'You didn't know that, did you?'

'No.' His voice was a weak croak.

'That's what I call trouble.'

In his anxiety he'd temporarily forgotten about his trousers. He shoved one thumb up to his mouth and began ravaging the nail. His face was working furiously, a shop-window display for what was going on inside his head.

'I don't know nothin' about it,' he said, after a minute. 'And you can't prove I do.'

'You're probably right.'

I laid the photograph of Rose and the soldier on the table.

'That don't prove nothin'.' He really was feeling perky again now. It was a pity I had to spoil it.

'I wasn't thinking of the police.'

'Police won't give you tuppence for that.'

'Perhaps you're right. But the boys out at Church Crookham would.'

'What? The Gurkhas?'

'They'd like to see this. They'd like to hear my story about the blackmail you pulled on their mate. That's all the evidence

142

they'll need, Mr McKenzie. Have you any idea what they do to people who kill their mates?'

'What you saying, I din't kill nobody . . .'

I waved his words away and continued in the same steady tone. 'You don't think they're going to hang around waiting for the police to make their minds up, do you? One morning, the police are going to find you with your balls in your mouth, Mr McKenzie.'

That did it. At first I thought he was going to hit the deck, but he hung on to the edge of the desk, and stood there swaying.

'Don't set them mad little buggers on to me.'

'Give him his trousers, Jamie.' She pulled them from behind the desk and threw them over to him. They fell to the tiles. 'And his keys.' She pushed his keys across. They lay between us, attached to a brass plate inscribed 'The World's Greatest Husband'. Still he didn't move.

'One name,' I said. 'Who was it? Who set it up?'

His lined face burst open in an expression he can't have used much: it was frightened, blazing honesty. 'I don't know. On my life, straight up, I don't know his name.'

'How did he find you?'

'Asking around. He said it was a stunt he wanted to pull. I had to get this little Keshar to do the shooting, and I came up with this idea of the picture. Anyway, it worked. I din't think it would but I suppose them little buggers know sod all, don't they? This bloke said his pal would drive down a road near the camp and get out and stand in his headlamps and all this Keshar had to do was to fire about six-foot away or something. So where's the harm in that, eh?'

'The harm is that he is dead.'

'Yeah. Well.' His head was down. All truculence gone.

'Describe this man.'

Description wasn't McKenzie's major talent. All I could learn was that the man was medium height, in his thirties, dressed like an office worker, and spoke posh. Which restricted it to about ten million middle-class males.

'Any details? Did he have buck teeth? What was his tie like? Did you see his watch? Think, for Christ's sake.'

'No.' He looked dull and hopeless. He knew this was the only way for him to buy his way out, but he couldn't find anything to give me. He was trying all right. 'Yeah, I know, there was one thing.' Eagerness flooded back into his face. 'He had this funny way, when he was talking, of making the end of his nose jump. Like a rabbit.'

'Or a hedgehog,' Jamie said.

'Or a hedgehog,' I repeated.

After he'd gone, Jamie insisted on bathing the swollen cut over my eye where the car door had got me. Charlie, out on his evening patrol, watched. He probably thought I was having my ticks removed.

'He was a horrible little sod. What got me was how you knew his name though.'

I handed her a card. It certified, for those who cared, that Mr Gary McKenzie was a fully paid-up member of the Glittering G-String Club. I'd found it in his pocket.

'Ah, but he was here to defend a lady's honour.' I told her a bit about Rose.

'Why'd you do it, Joe? Mixing with folk like that. You'll get yourself killed one of these days. Then what'll I do?'

'Have one less worry, that's what. I must say I was pretty impressed with the way you kept your nerve when we took his pants off.'

'If you've ever cooked spaghetti, there's nowt to frighten you in a pair of trousers.' She began to smear ointment on my forehead. 'So, that's why that Gurkha lad jumped off Beachy Head. Blackmail. They've got a lot to answer for, them two. Where you off to?'

'Out.'

I had to get out into the cool November night to calm myself. The more I thought about it, the angrier I became.

I didn't care about Rose and her man. The man I wanted to talk to was Charles Noble. All along I'd been dogged by the feeling that there was something wrong. I'd sent myself dizzy scouring my mind to imagine the events and motives which could lead the young soldier to fire at Charles, even though I knew he meant to miss. A fake assassination seemed to me even more mind-boggling than a real one. I'd een hunting a sensible explanation and of course there wasn't one.

At the back of it was Charles Noble's boy-scout bungling. He'd emerged from the school life where he lived like some protected species, preserved along with his pre-war comic-book principles, and tried dabbling in the real world. With his dangerous innocence, and the lame-brain scheming of two petty thieves, he'd dreamed up a plan that had driven a soldier to his death. I could never have worked that out myself because I'd never have believed that a big kid like Charles would ever try to concoct a blackmail trap. I'd been looking for wickedness, not for unworldly stupidity. Now look where his amateur dabbling had led. Jesus!

It wasn't until I saw people crossing the road to avoid me that I realised I was muttering out loud. My fury was boiling over, and I had to walk the streets, cursing between clenched teeth, to let it out. But why? For the life of me, I still couldn't see what he stood to gain from this elaborate fake assassination.

My first thought was to drive down to the school and kick it out of him. But I'd already got it so badly wrong, that this time I made myself sit back and think. I wanted to talk to someone else first, to see if I could get into the man's mind before I tackled him head-on. Then it struck me. Anna Mauch. And I didn't need more than half an excuse to phone her.

By the time I'd got home, dialled the number, and heard her measured voice, I was all sweetness and cheek.

'Is that Joe Hussy?'

'Himself it is, and if I may say so, you're looking as edible as ever tonight.'

'And how would you know?'

'Jesus, didn't I tell you, I've got one of these new video telephones. Wonderful inventions. But are you wise to take calls in the bath like this?'

She laughed. It was such a thrilling sound that my scalp fizzed. The million-pound woman. All my anger dimmed.

'I hope you're keeping my friend Charles safe from the perils of the world?'

145

'Trying, I'm trying, but he's not an easy man to protect, particularly from himself.'

I heard her blow out a mouthful of smoke. 'From himself? What do you mean?'

'He fixed for that soldier to take a shot at him. Making sure he missed, of course.'

'How . . . how . . . I mean, why? What would be the point?'

'I was hoping you might know.'

There was a silence. When she continued, she sounded genuine enough, and she'd certainly sounded surprised when I told her. But, as someone once said, she would, wouldn't she?

'No, I don't know, Joe, although I gather from your tone of voice that you will not believe me in any case. I can't begin to imagine why Charles would do such a foolish thing.'

Again I heard the smoke exhaled. 'He may be my lover, but that does not mean I know everything about him.'

'The honourable but penniless schoolmaster.'

'Have you asked him? I am sure he will have a good reason.'

'I thought I'd ask you first. The trouble is, I can't tell if you're telling the truth unless I look into those lustrous brown eyes of yours.'

The pause hung in the night air. When she replied, I felt my heart jump under my ribs.

'Then come and look into them. You never know what you might see.'

'And Charles?'

'I am not married to him. Even if I was, I somehow think that when they talk about forsaking all others, they don't intend to include Joe Hussy.'

'You'd be surprised the number of times those very words have crossed my lips.'

'So there you are then. As you can see, I'm getting out of the bath now, Joe. If only you were here you could help rub me down with a warm towel. I'm sure that would help me relax. You look to me like the sort of man who knows how to relax a woman.'

For some reason, my mouth had dried up and my voice came out like an unoiled gate. 'I got a badge for it in the cubs.'

'Did you really? And how long does it take to drive from your place down here? Or do you think,' she said, drawling out every word, 'I'd be biting off more than I could chew?'

'If you take the mickey out of an Irishman, you know there's nothing left.'

'I'm taking the mickey, am I? Well, there's only one way to find out.'

Women like that didn't come into my life very often, and when they did they were only ever through traffic. All my professional instincts told me there had to be a reason why a champagne woman like that would make a pass at a light-ale man like myself. And all my other instincts said what the hell, get in your car and burn the tyres off getting there. Morals and motivation could wait till morning.

When I touched the front door, it was ajar. I went in and closed it quietly behind me. I could see a dim light through in the rumpus room. She couldn't have heard me coming because she was standing by a small open bureau when I came through the door. Harrod the cat rubbed a curved back against her leg. She started when I spoke, dropped a white envelope into the bureau and closed the front.

'You got here quickly.'

'I got sort of motivated.'

She was wearing a dark blue robe with a hood. Inside it, her face shone like a lamp. Jesus, she was beautiful.

'How?' Her voice was breathy and she moved towards me.

'Well, I was thinking, God knows there's little enough happiness in this world and if the two of us have the chance to manufacture a little more, then surely we're honour-bound to do it, don't you reckon?'

Then she was touching me and the scents of her warm body weren't the ones you get out of a bottle, and I found out why they called it a rumpus room.

It was much later when we got upstairs to bed, and later still when she was asleep.

I listened to her breathing for a while before I moved. When I stood up, the duvet was on the floor and there was enough light from a street lamp to see her. For a moment, I wondered if I'd

147

been dreaming. Half-seen and half-imagined, her body had a sleek, cold beauty about it. One arm, shoulder and breast were brilliantly lit by the shaft of light. It silvered the curve of her thigh and touched the high points of half her face and one dangling foot.

She snuffled, sighed, and stirred, then settled down again. 'If you do that once more,' I'd whispered to her, 'you'll have serious brain damage.' All she said was: 'Try and stop me.' I did try, and I failed. Twice more, which made it seven-two to her. If her conscience was troubling her, it didn't interfere with her mechanics at all. At a million pounds she was very seriously under-priced.

The front of the bureau was unlocked and the envelope was where I'd seen her drop it. I tiptoed over to the window to see what it was. Two BWIA tickets from Heathrow to Barbados, on December 14th. In the names of Anna Mauch and Charles Noble. Single tickets.

I never think Christmas is the same in a tropical country.

# 22

Cassidy was right about Santos. At eight o'clock he was leafing through the *Independent* and toying one-handed with a croissant and coffee. I tucked into a healthy English breakfast: the night before I'd burned up a lot of fuel. I was still so dazed by it – by both the shock and the experience itself – that it was all I could do to remember why I was there at all. Even after a shower, I still bore the rich perfumes of her body. If I'd been eighteen, I'd've sworn I was in love but I was old enough to know it was only that delicious giddy guilt that you get from an excess of pleasure.

At eight-forty-five, he yawned, folded his newspaper, got up and sauntered through the tables. He was wearing a blazer striped broadly in dark green and white, and white trousers with old-fashioned razor-blade creases. He was working a toothpick between his front teeth with a studied air as he passed. In the same hand as his newspaper, he held a brown handbag. I watched him step into the lift, and finished my last sausage and another cup of tea before following.

I tapped on the door and when he asked who it was, I put on a squeaky voice and said it was room service. He was protesting that he hadn't asked for anything as he opened the door, but he never finished the sentence. Fist into stomach doubled him up with no more noise than a burst tyre, and I smacked his neck as he went down. He was unconscious before he hit the thick red carpet. I hauled him in, closed the door, and began looking.

I went round that room like a whirlwind trying to find the damned handbag before he began to take an interest in the world again. What the hell had he done with it? I'd seen it in his hand as he left the restaurant and now I couldn't see it anywhere. He began to groan, and I was thinking of ripping up one of his nice silk shirts to bind him, but when I turned him over the bag was dangling from his wrist.

It was that scaly stuff, crocodile I think it is. It had a flap over the main pocket, and a zip section on the back. I found a wallet with about two hundred pounds English currency in the main pocket, along with a card for Davina's, and an olive green passport with the Brazilian coat-of-arms on the front. Inside, his unsmiling frog-face stared out at me.

The same pouchy face looked at me out of the dark blue soft-backed passport I found in the zip section. Dark blue, with an eagle stamped in gold on the front, and although I couldn't read the Arabic lettering even my French could manage to interpret the bit about the Republic of Syria. In any case, anyone who's taken even the slightest interest in international terrorism could recognise a Syrian passport at a hundred yards in thick fog. I remembered enough to flick through it from back to front, which is the way they read. In both he was born on 17 November 1935, in both he was a company director; but in Rio he was Luis Santos, and in Damascus he was Ali Fattah Yaseen.

He was watching me from the floor. His eyes were almost black, quite flat and emotionless, as he watched to see how I was reacting to this discovery. Rubbing his throat, he pulled himself up into a sitting position.

'Mr Yaseen, I see.' I wagged the Syrian passport at him.

He didn't speak. He was brushing dust off his white trousers.

'Seems you're not a Brazilian after all, then, Mr Yaseen. Now why would you want to go round pretending to be Brazilian. Or, more to the point, pretending not to be Syrian?'

'I shall inform the police.' He spoke almost accentless English in a throaty voice.

'Don't be bloody silly, of course you won't. The only reason you run around under this phoney passport is in the hope that the cops won't know you're here. But I'd like to know why you are here, and I'd like to know why it is that you're so unlucky at cards.'

We looked at each other, and we both knew I was wasting my time. Look at the trouble I had getting information out of the Gurkha Rose; with a pro like him it would be noisy, messy and it would take hours. He held his hand up for the passports.

I dropped them into his lap and walked out. He was safe and he knew it.


'I suggest a turn around College Field,' Charles said as he stepped out of his front door.

I let him go ahead of me over the narrow stile that led to the sports field in front of the main school building, a cloistered affair with a pagoda clock on top. He was wearing a duffel coat, the first I'd seen for years. It wasn't one of the paint and drink stained models that used to be affected by those wishing to establish an artistic disposition. Like every other garment he owned, his was unmarked, pressed and cared for. That was enough: my anger flashed inside me again and if I hadn't been behind him he would've seen it on my face.

Compartmentalise. That's what one of our shrinks told me years ago in those early training sessions. When you find your

150

emotions running high and threatening to disrupt everything, chuck them in a box, seal it up, and stick it on the shelf until you're ready. It took an effort of will, and it made you feel a bit of a cold fish too, but it did give you elbow room to get on with whatever you had to do. That's what I'd done with my feelings over Charles and the Gurkha, while – in two very different ways – I'd sorted out Anna and Mr Yaseen. Soon, very soon, I'd have to let them out. But before then I had to get some information out of Charles.

It was one of those clean winter days that make you realise that winter's the season we do best in England. A brisk sweet wind scrubbed the sky to a sharp blue and everyone's cheeks to pink health, and chased the loitering leaves over the grass. Around the field, the trees posed in silhouette against the sky. Every time you breathed, the air scoured the muck out of your lungs.

'They only make days like this in England. Won't you miss them?'

'Miss them?'

'In Barbados. Take a tip from me, watch out for the mahi-mahi.'

He stopped and frowned down into my face, so I just went on. 'The dolphin. They'll tell you that it's some sort of fish, and that it's not real dolphin, but mine tried to jump through my napkin ring. Hardly seems right, does it? Eating Flipper, the smiling intellectual of the seas?'

He reached out and put his long fingers on my arm. 'Quite honestly, Hussy, I haven't understood a word you've said.'

If there's one thing that does get me a bit testy, it's being conned by an amateur. 'I've seen the tickets. BWIA, to Barbados, December 14th. You're skipping with Anna. I know, Noble, I mean I really know.'

He was such an odd bloke, Noble, such an incalculable mix of candour and downright shiftiness, and I watched with fascination as both drifted across his open face. He stuttered before he managed to get going again.

'Where . . . where . . . where did you see them, actually?'

'At Anna's.'

With a shifty sort of look, he said, 'For all you know, we might be going away for a holiday.'

'On one-way tickets?'

'Ah. You picked that up, I see.'

'Does Veronica know yet?'

That made his eyes spin. 'No, no. I, er, haven't had a chance to raise it yet, although of course I shall ensure that I do so before the . . .'

'Before you go.'

'Quite so.'

'That gives you just over a fortnight.' It was 28 November. 'Is that all?'

It was an odd response, but so was his reaction altogether: he looked more perplexed than guilty at being found out. Maybe I would've made more of that if I hadn't been focusing my attention on what came next.

In the shade of the pavilion and the high wall, there was still frost on the long grass at the side of the field, and it hissed as our shoes passed through. I took him by the arm and turned him to face me, then I told him about the Gurkha's suicide, and how I'd found Rose and Gary. Why? That's what I had to know. Why the hell had he done it? Because no matter how I switched angles on it, I couldn't for the life of me see any logic behind it.

I thought he might've heard about the suicide on the radio but it was obvious that he hadn't. His face paled, leaving the end of his nose raw red in the cold air, and he put his hand to his mouth as though to stop himself being sick. He turned away from me for a full minute, and supported himself against a tree.

When he turned back, he was drained by distress. But he pulled himself up and, with trembling lips, delivered a small speech.

'Hussy, I am truly sorry about that. I had no idea, no idea at all.' He reached out one hand as though to stop any protest. 'Of course, any moral responsibility is mine and I must bear it. That poor young man. That poor . . .'

'Why?' I worked my face up near his and struck him with the question. 'What the hell were you playing at?'

Across his face drifted a look of pure surprise and I realised then that I'd known the answer to that question all along. Known it, but rejected it as unbelievable.

'To keep you interested, of course,' he said, his eyes wide open, and how I kept my hands off his stringy throat I'll never know.

'Just a minute, let's get this right . . ' The re-run was for my benefit, while I tried to digest it. 'You set up this crazy charade to make sure I kept after your brother.'

'That's it.' He was almost eager to agree, as though in some way it justified him.

'You bloody eejit. You brainless bungling bloody eejit.' That was all I could manage, as the full realisation of what he'd done fell into place. He'd conceived the idea of getting someone to take a shot at him, and in trying to set it up he'd fallen into the hands of two piddling little crooks. Between them, with a mixture of incompetence and wickedness, they'd driven an honest man to take his own life, not to mention the uproar and confusion they'd caused the security forces.

I spun him round and leaned him against the tree and I told him. I told him what he'd done and what I'd like to do to him. I used several words they don't hear a lot in the masters' common room. I told him that clumsy amateurs who were blinkered by their own fine principles weren't equipped to mingle in the mess of the real world, and that his sawn-off ignorance was more dangerous than any shotgun.

I had to put my hands in my pockets to stop them reaching out for him. Not that I needed them. The hard force of what I was saying pinned him to the tree.

He took it. He stood there blinking while I gave it to him, until I ran out of rage.

'You are right,' he said in a hoarse whisper. 'It is a cross I shall have to bear.'

We continued walking then, and he spilled out the story of how they'd rigged it. Between them, they'd worked out that Dashera coincided with a day when Kesharsing had access to a rifle.

He was sure that the stunt would be enough to convince me

that someone was out to kill him. The plan – if that's the proper word for a shambles like that – went wrong when I realised the gunman was shooting to miss and went after him.

We'd stopped again, and Charles was leaning against a cricket roller. In the distance, I could hear a boys' choir singing one of those hymns you can never quite forget. From somewhere, a scattering of the words came back to me . . . 'there's no discouragement shall make him once relent, his first avowed intent . . .' That was him: once he got on track, nothing could knock him off.

'Anyway, since you're leaving the country you won't be bothered about your brother any more.'

He frowned at that. 'Oh no, you're quite wrong there, Hussy.' With the winter sunlight on his face, you could see the strain of it eating at his innocence. It was dragging him down, but he wouldn't leave it alone. 'I must find him before . . . before Anna and I leave. That is absolutely imperative.'

'Why?'

'I don't suppose it means much to you, but I am head of the family since father died. If I can help him, then I have a duty to do so.'

After what had happened, I'd assumed that he'd want to drop the whole business. But not Charles.

'I was hoping you'd agree . . .'

I knew what he was going to say. 'Okay, okay, I'll stay with it. But only to stop you screwing everything up again. By the way, I saw your brother the other night.'

I'd said it for effect, and I got it. At first, his face flooded with relief and pleasure that I was staying in the hunt, and he leaned forward to grab my hand. When I mentioned Richard, he froze in that position, his hand still held out.

'Richard? When? Saw him? For heaven's sake, Hussy, where was this?'

In the middle of this torrent of questions, he grabbed me by the shoulders and started to shake me. In his agitation, he was stronger than I'd expected. I knocked his hands down.

'Sorry,' he said, instantly. 'Awfully sorry, but I must know more about it.'

154

'So give me time.'

'Yes, but . . . I am sorry. You are quite right. I was a little over-excited. Perhaps now you could tell me.'

The air was cold enough to redden his hands. I dug mine down into my pockets. We were standing on the pavement now, only a hundred yards or so from the House. Two boys came round the corner on a bike together and as they saw him, the back one slid off so he was running behind. Noble didn't notice, and I remember thinking that he probably didn't miss many like that.

'It was in a casino. He was winning a lot of dough. A whole heap of dough in fact.'

'Was he?' Charles looked quite indignant. 'Gambling was never among his vices, or certainly not as far as I knew.'

'I think he was playing on behalf of someone else, in fact, but that's not important. You were right, he is running around with some bomb boys called Rich Pickings.'

'Where does he live? Have you got an address?' He was plucking at my clothes again, his eyes fired up with enthusiasm.

'Don't rush at it, Noble. He's living in Liverpool.'

'Whereabouts? Do you know?'

'Well, I'll tell you this for nothing. It'll be a district where the schools are only public in the sense that the doors and windows will've been kicked in. No, I don't know exactly where.'

'Can you find out? That's the one thing I must insist on knowing.'

'Hey, hang on, you can insist all you bloody like but if I don't know it you won't get to know it.'

'I do apologise.' He ran his fingers through his hair, pushing it to the back, but afterwards it immediately fell into the old sideways pattern. 'I know you'll turn up trumps. When are you going up there? Today?'

"Tomorrow, I think."

'Wouldn't today be better?'

'Not for me, no, it wouldn't be better. If you want to go and nose around the gutters of Liverpool, you do that today. Tomorrow's when I'm going.'

This time he got the message and backed off. That would be

155

fine. Would I be sure to let him know as soon as I'd made any progress. We stopped outside the House. At a third-floor window, I saw a small red glow flare up, then die again. I recognised Stephens' face. That made two crimes that Noble had missed in ten minutes.

I was already in my car when Veronica came hurrying out.

'Well, have you told him?'

Charles rubbed his hands together and began to mutter some apology.

'Told me what?'

She bent down so that I could see the turmoil of emotions in her face. The muscles in her cheeks were working.

'Someone's watching us.' Over her shoulder, she said: 'I know you say he won't believe us but that's what you're paying him for, isn't it? It's true. Someone is spying on us.'

Although Noble was signalling me to ignore it, I asked her what made her think that.

'I saw a face at the window the other night when I was sorting the boys' laundry, and that fifth-form boy, Carter, he says there's been a funny little man hanging around the house. Well, what are you going to do?'

'Another threat on your life, Noble?'

He pulled an apologetic face.

With a nervy quickness, his wife switched her gaze between the two of us. 'You haven't answered my question. What are you going to do?'

I put the car in first gear. 'Tell her, Charles,' I said, and drove off.

# 23

The first call was from Cassidy, giving no name, to say he'd see me down at the talking-shop in an hour. Cautious man, Cassidy. The second was from Caroline, with second thoughts.

'About what?' I'd just mucked out Charlie. From where I was standing I could see him giving me his betrayed look as he reluctantly settled down into his disgustingly crap-free nest.

'What I said the other day.' Each word was hand-picked for the job. 'When you asked about Richard's business trips.'

I dumped my mug of tea and sat down to concentrate. 'Yes?'

Hesitantly, she went on: 'Joe, if I use the phrase High-risk, would you have any idea what I'm talking about?'

'Do you mean High-risk Hussy, Death Delivered Daily, by any chance?'

Her laugh made the phone seem warm and almost human. 'What was the rest of it, I can't remember? Death Delivered Daily . . .'

'. . . Takeaway Mayhem, Bullets Caught in Teeth, Dogs Walked . . .'

'. . . and Windows Cleaned. That was always my favourite bit.' Her laughter faded. 'I had to be sure.'

'Well, there can't be all that many people know that bit of nonsense. You got it from Richard?'

'Yes. You were right. They weren't really business trips. Or not what most people mean by that. He always said he was doing a job for Liz and Phil.'

'I had an idea that was it.'

'I wouldn't have told you, but I was wondering if you were the same person and then I remembered your little rhyme. I gather you were quite a celebrated Hooligan.'

'Only because I kept laughing in the wrong place.'

'And weren't you a friend of Tiger Tomkins?'

157

'Jesus, I'm terrible at names, would you believe?'

'Oh yes, of course. Direct questions – sorry. Richard didn't know you personally, did he? – only by reputation?'

'It's wicked the things they say about a man behind his back now. And would I be right in thinking that Richard put Charles on to me?'

'Let's think. Veronica actually. You know I said she once asked Richard to check up on Charles? Well, at first he suggested she should hire an agency and I rather think he pointed out your ad to her in one of his security mags. She must've kept it, and passed it on to Charles. I remember him pointing it out to me. "That must be old High-risk," he said.'

'I gave him your message.'

The busy flow of chatter ceased. 'I know it's no use asking where or anything of that sort, but can you tell me what he said?'

'He said: "That's nice" and he gave a bloody big grin.'

'I only wish . . .' she began, then halted. 'It's no use wishing, is it?'

'Never did much for me. Have you had a visit?'

'Yes. Two of them came round. They were very helpful about it. They assured me that they would see the divorce goes through smoothly and that I needn't worry about money, not that that's any great problem. It was rather upsetting, I don't mind admitting.'

'Natural enough.'

'No. I mean about some of their questions. They seemed doubtful about Richard's . . . well, reliability, I suppose you'd call it.'

'Jesus, they can be desperate insensitive people sometimes. Anyway, you'd soon be able to reassure them on that.'

'Yes, I think so. I certainly tried to. This isn't something I would have said to them, but I think you'll understand. Richard was always his own man and so you couldn't always predict what he would do. Despite the training and everything, he somehow always kept a little bit of himself private and sealed off. They never quite got all of him, if you know what I mean.'

'I've a good idea.'

158

'Do you know why I decided to tell you?'

'No.'

'Because you remind me of him.'

It was my turn to weigh words. 'That's very flattering.'

'And I think you might be his friend.'

'Oddballs versus The Rest.'

'Something like that.'

'Caroline, I hear that brother Charles may be moving out too.'

'I don't think so. I'm sure I would have had Veronica on the telephone.'

'You could say this is a sneak preview. She doesn't know yet.'

'Gosh. I think I'll go and stay with friends. Veronica will be spitting with fury.'

'She's so fond of him?'

'Fond? Not Veronica. I don't think she would mind particularly if she had a cardboard cut-out of a husband – anything to show the neighbours and shout at from time to time. I am sorry, I shouldn't have said that. What a bitch I'm becoming. Awful thought – it's rather open season on the Noble wives at the moment, isn't it?'

As I was going out, I saw Jamie locking horns with one of those middle-class blokes who must have read an article urging dissatisfied customers to complain. He was trying to be forceful with Jamie, an attack strategy which had about the same success rate as throwing eggs at a tank.

'You tell 'im, Joe.' She grabbed my sleeve as I tried to scoot past. 'Feller 'ere says he brought his car in the other day and he reckons it's put on 150 miles on the clock.'

'Don't tell me, sir. Honda, is it?' I gave him the old respectful yet confident smile.

'Yes, that's right.'

'CRX?'

'As a matter of . . .'

'I knew it. Bring it in and I'll have a look at it personally. We've had two or three of them in with the same problem. It's what's known in Japan as the sayonara car – the equivalent of our Friday car. They're not all perfect even in Japan, sir.'

As he drove off, Jamie nudged me. 'Is that right? About those sayon-whatsit cars?'

'For all we know, Jamie, for all we know.'

At Speakers' Corner, I found Cassidy listening to a white-haired old character who was encased in sandwich-boards with the advice: Flee From the Wrath to Come. In an elaborate Geordie accent, he was explaining how the Lord came to him outside a greyhound stadium in Gateshead. 'Eee, Ah was reel surprised, and He says to me, He says, why now Bobby, you seem to like a canny bit sin, and Ah says, it's Satan what does it . . .'

'Do you reckon they could extradite Satan?'

'Not a chance, Joe, if he's in Dublin. How're you diddling?'

We were at the front of a crowd of about fifteen people. Three lads with cans of lager who wanted to know if there was any football in the hereafter, a potty old lady festooned with carrier bags who was doing a whooping war-dance, and a dwarf who said he was collecting money for a new pair of legs. The rest were tourists who were probably wondering if freedom of speech was some form of psychiatric therapy.

'Without you, I'd never meet these nice people.'

Cassidy grunted. 'Bloody phones. I know, cock. Yours'll be about as private as Radio Fucking One by now.'

We walked away from the speakers, across the beaten-down grass, and Cassidy mauled a hot-dog that steamed in the cold air. His grey hair looped down as he struggled with it and onions dripped on to his dirty donkey-jacket.

'Not much on Yaseen. Reckons to be chairman of some sort of Syrian commission on tourism, which is about as likely as a Syrian Yom Kippur party, but it does give him a lot of leeway on moving around. He don't usually bother with all that false papers crap. So he must be doing a naughty.'

'What is he really?'

'Couldn't get near the real stuff, Hussy, you know that. But I asked a mate in anti-terr, without looking too nosey, and I gather he's quite a big-shot in Damascus. Trusted government emissary, that sort of thing. Not the sort of geezer you'd shove off abroad to talk to people about buckets and fuckin' spades. The question is, why is he losin' all that cash?'

He threw the last inch of his hot-dog down on the ground. Instantly a dozen pigeons gathered to peck at it, like civil servants round a memo.

'Tell you something, Cassidy. I'm not sure about that.'

Idly, he swung his leg at the nearest pigeon. It slid beneath his scuffed shoe and stabbed a fleshy chunk of sausage. Then his hard face creased up and he looked at me. 'Course he's losing. You've seen him. Thousands and bloody thousands.'

'He's not losing cash.'

'He's not?' His hard eyes were on me.

'No. He's moving it.'

'Moving it?'

'From A to B.'

'Go on.'

'The banks have shut down on international terrorism. At one time, they used to be able to move their money around, no problem. You know, if the Iranians wanted to sponsor the micks, all they had to do was to call themselves the Committee for the Relief of Boredom in the Middle East or something, and bung a cheque in the post. If you want the best interest rates, shove it in the building society until the next delivery of Kalashnikovs comes through. Then the western governments started leaning on the bankers and at long bloody last they've knocked it on the head. Even the Swiss banks are discouraging them now, and at one time they'd open an account to encourage international child molesting.'

'So Yaseen's the delivery-boy for Damascus. Not old Colonel Dentures in Tripoli.'

'There's a lot of competition over who's the most sincere and generous in their support for the battle for freedom, and a lot of the readies flying about too.'

Cassidy turned to listen to a man with a Mayo accent who was shouting about the British murderers still doing Cromwell's work in Ireland. 'Rum fucking world,' he said.

'Rummish.'

'Too deep for me.'

161

'Me and all.'

'But I says to myself, when they put the lid on young Thaw, I says maybe I'd give little Joe some back-up. Course, your problem is that I could be put in to keep a beady on you, couldn't I? I could be telling you a load of porkies this time.'

'You could, and that's a fact. I was told hands-off by my head office at first. Now they're letting me in for the ride. What d'you make of that?'

'I was right about Richard Noble?'

'You were.'

He scratched his nails on his unshaven chin. Slowly, still thinking, he said: 'Then they do think he's gone sour.'

Out of the sky I saw a football curving down towards me and heard some kids shouting to me to watch out. I thought about heading it back to them, or trapping it beneath my foot before slamming it back to them. In the end I ducked and let it bounce out over towards Park Lane. I was never much good at football anyway.

'Those boys don't go sour,' I said.

'They don't.' Cassidy's jeering had a way of cutting through to the truth.

Caroline's words came back to me. 'Okay. It can happen. But I don't believe it.'

He screwed his face up in cynical amusement and shook his head. 'Always admired that, loyalty. Anyway, if he ain't gone sour, they've sussed him and he ain't working any more. Something's gone wrong and they're putting a ferret down the bunny-hole to see what's going on.'

'And a terrier behind the ferret, Jim?'

He gave a raucous laugh. 'I'm too big to be a fuckin' terrier. I knew you'd think that. You don't trust nobody, do you?'

'It's the difference between believing and knowing. We believe in each other, but we never know. Not really. Not for sure.'

'Yeah. That's about as far as we can go. You heading for Liverpool? Want someone to watch your back?' Even he had to laugh at that after what we'd just been saying. He held his hands up. 'Gospel truth, I mean just as a mate.'

162

'What – with your barrow-boy accent?'

'Yeah, you're right. Dead giveaway, ain't it? If you need me, bell me. Tell you what. All this cash, I reckon someone's gonna lay on a party.'

'What worries me, is who's the guest of honour.' I pointed at the sandwich-man lumbering off towards Marble Arch. 'But you can't say God didn't warn us. Flee From the Wrath to Come.'

# 24

For anyone who knew the old Liverpool, it's a sorry sight now. I can remember the place when every day brought ships to pump new life into the old seaport, you could hardly get across Lime Street for the traffic, and everyone was a poet, a musician or a comic. These days, what trade there is comes pre-packaged in containers, you could picnic in the middle of the road at rush hour, and the famous Scouse wit's about as keen as damp cardboard. It was always a tart of a town, all tits, gin and lipstick, but now it's just an old has-been whore who can't raise the price of a glass of stout. Breaks your heart to look at it.

I checked into a pub at the back of the London Road and got myself all dressed up, for the second time that week – and for that matter, the second time that decade. My one sharp suit, my one Jaeger-sale shirt, my one silk tie. Jesus, I even combed my hair. Then I set off to walk into Liverpool Eight, which, if you're not either black, a highly-qualified lawbreaker, or very very tough, is one of the most dangerous parts of Britain.

My problem was that I merge too easily in those places. There's something about me – a sort of second-hand, army-surplus quality – that makes me look like a man who's had a bad day in the betting-shop. When you want to merge into places like that, which is what I do want most of the time, it's a priceless talent. But this time I wanted to stand out, and for someone with my slum-clearance style, it isn't easy. Which accounts for the fancy-dress and the hair-combing.

I tucked a copy of *The Times* under my arm, and set off to walk across town. Past the Catholic cathedral, the one that looks as though it's just landed from Mars and is known to the locals as Paddy's wigwam, and up to the more traditional Anglican model, a looming mass of sandstone. I turned left into Upper Parliament Street, and I was there. Liverpool Eight. Toxteth, the newspapers called it during the last lot of rioting, but that's just because they don't like putting numbers in headlines. To the locals it's always been Liverpool Eight. Before the street riots of the mid-eighties, it used to have a Left Bank air about it, and they claimed that you couldn't throw a bottle without hitting a poet or an artist. These days they throw bottles at anyone, regardless of their aesthetic gifts. Once the casbah of colours and races you find down there made it colourful and exciting: now they make it threatening. It's definitely not smart-suit territory. I knew that – and I knew that my disguise as a respectable citizen was working – within a minute of walking down Parly, as it's known to the locals.

I felt like a rabbit at the greyhound derby. It was the end of the afternoon, but there was still light enough for me to be seen. In the tall terraces where Victorian merchants once lived, I could see boarded windows and peeling paintwork. I turned a corner. There were gaps where houses had been burned down, and everywhere the ornaments of modern urban living: broken glass in the roads, discarded cans in the gutter, twisted shopping trolleys and wheelless prams and the stripped carcases of stolen cars. I walked through it all, knowing I was watched. First a little black kid scampered up the steps to bring his parents to the window to see. Then a tall Sikh stopped when he saw me, and his disbelieving eyes followed me long after I'd gone past.

The first car, its windows dark with black faces, revved along behind me for a few yards, then roared off. The second tucked in behind me and stayed there. I didn't look round. Ahead, outside a barricaded shop, was a mob of twenty or thirty men: mostly young, mostly black, and all waiting for me as I headed towards them.

I could feel my scalp tingle and my mouth dry. Whatever the cops say, the only real law in Liverpool Eight is street law. You might as well hope for divine intervention as shout for the police. They stood waiting for me, spread out halfway across the road, as the chugging car prodded me slowly towards them. What the hell was I doing, wearing my best suit and a bright smile, striding cheerfully towards them, armed with nothing more lethal than today's copy of *The Times*? Somehow it didn't feel like enough.

A yard short of them, I stopped. I smiled. They didn't.

'My name's Alan Hamilton. I'm from the *Times* newspaper and I want to see Winston.'

Nothing showed on any of the faces. Then, from the back, a man in a red knitted cap and mustard-coloured waterproof ambled up to me. He was under twenty and he had a moustache no thicker than a mannequin's eyebrow.

'What you saying, man?' All the lilt of the Caribbean was in his voice.

'I'm saying I want to see Winston.'

Almost before I'd realised it, he'd slipped my wallet from inside my jacket pocket and passed it to someone behind him. 'Everyone want see Winston. Watch.'

He tapped my wristwatch.

As I unfastened it, I said: 'I know, but I think he'll want to see me. Will you ask him?'

'He not want see you, man. Not Winston.' As he spoke, he passed my watch back to his pals. Then he ran his weightless hands in and out of my remaining pockets, just in case.

'Tell him I'm here. He'll want to know.'

'Why he want know you, man?' This time the voice came from behind me. Imperceptibly, the crowd in front of me had fallen back. So too had the man who'd taken my wallet. I moved round slowly and saw, slumped against the side of a big Peugeot, a long-limbed black in a royal blue track-suit, with his

165

Rasta hair in one of those big baggy hats. A thin wisp of a beard trailed from his chin. He was older than the young highwaymen who'd just robbed me, and he carried a lot more weight.

'I'm Alan Hamilton from *The Times* newspaper. I'd like to talk to him.'

Half-stooping, he whispered something through the window of the car. From the crackle and buzz, I knew someone had got a radio set-up in there.

He stooped again to listen. 'He don' want see any reporters.'

He was opening the car when I gave him the second part of the message. 'Tell him it's about the Brazilian.'

After a moment's pause, he went through the same routine. This time, he opened the back door of the car and I got in.

It was two streets back, and Track-suit grabbed me by the arm and whirled me through the front door and up the stairs.

On the first landing, he had to pause to shout to someone downstairs, but he kept a grip on my elbow all the time. Two youngsters, mid-teens, opened a door, and from inside I heard a white and classless voice talking. 'The point about the soap flakes is that they turn the petrol and acid into a gelatinous mass so it sticks to clothes and to flesh. In many ways, it's every bit as good a bomb as napalm.' Evening classes in bomb-making. Sullen-faced, the youngster slammed the door and clattered down the stairs.

We went up two more flights. I had a flashing impression of more crumbling stonework and peeling paint, and more dark faces in doorways, bare stairs and the teasing smell of dope, until I was half-pushed through a door.

To my surprise, I found I was alone in an office – and, even more surprising, it was an office that wouldn't have disgraced a multi-national skyscraper in the City. Rosewood desk, matching unit covering one wall, long-backed swivel chair, two soft black leather armchairs, glass-topped brass-edged coffee table, computer at its own work station, and a massive telly in the corner. All illuminated by a large brass lamp. Only the poster on the wall told you it wasn't an oil executive's. It showed a knife slicing open a blue onion and the caption read: 'What's the difference between an onion and a policeman? You cry when you cut an onion.' That about summed up the philosophy of Rich Pickings.

A door opened and in came Winston. He was talking to someone over his shoulder but when he saw me he stopped mid-sentence. It didn't stun him for long. A second later, a high-watt smile was spread all over his face.

'You. Well, well. I don't believe it. Cracker!' He raised his voice, still without taking his eyes off me. 'Is he going to be pleased to see you.'

'What's dat den?' Cracker, his Scouse thicker than ever in his own territory, came into the room. As he saw me, his finger touched the ugly red seam which studded the side of his nose.

'That's what you get for picking your nose,' I said. I was on my feet and round the back of the chair as he ducked his head and started for me, but Winston flung an arm out and stopped him.

'You lirrel rats-arse . . ' he began.

'Get out, Cracker. I'll shout if you're wanted.'

He lowered himself into the swivel chair behind the desk and waved me back into the armchair. Although he was in shirt sleeves and jeans, he didn't look out of place behind the executive desk. There was lots of Africa in his hair and lips, there was Arabia in his fine hooked nose and cheekbones, but the predominant qualities in his face were intelligence and arrogance.

'You like it?' His glance took in the room. 'Looted. All of it.'

'Saves queuing.'

'Saves paying too. Mr Alan Hamilton of *The Times*, I believe.'

I ignored the snooty voice he'd adopted to make this announcement, and passed over my press card. I say mine, but really it was one I'd once nicked off a young Scottish gentleman, a Mr Alan Hamilton, of *The Times*, and forgotten to return. Then I held out a copy of the paper. Hamilton had got a royal story in that morning. Thank goodness: you never know with those journos, they're such an idle lot.

'I don't like to admit it, Mr Hamilton, but you've got me guessing. Everywhere I go I find you. At that house down in

167

Sussex. Then in that mews in London. *The Times* is getting around a lot these days, isn't it? I'd like to know why. Though it's only fair to tell you, I'm a *Guardian* man meself.'

His tone was friendly, conversational, and for the first time I noticed that behind the Merseyside accent there was the echo of an education. I couldn't read anything from his smoky black eyes.

'I was doing the same as you.'

'And that was?'

'Checking out Richard Noble.'

He sat back in the seat and laughed out loud in surprise and admiration. 'I've got to hand it to you, I wasn't expecting that. So you know Noble, do you?'

'Hoping to.'

He moved forward in the seat so that his arms rested on the desk again. He was making himself comfortable. 'Why?'

'If an ex-officer of the Gurkhas joins a revolutionary group like yours, that's a story.'

'Because he's a traitor to his class?'

'Maybe. *Times* readers would find that hard to believe. You must've found it hard to believe too, or you wouldn't have been checking him out.'

His laughter was full of confidence. 'Don't try that old stuff. Sowing seeds of doubt. Noble's on the side of the angels now, don't you worry. You wanta chat to him? No problem.'

He touched a button on the telephone deck in front of him and Cracker almost took the door off its hinges he came in so fast. When he saw me relaxed and cross-legged on my chair, he straightened out of his fighting crouch and uncurled his fists.

'It's okay Cracker, he's as good as gold. Get Noble, will you, and send him up here.'

'Tell him to finish his bomb-making lecture first.'

If he was worried I'd recognised Richard's voice, he didn't show it. 'You overheard that, did you? We're great believers in the power of education here. Tell him, Cracker. And don't bother telling him there's anyone here, right?' As the door closed, he went on: 'So. How does a posh scribbler like you know about weed-killer bombs?'

168

'Belfast.'

'Yeah?'

'I covered Belfast for two years. You learn a lot over there.'

'That right?' Thoughtfully, he added: 'A highly educated bloke, that Noble. Very useful for us – we've got plenty of dedication but not much experience in the field. He's full of useful tips, you'd be surprised.'

With one square-tipped finger, he tapped a toy-sized silver rocking-horse into motion so that it began to ride furiously, but without progress, over the gleaming desk. He even had executive toys. 'Someone said you were asking about a Brazilian.'

'Something like that.'

He held out his finger-end so that the jockey kept nodding his finger-nail. 'Don't know the gent myself. Would I like him?'

'I think you would.'

'Why's that?'

'He gives away money.'

His raised eyebrows ploughed furrows in his forehead. 'Is that right? Much?'

'Millions.'

He bunched up his big lips and put his head on one side, as though trying to visualise the stacks of money. 'Millions, eh? Who's he give it to?' His eyes were on me.

I pointed one finger at him.

He patted his clean yellow T-shirt. 'Me?' He gave a bubbling laugh. 'Why'd he wanna do that?'

'That's my next question.'

I watched the silver horse start its endless skidding journey again. Winston was rocking himself slightly now, as he slumped back in his chair. This was what he liked: playing games, and I was just another executive toy.

It was my turn. I saw his face willing me to answer, like a teacher with a hesitant pupil. It wasn't as though I hadn't already given it plenty of thought. Foreign money for English anarchists? Was that what it really was? It could be an arms deal, if there was anyone in Liverpool who could deliver on orders that size. There was the Irish connection too. Hell, in the spaghetti mess of international revolution, it could mean anything.

'I tell you, you put it on the front page? That it?'

'That's it.'

'Why'd I do that?'

'Because you live by propaganda. The Kalashnikov and the press statement, one in each hand.'

He tipped his head towards the door. 'My lads don't get to read your paper a lot. And how can I be sure you'd give us a nice little write-up?'

'That's the last thing you'd want off me. You know dam' well we'll slag you off as usual and that's what you want. But they'll read what you say in the City, and that's what you want too. Street cred and Threadneedle Street cred. Make the pinstripes shiver, eh?'

'And what is it I'm going to talk about?'

'About why you want Middle East money.'

'Middle East? The way I heard it you were going to ask me about a Brazilian.'

Slowly I shook my head. Between us, in the cool still air, the lies and truths lay there, as I'd shuffled and dealt them. His unfathomable eyes looked into mine.

'Ali Fattah Yaseen. A gentleman from Damascus. And he's the delivery-boy for the men with the biggish bucks in that part of the world.'

'Such as?'

'Would it matter?'

'And what does he deliver?'

'Wages.'

'Who for?'

'The hired help.'

'Hired for what?'

'There's only one thing they want to buy. Revolution.'

His gaze rested on me, without any of the signs of disturbance I'd been hoping for. After a moment, he rose from his vast soggy chair and moved over to a rosewood cabinet against the wall. 'Beer?'

'Now that's what I call civilised.'

170

'You'd be amazed.'

The front of the cabinet came down and he tugged two cans out of their plastic rings. He tossed one to me as he slid back behind the desk.

'Here's to revolution,' I said, and, as his eyebrows began to rise, I added: 'After all, isn't it keeping the two of us in regular work? You starting it, me writing about it.'

He raised his can, then drank from it. 'Alternatively, I could always get Cracker to lose you. Let's face it, you're only a chicken-shit hack.' His face was still set in its mask of pleasantness, but through it I could see the casual cruelty that was at the centre of his character. He was on his own ground: he could give me a beer one minute, wipe me away the next.

Unless I could give him a reason to keep me alive.

'Come on now. I'd die a disappointed man if you really thought that even a chicken-shit hack like me would walk into this set-up without leaving a bit of insurance behind. I've filed the full story on what happened at Davina's, and the fact that I was coming here to see you, with instructions to pass it on to those comical people with the invisible ink and the passwords in Whitehall.'

'We can handle that. We've had them before.'

'Course you had them before. Bloody panda patrol on a quick in-and-out hoping to pick up someone for possession of half a joint without starting a riot. I'm not talking about that. I'm talking about the serious gents up your arse with a searchlight. You wouldn't hang on to this nice shiny desk for long then.'

I was watching for anything, even an eyelash move, that might tell me which way his mood was going, but I never got it. At that moment the door behind me was flung open and Richard Noble strolled in.

His quick glance passed over me. 'What is it, boss?'

'Feller here wants to meet you. You know, the one I had to smack around for sticking his nose in when I was talking to your missus.'

Richard Noble gave one sharp nod. He was watching me, and Winston was watching him, and I was trying to watch both

171

of them. I suddenly realised, from the way Winston was looking at Noble, that he still didn't trust him.

'He's from *The Times*. He reckons his readers'd like to meet a real class traitor. What you think, Noble?'

'Do you want me to talk to him?'

'Yeah. Why not? No such thing as bad publicity. Anyway, I'd like to hear it again. We don't get many converts from your side.'

There was something about Richard Noble that made the black drop into a harsher Merseyside accent and put a jeer into his voice. I couldn't make up my mind if that was just his way of dominating the pack, or if it was personal: if he still saw him as a representative of the hated officer class. Either way, Noble didn't seem to notice.

'What do you want to know?' He made no attempt to sit down. Instead he stood, feet eighteen inches apart, hands by his sides. His clothes were baggy old items, a ragged green sweater and colourless canvas trousers that draped over the tops of his shoes.

With him there in front of me, I could see he was two inches shorter than Charles, stockier too, and he had a steady look about the eyes that made you think he'd seen more of the world. He hadn't spent all his time catching secret smokers, that was for sure.

'Tell him why you switched sides.' Winston cut in again, in a rasping tone.

Richard Noble's eyes stayed on mine. 'Okay. Did Winston say you went to see Caroline?'

'I did.' If he remembered the message I'd brought him from his wife, he wasn't showing it.

'He was checking you out,' Winston interrupted. 'We all were.'

He ignored that. 'Right, then, you've seen the set-up. There's Caroline with that house and her horses down in Sussex, there's my brother who's on the staff of a public school in Surrey, and there I was in Church Crookham with my Gurkhas. We were all living in clover, not because of hard work or any sort of merit, but simply because we were born to the right parents in the right part of the country. No logic to it, certainly no justice, it was our birthright.'

'It took a long while for it to hit you?' I could feel Winston's glance of approval: he liked my question.

'It did.' He tucked his chin in then so that he had to look from under a wrinkled brow. 'I'd always had what I suppose you'd call liberal sympathies – by the way, do you want to make notes or anything?'

'It's all right. I work off memory.'

'Fine. Let's see . . . I'm trying to put this in a way that your readers can recognise. There's no point in going off into polemics but if they can see how someone from the same background . . .'

'Like Patty Hearst,' Winston chipped in.

Without turning, Noble replied quietly: 'Like Patty Hearst, except you didn't kidnap me and you didn't fuck me.'

Winston's face twisted into a smile. 'So far.'

'Go on,' I said.

'Right. As I was saying, I'd always been a bit uneasy that we had so much when others have so little.' He made a quick movement with one hand to indicate the slums of Liverpool. 'To be honest, we only saw places like this on television documentaries. The thing about the Army is that the whole British class cock-up is there to see, all formalised and laid out in front of you. There's the chaps with the rich daddies who get a good education to make sure they speak nicely and use the right knife and fork, so that they too can qualify for the good things in life. Then there's the rest, who get to do all the work, clean out the lavatories in peacetime and get shot if there's a war on. I remember thinking to myself that all I had to do was to hang around drinking out of a silver mug in the Mess until I retired to a cottage in Hampshire. So I got out. Got that place in the Downs, the one you saw. I did adventure holidays stuff, Caroline played around with her horses.'

He'd hooked one thumb in the top of his trousers now. In his accentless voice, and his easy way of talking, you'd never have realised it was a revolutionary's confession.

'You got out, why wasn't that enough?'

'Yeah,' Winston said, from behind his desk. 'Tell us that.'

This time Noble did turn to look at him. 'You've heard it a dozen times – you're not sure if you believe it, that's all. But here goes again.' Winston tapped his beer can against his teeth as Noble turned back to me. 'Did I say I'd got a brother who's a housemaster at a school in Surrey? Okay, well his wife Veronica is something of a right-wing toughie. She's a neurotic too. They crystallised the whole thing for me. I was having dinner with them one night when they were telling me about some kid they thought I might help. He was a real thicko, apparently. He'd blown up all his exams. But you know how those people work it. Daddy forked out a fortune to put him through a crammer and have another go at them. Incredibly, even after all that, he crashed them again. So they wanted my help to slide him into the Army as an ordinary recruit – even though he didn't have the basics for that – whereupon after a suitable lapse of time they would spot his potential as an officer and haul him out from among the hairies. "But he isn't good enough," I said. Do you know what my lovely sister-in-law Veronica said? "He's one of ours," she said. "We look after our own." That's what she said.'

There was a silence in the room when he finished. Then I spoke: 'One pampered kid. That was enough to turn you into a terrorist?'

He gave another of those sharp nods. 'It sounds trivial but that's how it was. Somehow that brought it all home to me. They never allow one of theirs to fail, however undeserving he is. It was Veronica who showed me that. She even spelled it out for me. I remember I began to protest, and say how disgraceful it was that people like us should stoop to fixing and double-dealing just so we could hang on to our power and our privileges. And Veronica said that was the point of the ruling-class – that they had the power to ensure they went on ruling. "We've got it," she said, "and it's up to us to hang on to it." Democracy? This isn't democracy. It's a self-perpetuating oligarchy.'

I couldn't resist it. 'And you really believe that a schoolmaster and a junior army officer qualify as members of the ruling-class?'

'Worse. We're the guarantors. The public schools make sure that they have the edge in qualifications, just in case any question of merit ever does creep in, not that that's very bloody likely, I can tell you. And if your average working bloke realises he's stuck in the gutter forever, and decides to do something serious about it, then there's always the Army to herd him back into his hovel.'

Without warning, he smacked his fist into his palm, and his voice rose. 'And that's how it'll stay forever unless someone stands up and fights.'

I leaned forward on my chair, looking up at him. 'So if your weedkiller bombs blow the legs off a kid or the guts out of some old lady, you don't mind.'

His eyes tightened as he returned my stare. In a whisper he replied: 'In this war, we're all bloody squaddies.'

'You gave up your home, your business, that lovely wife of yours?'

He shrugged. 'Once I understood it all, I didn't have a choice. When I left the Army, that was running away from the truth. I had to face up to it, accept it, and do something about it. No choice.'

Winston spoke in a dreamy voice. 'She's a classy bit of talent, wouldn't you say, Hamilton?'

'She is that. Meself, I'd think twice before I moved off and left one like that smouldering in bed . . .'

Noble was good. He just folded his arms and breathed in deeply through his nose. 'I know what you're trying to do, but it won't work. If you want to know, I loved Caroline. Still do. But this was what I had to do, and you can't bring a woman into all this.'

'A matter of honour, eh?' I saw his cheek muscles move when I pulled that word out of his past.

'If you like. I wouldn't be ashamed to call it that.'

Standing there, so defiantly, he reminded me then of his brother. They could both identify honour as clearly as I could see traffic lights: stop, go, whatever the lights said.

175

'Don't you sometimes wish you'd stayed with Caroline?'

'Yes,' Winston repeated. 'Don't you?'

'Of course,' Noble said, flatly. 'Sometimes. At night mostly, I suppose. Is that something your readers can relate to?'

'What did you tell Caroline?'

He gave a heavy sigh. 'I told her I was going to another woman.'

'Why?'

'It was easier for her to take that than for her to think I would join a movement like this.'

'Easier? Another woman?' I didn't have to fake my surprise.

'Okay, more believable. She'd never believe that I would leave her because of . . . well, a matter of political morality.'

I studied his cool self-control. 'You seem a bit low on revolutionary zeal for this sort of life.'

A half-smile touched his sombre face. 'You forget. Dissembling is the first thing you learn at public school. I learned early how to contain emotion, but don't question my sincerity because of it. If Winston wants you to vanish, I can arrange it. How about it, boss?'

He raised one eyebrow at the black, and I saw nothing in his pale grey eyes to make me think he didn't mean it.

'You've scared him.' Winston chuckled at me. 'Don't crap yourself, I got uses for you.'

'By the way,' young Noble said, sliding my copy of *The Times* along the edge of the desk back towards me, 'if you're trying to pass that to me, I don't want it. Is that all, boss?'

As he left the room, the newspaper I'd placed on the desk slowly unfolded. Written in blue ballpoint, right across the top of the page was a telephone number. His eyes never leaving mine, Winston picked up the telephone and tapped out the numbers. I could hear it ringing, and I could hear the squeak of an answering voice.

He put the phone down. 'Staying at that old boozer up London Road, eh?'

I didn't say anything. What was the point? But it really made Winston's day. He was delighted that I'd thought I could lure his convert, and doubly delighted that Noble had betrayed me.

176

'Nice try. I thought the bastard was conning us an' all. I take a lorra convincing. The trouble with us, we're not used to mixing with men of honour. Now what was this rubbish about a gambling club?'

I went through it all in detail. The game, the odds, the chances of a run occuring like that night after night. I told him I had seen the Syrian lose, then leave the minute he began to win. I told him I had seen Richard Noble do all the winning, and I'd seen the two of them, Winston and Noble, leave together with the money. I even explained how you could rig a shoe so that one man won while the other one lost.

As he listened his only reaction was polite interest. At the end, he said: 'Why'd they wanna do that? That's no game.'

'It wasn't a game at all. It was an operation.'

'An operation?'

He was making me do the running but I didn't mind. 'A money-shifting operation. How to move over a million quid from those fat wallets in the Middle East to some of our naughty boys here in Britain. Via Mr Ali Fattah Yaseen the wages clerk. Without any complications with currency controls and awkward questions from intelligence authorities. It was a beautiful operation. The croupiers who rigged it are paid off, everyone else will put it down as one of those funny punter's stories, and the only guy who thought it was a bit too funny got knocked off by a burglar. Sweet stuff.'

Just then Noble strode back into the room. 'The boys thought maybe your visitor ought to have these back.' He dumped my watch and wallet on to the desk, and left.

'Take them.' Winston pushed them towards me. 'You've done pretty well, I reckon. You've got a good story about the lad who saw the light. Leave it at that.'

'Or what?'

'Or you'll go home with your face in a hankie.'

'One question?'

'What's that then?'

'How much? Altogether?'

He stood up and stretched, laughing at me. 'You don't give up, do you? Okay, Ali was going to announce it at his end anyway in a couple of days, so you've made me jump the gun. A gift of two million pounds to the people's movements in Britain.'

'Which people's movements? I didn't know we had any.'

He put his finger-ends on the desk and leaned on them so that they turned white with the pressure. 'Every kid who snatches a purse out of some rich scumbag's basket. Every man who has to jump a window-lock in a suburban house to nick one of their three tellies so his kids can eat. Every bloke who's ripped off a car that cost more than the stinking room he has to live in.'

'Crime, you mean.'

'Social redress, we call it. That's what I mean by people's movements. Anyone who's prepared to stand up against our oppressors. Anyone who'll lead a strike or a riot. Anyone who'll torch a factory or slice a pig.

'We've even got work for the little kids. Every time you see some rich bastard's Jag or Rolls, scratch it. Chuck bricks through the golf-club window. Dirty phone-calls to their wives when their husbands are away. Anything to put the pressure on them. Anything to let them know we're coming. They've had the rich pickings for years – now it's our turn.'

'What about rape? Isn't it a shame that you can't find a place for that in your revolutionary programme?'

'Maybe we could. Possibly.' He shot me a glance to see what effect his reply was having. Then, in the same even tone, he went on. 'If you stick to those brainless little judies you get round Kensington and Chelsea, I can see that would serve a purpose. You know the ones, those who live in a flat daddy bought them and drive round in white sports cars looking for a nice young subaltern. You could justify raping them. Let them feel our anger. Let them know that the world is going to be a dangerous place for expensive ornaments like them. That makes sense, doesn't it?'

'You won't swing it,' I said, trying to explode his ideas if only because they were so scary. 'Strikers aren't criminals, and burglars don't regard themselves as fighting for social equality. And just because a man will have the wheels off a parked car doesn't mean he wants to burn coppers alive.'

While I was talking he'd returned to the drinks cabinet and

got himself another beer. He tilted it towards me before he took a drink. Good manners, Winston. For a killer.

'It's already happened. You're doing the work for us, you know that? When we used to try to get stuck into strikes at first, all the lads had us down as another bunch of nutty anarchists. It was you – your readers anyway – who put striking miners in prison in the mid-eighties and told them they were criminals. They might not have believed us when we told them, but they believed those judges when they sent them down, and now they welcome us with open arms. We've got credibility.'

'That was years ago.'

'Yeah, but it was a turning-point. Do you know about the Revolutionare Zellen? The Red Cells? In Germany? They attacked a coal merchant in the Ruhr for exporting coal to Britain during that strike. They showed us how. That's why we get into all the social and industrial problems. That was what was wrong in the old Baader–Meinhof days. Middle-class intellectuals with a lot of romantic ideals about justice.'

'Like Richard Noble.'

'Fair enough. Like him. I don't give a stuff for his ideals but I want what he can teach us about bombs and small-arms.'

'So what are you saying? You've got support from international terrorism and financial backing from the Arabs?'

He walked past me to the door and opened it. 'See this reporter feller don't get damaged,' he shouted down the stairs. As I moved out he put his hand on my arm.

'The Frogs have got Action Directe. The Germans have got the Red Army Faction. We've got Rich Pickings, and we're all part of a revolutionary strategy that's going to knock the shit out of your nice cosy world. Tell your readers. They're going to need their Mogadons.'

'When? When does it start?'

'A symbol. That's what we go for first. We smash a symbol of all that's worst in this stinking corrupt society.'

'Military?' I saw the look on his face. 'Civil?'

'Both.'

'Human? You're going to knock someone over?'

He smiled down at me. 'A symbol, that's all. One symbol every day.'

'Until?'

He spread his hands in a gesture that could mean he didn't know. Or he didn't care.

'Starting when?'

Lazily he reached out his left hand and turned the pages of a stand-up calendar in a silver frame. 'The second.' He nodded, like a dentist confirming an appointment. 'Yes, it looks like December 2nd.'

# 25

I'd avoided the multi-storey hotels because once the lift rises off the ground you're cut off from humanity. At least the dog-eared old boozer I'd picked had fixed me up with a first-floor room that gave me a view both ways from the corner: down the brightly-lit main road and into the shadows of the side street. I wondered about opening the half-bottle in my holdall and decided against it: tonight I'd like to keep both brain cells ticking over. I even thought about starting smoking again but decided against that: what Jamie would do to me would be very bad for my health. Those are the ones I miss – the boredom cigarettes.

So I lay on the bed and listened to the sounds of a Liverpool night coming to a close. Once the dumpetty-dump of the juke-box had halted, the noise from the mob in the bar downstairs blended until it sounded like the snuffling and squealing of one large and untrained animal. A little later, I heard the landlord put it out of the door like an over-excited dog, and for a while the beast-sounds echoed in the damp street. It was the evening's death throes, and all that was left were the half-remembered scraps of earlier jokes, which they scraped up as re-runs of the night's highlights. 'So she says to him, she says, "Put it on the pillow an' I'll smoke it later", and he didn't know what the friggin' hell . . .' They coughed and spat and stamped out their tab-ends as the cold drove them grunting to their homes.

I watched television die a slow, hard death too, as the lively comedies and magazine programmes gave way to documentaries on Eskimo art, and finally a Japanese film about man's eternal soul, sub-titled in English: or maybe it was the other way round.

After that there were the noises of the night. In some distant part of the building, I heard doors close and boards creak and water-pipes hiss as the last ones went to bed. In the next room, which was really half my Victorian cavern separated only by a sheet of hardboard, my invisible companion clumped in, unloaded the ten pints of ale he'd swigged with a noisy gush, crashed on the bed and went to sleep snoring at one end and farting at the other. I bet his wife missed him when he was away. Long corridors away, I heard a phone ringing, and I wondered what would happen if the manager didn't bother to answer it. There wasn't much I could do about that. So I shifted the one chair nearer to the window, fixed the table lamp's broken shade for maximum effect, and curled up with P. G. Wodehouse. He didn't seem quite as funny as usual. Somehow, that night, Bertie was a bit too candyfloss.

Every now and then I'd stick my head out and take a look. The frost-bright moon gave a clear view of both roads, and apart from the occasional swoosh of passing tyres, the night was quiet. Even so, I wasn't aware of his presence until the door opened and in he stepped.

He gave a low whistle as he took in the indestructible smell of the last one thousand bodies that had stayed there. 'Expense account living, eh? Cringle's as generous as ever. High-risk Hussy – right? One of La Bill's boys.'

'Jesus, am I that old?' It was true though: I had caught the end of La Billiere when he was the SAS boss. 'I didn't see you.'

181

He jerked a thumb behind him. 'Thought I'd lost you, the time that damned manager took to answer the phone. I didn't want to stand around chucking stones at windows, so I slipped in the back way. Guest book, Mr Hamilton, Room 3, bingo.'

'Shot of Scotch?' I nodded toward my bag.

He shook his head and sat down on the edge of the bed. I dropped the window, drew the curtains, switched off the lamp and pulled my chair round to face him. A second later he was up on his feet all ready to go, with his hands up and his eyes everywhere.

'My room-mate,' I explained. 'Curry and gassy beer.'

'Home from home, just like life in the Lines.' Bradbury Lines, on the edge of Hereford, was where we'd both done our boy-scout stuff.

'You okay?' He didn't look it. The leftover light from the city penetrated the soiled windows enough for me to see how the tension had dug furrows in his young face and his eyes were sunken with strain. He had that nervy quickness that you only get from deep mental exhaustion.

When he'd been performing earlier, in front of Winston, none of this had shown. But now, in a few seconds' relaxation, it had all surfaced. He'd flopped back on the bed now and, to me, he didn't look far from the end.

'Tough?'

'Yes.' The word came in a small sigh. 'Winston's so damned sharp, he's on to everything. Thanks for the phone-number gag by the way. He went for that. Certainly helped with the old credibility.'

'You've been having problems.'

'Would you believe me?'

I shook my head. 'But they need you.'

'Yep. And now he just about does believe me.'

He lay there for a moment, and I left him to gather his thoughts. I had to clear my own mind too. He'd be like an actor who's just come off stage: he'd been playing the part for so long, twenty hours a day, that he'd still feel himself in character. I knew how it felt: bloody unreal. So it would be up to me to fish out of him the stuff we wanted. What Cringle wanted. What I wanted. And they weren't necessarily the same things.

'You got out all right.'

He nodded, and opened his eyes. 'Damned difficult. You've seen that place. Like prison.'

'They look like pros, these Rich Pickings blokes.'

'And how. They're not your average street villains. They don't do a lot on booze and they don't shoot or snort much either. Christ, they train. They really do. Every morning, in some gym they've put together in a burned-out factory. Would you believe it?'

'Good discipline?'

'Brigade of Guards with bloody dreadlocks, old man.' He looked at his watch, and immediately sat up, knuckled his eyes and ran his fingers through his scrubby hair. 'Let's get cracking.'

'What happens on December the second?'

'Come back on that, okay?' He was squeezing the bridge of his nose between finger and thumb and shaking his head.

'What's the money for? The two million?'

'Set up a united front for revolution. They'll back anything that will shake the social fabric. They're going to buy their way into any big strikes – you know, fraternal contributions from fellow workers, so they can get on the committees where the decisions are made to cause maximum damage. They'll pump money into any of the activist groups – blacks, Marxists, students, and they're going to use it to lay on a series of massive marches, demos, all that stuff.'

'Where does the money come in?'

'Hand-outs. Expenses. For food and travel. That's what they call it, but really it's an attendance fee of twenty-five quid a day. More like a riot grant. Legal centres for defence, compo for injuries or jail sentences.'

'Training?'

He stretched and did a few exercises with his arms. 'Christ, that feels better. I'll take you up on that Scotch now.' He drank from the neck: three short gulps, then belched, nursed the bottle in his hands. He was coming together again.

'You ever done one of these, Hussy?'

'Similar.'

'Keeping it up, day after day. Tricky. Like women.' He took one last belt at the bottle, then screwed the cap on and handed it back. 'Training. Plans to send their more promising lads off to Libya, maybe Cuba too, nothing firmed up as far as I know.'

'Weapons?'

He squinted his eyes as he concentrated. 'On the way. They've got the money now and as soon as they prove they can deliver, the real stuff will come flooding in. So far I think they've got a couple of nine-millis from well-wishers in Belfast tucked away and the odd shotgun. Enough for a kick-off.'

'I thought you'd been giving them small arms training?'

He sat up then. Slowly, he said: 'I have. With air pistols. They won't let me near the real stuff yet.'

'Ease off. I know what it's like. Will you be in on it?'

'Should be. I'm a helluva catch and I try to make it easy for them to believe it.'

'I saw you throwing the Molotovs. That was clever stuff – you managed to do it without barbecuing any cops.'

'Not clever. Lucky. For them.' He lay back and stared at the ceiling. Next door we heard the man stumble across the room and drain off another five pints of processed beer. This time the decibel level was halved, which could only mean that civilisation was losing its grip all around us: he was using the handbasin.

'Did he give you his line about politicising criminals?' Richard Noble said, again screwing up his face to get his mind in focus.

'Can he make it work?'

'Dunno. I'm too close. But he's going for it and he's got the rest of them sold on it. The idea is, get enough protesters, rioters, strikers, demonstrators – whatever you want to call them – to get themselves nicked. Try to needle the coppers into hammering a few of them as well. Eventually you make law-breaking respectable. That means you blur the distinction between criminals and the law-abiding members of society. I'm sorry about this, I may have got it a bit mixed.'

'That's the way I heard it.'

'That makes crime – some crime at least – acceptable.'

'That's just a propaganda drive?'

'At this stage.' He sounded calmer now, more settled. He gave a low laugh. 'They're printing up a load of posters. One of them shows a brick splintering a jeweller's window and the slogan says: "Property is Theft – Steal Some Yourself Today." He could get a job with Saatchi's.'

He sat up and rubbed his face again. He even looked better now. This was the first time he'd been able to be off-guard for weeks. 'Thanks for the message from Caroline. She's a good girl.'

As casually as I could, I said: 'You're not leaving her, then?'

His boy's face cracked open in a wild grin. The lamplight licked up the gleam in his eyes and put some life and colour into his face. 'That other woman rubbish? No, I laid that on for Winston. He had to run a check on me.'

'She believes it. So does Charles.'

'Best if she does. That way the story'll hold. Charles. Well, Charles is Charles, if you know what I mean. Is he still getting his leg over that tasty number in Doughty Mews?'

'I think he is. You've been round there too?'

It was a statement, not a question. Lightly he came back: 'That's right, but not for the same reasons as my big brother, sad to say. Veronica had asked me to see what he was up to. I should've left that well alone. She's trouble.' He began to laugh again. 'Trouble? Veronica? Christ, I wish she was the only trouble I had right now.'

'What about big brother? Didn't he mind you spying on him?'

He turned his eyes up to the ceiling in despair. 'The times I had to explain that to him. I was told he might be in money trouble. I was only trying to help out. In any case, I never told Veronica. He did, which shows you what sort of a brainless bastard he is. Correction: vicious brainless bastard.'

Even allowing for strain, it wasn't the sort of talk you expect from brothers. With some care I monitored his reaction as I told him that Charles was desperately worried about him and wanted to see him. The reaction was instantaneous. He gave a snort that mingled disbelief and indignation.

'Charles wants to see me dead, that's all.'

'He hired me to look for you. He even went digging down at your old regiment.' I didn't bother telling him that he'd faked a murder attempt to keep me interested.

He closed his eyes while he summoned his patience and then opened them again. 'Look, this isn't the time to give you my family history, but the truth is that Charles has hated and resented me all my life. One of these days, if he can ever find the nerve, he'll stick a knife in me. Now all I can say is that if you don't believe that, speak to Caroline.'

To close that line of questioning, he hauled himself up and went over to the handbasin and poured a glass of water. He drank it in one, and poured another. 'Got to get back, Hussy. Anything else?'

'Yes. You like Winston, don't you?'

He answered me clearly and immediately. 'Yes. I respect him. Up close, he's an impressive man, Hussy.'

'You think this scheme of his can work?'

'Not altogether. Not one great united move that will overthrow the government, no, I don't. That's sixth-form Marxist talk.' He moved and a bar of faded silver light touched his face. I saw something I wasn't expecting: what the courts call reasonable doubt.

'But.'

'Well, as I say, he won't change the world overnight, but if he can pull off even half the things he's planning it's bound to have some effect. When you hear these guys talk, Hussy, you realise that to them the law is the wall that the rich build round themselves. If people begin to see that, you've already got a change. Wouldn't you go along with that?'

'Where's the money?'

'The two million?'

'The two million.'

'Right. You know the office, the room you were in? His private room, bedroom and everything, is at the back of that. Third floor. He's got a wallsafe in there. Very flash job. PPI.'

186

'PPI?'

'Positive personal identification. Hand recognition to you. He looted it during the riots and a couple of sympathetic electronics students bunged it in for him.'

'And December 2nd?'

He tossed water over his face and shook it off like a dog. 'What did he tell you?'

'Something about destroying a symbol of capitalism. It was too vague to mean much.'

'Okay.' He gathered his thoughts, then dived in. 'Can't add a lot, but I do know it's a topping job. They're going to pop someone off.'

'Who?'

He shrugged. 'No idea. Don't think it's the PM or the Queen or a big name like that. It's not just one, either. Winston keeps giving out with this stuff about a series of symbolic executions.'

'He told me one every day.'

'Did he now? Well, you know more than me then.'

'But he's serious.'

When he looked at me then, I saw all Charles' innocence in his face. 'Very serious, Hussy. Very very serious.'

I believed him but I had to push him further. 'Maybe he's mouthing off. Get some headlines. Seemed a bit of a cheapo to me.'

He gave me a contemptuous look. 'You don't believe that. Or if you do, you're not the Joe Hussy I was told about. He's not joking. He'll do it.'

'What with – juvenile delinquents and air pistols?'

'The talk on the streets is that he's bringing in one of the big boys. An international name. That's one of the things he wants the money for. He'll do the job.'

'Name?'

He hesitated. 'No name.'

'El Gordo?'

He shook his head at Carlos's nickname. You wouldn't expect to find a passion for cream buns alongside an appetite for blood – hence The Fat One. 'I think he's out of it now. The man these young blacks like is Abu Nidal. They go for all that

187

Islamic aggression and they like Fatah's anti-American stuff. He's the one they want. Have you got any names?'

'No, no names.'

'I'm going back.'

I didn't want to do it to him then. The poor sod didn't know what he was walking back into, or if he'd ever get out again. In the half-hour we'd been talking, he'd come back to life. Now he had to face it all again. That takes guts, and he had them. But I still had to do it.

'Cringle reckons you're out of the game.'

He stopped halfway to the door. 'Out? Why?' His pale eyes pinned mine and he frowned.

'He says, Cringle that is,' I said, slowing it all down while I watched his reaction, 'that you've cracked. You've been in there too long. You've listened to them too much. It's all begun to make sense to you and now you don't know which way you're facing.'

'You mean, he thinks I've signed up with Winston.'

'Maybe. Or more likely you've lost sight of why you're there.' His face remained expressionless. 'It happens,' I added.

'It happens, I know.' He sounded more baffled than outraged. 'But why? What makes him think that? I've been out of touch, I know, but you've seen how it is. I can't exactly ask to borrow the phone, can I?'

He put his head back so he was looking at the ceiling, and we both stood there quietly in the darkness.

'What are you thinking?'

'I was wondering if it was beginning to happen to me. It does make a sort of sense, or does that mean I'm going doolally?' He exhaled wearily and shook his head. 'What does Cringle want?'

'He wants me to bring you in. For a once-over.'

That made him angry. 'If I do that, I really am out of it. I started it, I finish it. My canoe, I paddle it, right? You know that.'

'I know that, Noble.' I spoke in a quiet controlled voice.

'So what are you going to do about it?' His eyes were wide and I saw him get his body balanced so he'd be ready.

'I'll show you.' As I brushed past him, he leapt back. I reached forward and opened the door. 'On your way.'

Without a glance or a word, he slipped through the door. I listened but I didn't hear a thing. He was good. Not as good as me, but good.

# 26

'Is he folding?'

'I'd not say so myself.'

'Then what? He's not going to convert, obviously.'

If it was that obvious, Cringle wouldn't have bothered to say it. Or to wait for an answer.

'I'd say not.'

'Frame your replies more positively, Hussy. It helps. Noble's an experienced man. I'm confident he won't jettison all that training to take up some . . . some cause or other. Not at his age.'

I stopped in my tracks. 'He's my age.'

'Exactly. A little late in life to be taking perfectionist principles on board, wouldn't you say? Damn, I've trodden in it.'

Cringle – 'your posh friend,' Jamie said, with the wrinkled nose she employed to indicate haughtiness and high birth – had arrived just as I was setting off for my late-night run. We'd decided to walk the course instead. I must admit it had struck me that if he strayed off the path anything over a centimetre he might get unlucky. On the other hand, those of us who use London's parks have come to regard it the way Cockneys did doodlebugs during the blitz. That one obviously had his name on it. The thought struck me when I saw he was going to put his foot in it, and it was only my respect for destiny that stopped me warning him.

We were crossing the old recreation ground at the back of the main road. It was only just after ten, a time of romance in London's quiet sidestreets and open spaces.

Young lovers were everywhere. They were the ones who were too young to have places of their own, and too old to want to watch telly with their parents. We'd passed them huddled in bus shelters and shop doorways, lit by lust and neon. On the rec, they shared swings and lolled together on the roundabouts, all fumbles and whispers. Although we were careful not to look, we were aware of their black bundled forms in the darkness, and the suspended breathing as we passed. It was one way of keeping your hands warm on a cold November night. The thought made me feel old.

'Do you and your missus ever do it out of doors?'

I like to play the odd wild card with Cringle, if only to keep him on his toes. 'There are times when I question your grasp on reality, Hussy,' he replied, and I made a note of it for the next reunion.

Without shifting gear, he carried on: 'Tell me if this corresponds with your thinking. He's been in a long time, over seven months now, and he's stopped acting and started taking on protective colouring.'

I made a non-committal noise.

'Natural enough. He probably realises it's happening and he's wise enough to go along with it. Agreed?'

I made the same noise, which seemed enough for Cringle.

'That doesn't mean he's lost sight of himself or the objective, and need not in any way interfere with his ability to complete the operation. Go along with that?'

'What about the shrinks' report on his phone reports?'

'For once, I think they're wrong. Clearly they picked up some wavering, some uncertainties, but now I've heard your report I think we can put all that down to the circumstances. First-hand intelligence from the man on the ground over-rules everything. Agreed?'

'Uhuh.' That passed as agreement. At the same time I was

wondering what he would've said if I'd told him everything that Noble had said about Winston's grand plan. 'It does make a sort of sense.' Cringle would be sending in tanks if he knew about that.

I led the way through a sagging wicket gate out on to the road. Cringle stopped to clean his shoe on the pavement edge, by the light from a corner shop. Inside, a bald-headed Asian was humping cardboard boxes around. His wife, in milky blue robes, was balanced on top of a ladder stacking cereals on the shelves.

'Damnation, dogs. Should ban them in cities.' That seemed to remind him. 'Have you still got that hedgehog?'

'Yes, but I don't let it foul the footpath or bite the postman or anything of an anti-social nature.'

'Quite right,' he muttered, picking up a stick to finish the job. He wasn't listening. He straightened and pulled his tweed cap down to a crisper angle. 'What about your cohabitee? Not having any trouble, I trust.'

That was to remind me how easily she could be made to have trouble. I ignored it.

'It looks as though we're going to see Herr Koch in action,' he said.

'I gathered that when you came round to ask me about the report on him. He's here to do a gig, yes?'

I looked to see if he flinched at my phrase. He did.

'What's his motivation, Hussy? You've been up close to the man. It's a great help to us if we have some indication on what makes these chaps tick. Gives us some idea as to how he might tackle things. How much of a fanatic is he? Reasonably rational, would you say? Or is he another of the homicidal maniacs they seem to produce with such depressing regularity?'

'His motivation is money and he's as sane as . . .' I was going to say as sane as Cringle, but I thought he might not welcome the comparison. 'As sane as me,' I finished.

In the long terraces that lined the treeless sidestreets, curtains closed in the comforting glow of fireside families and held at bay the unfriendly forces of the city. Cringle's heels cracked spitefully on the pavings.

191

'Hardly as simple as that. The terrorist's psyche is a good deal more complicated than cash. However, I take your point. You found him . . . normal? Superficially, of course.'

'I did. Superficially, and every other way.'

'Interesting, that passion of his for Fortnum's pies. Glad you put that on file, you never know when those little snippets might come in useful.'

'Are you thinking of sending him an exploding pastie, sir?' As he spun round, I held up my hands in apology. 'I'm sorry, I opened me mouth and out it popped. It's just my casual way of expressing myself.'

His hard face softened. 'That's all right, Hussy. You did a good job in Liverpool. Not without its moments of strain, I dare say. Funny they would go for Koch and not for his more illustrious colleagues.'

'Abu's after the Great Satan – the Yanks.'

'Yes, and he may also find London a shade too hot since we picked up Hindawi.'

'Since Mossad picked up Hindawi,' I corrected him. I don't know why I bothered: he knew we had sod-all to do with it. 'Anyway, that wouldn't stop him coming. Talk about nutters, he's the original.'

'And Carlos is enjoying family life these days, so we're told.'

'That's the word. But anyway, if you were buying the best, you'd go for Koch.'

He stopped and gave me a critical look. 'Is that a professional judgement, Hussy?'

'It is. For VFM, it's Koch every time. Technically he's first class. The last thing you want is a holy warrior and Koch doesn't have any loony ideas. He's a craftsman. Give him the cash, give him the job, wallop, he's in there and it's all over, no problem. He's the man, no doubt about that.'

'What's this VFM?'

'Value for money. Though mind you, revolution's so well-funded these days that maybe that's not so important.'

We walked on for a few steps while Cringle took that in. On a low stone wall, a couple entwined over a shared bag of chips. In the frosty air, the smell was as sweet and warm as a kiss.

'It fits the facts, certainly. He's tied up with FARL. I suppose Christian Lebanese Marxists aren't too far away from him ideologically. They've strong links with the Red Army Faction and Action Directe, and they don't mind working outside the Middle East either. They've hit targets in Paris and Rome. It all ties in.'

'And he's here, which helps.'

'That's right. He's here. Craftsman. Funny word to use, Hussy.' He came to a halt on the pavement and looked around as though trying to scent his enemy. Over the ragged chimney tops, London glowed as though it was on fire.

Craftsman. It was his own word, of course. Not that I'd tell Cringle that. Using it made me think about Koch and the way he'd talked about all the lost passion of his life. Where had it all gone? When did it slip away?

I knew what he meant. The sharpest betrayal of all is the way we each betray our youth. At sixteen or so, you take a look at the mess that older people have made of their lives and of the world and you know it will never happen to you. You set off with a batch of fresh-baked beliefs, every one still warm from the oven. But they don't last. They go cold, they go stale; they lose their flavour, or maybe you lose your appetite. You compromise. You change your mind. Hell, you just change: everyone does. Every change is a betrayal, not of anyone else, but of the way you used to be.

Like the first time you fall for a girl, you tell her you love her and promise you're hers for ever. A week, a month, a year later you're saying the same words to another girl. Love, ideals, beliefs, it's all the same. You chip away at them. Each time you have a new name for it. Flexibility. Learning. Give and take. Pragmatism, for god's sake. Then one day you look down and they've all gone. All you have left then is the trade in your hands and the will to survive: that's the one thing that never changes.

That's when you glance back at your own shadow. The young you, who talked about the Truth as though it was an exam he'd just passed and doubt was a disease of the middle-aged, like bleeding gums and falling hair.

It had hit them both, Koch that night in Beirut and Richard

Noble in his Liverpool slum. And me? How the hell would I know – I'm one of life's actors, not a bloody critic.

Koch. Richard Noble. Me. We'd signed on at eighteen and now we couldn't remember why. The blacks and whites had all gone grey on us. They do. A bastard, isn't it?

Cringle was good on revolutionary politics, which is more than you could say for me, so I asked him what he thought about Winston's United Front. To my surprise he didn't dismiss it, and he was able to surmount his own prejudices to analyse it.

'In my book, of course, they've nothing in common. Strikers in some industrial row, criminals trying to make a dishonest living, and international assassins from the Middle East. Highly disparate groups, I would say. But find common ground to bring them together and you'd set a lot of problems. Chap's right about the Red Cells in Germany too. They have managed to get into one or two industrial situations. That's what's so worrying about these damned riots here. They do bring together some of these elements. Easiest thing in the world to exploit social injustice, and we've got plenty, I'm afraid to say. Ask any young black. They may get involved in street actions or demos with the highest motives in the world, and before they know it they're in conflict with police and society. Then they're criminals. That's what they're after, no doubt about that.'

'At local level. But at international level, they've got to bring in a professional to show they can up the stakes from bricks and bottles to first-division terror.'

'A fair summary, Hussy.' He stopped under a lamp to check his shoe again. 'That's possible too, as we are beginning to see. Your friend Koch and the rest of them, these days they switch around like footballers changing clubs. For a fee, of course.'

'Superstars.'

He gave a disapproving cough. 'Not the phrase I'd use, but I suspect you may be right.'

# 27

I was under a Mini when I heard it had started. It came squeaking over the old battery radio I keep on my workbench, so I had to stick my head out to hear it properly. The phrases were as simple as semaphore: drugs raid, police, clashes with youths, gangs. It was while I was lying there with my head touching a rusty exhaust that I saw the date on an oil-fingered wall calendar. The first of December. Saturday.

By the late evening they were waving bigger flags. Reinforcements, injuries, overturned cars, burning buildings. Television showed the familiar scenes of smoky streets, stooping darkened figures running, and the huddled ebb and flow of opposing armies; and – as television always does – it took the pain out of the shouts and the heat out of the flames. In the studio, experts analysed it as they would a football match. It was, after all, only an alternative entertainment to Benny Hill on the other channel.

But I felt the heat and heard the pain, because I remembered what Winston had said. 'You don't wanna get hurt, stay off the streets.'

I had to go over to Jamie's to watch it on her box. We sat on the sofa, snug as you like, drinking Ovaltine, with Charlie tucked down between us. Even so, I must have given off something, a flicker of anxiety maybe, because Jamie picked it up.

'They won't want you to go there, will they?' Jamie didn't know who they were, only that they gave her grey hair by sending a useless devil like me to some damn funny places. I could see her point.

'Me? No chance.'

'Tell 'em you can't. Tell 'em you've got to watch the garridge.'

'I will, Jamie, I promise.'

Fire suddenly filled the screen with red and orange daggers. 'I don't know what they want to do it for,' she said. 'It'll get them no sympathy.'

I didn't say anything because I didn't want to offend her. But most people are sheep and you don't need many dogs to turn a flock any way you want. As my old da was fond of saying, when he recalled the glorious Easter Monday of 1916 when they proclaimed the Irish Republic, they couldn't have raised two football teams from the heroes who were actually in the Dublin Post Office that day. Though, Jesus Christ, if you were to include all the ones who now swear they were there, you could fill the Albert Hall twice over. Power, legal or illegal, doesn't need a plebiscite, but if it's public sympathy you're after, that's easy enough: join the RSPCA.

Was Richard Noble there? It seemed an unreal thought, sitting there sipping my Ovaltine with Jamie making her pronouncements and Charlie doing his little snorts. Richard and Charles. The two brothers. Somehow it all swung around them. At the centre of everything was the emotion that held those two together – or drove them apart. From Charles, all I'd seen was big brother stuff, heavily laced with social duty. According to the feckless and reckless Richard, it was hatred. It was worth a call. Although I'd no intention of telling Charles where to find his brother, there was always a chance of getting Veronica on the phone. And, if her dutiful husband hadn't yet announced his plans for a new life with Anna Mauch, Veronica wasn't too inhibited about discussing private lives. On the other hand, if he had made his declaration, then she'd probably be on a murder charge somewhere.

'Charles has been trying to get you for days,' she said, at the sound of my voice. 'There's something I wanted to ask you too. You know I thought we were being watched – well, I'm quite sure of it now.'

I didn't want to get pulled into that. On a bad day, Veronica could've seen vultures gathering on the towel rail.

'I'll go into that with Charles. Is he there?'

'He's on his last rounds, but he should be back in twenty

minutes or so.' She sounded as though she'd been wound too tight, but then, Veronica always sounded like that. 'I see from the television that brother Richard has been busy again. You didn't get to see him, I take it?'

I skipped that question. 'One thing you can tell me – what was the relationship between Charles and his brother?'

'Relationship?' She said it as though it was something you caught off lavatory seats. 'I should have thought that was perfectly obvious.'

'Describe it.'

'Well. Well. You've seen for yourself.'

'Seen what?'

'How Charles is always trying to help Richard. Trying to get him out of trouble. I've told him he is wasting his time but Charles is a rather old-fashioned man in that respect and he doesn't take his responsibilities lightly.' I had that feeling, one I'd had before with Veronica, that we were in parallel conversations; if she kept saying it, with conviction and force, she somehow believed she could make it happen that way.

'You wouldn't say he hated Richard.'

I could hear her gasp down the telephone. 'Not at all. Charles hates no one. It would be quite out of character. In any case, Richard is his brother and however worthless he may be Charles would never desert him.' There was a pause while she waited for me to respond. I didn't, so she went on: 'If, of course, you were putting the question the other way round, I should have to give you an emphatic yes.'

'What? Richard hates Charles?'

'Passionately. For a person who is supposed to study his fellow man, you are surprisingly unobservant, Mr Hussy.'

'So I'm told. But that's true, is it?'

'My dear man, Richard has hated Charles from day one. It's quite simple really. The poor man was always in Charles' shadow, academically, personally, in every possible way. He could never hope to compete. He resented Charles, which was most unfair after all Charles did to try to help him. Ah, here he is now . . .'

197

I could hear him asking who it was, and the next thing Charles was almost leaping down the line at me.

'You've found him? Excellent work, can you give me the address now?'

That was the start of a very tough three minutes. Even if I wanted to, I couldn't have sent him to that house in Liverpool Eight. He would've got killed. And he would very likely have got Richard killed too. So I lied. I said Richard was moving around and didn't have a fixed base. He said there must be contact points and he would go there. It went on like that until Charles realised he was getting nowhere. Immediately his tone changed from gushing curiosity to suspicion.

'Very well. All I can say is that I am sorry you are taking this attitude, Hussy. I presume he paid you not to divulge the information.'

'No, I can't give you a firm lead, that's all.' Into the silence which followed, I said: 'What about Barbados? Is that still on?'

I could hear hard breathing while he got himself under control, and when he spoke it was more in the nature of a verdict than a reply. 'You have behaved most unethically, Hussy, most unethically. You are a disgrace to your . . . to your calling.'

Bang. Down went the phone.

When I went to bed, the late night news said the trouble, which had started in the St Paul's area of Bristol with a mix of blacks and whites, had spread to Handsworth, in Birmingham, where it involved mainly West Indians and a few Asians. They were still getting unconfirmed reports of petrol bombs in the Toxteth area of Liverpool. A man who purported to represent the rioters had telephoned the Press Association to say that they would rise up against the police brutality and oppression. 'The state has declared war on the people,' the newsreader repeated, without any emphasis. 'The people will now declare war on the state and all its servants.'

I thought about that when I went to bed, and I remembered Winston saying what they were going to do. They were going to smash a symbol of this corrupt society. One every day, he'd said.

198

I didn't know what he meant until about noon the next day. Sunday the second. I was shoving a clutch into an old Cortina when I heard it on my tinny little radio. Someone had shot a Beefeater at the Tower of London.

Now that's what I call symbolic.

# 28

All the Beefeaters are ex-NCO's and Vic Wilshaw had been a sergeant with the Duke of Wellington's. Now he lay beneath a blue plastic sheet in front of a small grassy mound near the main entrance to the Tower of London. His hat, one of those black boater affairs, had been placed on the grass to one side. It looked strangely bereft.

I'd had a look at him as soon as I got there. He was a hell of a mess. One bullet had hit him centre chest, hit a rib and flown up in such a way it had blown his shoulder-blade out. The next had taken the bottom half of his face.

'What you think?' Cassidy asked.

They'd put him in to advise on liaison and it was just as well. There must've been two dozen blokes from the police and security agencies of one sort and another, milling around beneath the clean grey walls. It was a Sunday morning, cold but sunny for early December, and the Tower had been packed when the shooting happened. There'd been a bit of crowd panic at first, but fortunately the other Beefeaters – all old sweats – had got a grip of the situation in no time and soon cleared the place. Now the gates had been shut against the public, and the reporters and the cameras would be let in later when the police had straightened out their story. That was one of the benefits of having assassinations carried out in an ancient fortress.

'I'd like to bet that Sergeant Wilshaw never had this much interest from the brass when he was alive,' I muttered.

'Here's another one, sir.' A boy-faced copper, one of four who'd put on overalls to comb the ground, sprang up and hurried over to a superintendent with his hand cupped in front of him. Another bullet.

The super, who didn't look much older himself, dropped the bullet into a small plastic bag and walked over towards us.

'Not much of a marksman, your chap,' he said, as though I had selected and employed the killer personally.

'No?'

'Four shots, and only two hits. Not exactly brilliant, is it, for an international assassin?'

I'd been studying the lie of the body and the surrounding buildings for about fifteen minutes. 'Have you got someone looking over that place?' I pointed out a half-built office block by the roundabout to the north of the Tower.

'We will be having a look at it, of course, but it must be six hundred yards,' he said, which was about as far as he dare go to questioning my expertise. 'It wouldn't be top of my list.'

'Then make it the top.'

Twenty minutes later I saw two cops hurrying through the crowd with a thickset man, Mediterranean in appearance, and a little girl hanging on to his hand. They came through the gate, and the superintendent conferred with them before coming over to Cassidy and myself. He looked surprised.

'Could've struck lucky there. This Greek chap's a labourer on the site and with it being Sunday, he'd sneaked up with his little girl to show her the view. On the way up the stairs, they were passed by a man coming down. In a rush, so he says. We're taking a full statement and then we'll see . . .'

I pushed past him and walked over to the Greek. 'This man. Was he carrying a golf bag?'

'Golf bag?'

I mimed a bag over the shoulder and immediately his face lit up. 'Bag for golf, golf bag, yes yes, he carry one.'

'Green? Green and white?'

'Green, that is it. Green golf bag.' He waved his hands to

200

describe a green golf bag, and I turned back to the super.

'That's him okay.' I looked up at the flags which shook in the wind off the river, and again tried to assess how Koch would set about it from the top of that building. The newspapers and television would have reconstruction pictures of a Beefeater in the telescopic sights of a rifle, but that isn't how it goes.

'Six hundred yards, wind like that, even Koch would have to go for a chest shot. Shooting downhill, he'd have to aim low. Probably around the target's bollocks. With that wind, left to right, he'd have to allow about five foot. Say, one shot aimed five foot to the left, move in to four foot for the next, and then three foot, so he'd bracket the target. First bullet in the ground, second hits him in the chest, third in the grass on the other side. Then back to the centre position for one last go, a head shot now he's got the range.'

Cassidy squinted up at the distant building and gave a short whistle of admiration. 'Handy lad.'

'If you can do any better,' I said to the now silent super, 'you can give me lessons.'

With new respect, he briskly snapped out: 'We'll put some more men over there immediately, sir, and strip that place to the ground. There should be four cartridge cases over there.'

As he set off, he turned and asked me: 'If you don't mind my asking, sir, how did you know about the golf bag?'

Sir now, was I? Jesus, there's promotion for you. 'Sunday morning,' I said, unsmiling. 'I guessed he would've been out for a round.'

We watched him go with a stunned look about his face, and I said to Cassidy: 'He'll stand about as much chance of finding a signed confession as he will of finding any cartridge cases.'

'Don't suppose pro's like him leave 'em lying around.'

'Not as a rule.'

'Three days and two nights, they hung on,' the old dear was saying. 'The Chinkies were coming at them in waves. They called it the Battle of the Hook but they got no credit in the papers because it was on Coronation Day, nineteen fifty-three.

201

Vic was on the mortar. He said you could always tell an old mortar man because they were deaf in their left ears.'

Then she began crying and saying how awful it was to live through the horrors of the Korean War to die like this. It was a fair point. Sergeant Wilshaw been shot down on a clear Sunday morning, standing among the waves of tourists at the Tower of London. No death for an old mortar man.

I was listening to it on Radio Four as I drove up the motorway. They'd got it half right, which wasn't bad for journalists. They said he'd been shot in the head which had killed him outright, but as he crashed backwards the callous assassin had put another into his chest to make sure. He'd been shot by a high-velocity weapon, the radio reporter said, and police were examining several possible vantage points the killer might have used within a range of several hundred yards.

There was no mention of Klaus Koch and the Dragunov, with its pretty little green and white pom-pom hat, that he carried in his golf bag. He'd be on his way now. On his way to his next appointment. One a day, Winston had said. One symbolic slaying a day. If he was going to pick soft targets like that, nothing could be done to stop him.

Cringle's phone call had got me almost before the Beefeater hit the ground. Had I heard? Get down to the Tower, see if it looks like Koch. When I'd reported back, he switched me up to the north. The rioting was getting worse by the hour. They desperately needed Noble's information from the inside but he hadn't been able to make contact. Who, what, where, they wanted to know every scrap they could, but most of all they wanted to know: what next?

I didn't bother mentioning that if Richard Noble had been sussed, they'd need a spiritualist to get his information. Cringle wasn't susceptible to sentiment when under stress. Before I could ask why me, he added in his coolest and most clipped tone, that I was their only man who had immediate access.

It wasn't a request. Go, that was all.

I went. I didn't go for him and I didn't go for the Unit, and I certainly didn't go on behalf of this rough island race of ours. I went for the same reason I went in for Chris Clark that time.

One day I might want someone to haul me out, and I wouldn't want to think they'd stand about debating it too long. I thought of telling him that. Then I realised he would know. What's more he would approve.

I was heading for Manchester where, according to Cringle's latest intelligence, Winston and a white man in his thirties had been spotted at the back of the mobs. The trouble there was in Moss Side: it was the usual backcloth of inner city dereliction, unemployment, and blacks who found it hard to believe they have a stake in society. Yet it was still surprising, because Moss Side, for all that, was a well-established community where they hadn't seen any street fighting on this scale since the mid-eighties. The flashpoint had been a jobs march which had turned into a push and shove with the police. Then came the bricks over the top, the police charges, petrol bombs, and rumours that a pistol had been fired.

Already the police were talking about using rubber bullets. St Paul's was still simmering, but Birmingham had quietened down. There was something inevitable about the same old dreary escalation, except this time it seemed to accelerate more quickly from one stage to the next.

As I drove nearer, I listened. A senior policeman was insisting that this time there were indications that the disturbances throughout the country had been co-ordinated and centrally organised.

At that moment they got the announcement from Rich Pickings claiming credit for the Beefeater's death. He was a 'militaristic puppet', the newsreader said – changing his tone to dissociate himself from what he was reading – who had chosen to use force to inflict imperialism on freedom-loving people throughout the world. He was a symbol of Britain's shameful past. With a triumphant note that even penetrated the newsreader's voice, Rich Pickings announced that they had the active support of other freedom fighters throughout the world who had given financial aid and technical advice to their brothers in Britain. It finished with the bald declaration that they would destroy a similar symbol every day.

At the same time: around noon.

For the next few minutes, all I could hear was a sort of radio rioting.

The senior copper said there was no doubt that the assassination had been carried out by a professional hit-man who had been specially imported for that job. If not actually Carlos the Jackal, he said, it was definitely one of a handful of similar international killers. All around him politicians were competing for who could claim the most fervent outrage. The people of Britain, they said, would never allow themselves to be dictated to by agents of fear and terrorism. The people of Britain – suddenly everyone was plugged into the national psyche – were repelled by savages who were prepared to shed innocent blood in their murderous bid to destroy democracy . . .

I switched it off. The truth was that the people of Britain would sit and watch their tellies. It didn't have a nice clear story-line like *The Dirty Dozen*, say, but at least you had the satisfaction of knowing the bullets were real. Well done, Winst. He'd got the street violence cooking nicely, and he'd already dragged in a jobs march. But it was the killing of the Beefeater that was a stroke of genius. Stars of millions of tourists' snaps and postcards, they were recognisable world-wide; in almost every country in the world, the television screens and the newspapers would carry news along with a picture of the familiar figure. And however repelled the people of Britain might be, in Tripoli and Tehran and Damascus, Winston and Rich Pickings would have instant credibility. If he could keep up his daily symbol-slaying, and claim it was all part of the people's struggle, he'd get all the backing he needed from the terrorist capitals of the world.

That's why Cringle was sending me back. Richard Noble was his only line in, and I was the connection.

Drizzle smeared the windscreen as I hammered up the fast lane. Perhaps it was the isolation of the car, with the night brushing hard against the windows while I listened to living history, that made me feel that events were gathering pace too quickly, and that however fast I drove I was falling behind.

The fourteenth. I had to keep reminding myself that the date on the airline tickets – which I'd got fixed in my mind as the backstop position for us all – was still twelve days away. No one was going anywhere until then.

As I drove up through south Manchester, I found the Chinese takeaway with a Union Jack outside. A fat man in a brown trilby stepped out of the doorway and flagged me down with a rolled-up newspaper. Through the passenger window he handed me a ripped-out sheet of street map, with some streets marked in green. For my purposes, it was no use going in behind the police. Somehow I had to surface with the freedom fighters and do some rapid blending. I was lucky. Either the local Branch man had made a cock-up of the map, or I misread it, because I got lost along the grimy high-rise ruins of Hulme – a place that drives angels to insurrection – and I put in a lot of solid cursing and three-point turns that roasted the rubber off the tyres of the old Chevette I'd taken from Jamie. Then I bobbed up in the old Victorian terraces, and suddenly I could see the fires burning an angry silhouette around the chimney pots in front of me.

The minute I got out of the car I was hit by the excitement all around me. One street away, the sky was leaping with flames, and clouds of magic sparks rose in sizzling spirals. The air was a vital cocktail of winter frost and the acrid aftertaste of a bonfire, and in the high hollow shouts which accompanied the crackling and crashing, I could hear the thrill of terror.

What was even more exciting, even more alarming, was that in myself I felt all the old responses: my skin tightened, all my senses sharpened so that the night city fell into clear-edged focus, and I knew for sure that now I was truly alive. That's the factor all the analysts forget when they wonder why civilised men fight in the streets: and that is that most of us still have plenty of battle blood in our veins. We like war: it's as simple as that.

I ran down to the corner of what I thought was Moss Lane and cut up to the junction with Princes Road. As soon as I stepped out of the cover of the houses, the heat and the uproar hit me with an intensity that shook me. Sixty or seventy yards up the road, ignorant armies clashed. I'd come out at the back of the street gangs. Half lit by flames, muffled in smoke, the bank of rioters swirled backwards and forwards. Inevitably, they were mostly young and mostly black, yet they moved in patterns that seemed as set as old-tyme dances. At the back, foragers smashed paving stones for more ammunition. Between billows of smoke, I could see that the shops on my right, whose windows were still boarded and bricked from the last riots, were again in flames. Black holes of windows suddenly blossomed with flowers of searing gold and yellow, orange and roaring red. After a shuttering of sliding masonry, a spinnaker of flame filled with the wind and billowed out through a ripped roof.

I'd been so busy taking in the main drama that I'd missed the action in the shadows closer to me. Half a dozen men in donkey jackets and stocking masks ran along a row of shops smashing in the windows with clubs. Behind them, bands of kids and older people stepped through the shattered glass to help themselves.

At that moment, the balance of the battle shifted. From the rushed thunder of feet and the drumming of truncheons on shields, I knew the invisible lines of police were on the move. The solid line of street fighters in front of me broke and I saw for the first time the squads of police, faceless behind their shields and helmet visors, burst into sight, and now the mob broke up into packs of two or three, plunging in to fight, pulling back before another rush, and re-forming to charge again.

A patch of road burst into flame where a petrol bomb had landed and a tall white man with braided hair screamed and danced with high frantic knees as his legs blazed.

They were back-pedalling. Seeing this, the looters began to pour out to escape with their trophies. One solid black woman, her rump rolling, unhurriedly wheeled away a supermarket trolley laden with stereo equipment. 'Help yoursel, an' gerra move on,' she shouted over to me, and her homely Lancashire accent hit a strange note in this scene of tropical heat and colour.

'I want Winston, quick.'

She pointed up a side street fifty yards back from the fighting.

'They're all up there,' she said, and set off in a clumsy run down the road. That gave me the last bit of confidence I needed. She'd taken me for one of their own, which meant that my natural hooligan look – with a bit of help from my filthy old track-suit – had passed the test.

The house she meant, with flickering candlelight in the front room, was the only one in the terrace that wasn't in darkness. Outside, a small bunch of men, six or seven maybe, were gathered around the steps and I could see Winston over their heads. He held up two petrol bombs, then passed them down into the reaching hands. 'That's the last of 'em for now, lads. Remember, don't chuck the fuckers anywhere, go for a pig and fry him. Then pull back down the road and we'll have another go at the bastards.'

They bundled past me as I walked up. He half turned, then stopped. 'What's all this then? Are they giving medals for gallantry at the *Times* these days?'

# 29

'Thought I'd try a taste of life at the front.'

'Great idea. We're shifting quarters but come in anyway. Noble's inside. Your readers will be proud to know he's done a great job here tonight.' I might've called round for afternoon tea for all the surprise he showed.

I followed him down the passage and into the candlelit room I'd seen from the street. Down on his knees away from the window, Richard was draining the dregs into one petrol can, and tossing the empties into a corner.

He gave me his quick nod. 'Giving the boys good value.' His eyes flickered up towards the fighting.

'So I see.'

'The Beefeater – it was Koch, not Abu.'

'Shit hot, eh? Reckon he wins a goldfish for that.'

'I reckon.'

He came quietly to his feet and gave me a sequence of signals I couldn't follow. First his eyes held mine, then swung towards Winston, then back to me. He mouthed something I couldn't catch, but I could see the urgency in his actions.

Winston saw none of this. He was standing by the window, looking out into his night of triumph. When he spoke, it was in almost awestruck tones. 'See that, *Times* man? What did I tell you? I did it. I said I would, and shit, I did.' It was all there in his voice: he was transported by his own power.

So he didn't hear Richard move at speed across the room. The first he knew was the hand clasped round his forehead and the other round his jaw, and if he heard his spine make a noise like someone dropping a hundred pennies on to a tin roof, it was the last thing he did hear. Richard lowered him to the floor like last week's washing.

'Got a car?'

'Chevette. Over there.'

He looked quickly where I was pointing. 'Great. Give me that axe.'

He was on his knees beside the body, lifting Winston by the back of the neck and at the same time trying to tug his jacket off. He looked up and snapped: 'Come on, don't piss about, the axe.'

Maybe I knew, maybe I only half knew, but I still stood there, so he spun round and reached out for the old-fashioned firewood axe which stood against the wall by the petrol cans.

Just then, a vast flare of fire ran up the sky and lit the whole room, walls and floor and cans and the three of us, and washed us the colour of blood. I saw Winston's blood-coloured face flopped over to one side, and his blood-coloured right arm stretched out, palm up, on the bare floorboards. I saw Richard, stooping, lift the blood-coloured axe and his blood-coloured hand, and I heard it make a soft gritty sound as it sunk into the joint. It was like a scene from Judgement Day.

'Holy bloody Jasus, Noble,' I shouted and went to stop him. At the last minute I hesitated when I saw the real blood pumping out of the half-severed arm on the floor. He was straightening and although he looked surprised, that moment gave him all the time he needed. Feet apart, sideways on to me, he swung the axe in a short backhand arc that struck the flat head of the axe against my neck.

I half came to once, and felt my track-suit top being opened and my heels dragging over hard ground, then I slid away again. The next time I woke I thought I was still in the house as fiery red lights filled my swimming vision. Jesus. I closed them again and immediately felt the block of solid pain where he'd hit me. Bloody Jesus. Someone had parked a ten-wheel timber-hauling lorry on my neck. Ease the eyes open this time. That's right, slowly slowly, don't let the light in till you're ready. The flames, which somehow looked more orange than red now, were passing one at a time, great gobs of fire in the sky. Then I realised: beneath me, I could feel the tyres humming and bumping over a road, and overhead I was seeing sodium street lamps. I was on my back in a car.

I tried to move my head a fraction and – Christ Al-bloody-mighty – my neck nearly snapped in two. But at least I could see where I was. Which was in the front passenger seat of the Chevette, with the backrest in the half-flat position so that I was stretched out like an invalid. Richard was driving. I could only see the back of his head from the left-hand side, but it was unmistakably him.

As he drove, he whistled through his teeth. I recognised the tune. It was that old Beatles thing, 'Penny Lane.'

Full consciousness blew aside the mists then, and I realised that I couldn't move my hands or my feet. Gently – I didn't want Richard to know I'd come round – I tested them again. My hands were fastened at the wrists, my feet at the ankles, and both too tight to allow any movement. Even though my hands were in front of me, I couldn't seem to see them. As we passed beneath another orange light, I saw that my zip-up jacket was humped beneath my chin in a clumsy bulge. A little pressure on my heels tensed my body so that I could twist the muscles of my

209

chest and stomach. I could feel that something heavy had been jammed inside the top of my track-suit and then zipped up. It was wet too. There was a damp patch around the elastic band at the bottom that kept sticking to my belly.

'How you feeing?' Cautious as I was, he'd picked up the movement.

'Sitting up and taking a soft-boiled egg.'

'Glad to hear it. Sorry I had to smack you down.'

'As my old embroidery teacher used to say, ten out of ten for neat work.'

'You're okay. I checked. Nothing broken, just bruising. You're never sure with necks.'

'They're a devil to judge, are necks. If I could just try it out with my hand now . . .' By then I'd worked out that my wrists were taped up.

'Couldn't take a chance. I wasn't sure which way you were going to jump so I had to put you on the shelf for a while.' He jammed on the brakes and I felt the car swerve. 'Bloody drunks. Sorry about that.'

'No problem.' He was taking it easy, thirty according to the speedo, and the way the lamps passed overhead meant we must still be in the city. But which city? My memory was still full of holes. Then the orange light reminded me of the blood-light in the room. I didn't try to turn my head because of the solid block of pain in my neck. 'No Winston?'

'No Winston,' he repeated, changing down and then accelerating away. 'Had to barbecue old Winst, I'm afraid.'

'What? With the petrol?'

'Yes, plenty left in those cans, luckily. Splash it all over, as the ads say, then chuck in a match. I mean, I could never have got him out, even unconscious. Not in one piece. The boys would never let me take him away.'

'Whereas no one would care about me?'

'Fraid that's it.' I saw the turn of his head and his tight smile in the passing lights. 'Still, better here than there, eh?'

'Is that right now?'

He laughed, then came out with the old joke: 'Is it true what

I've always heard, that an Irishman will always answer a question with another question?'

'Whoever told you that now?' I replied obligingly, and he laughed again. 'Are we going back to the 'pool'?

'Yep.' He slowed right down, then took off again. From my slumped position I could just see the traffic lights. 'Are you warm enough? God, you mustn't get cold.' He put the fan on the full and directed it towards me and I had to half close my eyes in the blast. His voice was full of concern. 'Are you sure you're warm?'

'Holy mother, are you trying to barbecue me too?'

That made me try to push myself a bit higher, and as I did I felt the lump in my cotton top sink lower. It felt soft, yet cold and somehow weighty. The rest of the scene in that house in Moss Side flicked up into my mind and I remembered what he'd said: 'not in one piece.' Doubts vanished: now I knew what it was.

As I looked down I saw that the shifting of the weight had pulled at the front of my track-suit. The zip was slipping down. An inch. Stop. Another fraction. Stop. I jerked my stomach to start it again. Slowly, it edged down, another inch or so, leaving a black gap open at the top. I tried another wriggle. Nothing. The zip was jammed on the uphill side of a crease. I worked my shoulders. Again, nothing. It was still stuck. With my thumbs, which I could just move, I gave my top a tug, the crease vanished, and the zip charged away downhill, opening my jacket as it went.

Even though the hand fell out pale palm up, I knew it was Winston's because I could see the dark shading between the fingers. What I'd got inside my jacket was his arm, from the elbow down.

The only thought that sprang into my mind was what they'd said about Clarky: 'He can do everything except take the top off an egg.'

'Careful,' Noble said, reaching down to tuck the arm back in. 'Your job's to keep old Winston warm.'

211

# 30

We were up the front steps and in through the open door, me first with Richard close behind, before we saw them.

Until then, we'd hardly seen a soul, just as Richard said. Winston had got his troops deployed around the country; he wasn't turning the heat on in Liverpool Eight until the next night. One or two people glanced up as we drove past, but apart from that the streets looked eerily deserted, and the house, its windows in darkness, even more so.

'What's he doin' 'ere den?' Cracker, his bunched face lunging towards me, stepped out of the back room. Behind him, on a plastic-topped kitchen table, I could see the tinfoil remains of a takeaway meal and some lager cans, and a gasp of sweaty heat and old curry came out of the room with him. The three of us were jammed in the space at the bottom of the stairs.

'Won't they let you go out and play with the big boys?' I asked.

He reached for me, but Noble was too quick for him. His arm dropped between us. 'Don't let him do it to you,' he said to Cracker, the way postmen talk to snarling dogs.

'I'll do it to him,' he said, his curled fingers paddling the air in front of me.

Noble took hold of his thick wrist and returned the hand to him, like an unwanted bunch of bananas. If Cracker knew what had happened to the last arm he'd held, he might've been more nervous.

'He's mine,' Noble said, 'leave him.' This time his tone was different and Cracker let his hand drop by his side and stood silently glaring at me.

'Why you bring him here, man?' A tall Rastafarian was silhouetted in the doorway. With a vast cap to contain all his hair, he looked like a lollipop at first, but as my eyes adjusted I saw he was the man who'd brought me to see Winston the last time. He was still wearing the same royal blue track-suit.

Noble, who'd been herding me towards the stairs, paused. 'Winston wants him here.'

'Then why Winston not here?' Aggression and suspicion ran over his high-boned face. His eyes looked red and sore from smoking dope. 'Stay there, you.'

He was speaking to me. He'd seen Noble push me towards the first step. It was a dangerous position for me. Cracker, looking confused, had fallen back, but the Rasta had taken his place: and I could see in his face how he felt his command of the situation increasing. He loomed over Noble and when he spoke it was with the stubborn truculence of a lifetime of injured pride.

'You gimme this shit about Winston saying this and Winston saying that. I know nottin' about that.'

'I told you, Winston wants me to keep him here until he gets back from Manchester. Let's just relax, shall we?'

The way Noble spoke, he wasn't trying to back the Rastafarian down like he had Cracker. He wasn't backing down himself either. He was keeping it neutral but the young black wasn't relaxing. He was still probing and testing.

'You walk in here and say Winston send you, I know nottin' about that, man. I know Winston tell me watch this place, don't let people run roun', and don't take no shit from no one. Why you think I'm here, man? This is his headquarters, this very very private. So you think you can walk in with this reporter man, going up to the office, stickin' your fuckin' nose in everything. How you think you gettin' in for start, you tell me that.'

Without any hesitation, Noble reached into his pocket and pulled out two Chubb keys on a ring. 'Catch.' The black had no choice: he grabbed them as they hit his chest. 'You can have him.'

He set off down the long dark hallway towards the open front door and I had to stop myself shouting after him. It was a risk, and I was the stake.

'Hey.' It was an aggressive shout but when Noble turned

slowly in the doorway, the young black didn't know how to follow it up. In a weaker voice, he asked: 'What we do with him, man?'

'Please yourself.' Noble gestured vaguely. 'His hands are strapped so he shouldn't give you trouble.'

They hadn't noticed that because I'd had my hands pressed against my stomach to prevent my grisly package from falling out.

Then they looked and it was Cracker who noticed. 'He's bleeding,' he said, and he pointed at the dark stain on my track-suit and the line of drips down the front of my trousers.

Quickly, the Rastafarian shouted: 'He not my problem. You take him. Take him upstairs, anywhere you fuckin' want. He nuttin' to do with me, man.' He waved us away and began to retreat into his own room.

With a resigned air, Noble strolled down the hall, took the keys out of his hand and motioned me up the stairs. He'd worked it, and now we were guaranteed no interference either.

The keys got us into the office where I'd interviewed Winston, and then through into the room Richard Noble had told me about. One switch lit up three table lamps. By the look of it, they must've looted Habitat too. It was all low, soft sofas in black leather and glass-topped coffee tables; on wall shelves, there were art books and sculptures of what looked like African heads in bronze and rosewood, and those prints of coloured geometry exercises in chrome frames. That was all I had time to take in because the moment the door closed, he zipped open the front of my jacket and lifted out the sagging limb.

'Hope to Christ you've kept him nice and warm, Hussy.'

I dropped on to one of the sofas. I deliberately didn't look as he pulled it out. Dear God, was I glad to get rid of that sickening burden. I don't rate myself as over-squeamish but the feel of that cold flesh against mine all the way there, and even worse the touch of those dead fingers, made me crawl. I could still feel its graveyard caress, even though I could see the open flaps of my jacket where he'd taken it.

'Watch this, Hussy.' Richard Noble laid the severed arm along the top of a convector heater and tugged down the blinds at the wide bay window . . . 'Got to keep old Winston warm or he won't do his stuff.'

I sat up, still feeling sick. Maybe from the arm, or maybe the belt on the neck, I didn't know which.

In the corner by the window, he was tipping books and potted plants off the shelf. They crashed to the floor, breaking and spilling soil in black heaps on to the moss green carpet, but he carried on like a man with plenty of purpose and not much time.

He wrenched the shelf off its bearers and dropped that on the floor too, and then knelt down and reached right into the corner by the floor. With finger and thumb, he took hold of the heavy striped wallpaper. It lifted easily at first, and then he ripped it so that a square yard or more tore free. All I could see behind it was the plaster of the wall. Quickly, he took a knife from his pocket and ran the blade sideways down the wall. As it slipped over the surface all the way down to the skirting board, he swore to himself and did it again, this time with greater care. Two foot above the skirting board, the blade jammed.

'Aha.' He winked up at me. He turned the blade and eased it into the plasterwork. With one move of the hand, he slid it along so that flakes of plaster peeled off as its cutting edge opened up a thin seam in the wall. He did that on four sides of a square, and then lifted out a plastic panel, about eighteen inches square.

His eyes and mouth tightened in a small smile of triumph. 'Bingo.'

On the wall, I could see a metal plate and sunk into the plate were five grooves set out in the shape of an open hand. Each groove contained rows of tiny buttons. I bent down to watch over his shoulder. Somehow I didn't feel sick any more. I'd never been that near to two million pounds.

As he delicately dusted away the dust and scraps of plaster he talked. 'You know about these things? No? Positive personal identification. As I said, perfect security. No keys or cards to get stolen, no password so people aren't tempted to wire your donger up to the mains. Look. In each of those slots there's a strip of light detectors. They can measure anything you want –

215

length of fingers, width of fingers, perimeter of the whole hand, even your wedding-ring. You set it up so there's only one hand in the world it will recognise, and if it doesn't see that hand, it doesn't open, and we don't get the goodies. Which is why we had to borrow Winston's arm. Pass it over. Come on, Hussy, you've seen cold meat before.'

I held up my strapped wrists to remind him. Without even thinking, he quickly crossed to me and sliced through the bindings.

He was right. I had seen plenty of cold meat before, but never quite served like that. But I picked up the arm with my two hands and I must say it didn't feel much different from a good-sized salmon.

A lot less gingerly, he grabbed it by the wrist, and I saw for the first time that he'd tied a tourniquet of twisted fuse-wire around the severed end.

'It's cold,' I said.

'Bugger. Trouble with some of these access systems is that they have a heat sensor built in. Tht's why I stuffed old Winston down your shirt. Let's give him a go.'

Holding the wrist and the back of the middle finger, he laid the hand into the grooves.

Nothing happened.

'Did Caroline really say that?' Noble adjusted the fingers.

'Yeah. Thanks for everything. Some girl. And you're going back to her?'

'Why? Fancy your chances?'

'Maybe.'

'Tough. I'm going back. Sod it!' The arm turned in his grip so that the hand flopped down. He began to set the fingers in position one by one.

'Ease up on the pressure.'

'Okay. Bloody difficult. If I don't press, the hand falls down.'

Winston's skin had changed from his near-blue colour to a sort of dull grey and it seemed to be creasing up into wrinkles. Every time he moved it from the wrist, the rest of the arm swung like a club.

'Here.' I grabbed the arm and held out the hand so he could

216

interlock his own fingernails into Winston's. He did it as I'd indicated and when I looked up I saw he was giving a tough little grin over this grotesque charade. But it worked. With the extra control from him, the fingers dropped neatly into their grooves. I worked the thumb into position. Again nothing happened.

'It's the heat sensor. It must have cut out.' Noble's young face darkened with frustration as the two of us crouched there, holding the dead man's arm.

'Jesus.' I stared at the square metal panel. It was there on the other side. 'Two million quid.'

'My two million.' He gave me a quick hard look.

'Where it is now,' I said, 'you might as well give it to charity. At least you'd get a bloody flag out of it.'

He'd opened his mouth to say something when we both heard the single heavy click and felt the dead hand jump. We dropped it. The door swung open.

Whatever length of time it takes to flick through dreams of pastel-shaded villas on lush hillsides, where men in short white jackets delivered long glittering drinks on silver trays beside water almost as blue as the eyes which stared into mine . . . however long that takes, that's what it took us.

Nature doesn't make many things which stop time; when it's in twenty stacks and each stack is over six inches deep, money's one of the few that can do it. It couldn't be entirely accident that when the safe door opened, the two of us were kneeling in front of it in an attitude of prayer.

Then we turned and looked at each other. By instinct – his too, I could tell – what we both wanted to do was to grab each other and do quite a lot of the old back-slapping and shouting. Because, any way you looked at it, it was a big big hit, and while we'd been kneeling there, both holding the dead man's arm, we'd somehow been bonded by the tension and the high excitement. Perhaps our training and temperament pulled us together too. But now, with the suspense snapped, we both had to face up to the fact that we weren't even on the same side.

From his jacket pocket Noble drew a .38 Smith. It was the

217

model with the two-inch barrel, the one the Met chose because it has six chambers instead of five. Personally I never rated the Model 64. Anything over thirty yards and you'd be struggling. On the other hand, I was about three foot away from Noble. At that range he could spit the bullets at me.

He held it on me. I felt the back of my neck tingle. But before either of us could speak, the ring of the telephone cracked the silence. Signalling me to stay there, Noble rose and crossed the room to pick it up, the gun dangling by his side.

'Yes. Koch? Noble. No, he's not here. What's the problem?' Whatever the call was, he wanted me to know about it. He caught my eye and moved his head in a way that brought us into a silent conspiracy against the caller. Once that was done, he pulled a wry face at me while nodding and grunting into the phone.

'Shit, are you sure?' This time he flicked his eyes towards the arm which we'd dropped in front of the safe. 'And they think it's Winston? Shit. I don't know. I mean, what the hell can I say? He was okay when I left Manchester. Two or three hours ago. Dead? I don't believe it. Doesn't make sense. How the hell could he burn to death, he was lighting the fires?'

He listened again, giving the odd grunt to let him know he was still there. 'I didn't hear the news. Yes, yes, sounds as though they know what they're talking about. Shit. Dead.'

He shook his head sorrowfully at the same time as giving me a wide smile.

Then he straightened and his face turned serious, almost angry. 'Don't ask me, Koch. You know Winston, it was his show.' He paused, then carried on in the same fast staccato. 'Ease off. I told you, I don't know. He handled all the cash. Like he fixed up the punto game with the club and Yaseen.'

Again, he listened. Even I could hear the fierce pitch of the voice on the other end. 'All I can say is the same thing. If Winston's out, there's no number two. Me? I do evening classes, ask anyone.'

Finally he raised his voice too. 'You're wasting your time. No one here knows about the money. The boys said he had a safe somewhere, but I don't know where and I don't know how you'd get into it. Come round, turn the bloody place upside down if you want to.' He put the hand holding the gun on his chest like an amateur actor miming innocence. 'I told you, I don't know. Do the job, don't do the job tomorrow. Your problem, pal. I'll tell you this, though. If Winston's down the tube, so's the whole thing. I'm out. As of now.'

He dropped the receiver noisily on to its stand, picked it up to make sure the line had been cut, and then laid it on the table. He wasn't taking any more calls.

He held the gun out for me to see without pointing it at me. 'Clears the air,' he said, in the voice of a man who's anxious to be reasonable. He glanced towards the money. 'In case you're feeling ambitious or anything.'

I nodded. He was right. It did clear the air. It was his game.

'I think,' I said, still kneeling on the floor, 'that you might end up having to give me the little lead sleeping pill.'

'Drink?' He dumped the gun on the table next to the telephone and selected a bottle of brandy from a tray of drinks. He poured out two hefty measures, sank into a sofa and put the gun beside him. I walked over and picked up mine and sat down on a sofa at right angles to his. I thought he hadn't heard what I'd said until he spoke again. 'Maybe you're right.' he said, after taking a sip. 'I've been thinking about that. The way I see it, you're not going to want me to walk away with that cash under my arm, are you?'

'I could say yes.'

He read the next sentence in my face. 'You could say that, yeah.'

Yeah. Whatever would Charles say if he heard such sloppy talk from his little brother? But I'd noticed before that Richard could tailor his talk to the company. I found myself wondering if Richard had ever been like Charles, and if any of it remained under his cool pro veneer.

He squinted up at the ceiling, thought for a minute, and then began talking in a salesman's voice. 'When you think about it, it's only dirty old Arab dough, isn't it?' The only losers are the Syrians who put up the readies, and do they lie awake at night worrying about your finances, ask yourself that?'

I had a belt of the brandy. It made me shudder. I thought about what he'd said, and took another belt of the brandy. Maybe he was right after all. Or maybe he was yet another Noble brother trying to manipulate me. That was one thing they still had in common.

'That was Koch, you gathered. Tomorrow, noonish, he was due to drop a village policeman in Chipping Campden in the Cotswolds. Another traditional English figure, shock-shock headlines here, happy hats for the loony left. Next day a Tory grouse-shooter in Scotland. Magistrate in Guildford after that. And so on. You probably heard, he's not best pleased. The radio put out a piece saying they'd found Winston's body. He thinks he won't get paid. He's right.'

'What was he on?' I was interested what the going rate was these days.

'Ten jobs, a million quid.' When he saw the expression on my face, he explained: 'They were all bespoke jobs. That Beefeater was kindergarten stuff, but the pressure would be on him after two or three. And he is the best. Hell, you know, you've met him. What's he like? I don't mean as a pro, I mean as a bloke.'

'Another spoiled romantic.' I watched him over the edge of my glass and he gave a little nod at the accuracy of the shot.

'Lot of it about,' he said. 'Wants the money and out?'

'Doesn't like the pension prospects in his present employment.'

'What did you think of him?'

'Good feller.'

'One of us?'

'One of us.'

Almost dreamily, Noble added: 'And he's got tired of playing Cowboys and Indians. You know, Hussy, I was thinking the other day, I can't remember now why I came into this trade.'

'Fun?'

He rested his head on the back of the sofa. He looked tired. It was odd, because although they'd come at it from opposite ends, Richard Noble and Koch had ended up in the same place. Perhaps I had too. But until they built a Home for Disheartened Hooligans, there was nowhere for us to go.

220

'It must've been fun, I suppose. Fun and guns and excitement, all that. But I was serious about it too. There were one or two big principles in there.'

'Making the world a better place to live in maybe? You've done a great job on it.'

He gave a short bark of a laugh. 'Tremendous. Seriously, I think I did it more than anything to show Charles.'

'I thought you hated his guts.'

He shook his head. 'I think he hates mine. What it was, Hussy, he was always so bloody smug. He was forever lecturing me about duty. Duty to the family. Duty to the school. Duty to the country. I was always failing in my duty, he was always a hundred per cent. The only thing I could do better than him was rough-arsing and girls. So I joined a profession where you could rough-arse in the name of patriotism.'

'And the girls?'

He looked at me from beneath half-lowered eyelids. 'Not found anyone who'll pay me for that yet. No, after all those lectures when I was a kid, I had to show him. I had to hurt him.'

'You're happy now? You think you've made your point? You're as good a man as he is, or whatever it was you were trying to prove.'

He thought about that. 'That must be it. The sad thing is, I don't know. I don't know what young Richard Noble thought and felt all those years ago. It must've been important then, now it's dead memories, that's all. All those fine principles – gone. Can you imagine what Charles will say when he hears about this? God, he'd love to put it on my school report. "Noble Junior has once again demonstrated that the only talent which he is capable of sustaining is that of treachery." Shit, I can hear him now.'

His laugh had a tinge of bitterness that suggested it wasn't all burnt out. My first instincts had been right: drain away the politics and the death and the terror, and swirling at the centre was this ancient black rivalry between the two brothers. It'd be a great old world if it wasn't for the people.

'You still want to hurt him?'

He rose and drained his glass. 'Not now. Oddly enough, I'm

going to have to smash him again, but that'll be accidental. Not that the honourable Charles will ever believe that.'

He crossed the room to a small cloakroom, reached in and pulled out a black leather flight bag. He tossed it on the floor by the safe, and knelt down beside it. As he picked up the first wad of notes, he hesitated. He threw it up to me, and I caught it. I saw from the top note that they were fifties.

'Two thousand notes, one hundred grand. You'd have to do a lot of MoTs to get that. Would that make life simpler for both of us?'

I held it in my hand. I'd never held that much money before. I'd never even seen that much money before. What would I do with it? Buy things. That's the trouble with me, I don't like things very much. It's a sort of a blind spot with me. So, with an apologetic grin, I gently lobbed it back to him.

'It'd be wasted.'

He crouched on his knees, looked up at me, thinking, and running his tongue around his teeth. I was a problem. Suddenly he began to throw the money into the bag.

'London,' he said. 'You drive.'

'Cringle would bollock you senseless for that. Sentiment, he'd say.'

'Well, Cringle would be wrong for once in his life,' he snapped. 'I don't like driving at night, that's all.'

I picked up Winston's arm and for a minute I saw him wonder what I was going to do with it. When I told him, he laughed.

At the bottom of the stairs, I kicked open the door and Cracker and the tall black were only halfway off their chairs when the dismembered arm landed on the table and sent their beer cans tumbling. It landed with a sullen clump, half-rolled over, turned back again as though it was alive, and came to rest with the hand dangling over the edge.

'What the fuck . . .' – the black immediately started pedalling backwards. Cracker froze twelve inches above his seat, his hand on the back: he couldn't move at all. Neither of them could take their eyes from it.

'That's what'll happen to you, Cracker, if you keep playing

with yourself,' I said, from the doorway. No one moved. No one spoke.

'Winston's,' I added. 'That's all there is left now. It's over. Piss off.'

I stood to one side. Slowly at first, they edged around the table, and with one last white-eyed look they clattered down the dark passageway and their stampeding feet echoed away into the night.

'You were right,' Richard said. 'It did flush 'em out.'

# 31

As soon as we crossed the North Circular he taped me up again. You'd've thought we were old mates to hear us talking on the way down, me at the wheel and him with the bulging pocket. If I'd been a telly star, I would've disarmed him one-handed while doing a hundred and fifty in the fast lane. In real life, just knowing there's a .38 on the premises is enough to make you very particular about your behaviour.

He did hop into the back seat to bind me again, because if I'd fancied my chances at having a go that would've been the time. As it was, with the gun on the back seat beside him, he had me trussed up in a minute, and a lot more thoroughly than before. Hands behind my back, my mouth bound tight, and he explained as he did it that he was buying time; after a few hours to get clear, he'd put in a call to make sure I was picked up. Then he jammed cotton wool in my ears and taped over my ears and eyes too. So I was pretty well sealed up while he drove the rest of the way.

After a while, I felt the vibrations of the car stop, the door open and Richard take me by the arm. I felt cold night air on my neck, followed by the warmer air of a house, with a carpet beneath my feet. The buzz of voices just penetrated the earplugs, which meant that he wasn't alone.

I was sat on a bed while he taped up my ankles. I felt a goodbye pat on the shoulder and there I was, oven-ready and stuffed in every way you can think of.

Now, I said to myself, they'll really see what old High-risk Hussy is made of. Escape from sealed room while bound. What, in the trade, is known as a piece of piss. I rolled on to the floor, hauled myself into a sitting position, and began to bounce around the room on my bum. It was slow work and when I finished the sweat was streaming down my body.

But I did know that I was in a room about twelve foot by eighteen, bare apart from a double bed and fitted wardrobe.

I hauled myself back to the bed and leaned against it. For the next hour or so I worked on the tapes. Again that left me soaked in sweat and aching, and with the sure knowledge that Richard Noble hadn't made any mistakes. I wasn't going anywhere. Some piece of piss.

I got as comfortable as I could, which wasn't very comfortable with my arms behind my back and my head halfway into my neck, and began to think. What time would it be? Say two o'clock in the morning. Presumably Richard Noble wasn't planning to launch my rescuers until the next morning . . .

If he meant to at all. My blood iced over at the thought. Dumping me there was the perfect way to get rid of me. Locked in an empty house, unable to move, see or make a sound, I would lie there until I died. Jesus. What a bloody death. How long could I last? Three days without water – but not trussed like this. Panic knotted my stomach, so I got my breathing under control, and tried to remember anything he'd said that would tell me what he might do.

We'd talked on the way down. As I say, apart from the .38 we could've been a couple of pals who'd been for a night out. And why not? Then, at any rate, he wasn't hurting me, and I couldn't do a thing to stop him, so why not chat to pass the time? But what had he said? I cleared my mind and focused on that. He'd asked me what Koch was going to do with the money. I'd told him what Koch had said to me: that he'd maybe go to South America. I'd asked Noble what he'd got planned. He'd laughed and said he liked Koch's idea. What was it he'd said? Sit in the sun and pluck the daiquiris off the trees. That was what he'd said. What was it worth? Slightly less than sod-all. He wasn't going to give me a schedule for his movements for the next ten years, now was he?

What else had we talked about? Oh yes. He'd asked me how Koch would take it when he knew the money had been lifted. 'Personally,' I'd said. 'Very very personally.' Meant it too. In Koch's mind that money was his. The superstar's pay cheque. His pension. That was business to him, and he struck me as a man who was exceedingly serious when it came to business. He would not take kindly to anyone making off with his money. Was there anything in that for me? Not that I could see.

We'd talked about Charles. I'd told him about the faked assassination, and Richard had whistled his surprise. 'But he was right, wasn't he?' I didn't know what he meant. 'He was right, you were the only one who could get to me.' I hadn't thought of that. Perhaps Charles wasn't such a stiff-necked dummy after all.

Then we'd talked about why it was so important to Charles. Richard said it was the old feud between them: his brother wouldn't leave him alone. I'd also told him about Charles' plan to scarper to Barbados with Anna on the fourteenth. He was fascinated by that. He wanted to know how I knew. I'd told him about the airline tickets, but I didn't mention how I came to be in the house at the time. Hussy would never impugn a woman's honour. Well, only about seven times. I hoped Charles was taking plenty of multi-vitamins with him. I didn't tell Richard either. Even so, it was mostly me feeding him information. When I thought about it, I'd told him a lot more than he'd told me. But then, he was the man with the .38, wasn't he?

Then I'd told him about the little Gurkha going over the top of Beachy Head and that had stunned him. That was genuine enough, no doubt about that. He was distressed, no messing. 'They're the last innocents, those little buggers.' That was what he'd said. I said I thought they were supposed to be brilliant

225

soldiers. 'The best. The bloody best. It's the same thing, isn't it? A primitive innocence.'

I knew what he meant well enough. To believe in honour and duty and all those corny old things, you had to be an innocent. Do something dishonourable these days and you go down to the pub to swank about it; you don't jump off a cliff.

Somehow I could see the Gurkha falling then. He was spinning, smiling and falling down towards me, and above I could see a hard winter blue sky and the sludge-white chalk cliffs, and then he was flying, as though he had an invisible hang-glider.

My mind flew around the sky too. Dreams swelled and burst in my head. Charlie's nose, and Charles' nose, twitch twitch. The Gurkha dancer. The sky filled with flames. The ragged-ended arm clumping on to the table in front of Cracker. Each dream ended with a lacerating pain when, in my dozing, I tried to move. It was worst in my shoulders and neck, bright yellow shafts of pain that dragged my mind back into the conscious world. Then I slipped away again. Several times I thought I heard sounds: buzzing, drumming, and what I was sure was a ringing noise, but whether they were sounds from the world outside my head, or my dreams, I'd no means of telling.

But when I knew – really knew – there was someone in the room, it wasn't anything I heard or felt: somehow I sensed another presence. It was an eerie feeling. Whoever it was came in without making a sound, and I felt no vibrations from footsteps or draughts from moving doors. But I was as sure of another person's presence as I would've been if I could see him with my eyes. Involuntarily I snapped upright and I desperately fought to concentrate what remained of my senses on the room around me. Nothing. Nothing at all. Nothing for eyes or ears, yet my scalp kept on wriggling and the hairs at the back of my neck were rising from the skin, and those were danger signals when men lived in caves. Someone was in that room. I don't know how long I held myself in that tensed upright position. Eventually, I collapsed backwards, and exhaustion must have pulled me down into some sort of sleep. The next time someone came in, I was in no doubt at all.

When the hand lifted my chin up, I jumped so much I almost jack-knifed backwards. Someone wanted to see my face. The tape ripped, light and noise roared over me, and I saw a blurred and bleary Charles Noble bending over me.

'You have let me down totally, Hussy.'

# 32

'I call that dereliction of duty, Hussy. You let him get away.'

Charles Noble's face was pinched with fury, and I had to bite my own anger back. I pointed at the two BWIA tickets on the table. 'If you remember, you as good as told me those were yours. You were going away with her. On the fourteenth.'

His mouth tightened. 'It was a complete shock to me to learn she was planning to go anywhere. You would hardly expect me to admit she was going away with my own brother.'

'So you had to pretend it was you to save your pride. See what happened.'

We were standing downstairs by the window in Anna's house in Doughty Mews. Outside I could see the stain where I'd smashed the milk into Cracker's face. That seemed a long time ago now. Once I knew where I was, everything became clear. Richard had dumped me here and he'd taken off with Anna and the two million. So simple it hurt.

It also hurt to remember how cleverly Anna had made sure that I saw the tickets. That was their dummy run. While I had my eyes on the fourteenth, they slipped away eleven days earlier. They'd gone. And we'd no idea where.

It had taken me half-an-hour's stretching to get the worst of the pain out of my limbs. Even now, every time I moved I felt as though my muscles were on fire. And all the time I'd had

Charles Noble following me round the house cursing his brother for his treachery, lamenting his lost love, and trying to blame me for both.

He'd telephoned to speak to Anna while the boys were having breakfast, as he often did apparently, and when there was no answer he'd shot up here. To find me, and an empty house. Almost empty, anyway. Curtains and carpets and basic items like beds and kitchen tables were still there, but the good stuff, like the near Vermeer, had gone.

With Charles moaning along behind, I gave the house a complete turn-over. I even went through the dustbin. But the place had been stripped of any sort of documentation or personal property and the speckled remains of ashes around the bathroom handbasin told me the rest.

At the end of my trawl, I assembled all my loot on the kitchen table: a couple of gas bills which I'd found behind the boiler; a letter from the agency handling the house thanking her for the last payment, which was on the stairs; a commercial telephone directory, next to the phone in the room beside the front door; one of those glossy give-away magazines that are packed with house sales which I found inside the door; an invitation to a fashion show at Grosvenor House the following month; and cards from a selection of mini-cab firms. They weren't worth a lot.

'I wonder how he tricked her into it,' Charles said, hovering over me.

'Into what?'

'Into going with him, of course. He only knew her because Veronica asked him to keep an eye on me.'

As gently as I could, I said that I thought a fair bit of forward planning had gone into this. I didn't bother telling him that the only reason I'd gone to the mews in the first place was because Richard had been picking up parking tickets there; somehow I'd lost sight of that myself when Winston rolled up. That was to save Charles' pride. Mine was seriously dented every time I thought how she'd led me to the air tickets. That was Oscar-winning stuff, all right, but I was still convinced that every one of the magnificent seven was authentic: no one, not even Anna Mauch, could act that well.

Any way you looked at it, we'd both been very deftly conned. Charles wasn't so sure.

'Allow me to point out that you don't really know either of them. You can take my word for it that my brother is a nasty piece of work, but I must concede that he can be quite convincing at times. And for all her apparent sophistication, Anna is an innocent in many ways. Yes, I think we'll find that he has deceived her in some way.'

I looked up at him as I sorted through these bits of paper, and I couldn't help but feel sorry for him. His face was pink with emotion and his eyes were suspiciously moist. He loved her all right, I could see that. She must've been an obsession for him, and even now he wouldn't let go. The truth was that he was the victim and she was the deceiver, but I couldn't tell him that.

'Although admittedly I did mislead you over those tickets, Hussy, Anna and I had devoted quite a lot of time and thought to our new life together.'

'In Barbados?'

'Heavens, no. I thought we might start a business somewhere. Perhaps down in Dorset. My father was a Dorset man, you know.'

'What sort of business?'

His bottom lip was wobbling dangerously. 'We hadn't discussed it in specific terms, but I did wonder about a tea-shop.'

'A tea-shop?'

'Yes. Scones and jam and things.'

It was hard to believe that even his optimism could stretch to Anna Mauch in a mob cap. As kindly as I could, I said: 'You don't really believe Anna would go for that, do you?'

He blinked at me. 'You think not?'

I shook my head. 'Not.'

He gave several rapid blinks then, and a small desperate sigh. 'That's why she preferred Richard, I suppose. He is much more worldly than I am.' As he thought about his brother, his face hardened again. 'Although I strongly suspect Richard is only doing this to get at me. He always . . .'

229

'Charles.'

'Yes?'

'Give it a fucking rest.'

In his obsession with his old rivalry, he didn't seem to have grasped the idea that an awful lot of men would be happy to run away with Anna Mauch regardless of the effect it would have on him. As for running away with Anna Mauch and two million quid, I personally couldn't believe anyone would turn that down, up to – and very likely including – the Pope. But he saw it all as another twist in his lifelong rivalry with Richard.

That reminded me of what Richard had said. The next time he hurt his brother, it would be by accident. That's what he said. Was this what he meant? Running away with Anna. Again, it wasn't something I could ask Charles. Whatever it was they'd done to each other over the years, they'd long since cauterised any form of understanding. The only nerve-ends flickering with life were the ones that triggered suspicion and fear. Then, just as I was beginning to feel sorry for him, he did it again: he tried to dump the whole thing back in my lap. 'So,' he said, with forced brightness. 'What are you going to do to find them?'

'What I am going to do, is to stuff bacon, egg, tomatoes and sausage into my face, along with a gallon of tea.'

'Oh.' He didn't even try to hide his displeasure. 'May I remind you that you are supposed to be working for me and I would've thought . . . where are you going, Hussy . . ?'

I found a workman's cafe down the Gray's Inn Road. I asked for several samples of everything they produced by way of breakfast, and expressed the hope that it was guaranteed stratospherically high in cholesterol and suicidally fattening. They said they'd do their best. They did. And when it came, I didn't just eat it. I consumed it. Since Richard felled me with the axe and left me trussed and helpless, I'd experienced quite enough condemnation to enjoy a dozen hearty breakfasts.

Even Charles' accusing eyes couldn't spoil it. He'd trailed along behind me, of course. I banned him from speaking, but the moment the last forkful had gone in, he started again. 'I expect chaps like you have your means of finding missing persons.'

230

'No.' I polished off the last corner of toast. 'Some chaps may have, but they are not chaps like me.'

'Oh. Where do we go next, in that case?'

'Where you go, I don't know. I'm going to find a phone box.'

I had to report in to Cringle. First, I had to tell him about the plan to kill the copper in Chipping Campden, even though I doubted if Koch would want to stick to schedule once he thought he wasn't being paid. And I told him what I could about the Rich Pickings set up too, or whatever would be left of it after Winston's death. Without his leadership, and the cash he was pumping in, it would almost certainly be in shreds.

Richard Noble had wrecked the entire operation, no doubt about that, and he would've been up for herograms if he'd stayed around for the speeches. As it was, I think Cringle wanted him even more than Koch.

'Damnation. Still, what matters now is that he's not seen to get away with it. That would be irreversibly bad for business. Any idea where to look?'

All I could suggest was anywhere except Barbados. With his expertise, and that sort of cash, he could be anywhere in the world, up to his ears in camouflage.

'Is that the best you can come up with?'

Christ! Now he was trying to pin it on me. 'Look, the riots are over, Winston's dead and Rich Pickings is in bits of pieces. Won't that do for now?'

'We want him back, Hussy.'

I didn't like the measured way he spoke. 'We don't always get what we want, Cringle.'

'We must have him, I'm afraid.'

'I haven't got him.'

We both let the silence swell between us. Eventually Cringle broke it, and when he spoke again it was in an almost jovial tone. 'So. You're back to the garage, are you?'

'That's the idea.'

'Good. Keep in touch. Let me know if you have any ideas.'

I should've known. Cringle never gives in. Not like that anyway. Richard had left the Chevette in the mews, with the keys in the glove compartment, so I hopped in and headed for home. The minute I saw the police car on the garage forecourt, I knew.

The sergeant in the hall tried to stop me but I knocked his arm out of the way and ran through into the kitchen. Jamie was slumped over the dark-polished table, head in hands, shaking with sobs. A WPC with wrestler's shoulders was trying to console her.

'What's going on, Jamie?' I wasn't feeling anywhere near as gentle as my tone might've indicated.

'I didn't do owt. I didn't tek owt. Bloody lies, it's all bloody lies.'

'Take what?' I asked, as gently as I could, but she wouldn't lift her face from her hands. The sergeant had followed me in, so I took him by the arm and whisked him outside. He was a fat old chap who was within touching distance of his pension and had lost interest in persecuting the public. After a bit of pratting about, I eventually got the story out of him. Jamie had been picked up in a supermarket for shoplifting. Another shopper had seen her slip two items into her own bag which she had not declared at the cash-point. She'd denied it, but when her bag was searched, the two items were there.

'What were they?'

'I believe one was an artichoke – some sort of vegetable, as I understand it – valued at 59 pence, and the other was a tin of marrowfat peas, valued at 18 pence. I can see you're distressed, sir, but believe me, among women of a certain age, this is not at all uncommon . . .'

'Who's the witness? The other shopper?'

'I'm afraid I cannot reveal . . .'

'Don't piss me about, sergeant. She's not local, is she?'

'Well, as a matter of fact, the lady concerned was a visitor . . .'

Surprise surprise. I went over to my room to ring Cringle. I couldn't get him. He'd know it was me and he'd know why I was phoning: course he wouldn't take the call. 'Just tell him,' I said, slowly so his secretary would get every word, 'that even a bastard snake like him has to have some family or friends, and if I have to, I can find them.'

232

Peas, I might have believed. But an artichoke? For Jamie? She thought Brussel sprouts were a bit exotic. You'd think one of Cringle's bright young ladies would try to collect evidence that was more in character.

But when I went back over to see Jamie, by then she'd half convinced herself she was guilty. The cops had gone. I put the kettle on, and sat with her by a neglected fire. Christ, but the poor soul looked a mess. Her squashed-in face was blotched and bleary and her eyes were stencilled with crimson lines. She'd gone very Yorkshire again.

'Appen I did,' she said. 'I'm that damn smock-raffled I don't know what the 'ell I'm doing. Appen they're right. Appen I'm off me trolley.'

'Don't worry. You didn't.'

She lifted her weepy face up to me. 'You don't know, Joe. You wasn't there, was you?'

I couldn't tell her it was a set-up to put pressure on me. 'It's a mistake, we'll sort it out.' That was the best I could manage.

She dabbed at her eyes with a rag that left oil smears on her cheek. 'If they take me to court, I'll never set foot outside this door again, I'll be that shamed.'

I made her a mug of tea and sat across the table from her, holding her knobbly hands. Right then, I hated myself. I hated myself for doing a job that was so dirty that the mess spilled over to honest people like Jamie, and soiled them too. Most of all I hated Cringle for doing it. I meant the message I'd left. Somewhere there must be someone he loved, or liked, and at least someone he wasn't totally indifferent to. If he could dabble in my life, I could dabble in his. See how he liked it.

I went over to my place and cleaned out Charlie while I cooled down. The more I thought about it, the more I could see that – for the moment at any rate – the only way I could get Jamie off the hook was to give Cringle what he wanted. Or at least to try. But how the hell could I find Richard? I didn't even know where to start.

As I washed out Charlie's dishes under the tap and replaced the newspaper, I ran the sequence of events through my mind, looking for leads. Moss Side, Liverpool, back to London.

233

Then I remembered that I hadn't checked out the Barbados tickets. It was worth a go. When I rang the airline, they were engaged. I left it a minute, then picked up the phone and pushed the re-call button. Then it struck me. It was a long shot, but it was better than anything else I had going for me . . .

Without even asking, I took the Honda. Luckily, it's a nippy little model, if you're allowed to say that about Japanese cars, because it was all second and third gears, lane changing, swerving out and dodging back in again, and I collected plenty of shaken fists and mouthed oaths. It was only when I swung in to Doughty Mews that I realised how much the engine was squealing. I rang the bell. Christ, I was doing everything wrong. I hadn't got a key. Charles would probably have gone back to school. I rang it again. A gentle drizzle had begun to fall and in the window across the street I could see the Mediterranean woman watching from a window. She probably wondered who I'd be smashing milk bottles over this time.

'Holy bloody . . .' I banged on the door once with my fist when it opened. Charles stood there.

'I thought we'd seen the last of you,' he said, in a petulant voice.

'You haven't used that telephone, have you?' I jinked round him into the sitting-room where I'd pretended to phone the first time I went to the house. The white telephone, which had been on a table near the window, was now on the floor. The table had gone.

'The telephone? No, I don't think . . .'

I picked up the handset. Thank God. I'd remembered correctly. It was one of those with the buttons in the handset itself, and – like mine – it had a recall button. Which meant it would recall the last number. Whatever that was.

I pressed the recall button. I held it tight against my ear. I only half saw Charles follow me into the room but I knew from the anxious look on his face that he realised I was on to something.

The line hummed, then gave out a series of clicks. At last it began to ring.

That was the point when I began to think that in my

234

weariness I'd got it all wrong. But when the woman answered, my heart soared and I knew for sure I'd got it right.

'Cosy Cat Hotel, can I help you?'

The proprietor was a Miss Eridge who was thrilled to hear from a friend of Harrod's. 'It's so important to keep the human connection.'

Fifteen stone, moleskin trousers, tartan shirt, shorn hair, living in some broken-down smallholding. I put the picture together as I listened. Eccentric posh. A talkaholic.

Mrs Lord had quite forgotten to say that Harrod had so many caring friends. Although he'd settled in marvellously since she'd brought him the previous day, she was sure he'd be delighted to see me. It would be such a comfort, particularly since Mrs Lord couldn't be sure when she would be able to take him to his new home.

Lord. Noble. I wasn't surprised. When people choose fake names they often go for variations of their own.

'Do you think he'll like it there, Mis Eridge?'

'Where, Mr Hussy?'

'You know, this new home of his.'

'I really couldn't say.' I knew from her tone that I'd said the wrong thing. 'I don't know where Harrod's new home will be. Mrs Lord led me to believe that she will be travelling for several weeks, if not months.'

So much for that idea. I might've known that they wouldn't be so stupid as to leave a forwarding address with a cattery.

I sat on the floor looking at the telephone as Miss Eridge purred on about what a wonderfully adaptable little fellow Harrod was, and such a character!

But he had had a teeny tummy upset and Miss Eridge wondered if plaice upset him. Did I know if plaice upset him? No, I didn't know if plaice upset him. With an injured sigh, she said that this was exactly the sort of situation she had in mind when she'd asked Mrs Lord to leave an emergency telephone number.

Did she actually have a number? No, that was what made it so annoying. Mrs Lord had started to give her the number, and then said she'd rather not leave one after all. She'd seemed quite agitated about it, which was entirely unnecessary since everyone did it. Miss Eridge expressed the opinion that no doubt Mrs Lord knew her own business best. All that Miss Eridge was saying was that it did seem odd, particularly since it was clear to her that Mrs Lord was a genuine cat-lover, which was why she wanted only the very best for her Harrod.

Weariness weighed on me as I listened to the droning voice. So she didn't have a number after all? No, she snapped, that was exactly what she was trying to explain. Mrs Lord changed her mind, so that was that.

In that case, I said . . . But Miss Eridge was in verbal spate. She had all the emergency numbers of her customers on the board in the office where she was sitting at that very moment. She could even see the scribble where she'd begun to write it down. Started writing it, and then had to cross it out, and here was poor Harrod feeling bilious and they couldn't get in touch with his mistress. Shame, shame.

Started writing it? Mrs Lord's number?

Of course. She'd just told me that, hadn't she?

Could she perhaps read any of it? The number was incomplete, she began again, exasperation showing through. She hadn't even finished writing it down when Mrs Lord had changed her mind so it was quite useless.

'All I have is . . . just one moment, where are my glasses . . . yes . . . just the start of it, that's all. O-one-o, another one, four-o-three, eight-six-five, a seven, and then she stopped. (0101–403–865–7 . . .) So you see, only half a number. Quite meaningless, I'm afraid.'

'Ah well, never mind,' I said in what I thought was a philosophical tone. Then I checked the number with her again.

'A waste of time. That's exactly what I told the other man too.'

'The other man?' I could see my fingers tighten around the handset.

'Yes, the foreigner. Another of Mrs Lord's friends.'

'Did you give him the number too?'

'Rather like you, I'm afraid he wouldn't take no for an answer.'

236

'But you read it out to him?'

Whatever sympathy I'd had to start with had gone. She sounded steely when she replied. 'Mr Hussy, I do not have time for frivolous inquiries. I have my cats to care for. Good day.'

I put the phone down and looked at the number I'd written on the front of the glossy magazine. I inked over it, underlined it, and boxed it in. 0 1 0 – 1 – 4 0 3 – 8 6 5 – 7

The States. 0101 was America, I was sure of that.

I wasn't far off. Like most people, the duty officer at British Telecom was glad of the opportunity to demonstrate his expertise. The first three figures were the international code. The single 1 got me to North America. The 403 took me over to Alberta and the North West Territories. And 865 – he hummed as he flipped through his guide – narrowed it down to a place called Hinton. Wherever that was. That was it. Hinton, Alberta. Easy as that.

Easy as that for me. And for anyone else who'd got the number.

The next bit wasn't quite so straightforward. I settled myself down with the telephone. First I tried the Canadian High Commission. Even they didn't know much about Hinton without looking in the reference books. The girl came back in a couple of minutes. It was on the Yellowhead Highway which led from Edmonton to Jasper, the mountain resort in the Rockies, but Hinton wasn't exactly a holiday town. Most of its population of 8,350 worked in the paper mill or the coal mine. 'Colleague of mine here says it smells quite a lot,' she said.

Why would Richard and Anna want to go to a smelly town in Alberta? I couldn't find an answer to that. I began to ring round all the airlines who flew to western Canada. British Airways. Air Canada. Ward-Air.

The checked through their passenger schedules chuckling merrily over the two names I gave them: Noble and Lord. But at BA and Air Canada, they couldn't find either.

'We don't have any record of passengers under those names. Some kind of aristocrats you're looking for?' The girl at Ward-Air was most amused.

'Something like that. Nothing at all?'

237

She started giggling again. 'I'm afraid not, sir.'

'What's so funny?'

'Oh, it's just those names you were looking for. I guess there must be a lot of blue-bloods travelling around at the moment. We had a Mr and Mrs Peers flew out this morning.'

I was kneeling on the floor and the schoolmaster was hovering over me. He must've seen my face change. 'Have you found them?'

I waved him into silence while I took details of their flight.

'Well?' Charles' face, as keen and sharp as a fox, was pushed out in his eagerness.

'They flew to Edmonton this morning.'

Noble. Lord. Peers. It was the same joke. It had to be them.

'I'm coming with you, Hussy.'

I did protest. The last thing I wanted was a boy scout tied round my neck on a job like that. But when he started saying he'd go anyway, with or without me, I relented.

If he was going to clutter up the scenery, at least I could have him where I could see him. There was already one mystery man heading towards Hinton.

I looked at my watch. Ten past four. I wondered how long it had taken the foreigner to trace the phone number back to Hinton. And if he'd set off himself yet.

'Okay,' I told him. 'Go get your tuck box or whatever it is you travel with.'

# 33

The signs at the side of the road bear one word: West. That's all you need to know. The Yellowhead Highway runs in a straight line right across Alberta and out to the Rocky Mountains. I settled my foot on the accelerator of the hired Sunbird, hooked my fingers over the steering wheel, and concentrated on staying awake.

We hadn't been able to get a flight until the next day. I was quite glad about that because at least it gave me another night with Jamie. For all her gruff cynicism, at heart she was an old-fashioned traditionalist, and by the time evening came she'd convinced herself she was guilty: after all, the British bobbies don't tell lies, do they? She was a little toughie, and I'd've backed her to stand up to any sort of attack or personal disaster. But Cringle had got it exactly right: what she couldn't face was the possibility of her own dishonesty. It had thrown her so much that she was talking about selling up and returning to Yorkshire. There was nothing I could do but listen and keep the mugs of tea coming: she was too honest to understand the truth.

We had to fly to Calgary, all skyscrapers and stetsons, and then take a half-hour hop up to Edmonton, where I picked up the Tilden hire-car. The man on the desk was an Indian – takeaway rather than totem-pole – who'd lived in Lewes and before I knew it, he and Charles were deep in a discussion about whether Imran Khan was well-advised to play cricket for Sussex for another year.

All I could think of was Jamie's flat, sad face and her swollen eyes, and they were there before me as I drove out along the Yellowhead.

'Fascinating when you think about it.' Charles was wearing a brown tweed sports jacket and his flannels: somehow he'd emerged creaseless from the eight-hour flight.

'What's that?'

'The influence we still have throughout the world.'

'We? You mean schoolmasters?'

'The British.'

'I must've missed that.'

'That Asian chap. He would never have come to England if we hadn't ruled India, and then he came over here for the same reason. The mysterious swirling currents of history, you might say.'

God save us. He was off again. 'He's here,' I said slowly, so he could take it in, 'because he wanted to get out of Britain before the place fell down round his ears. Countries like this are the future. We're the past.'

'Really, Hussy. We teach our boys that England is rather a remarkable country.'

'The only thing it's remarkable for is the way the peasantry still tolerate the balls-aching jackasses who run the place.'

I could feel his eyes on me. 'I honestly don't know how you're able to do your job holding the opinions you do.'

'Someone's got to keep an eye on the jackasses.'

After that we sat in silence. To be fair, I suppose we both had a lot on our minds: he was thinking about his brother and Anna, and I was thinking about Jamie. And maybe a bit about Anna too. We were tired. At home, I'd just about be getting in a last pint before closing time and Charles would be on his last smokers' round-up.

It was a fast road, long and straight, cutting through the endless acres of dark pines. All the way we passed the truckers in their thundering lorries, their high-prowed fronts and chimney exhausts all chrome-plated and shiny like fifties juke-boxes. We were lucky. It hadn't snowed for a few days, and the remains of the last fall was banked at the sides of the road and scattered among the trees. In the fading light of the afternoon, I could see specks of dry snow drifting in the cold air as we swept along.

We saw the Rockies long before we got to Hinton. At first you couldn't tell where horizon ended and cloud began but, as we got nearer and as the sun slid down, earth and sky fell apart to reveal a mountain range that ran all the way along the edge of the earth. Backlit by the sun, they were as sharp and ragged as sharks' teeth. As we got nearer, we saw different facets and angles where the light lay, so that the whole range began to look more like a wedding cake the mice had got at. Beneath blue-pink clouds, the snow was every shade between a shimmering pure white and glowing dark crimson. Even in the distance it was a sight of extraordinary beauty and it pulled us down the road as it must have drawn the pioneers when they were heading westwards.

Then Hinton reared up in the lights, without quite the same effect on the soul, I must say. I slowed down to a walk as we cruised through the scrawled neon of the motels and shadow-less filling-stations, where the tall trucks were lined up for rest or fuel. 'Sleepy Drivers Stop Here' one sign said, and the night sky was filled with promises of everything from discos to buffalo burgers.

'Buffalo burgers? Do you imagine that's a joke?' Charles asked.

'No one would joke about a thing like that.'

We checked into one of the smaller motels back from the highway. It wasn't much more than a central reception area and bar, with the bedrooms in two long single-storey wings. We got adjoining rooms at the end of one wing. I had a shower to wake me up and Charles was knocking at the door before I'd even towelled myself dry. He was wearing his duffel coat, and I was glad of the old fake sheepskin Jamie had once picked up for me in a jumble sale: the cold air nipped like a terrier, and it had the sulphur taste you get around coal mines. I managed to slow him down long enough to grab a quick meal in a diner, a steamy cavern raucous with lorry drivers in baseball caps.

Then we began to search for Richard. It didn't take us long to realise that the task was almost impossible.

We tried to work the town section by section. We'd park, and I'd take one side of the street while he did the other. Bars, hotels, motels, any shops or supermarkets that were still open, petrol stations, anywhere we could find a light. I'd thought that an Englishman might not be too hard to trace in a town with a population of a few thousand. I had it somewhere at the back of my mind that in Alberta you can find every nationality from Ukrainian to Japanese. What I didn't know was that Hinton was a stopover for all the east–west traffic, like the high shining lorries with their loads of paper and coal that I'd seen on the road. To make it even worse, the town is on the edge of the national park, and people came halfway round the world for the ski-ing and fishing and climbing. It's a mill-and-pit town, certainly, but plenty of tourists stop there, if only to get fed and watered.

One thing was for sure: they weren't going to gasp in amazement when they saw an Englishman.

Everywhere I went I was offered plenty of information. I was told that the Brits wouldn't get off their butts to work, that Hinton was a union town with big wages, that Tyson would've beat the shit out of Ali on the best day he ever had, that Princess Di was just terrific, that there was an old grizzly scavenging on the town tip, that everyone round here had a jacuzzi and a snowmobile, and that – what the hell – the Brits weren't all that bad and did I want a drink? In other words, the locals were pretty much like locals anywhere: curious, proud, and courteous. But they hadn't seen hide nor hair of anyone who sounded anything like Richard Noble-Lord-Peers.

We were both pretty knocked out as we made our way through the soiled stacks of roadside snow back to the motel. Charles was saying that he seriously suspected that, in some of the places, they might have been laughing at him. I looked at him. Dear God, wouldn't they just? He'd probably been offering them strings of bright beads. There was something he said then that tinkled a distant bell but I was too tired to pick it up, and anyway my mind had gone off down a different track.

'Tell me, Charles, what exactly are you going to do if we do find your brother and Anna?'

'I should have thought that was quite clear.'

'Not to me it isn't.'

'I shall point out to them the folly of their actions and give them the chance to return.'

'And if they don't want to?'

I felt him turn and look at me and I knew it was a look of utter incredulity. 'Then it will be our duty to see that they do return. Surely that's inescapable?'

'Mmm.' I couldn't really trust myself to say more than that.

'Well. What did you have in mind?'

'I think I'll follow your lead.'

I hit the bed like a dead man. Then, around the time when the first customers would be rolling up at the garage at home, I snapped into wakefulness. If only I'd been there, it would've been the first day I'd been on time for work for years.

242

I looked at my watch. One o'clock. I tried to get back to sleep but my brain kept adding up six gallons of four-star, so in the end I got up and went over to the window. A fresh fall of snow had cleansed the scruffy little town, and although I could see the highway lights and hear the grumbling of the lorries, I looked out on a scene of peace and silence. Fat cushions of soft snow bulged on the branches of the trees and the roofs of the houses, and I could sense more than see the presence of the mountains up there in the clouds. It was the sort of scene that sweeps your mind, and that's exactly what it did to mine. In that moment, I remembered the significance of what Charles had said.

'A Big Boy's Milkshake.'

In one of the bars. That was the drink they'd offered him. Not surprisingly, he assumed they were suggesting that Englishmen weren't quite as muscular as they might be. For once, they weren't.

'That's what they said?'

I'd got Charles out of bed and half dressed before his eyes were open. 'I think so. Pass my jacket, please.'

'Who said it? Who exactly? Oh, for God's sake, would you ever look at the man – do you have to comb your hair now?'

'I most certainly do. In any case, I find it difficult to believe that any catering establishment will be open at this time of night. Or morning.'

'You'd be amazed, Cinders. But it won't be if you're going to spend all night combing your bloody plaits.'

He was stooping to peer into a mirror to make sure that not one hair crossed the pink no-man's-land of his parting. With a draughtsman's precision, he dragged the comb down the short side first, then up over the top towards the other ear.

'It was the proprietor. The man behind the bar.'

I held the door open while he came through and hustled him down the corridor. 'And those were the words he used?'

'Look, what on earth are you going on about, Hussy? I'm absolutely exhausted and you come and drag me out of bed in the middle of the night . . .'

'A Big Boy's Milkshake?'

'Yes. At least, as far as I can remember.'

'The bar behind the second filling station as you come in?'

'I believe it was. Rather a small one, if I remember correctly, with a tropical fish tank in the corner. I must say the significance of all this eludes me . . .'

'It would. Now shut up.'

It didn't take more than five minutes to find the place he meant. At first I thought it had closed up for the night. But it was only because it looked dark alongside the blinding white floodlights of the filling station. When I got closer I could see the modest glimmer of red table lamps, and the outline of the people inside: two sitting, two standing.

As the door hissed shut behind us, I heard Charles whisper: 'The fellow in the blue jacket.'

He was the barman, and he looked up from his task of taking glasses from a steaming washer. A customer sat on a stool at the bar, his back towards us.

In the corner, a young couple arm-wrestled for fun, and beyond them a small Asian woman was hunched over a cup.

'Just closing, friend,' the barman said, in a transatlantic accent that still had a touch of Eastern Europe in it. He was young, almost totally bald, and he had an apologetic air about him.

'Not even time for one drink?'

'Well . . .' He lifted out four glasses in each hand and still managed to glimpse his wristwatch. 'Maybe a quickie.'

'How about a Big Boy's Milkshake?'

'Hey.' He turned, grinned at me, turned back again so he could put the glasses down and then spoke to the man at the bar. 'What'd I tell you, Harry?'

'Not the same guy.' Harry, the man at the bar, inspected me from the other side of a bloodhound face.

'Well. Jesus. Twice, huh?' He stood there smiling, looking around the place, and then he leaned forward to look at Charles again. 'Excuse me, sir, weren't you the gentleman who was in earlier?'

'As a matter of fact, I . . .'

'Harry'n me were just joking about the milkshake thing,

244

hope you didn't take no offence nor nothin'.' He switched his gaze to me. 'Mind if I check this one, sir, last night was the first time I ever made it.'

He stood on the other side of the bar, and tapped his left thumb with his right forefinger. 'Two of tequila, right?'

'Right.'

He tapped forefinger on forefinger. 'One of kahlua, right?'

'Right.'

He spun on his heel, and began to measure out into his shaker. 'Then fill her up with iced milk?' Without waiting for my confirmation, he took a carton of milk from a fridge and began to pour.

'Helluva drink,' said Harry. He was wearing blue overalls under a fleecy-lined tartan jacket.

'You tried it?'

'With the guy last night. He a pal of yours?'

'Old pal.'

'What on earth is it?' Charles whispered.

'A Big Boy's Milkshake. Favourite drink at the Intercontinental Hotel in Muscat.'

'Muscat?' He blinked foolishly at me.

'In the Sultanate of Oman. The place where our lads go for a quiet drink when they've finished a stint down at the Yemeni border.'

'Soldiers, do you mean?'

'Of a sort, Charles. But very very irregular soldiers.'

'Your pal sure likes 'em,' Harry said.

'If he's the man I'm thinking of. Taller than me, shorter than him,' – I nodded towards Charles – 'more solid too.'

Harry gave a slow nod. He examined Charles without seeming to like what he saw. 'Looked a bit like that one with you. Only your pal was a bright kinda guy, feisty I reckon.'

He obviously didn't rate Charles as feisty.

'There you go, sir.' The barman poured out two glasses.

'Smells of coffee.' Charles sniffed before tasting.

'Best Mexican coffee beans,' I said. 'Last night my pal was here?'

'Yessir.'

'Was he with a woman?' Charles pushed his face forward in his anxiety to hear the answer. His nose was going like an anteater's.

'No, he was by himself. Alone, right, Harry?'

'He was alone okay.'

'Beautiful drink,' I said to the barman. 'Though the last time I had one it was a bit warmer. Is my pal staying around here, do you know?'

He was back to moving glasses again and he shook his shining head in doubt. 'I dunno. He didn't say, you know.'

Harry had a twice-folded newspaper in his fist and he drank slowly from a glass of beer while he read. Without looking up, he said: 'Staying local, I guess.'

'And what makes you think that exactly?' Charles homed in on him as though he was one of his less trustworthy homework-dodgers. I shuddered at his clumsiness, and I saw the man raise his eyes in surprise at his treatment.

'I'll tell you what makes me think that. Cause I saw him coming out of Les Daly's store with his provisions, that's why. And you wouldn't shop here if you was going to Vancouver and you wouldn't buy food if you was staying in a hotel, that's why.'

Deliberately, he returned to his newspaper. An awkward silence grew in the wake of his words.

'You wouldn't know where he's living?' However easily I asked it, the question sounded intrusive now.

He shook his head and went on reading.

'He didn't say.' The bald barman spoke quietly. 'He had a couple of these milkshake drinks, cracked a few jokes, and then went. He didn't say anything about where he was staying. Does he have kids?'

'No.'

'Funny. He had a big model in a box. You know, plane or boat or crane or something. You see what he had in that box, Harry?'

Harry grunted and went on reading, but one of the arm-wrestling lovers called out.

'You mean the English guy who was here last night?'

I felt Charles tense up and lean forward and I grabbed his

246

wrist before he could move or speak. It was the female half of
the wrestling act who was speaking: in the shadows of the
corner, and interlocked with her boyfriend, all I could see was
that she was eighteen or so, with a long face half hidden by a
swatch of hair.

'You know him, Jackie?' the barman called out.

'You don't know him,' her boyfriend said, in a teasing voice,
and he began to force her hand backwards.

'Oh, you vicious bastard,' she said, giggling. 'No, Ray's
right, I don't know him.'

Harry looked up from his paper. 'You weren't in here last
night anyway.'

'No.' Their arms were upright and tussling and she was
giggling again. 'But I heard you talking about him and I guess
he was the guy my father was talking about today.'

The barman gave me a hopeful smile. 'Your father knows
him?'

'Ray, you squeeze my ring like that again and I won't tell you
what I'll do . . . oh fuck!' Swiftly she put her fingers to her lips
and peeped at the tiny Asian woman sitting behind her. 'Sorry
'bout that,' she said, but the woman never looked up. Then she
turned back to us. 'He's moved into the Thrupps' place. Up
past Winter Creek.'

'Thrupp's?' Harry swore mildly to himself. 'Must be one of
the goddam Rothschilds if he's bought that place.'

'Renting. My father says he's renting.'

'Has he got a woman with him?' Charles was in too quick for
me.

'Dunno. Ouch, Ray, you know something, you're a sadist. I
dunno if he's got a woman with him. That kinda money, he'd
find one soon enough round here. Maybe me, oh Ray . . .'

The barman drew me a map on the back of a bar bill. He did
a straight line for the Yellowstone Highway and drew in Hinton
on the hill, the bit of Hinton that was down in the valley, the
mill, the coal mine, the liquor store.

He drew in the Athabasca River, and Ogre Canyon and the
Black Cat Ranch, and the road that led up to Peppers Lake,
going towards Grande Cache. He scribbled in Winter Creek

and did a big circle for Mount Solomon, and then marked a cross.

'Thrupps' place is right there. You'll have to park back there and walk the rest.'

'Thanks.'

'That's okay. Like Jackie says, he's renting the Thrupps', he's loaded.'

'It's a nice place?'

'Five, six bedrooms, same number bathrooms. I guess six hundred dollars a week, maybe more. Furnished fit for a lord.' The wrestling girl giggled again. 'Good thing too.'

'Why's that?' The barman winked at me as he looked past me at the young lovers.

'Why? Hell, he's only called Dook, that's all. Mistah Duke,' she added, in a posh English accent.

Duke. If there was any doubt, that disposed of it.

If Charles could've got the map off me he would have gone up the mountain there and then, on foot if necessary. As soon as we got outside, I told him: this time he isn't going anywhere. We know where he is, and he'll still be there in the morning.

I found myself trying to stare out into the darkness then, in the direction of the mountain. Anna. Two million pounds.

And, if I'd reckoned it right, three of them. One who wanted the money. One who wanted the woman. One who wanted both. Plus me. What did I want? I never answer direct questions. Not even my own.

# 34

'What can you see?'

'Not so bloody much through these things.' The cheapo binoculars I'd picked up in duty-free weren't exactly up to military standard but I could see all I needed to. I just didn't want to tell him. 'Give us some more of that coffee.'

I adjusted them and looked again. It was Anna. I could only just see her because, although the bedroom light was now switched on, she was at the back of the room.

'Is Richard there?'

'Coffee.'

I heard him murmur something impatient as he turned round to open the flask. To him it was blurred movement at a lighted window, but I could see what it was; it struck me that Charles was quite fidgety enough without being provoked by the sight of a naked Anna.

'Here.'

I managed to drink from the thermos cap without moving the glasses. Partly because I didn't want him to take them, and partly because I couldn't stop watching myself. Which made me a sort of peeping Davy Crockett or something. But I was glad to see that neither my memory nor my finger-ends had let me down: she was lovely.

'Is that someone at the window?'

'Richard.'

At that moment, she turned her head – I could distinctly see her crisp black curls bounce – and Richard Noble appeared behind her. He was fastening his shirt cuff.

I watched her protest, laughing, as he moved her away from the window and pulled one curtain over so the window was half covered. More modesty than security, I'd say. But then we were more voyeurs than a serious stake-out team.

All you could see of Charles was the end of his nose, radish-red in the cold, and his blue eyes peeping out from beneath his duffel-coat hood. I had my phoney sheepskin on over the top of every item of clothing I'd got with me, and I was still freezing, even tucked up in my snow-hole. The night porter was still on when we'd got up, but we'd managed to coax the flask of coffee off him for what we'd said was some early morning hill walking. With the barman's map, I'd had no trouble finding the place. It was only a twenty-minute drive. Across the highway, over the river, up along the road to Grand Cache, and then we'd swung up into what they called the wilderness country. As the dawn came, it wasn't hard to see why.

I parked where he'd marked it, and then we started the long haul up the mountainside. That was an hour up a steep track through the pine trees and, although there was enough light to see our way, with the loose snow over a foot deep we had to work to keep going. We walked bent double, sucking in pine-scented air that had never been breathed before, and when we got to the clearing, what we saw there made us both straighten up and stare.

Brother Richard had done himself proud. Brown Bear Ranch looked like an English country mansion built from timber.

Two-storey, long, low, it was constructed entirely from logs the size of telegraph poles. It had a central door – a vast studded affair – which opened onto a wide porch supported by four wooden columns. A verandah ran along the front of the house.

In front of the house there was a fenced paddock and to one side a tarred outbuilding. At the nearest point, the thick forest was no closer than two hundred yards, which meant that the house stood in two or three acres of clear parkland. For a nervous man, that must've been a good selling point.

Keeping in the trees, we skirted the clearing and worked our way further up the mountainside, so we could look on the house from a three-quarter view – to see both front and side. Then we tucked our clothes in wherever we could and settled down among the evergreens and the snow. By then, dawn was flickering in the sky. From a pale yellow streak, to rags of brown and pink, and finally a rose-gold fire which ascended the skies and showed us the world into which we'd climbed. We looked at it, open-mouthed. One by one, it lit up the mountains which ringed the valley we overlooked. Above the trees, the mountain tops rose sharp, steep and ragged, like clumsily sharpened pencils. The hard grey rock glowed a dim pink in the light, but the snow which lay in the gulleys and on the flanks and ledges soaked up the sky's blood. As the light grew clearer, we could

250

see a lake at the foot of the hills: it was the sort of crude blue-green that I'd last seen on the Gurkha Rose's eyelids.

The twentieth century hadn't touched the place. It was beautiful, it was remote, it was protected. A wilderness. Exactly what a man like Noble would be looking for.

'Not a bad li'l ol' place,' I said, but Charles made no reply. He'd be thinking about Anna, inside.

We were pushing our way through the stiff, brittle lower branches and ducking under the green springy ones when I saw it. On the edge of the tree-line, in the hollow beneath a broad pine branch, someone had made a shelter. I would never have seen it at all if I hadn't first spotted the fresh wood further up where branches had been snapped off. It was half snow-hole, half a lean-to made from boughs. The long thick branches had been leaned against the lowest bough of the tree and were now almost completely covered in snow.

'Animal's den?' Charles inquired, as I stooped to look in. It would only take one person, and I could see the packed snow where body heat had melted it before it again froze over. I slid in. The snow had been cleared away to give a clear view of the house. Whoever had gone to all this trouble must've been there for hours.

'I say, that's very handy,' Charles said. I don't think he read any more into it than that and I was wondering if I should say something when an upstairs light in the house came on. With the cold biting hard, and the wind just beginning to take the top powder off the snow, it looked warm and civilised.

'What now?' Charles was standing beside me as though he was on the touchline watching the school second fifteen.

'Get down, for Christ's sake. We watch.'

He knelt down beside me.

The way I saw it, Richard hadn't had time to tuck the money away into the financial system. I didn't think he'd be expecting anyone on his tail quite this quick and in any case he hadn't had time to do anything serious about locks and safes and guard-dogs. The thick end of two million quid was down there somewhere, and this would be when he was most vulnerable.

'Just watch?'

251

'Just watch.'

He crouched quietly after that, narrowing his eyes into the brightening light off the snow. Sunlight took the edge off the night cold, but our coffee had gone and I felt hollow with hunger. It wasn't helped when I picked out the kitchen on the side of the house and saw figures moving around: immediately I could taste bacon and egg and hot toast.

'Do we confront them now?'

'Shut up.'

Half an hour later, I heard a door slam. I got the glasses on the house quick. In the silence of that great bowl, silver snow polished gold by the sun, I could catch voices like the scratching of insects, distant but clear. From the back of the house, I saw two figures, one in a heavy-duty olive green anorak, the other in a fur built more for fashion than warmth, head down the hill.

'All clear, I dare say,' Charles said, rising.

'Get down.' I had to grab his sleeve to pull him down again.

We waited. We watched. We saw our breath plume in the icy air. Soon we could move.

'You know that brother of yours is likely to get a bit rough.'

Charles gave me a pitying look. 'He is my younger brother, you know. I do think I know how to handle him.'

I rose and beckoned him to get behind me as I made my way down the mountainside again, still behind the cover of the trees. When we got as close to the house as we could, we sprinted across the open ground to get there. I stuck Charles in an outbuilding at the side of the house – apart from some riding tackle it was quite bare – and left him there to keep watch while I went round to the back. First I emptied the two trash cans. Two or three tins clattered out. A carton of orange juice. Had they got into the Bucks' Fizz already? A packet of frozen plaice fillets. An empty box that had held a toy he must've bought in the model shop. Did Anna have a child somewhere? I'd have to ask Charles.

To get into the house itself, I used a stone to smash a pane in the front hall window, opened the window and hopped through. Easy as that. I was right: there was scarcely even average household security.

I started at the top and worked down. Discretion had gone now. All that mattered was speed. I ripped through the place as fast as I could. Even if he'd split it, the money wasn't something you could hide in a tea-caddy, which made my task easier. I went through the loft, then the master bedroom, the one I'd watched from the hillside.

Anna had begun to empty two matching Vuitton cases and one big shoulder bag into the fitted wardrobes. It was all clothes and hairbrushes and woman's personal stuff and the smell touched off fireworks in my memory. Richard's, one suit, jeans, sweater and four shirts, all cheap and all well-worn, were carefully folded in a scarred canvas hold-all. I flicked through quickly looking for the Smith, but all I found was a black plastic control panel for the model toy. I even checked the clothes, pockets and seams, and of course the collection of handbags that Anna had brought. Nothing.

After that, I went through the other bedrooms and bathrooms, all the drawers and cupboards and wardrobes, under the beds, behind radiators, under the baths and basins, inside cisterns and the linen and boiler cupboards. Then I moved downstairs, checking floorboards and looking on top of pelmets, under tables and shelves, and inside the oven, the microwave, the fridge, the freezer, the washer, the drier, the washing-up machine and even the toaster and the electric kettle which were still warm from their breakfast. I chucked out books and clothes and checked under all the loose floorboards.

Not a note. Not a penny. Not a damn thing.

Richard must be carrying it with him. All of it. Begrudgingly I decided that made sense. But I still went through the main sitting-room again.

It was a huge, beautiful room. One wall had a staircase and gallery that led on to the bedrooms, another was a vast window which looked out over the crude blue lake and the dazzling mountains, and the end wall was a brick chimney breast that was loaded with hunting trophies: black-eyed deer with high

253

antlers and cougars caught in mid-snarl. The floor was polished woodblocks covered with animal skins and it was only when I moved a flattened green-toothed wolf that I saw the trap door. I looked at my watch. I'd been searching for nearly an hour. It didn't matter. There was no going back now.

It was a yard square and I lifted it with the brass handle, a ring counter-sunk into a brass panel. As it opened, it belched stale cold air into the warm house, and I had the impression of an odd echo sound, and a glimpse of dancing lights in the black below.

I dropped to my knees and, one hand on either side of the hole, I lowered my face to look in. It was a cellar flooded almost to the brim. I lowered myself on to one hip so I could see in better. With my body to one side, to let in light, I could see the clear sheet of dark water, here and there skimmed with a fine skin of ice. Now I was closer I could see it was about a yard below the floor level. I stooped lower, to see and listen, but again there were only the dancing lights and eerie echo of my own breathing.

It wasn't a flood at all. It was a watertank, a winter's supply, kept beneath the house to stop it from freezing.

'Bathtime?'

I heard his voice as I felt his foot press hard on the small of my back. Hanging on the edge, It was only my right arm rigid against the far rim that prevented me from going in.

'Eight foot deep, must be fifty yards wide and thirty across,' Richard went on. 'How many hundred gallons is that?'

I didn't try to answer. He was increasing the pressure on my back so that I needed all my strength to keep myself from crashing through.

'And the only way out is through the taps. Fancy it, Hussy?'

'I showered already.'

He gave a sharp laugh, one kick of the heel to give me a last scare, and took his foot off. I spun away from the hole in case he changed his mind and flipped to my feet. I was aware of the speed of my heart.

He'd got the heavy jacket unzipped and was taking out some cigarettes. He lit one from a plastic lighter.

254

'Breaking training.'

'Out of training.' He tugged in a stream of escaping smoke, imprisoned it behind closed lips, then released it in a rush. 'For ever.'

He looked good. There was colour in his square face that hadn't been there in Liverpool and he had a touch of swagger about his shoulders. He didn't seem aware of the .38 that cluttered his left hand as he lifted the trap door and let it crash down. He glanced quickly out of the big window to his left and then back at me. This time he smiled.

'How the hell did you get here so quick?'

'Hit more ladders than snakes for once.'

'Why bring him along?' Anger tightened his mouth this time. 'Charles? He's supposed to be watching my back.'

'He was watching the path. I didn't come up the path.'

'Ah. Anna?'

'She'll be up in a few minutes. I told her to give me time to tidy up.'

I tapped the floor with my foot. 'Like tidying me down there, I suppose.'

He shrugged. His blue eyes vanished in smiling wrinkles. 'Maybe. What's your stake in this?'

I'd wondered that a few times since we flew into Canada. My country wanted its money and its traitor back. My employer, Charles, wanted his woman back. All I wanted was to give Jamie her self-respect back.

Without waiting for me to answer, Richard went on: 'You've got problems here, Hussy. Officially the Canadians won't want to know about me. Two million quid of Arab money gone missing and connections that run right from Tripoli to bloody Tehran . . . they could lose every third-world friend they've got by letting you take me back to London. And do you think Whitehall are going to thank you if you get this all over the front pages? Another British security cock-up, with the left wing saying Winston's death was a state assassination. They'd love that, oh yes, they'd really bloody love that. You only had one chance, Joe.'

'Which was?'

'Not finding me.'

I glanced down at the pistol. 'Which is tricky the way it's worked out.'

'Like I said, a problem. Unless you reckon you can get me back to London without anyone noticing. And you've no way at all of doing that.'

'You're wrong, Noble. I have two chances of getting you out.'

He frowned and I saw the short barrel of the pistol twitch. 'Two chances?'

'That's right. Fat chance. And no chance.'

He gave a soft laugh. 'That's about the way it is. Tell me, do you know if Koch carried on with his programme?'

'He didn't. I believe he lost confidence in the financial stability of his employers.'

A persuasive note came into his voice. 'What's the chance of convincing London that they came out of it well? One blocked revolution. Innocent lives saved. Goodbye Winston. It wasn't their money anyway.'

'Talking of money, and since I did help you to pack it in the first place, where is it now?'

'Invested. Answer my question.'

'Okay, I'd buy that and so would you, but you know the Unit won't have it. You know how it is, naughty boys must have their legs slapped, otherwise all other boys might be naughty too – that's rule number one, or somewhere up at the top of the list, isn't it?'

I could see him chewing the inside of his mouth as he thought and his eyes flickered around the room. But there was only one conclusion. I could've told him that.

He almost shouted it, his eyes suddenly wide in his face. 'I can't leave you taped up again, can I? What the fuck do I do, Joe? Tell me that. Down there – that's the only way.' He stamped on the floor.

'That's right. It's the little lead sleeping pill.'

He studied my face. After a few moments, more quietly he added: 'You think I won't. You think I can't. That's what you think, isn't it?'

'That's what I hope.'

What I did want to do was to make him think about it. Nervous, scared maybe, under pressure, it's fairly easy to kill someone if you don't think too much about what you're doing. That's how domestic murders happen. But we'd both been through the same academy, we'd been in the same club, and we'd heard the same words and thought the same thoughts. If I laid it out in front of him and forced him to look at what he was doing, maybe it wouldn't be so easy.

The pistol muzzle rose. Thoughtfully, he said: 'I don't want to do it, because if there are any good guys in this stinking world, then it's us. But you know how it is. I've done my turn. I'm getting out. If I have to lose you, I can. I can and I will.'

All the thoughts came in a rush. How stupid. To be shot simply because I was in the way. And by one of the good guys – because I was too much like Richard not to believe that too. I hadn't even got a gun I could try for, which might've made me feel vaguely heroic. I wouldn't get half way to his if I tried, so all I could do was to stand there and let it happen. I've often wondered how I'd go in the end, and sinking with the ship, saluting as the waves lapped round my knees, was never one of them. But that's the way it had to be. All those ideas cascaded through, along with the humiliating ordinariness of it all, but worst by far was the sudden memory of Jamie. Who the hell was going to dig her out with me gone?

'What will you do with Charles?'

His face hardened. 'I'll sort out bloody Charles, don't you worry. Lift the hatch.'

I hesitated. I mean, did he want me to dig my own damned grave? He spoke softly: 'Look, let's make it easy, eh? You lift the hatch, stand quite still, and I'll make sure it's a head shot. No mess. Fair enough?'

I still hesitated and I saw his tough face move into a frown of determination. As quickly it was wiped out by a look of amazement: eyes widened, eyebrows shot up, mouth gaped – but neither his gaze nor the gun moved off me.

'Shit.' His eyes switched in their sockets, trying to see behind him, then they came back to me. 'What the fuck is it? What's going on?'

From somewhere outside, out of sight of the window, a woman had called his name.

A shout. A scream almost. We faced each other, every sense fine-tuned, every nerve twitching.

The next time it was louder and clearer. 'Richard! Richard!' It was Anna. It had to be Anna.

# 35

The smooth soft pillows of snow had been trampled and flattened and the silence was a jumble of harsh cries and shouts. Between the house and the outbuilding, Charles and Anna were fighting. He had her by the left wrist, which he held with both hands as he tried to pull her towards the path. She was beating at him with her free hand as she tugged towards the house.

She was screaming for Richard and cursing Charles in hot teeth-clenched rage, while he tried to raise his head over her fist to reprimand her. As they kicked and stamped and slithered, the snow flew in the air and they breathed like dragons in the ice-clear air, so that the whole peaceful valley echoed to their fury.

Richard didn't have to tell me to go first – I know the rules when I'm the one without a gun – and he wasn't a yard behind me as I whirled out of the front door and round to the scene of the struggle. The two of them stopped when they saw us, Charles in his buttoned-up duffel-coat and Anna in her long silver fur froze like a couple of Arctic rock-and-rollers, and behind me I knew that Richard had halted at the corner of the house. He'd choreographed it so that all three of us were neatly grouped under his gun. That didn't seem to matter.

'Let her go,' I said, and I was surprised how hard I was breathing.

Anna looked from me to Richard and back again. She'd seen the gun, but she wasn't sure who was in charge. It was ridiculous: with death bubbling all around, I still found myself thinking how beautiful she was.

Against the piled white of the snow and skies, and her silver coat, the colours of her face were strong and clear: her eyes were bright black with danger, and flying snow rested in the angry black curls of her hair. I looked for fear in her face and saw only fury and resolution.

'Tell him,' she said, almost shouting, and twisting her body in her efforts to rescue her arm.

Charles hung on. Somehow he'd got hold of her wrist beneath the coat, with both his hands. Because he was so much taller, when they moved again she almost seemed to be dangling, like a child in a tantrum.

'Oh no you don't,' he said. And he even talked in one of those firm-but-fair voices that you hear from patient parents in supermarkets. But his face was a dark red and he panted with the effort.

'Jasus Christ, Charles, would you take your hands . . .' I touched his arm, only touched it, and he lashed out quickly with one hand, then as quickly put it back.

'Don't interfere, Hussy. I'm looking after Anna. If I don't she says she'll go with him.'

I rubbed my ear where his knuckles had caught me. 'She is with him, Charles. It's too late.'

At that she wriggled and squirmed but that seemed somehow to give him justification. 'Oh no you don't,' he said, grimly. To me, through gritted teeth he said: 'Never too late. I think you'll see that she'll come to her senses.'

At that, she lowered her head to look down and began to kick at his legs with her soggy brown leather boots. Charles skipped as he tried to avoid her attack, and with the two of them jerking about to hold their balance on the snow, it looked even more like a comic dance.

259

'Where the hell do you think you're taking her?' The harshness in Richard's voice blasted the false frivolity away.

Charles turned to face him. Anna stopped kicking.

'Home.'

'To Veronica?' There was a jeer in his voice too.

'No, we were going to find a place in Dorset . . .'

'You weren't. Never. You were dreaming.'

'Look, Richard.' Charles got a firm grip on Anna so he could concentrate on speaking to his brother. 'You have behaved absolutely despicably. You have betrayed every trust that has been put in you and now you have become a traitor. You have somehow blinded Anna into believing that you can give her happiness with the money you have stolen.'

He paused to swallow. Richard was watching him intently. Anna's face, expressionless, was turned up towards him. When he began again, his voice was still clear and confident. 'It won't work. It is dishonest money, criminal money soiled by the blood of others. I have a duty towards you, Richard, which I have always endeavoured to discharge. However, you now seem determined to place yourself beyond the pale. So be it. But not Anna. Before you say it, yes, I am perfectly aware that I am acting out of self-interest. I do want her for myself, that is true and I do not try to conceal it. But also I have a duty to save her from the consequences of your wickedness. You are still my brother. So she is coming with me.'

It was quite a speech. I'd never quite believed the things he'd said about honour, family, and duty, and once I'd realised that he was using me to get to Richard, I'd believed it less and less. But, in his own odd way, he did.

'Anna's my woman,' Richard said, in an ugly growl of a voice. 'That's why she came away with me. All the rest is just crap.'

'She loves me. You have tempted her with your stained money and your absurd heroics.'

'She's heard what you say. Let her go. If she believes you, she'll stay.'

'We . . . we are lovers.' Charles said that with a sort of puzzled pride, shaking his head as he spoke.

260

His brother's voice was filled with grating mockery. 'You pillock, you were just keeping the sheets warm. Hussy did too.'

It wasn't so much the shock of his knowing, or even saying it, as the way Charles turned his hurt boy's face towards me. 'That isn't true, is it?' In a righteous tone, he added: 'Not when you were in my employ, surely.'

Luckily I was saved having to reply by Anna. Again she began tugging at his arm. 'I won't go with you, Charles. I am not going anywhere with you.'

When Richard spoke this time it was in a low, hard voice that contained all the power he could find. 'Get out, Charles. Take your hands off her and get out. This is the last time.'

Charles raised himself so that he could look over Anna at his brother. It was between the two of them now. This was the one simple truth that lay at the bottom of all the deception and death. The two brothers. This was how it had been all their lives, and now, at last, it was out in the open and we all knew it would be ended here.

Charles had stopped panting and had gone pale and grave. Richard was bent, tense, with the gun in his right hand and his left out for protection, like we'd all been taught. The short-barrelled weapon shone like a new toy in his hand. Anna went still and her huge black eyes found mine: in the end, we were only the spectators. Perhaps that's all we'd ever been.

'Are you going to shoot me, Richard?' Under threat, Charles had a new dignity and authority.

'I'll shoot you, don't bloody worry about that. Unless you let her go.'

Charles stared at him, thinking, and when he spoke again it was a declaration of intent. 'Listen carefully,' he said – addressing his fourth-formers again. 'I am going to take Anna down to the car now. The only way you can prevent my taking this course of action is to shoot me, so I suggest you commence your arrangements now.'

Hoarse, urgent, Richard yelled: 'Get out of the way, Anna.'

With a look of contempt, Charles grabbed hold of her and swung her to the far side so that he presented a clear view of his

261

back to his brother. Then he began to walk, holding Anna in front of him.

'Shoot,' he called out, without turning. 'Father would've been very proud of you, Rich.'

It was the only time I'd heard Charles call him by a familiar name. Afterwards I wondered why it should come out then.

'Don't!' Anna squealed, and I caught a glimpse of her face, blown open in horror at the inevitability of what was happening. 'Stop them, Joe.' Then her voice subsided in sobs.

Richard spread his legs and raised the gun in both hands. I saw him adjust it down for the kick.

Then I spoke. 'No.'

'Don't balls me up, Joe.'

'You don't shoot him. Not your brother.' Four scampered steps had got me covering Charles' back with mine. I faced Richard and the gun, and neither of them was wavering.

'You're in the way.'

'You can't have him.'

I backed through the snow to keep me close to Charles as he struggled along, with Anna enfolded in his long arms, in his retreat. I could hear his breathing and Anna's sobs, but I kept my face to Richard. I couldn't let him shoot his brother. That's all there was to it. Stooping, shaking the revolver to try to move me, Richard moved after us.

'I'm not counting five or bloody three or anything. You first, then him. Got that?'

'You can't.' That was all I could say. 'You can't shoot your brother.'

'You, Hussy. I mean you. Then him.'

He stopped, bent his knees, straightened his arms and I held my breath, waiting to see if he had enough anger or love or whatever it took to kill his brother. I still didn't know which way he'd go. All I could do was to wait for the snapping stick sound. It came exactly as I expected it. Only it sounded far away, and it was followed by the muffled bump of a rifle.

Richard dropped the Smith and put his hands to his chest like a Victorian soprano. He looked at me in an odd way that was part reproach, part admiration, and then he lowered his eyes and saw what I'd seen. Where his green waterproof hung open, the front of his chest had been blown open. When he opened his hands, they were filled with blood and mush where the bullet had come out.

Charles and Anna had halted and turned to watch the dreadful sight. Unbelievingly, Richard studied the dripping crimson contents of his hands. He made an attempt to move round to see where the shot had come from but it was beyond him. Instead he lifted his face and stared at me. His face moved in a wince of a smile.

'Where's your mate, Joe? I didn't know you had a mate. You bastard.'

With his limbs locked as stiff as sticks, still nursing his own guts in his hand, he crashed forward face down in the snow. After a moment, his body jack-knifed, as though snapped by one last surge of pain, then he straightened out with a grunt. As we watched, his right hand crept slowly over the snow, stopped and clenched tight. Suddenly, the fingers opened and from them fell a small, hard snowball. It was bright red. He was dead.

From his fallen figure, I raised my eyes. There was a man walking down the open hillside from the forest. If it hadn't been for the golf bag I would never have recognised him.

It was Koch with his Dragunov under his arm.

Together, Anna and Charles went over to Richard. I suppose they had tributes to pay or goodbyes to say, the lover and brother, and I was sorry to see his lifeless body in the snow. But that was the business we were in – crossing the cemetery without falling into graves; he'd taken the most dangerous route of all, and he'd slipped. Right now I was busy watching my own footwork. I stood watching Koch march down the hillside. When he got within shouting distance, he raised one hand. 'Nobody shoots my friend the pieman.' His laughter rang around the valley, and when he came up to us, he halted and looked around at all three of us. 'Okay, I wanna know, who got my pension?'

He asked the same question when he got us back inside the house and his thin hawk face was darkened by black stubble.

263

Charles, who hadn't shown a second's fear in front of his brother, was a different man now he had seen death in all its meaningless mess. He couldn't take his eyes off Koch. I don't suppose he'd ever met anyone who regarded a human being as just so much meat. Anna was less frightened. Her eyes moved from Koch to me, trying to see which way it was going; behind all that gentle breeding, there was an awful lot of animal instinct.

'I tell you,' he said, shivering as he leaned against the chimney breast, 'bloody cold. I like sun. Sun, not goddam bloody snow.'

Somewhere he'd managed to get equipped. He was wearing a white snow-suit and a stocking-hat which he'd rolled up above his eyes. Even though I'd told him that Charles and Anna were spectators, it didn't relax him. I noticed when he took his gloves off, he was careful to keep his rifle ready to go. It was fair enough. In his world, all men were potential enemies. Yet I didn't feel there was any edge between the two of us. He'd saved my life, but only because he knew he'd have to eliminate Richard anyway – and it was understood between us that he'd kill me as easily if he had to. That's how he stayed a superstar so long. But I wasn't too worried. Men in his trade never kill for fun or out of temper. He killed only out of necessity, and if we gave him no cause, and he got what he wanted, we were safe. The problem was: could we give him what he wanted?

But first he had some questions about Richard. 'That guy, he was a traitor. He steal my pension, you know.' He sounded mildly irritated.

'He was more of a traitor than you know. He was one of ours.'

His eyebrows rode up. 'An agent?'

'That's right.'

A mellow pleasant laugh burst from him. 'That is funny. You are saying he was spying on Winston and Rich Pickings and he run away with the money.'

'He did the job first.'

He gave a murmur of approval. 'He did. Winston, Rich Pickings, whoosh.' He moved his hand in a downward slide. 'So. Now, my pension.' His quick eyes flicked round the three of us. Charles, who was standing with both arms round Anna as though to support and protect her, looked at me.

'The money,' I explained. To Koch I said: 'You should know better than us. How long were you up there?'

'One and a half day.'

'I saw your snow-hole.'

He looked puzzled. 'Not mine. I stay in mine. I watch you come. With this guy here.'

That made me wonder for a moment, but not for long.

'Hussy, I know you, you know me. We trade before. Tell me where the money is, I go. No hassles, eh? No hassles.'

'That's what I mean. You saw a lot more than we did. You ought to know where it is.'

He examined my face for a full minute before giving a small sigh. Water had formed a pool around his boots. He'd been on the mountain all night but you might think he'd been for a stroll around the garden.

'We ask the woman.'

'I don't know where he put it.' Anna answered so quickly she must've been waiting for the question. This time the two of us examined her face, and Charles' arm tightened around her shoulders.

Koch shot me a quick glance then turned to her. 'You run away with him but he keep money secret? You buy that, Hussy?'

He didn't, there was no doubt about that.

'Tell him where it is, Anna.'

'I told you, I don't know.' Chin up, she glared at me.

Koch made an impatient clicking noise with his mouth. He flicked a glance at the ceiling, adjusted the Dragunov in his right arm, and then spoke to me. 'Explain,' he said. I knew what he meant.

'If she says she doesn't . . .'

'Shut your face, Charles. Anna, this gentleman here has followed you six thousand miles for the money. He's not about to leave without it.'

Almost angrily, she snapped: 'And I've just told you I have no idea where he hid it.'

Koch was looking down at the rifle. I wondered how much of this he'd listen to before he started his own inquiries.

'Listen, Anna. Listen to what I say. Trust me. Koch knows that I don't know where the money is, because he was here before me. The same goes for Charles. But you were with Richard and he knows that too. If you don't tell us where it is, there's only one thing he can do. Save yourself a lot of pain.'

In the dark depths of her eyes, I could see so many levels of meaning and understanding that I couldn't begin to interpret them. With her arms under the heavy fur, she hugged herself, and shook her head so that the melting snow flew off in a glittering spray.

'He did not let me see. Honestly.'

I opened my hands to both her and the German. 'It's your life.'

Koch coughed and raised his face. His stone eyes fixed on her eyes. In her life, a lot of men had looked at her in many ways, but no man had ever looked at her like that before. I could hear the noisy nervousness of her breath when she spoke again.

'I have an idea what he may have done with it.'

Koch sighed again and ran one finger along the wooden butt of his gun. He was not concerning himself with any of these minor negotiations.

'I think that's why he bought the model,' she said.

The minute she said that it all fell into place. With Koch's permission, I ran upstairs and got the control panel. It was printed on the top. 'The Mississippi Belle, scale model of one of the historic old paddle-steamers of America.' I lifted the hatch to the water tank and once more it was like opening a coffin. I lay down to get a better angle, so that I could see at least a few feet across the black shining surface of the water beneath the house. Then I concentrated on the control panel in my hand.

I've never been any good with toy models. When the other boys were playing with them, I was practising rolling cigarettes and undoing bra-fasteners with one hand in the dark. But this looked easy enough – a slim black box, with two silver levers in the middle which moved around like a gear-stick for different functions. Even I couldn't cock this up, surely?

I moved one lever towards F, presumably for Forward, and tilted my head towards the opening to listen for results. Nothing. Christ. I pushed it over to R, which I assumed meant Reverse. Again nothing. I tried again, first one then the other. Still nothing.

I could feel the eyes of the other three drilling into me. I couldn't bring myself to look at them. 'Are you sure about this?' I asked, and I was surprised to hear my voice so hoarse. Anna's reply was no comfort. 'I don't know,' she said. 'I never said I was sure.'

The more I thought about it, the crazier it began to sound. Swearing softly to myself, I tried the other lever. That was marked for left and right, although I didn't see how I could steer something that wasn't moving – and probably wasn't even there. Inevitably, nothing.

Koch made that regretful clicking noise again. 'See – no good. You're wrong.' If I was wrong, Koch would ask Anna in his own way. I didn't like to think what that might mean.

I had another go. This time I moved both levers together. From the yawning mouth of the hatch, there was only the echo of a damp silence, and my own ragged breathing.

'What's that?' Anna bent down and turned the control panel so that I saw a button on the side. I pressed it. While she was bending down beside me, she whispered close to my ear. 'Remember – I go with the money.'

What did she mean? I was concentrating so intently on getting the controls to work that her message – whatever it meant – threw my mind into a spin. Then, through the hatch, came the sound I'd been hoping for: the faint, distant but distinct sound of splashing. I was right. We'd found the Mississippi Belle.

I pushed the lever to the Forward position. From beneath there came a scraping sound. It must be up against the side of the tank. What if it sank? I'd found her all right, but how did I get her back? I steered to the left. I listened, then steered to the right. More scratching sounds, so I quickly moved it to the left again.

Below, where the light shone, tiny waves corrugated the

surface of the inky water. Slowly the splashing became stronger and more regular, drawing all three of us around the hatch, until at last the Mississippi Belle, its paddles turning steadily, rode out of the echoing emptiness and into the light. At that moment, the bell above the ship's bridge rang out twice. No marooned sailor was ever happier to see a ship, I can tell you.

It was about three foot long and half that again in height, and I had to lie down and use both hands to get it out of the water. All around me I could feel their excitement as I set it dripping on the floor. It was a lovely thing – all gaudy colours, flags and bunting, and on the foredeck at the front of the superstructure, toy bandsmen played tiny trumpets to an equally tiny audience.

I brushed them all aside as I gripped my finger ends around the top of the housing and held the hull of the boat between my feet. It came free with a jerk that almost threw me backwards.

The money had been packed so tight it spilled out over the wooden floor. Twenty stacks of fifty-pound notes, each one about six inches deep, tipped out, heaped and tumbled in front of us. It looked a lot of money. It looked a lot of trouble too. How many deaths had it taken to get those neat notes fastened into their tight bands? And how many more? One of them was out there in the snow. With a quick stab, I remembered how we'd talked about spoiled romantics: now here we were fighting and dying for this money, but we were the real brothers. Richard, Koch and me.

'Two million pounds.' Koch dropped to his knees and reached out one finger to touch it. He lifted his face to mine and his grin had squeezed his eyes to slits. 'Some pension, hey Hussy? Better than a schoolteacher, I reckon.'

Maybe it was the sight of the money, or maybe the thought of the freedom it would buy him, that made him careless for that one minute. Out of the corner of my eye, I saw Anna pull back, but he was too busy touching the stiff notes and shaking his head.

'Drop the rifle.'

His eyes rose to mine and I watched his smile sink back into his face like water into sand. With great care, he laid the

Dragunov on the floor beside him, and moved around so that he could see Anna. She'd got to her feet and was standing, holding the Smith in both hands. It was cocked. The safety was off. And she was as steady and composed as she was the day she'd held out the Bucks' Fizz to me. That was all we needed to know.

'Joe.' You could hear the thrill in her voice, but it was under control. Christ, but she had good nerves.

'Yeah.'

'I told you. I go with the money.'

'I heard you.'

'Well?' She never once moved her gaze from Koch, who was still kneeling on the floor. 'Do you want us?'

'Us?'

'Me and the money.'

There was a gasp and the sound of movement as her words registered with Charles. 'Anna, darling, surely . . .'

'Quiet, Charles. You heard what I said. What do you say, Joe?'

I looked at the wads of notes piled on the floor. I looked at her exquisite face, skin glowing and eyes shining, framed in the fur of her collar.

'If I take the two million, I've got to take you too?'

Her lips tightened. 'That's what I am saying.'

'Ah well.' I looked around them all. 'There's always a snag in everything. What'll I put the cash in?'

She damn near smiled and risked a quick glance at me. 'My shoulder bag, beside the chair.'

It was one of those overnight cases. I unzipped it and began to load the money. I tried to keep an eye on the other two men. Charles stood bolt upright with his mouth open. He couldn't take in what was happening. Koch's face had closed down; whatever he was thinking wasn't on display.

'What about the German?'

The bag was full. I zipped it up and rose with it in my hand. 'Koch? We have to lose him.'

'Kill him?' She wasn't afraid to face it.

'Unless you want to spend the rest of your life looking over your shoulder. I told you, he won't give up.'

Koch had been studying Anna but once he saw how steady she was he moved his gaze to me. He nodded his head to where Richard lay outside. 'I save your life. You know that. When I shoot him, I save you.'

'That's true. The way things turn out, it was a mistake.'

He chewed his bottom lip in thought. 'Okay, we share the money. One million each. Good, eh?'

I shook my head. 'No, Koch. You'd look silly in a nightie.'

'One million, you buy a lot of girls.'

'Not like her you don't.' I gave Anna a cheeky little wink. 'Ready?'

Minute signs of doubt moved her face. Mouth hardening, eyebrows tensing, eyes narrowing. I hardly dared breathe.

'Put a couple into his chest,' I said, and casually hitched the bag up over my shoulder.

I thought she was going to for a minute. Then, moving her head towards me but keeping her eyes on Koch, she said what I'd been praying she would. 'I don't think I can, Joe. Will you do it?'

I gave an understanding chuckle. 'Okay. Careful when you hand it over.'

I stepped over towards her, keeping out of the line of fire. From behind her elbow, I slid my hand in and took the revolver. All the time Koch's eyes were on the gun, but it never shook, and there was never a moment when there wasn't a finger on the trigger. I waited until Anna moved across the room and turned to face out of the window. If she had to, she could shoot a man. But if it wasn't necessary then she'd rather not watch.

'Now, Joe,' she said, in a soft feminine voice.

'Fine,' I said, 'here goes.'

'You bastard, Hussy. One bloody minute there, I think maybe you kill me.' His voice bubbled with relief and delight.

Anna spun round. She saw Koch with the gun in his hand. She saw me sliding the bag off my shoulder and handing that over to him too.

'Why? Why on earth did you do that, Joe?'

All along I knew that was what I wanted, but I hadn't tried

to analyse my motives. Maybe because we were two of a kind. Maybe because it was bloodstained money. Maybe because if it belonged to anyone, then it belonged to him. I wasn't sure, and it wasn't anything I could explain to Anna, then or any other time.

'You got to watch that money stuff, Anna. Too much of it and it can get to change your personality – you know, like drink.'

It wasn't really what I meant but it wasn't all that far off either. Anna's face didn't move.

'When you did that, you gave me away too.'

I shrugged. 'I thought perhaps that was the way of it.'

The two of us stood looking at each other across the room. One by one, all the things that might have happened between us died like dreams in the daylight. She turned and looked out of the window again.

Koch had opened the case again and was fishing inside. He pulled out a pack of the notes. 'Here. I said half. You can have your million.'

I shook my head. Weariness was running through my veins now. 'No thanks. Take it. On your way.'

'Good for you, Hussy.' Charles' face swam up into my vision. Pink and eager and nodding with enthusiasm. If he thought I was right, that really was worrying.

'You sure?' Koch was holding the wad over the bag and when I nodded he dropped it back in and zipped it up again.

From the window, the three of us watched him climb the hill, the golf bag over one shoulder, the money bag over the other. It was snowing heavily again, and long before he reached the trees his white-suited figure had vanished from sight.

'I could telephone the police,' Charles said, with a glance at me.

'No, you couldn't,' I said, and that was the end of that.

Charles helped me to take Richard's body up into the trees and bury it in the snow-hole where I'd laid up. The snow covered him quickly. He wouldn't be found until the spring. Even then, no one would be in a hurry to claim him. He'd signed himself off everybody's team.

With his hands clasped and his head down, Charles stood

over the stamped-down snow of his brother's grave. Yet again, I found myself wondering about the two of them.

He said nothing until we were walking back down. 'Do you know, Hussy, I've been thinking. You remember when Richard was threatening me and I turned my back? Well, I am quite confident that he never intended to shoot me. He would never have killed his own brother. You do realise that, don't you?'

'I do.' If that was what he wanted to tell himself, I wasn't going to spoil it. We all have our own fairy tales.

'Incidentally, Hussy, I realise that you and I haven't always seen eye to eye over this business, but I would like you to know that I admired the stand you took when that German fellow tried to bribe you. You are a man of principle.'

'We're all men of principle, Noble. The question is, which bloody principle?

# 36

Too much had happened for the three of us to be easy in each other's company.

Anna had lost her man and her future. That was enough to shake anyone, and on top of that she'd offered herself, and been rejected. I don't suppose anyone had ever turned her down before, particularly when she came with a cash bonus, and it all must've been hard for her to bear. Whatever there had been between us was over. She ignored me.

Charles hung around her, fussing and cossetting her as we made our way back to the car, and once inside he held her in his arms. I couldn't see what she thought of that. She certainly didn't collapse on him, which was what he probably hoped for. Instead, she sat upright, her face as expressionless as marble.

I couldn't stand it. Not his slavering, her indifference, or the pain in my heart when I looked at the two of them. I took the car and drove off into the Rockies for the rest of the day. I drove, I looked at the mountains, I wondered where Koch was now and where he was heading for. Men of principle. Christ, the only man of principle among us was Winston, and look where it got him. But at least he'd been playing the same game as the rest of us, with the same risks. Poor little Kesharsing had been a passer-by who got dragged into the whole damned mess. He was an innocent. But innocence and principles don't make good armour.

I left it till late when I returned to the motel. There was a light in Charles' room and I could hear low voices that could've been him and Anna, or maybe the television. It was none of my business now. He'd left a note on my bed to say he'd booked us back on a flight the next afternoon.

I went to bed and I was out the second I hit the sack. Only that sort of sleep can restore you after a mental and physical pounding and I gladly gave in to it.

The first scream snapped me upright in bed with the hair rising at the back of my neck. The second almost took the top off my head. I was out of my room and through the open door into Charles' when the third one came. Anna was sitting up in bed wide-mouthed and she never even saw me come in. Her eyes were fixed on the figure in the next bed.

At first sight I thought Charles was laughing. Then I saw the gaping mouth was too low. It was beneath his chin, where his throat had been slashed open. It took only a second to see that his neck was half-severed: larynx, carotid arteries, jugular, it had got the lot, and the bed was swimming in blood. His head was flopped back so far that he was almost facing the wall behind him. He was naked. I checked his hands: no wounds, so he hadn't had a chance to defend himself.

Anna screamed again. It was a shrill, high blast of noise that was enough to shake your sanity. She too was naked, but for once that didn't matter. She was kneeling up on the bed with both hands pushing knuckles into her mouth between screams and her eyes were halfway out of her head.

273

Outside I could hear voices and footsteps. I grabbed Anna's fur coat from the back of a chair and bundled her into it just as other people started arriving. While the police were coming, I got her to myself for a moment in my room. She had seen nothing. She had heard something – perhaps a groan – and had woken up. She saw the door was open, put the light on at the bedside switch, and then saw Charles.

I held her in my arms, but it was only out of warmth and pity.

'Was it that German? Did he come back to kill Charles?' Her voice was no more than a whisper.

'No. It wasn't him.'

She looked at me oddly. 'Do you know who did it?'

'I think so.'

I wasn't completely sure until late the next afternoon when the police started getting their reports together. The significant thing was that it wasn't the usual tentative, clumsy stabbing. This was a professional job by a man who knew how to use a knife. The wound had been caused by one decisive blow from a broad-bladed weapon that had been exceptionally sharp. They could find no fingerprints, and he'd stuck to the trodden paths so there were no footprints either.

There was one possibility. At first, they thought there was no chance of witnesses – it was five in the morning. But then a truck driver who'd been passing on the main road said he'd seen someone moving along the shadows, and as he rounded a bend his lights had picked out the passer-by.

It was a woman. The cops went to great lengths to explain that they only wanted to see her as a possible witness. No woman would have the strength or skill to inflict such a wound – it had been done with one slash of the knife – but they thought she might have seen something or someone that would give them a lead.

What made it even more hopeful was that the woman shouldn't be too hard to find. Because, according to the truck driver, she was either in some sort of long evening dress, which meant she was maybe going home from a party, or it was an Asian woman in a sari. Whichever she was, the driver had the impression she was quite something to look at.

I remembered the pleas of the little Gurkha when he gave me the pouch of letters in the car park. I remembered his face at the top of the Sussex cliffs when they brought up his friend's body. I remembered Veronica saying someone was watching her house. I remembered the little Asian woman in the bar where I'd found the Big Boy's Milkshakes. I remembered the snow-hole on the hillside that I thought had been left by Koch. I remembered the *maruni* dancer who made such a beautiful woman. And the kukri that could behead a goat.

We weren't allowed to leave until a week later, and the vital woman witness still hadn't come forward then. I made the long flight back alone. Anna appeared briefly at my bedroom door to tell me that she was going to Montreal to visit some friends, and then she'd make her own way back to London. We knew too much about each other now ever to be comfortable together.

There was a moment then when we said goodbye that I thought I saw something in her eye, but it was gone before I could think of any words. Then she was gone too, her black curls bobbing in the crowd.

I had three women to see, but first I had to phone Cringle. I leaned against the wall in the arrivals hall at Heathrow, listening to what he was saying and wondering how we'd managed to turn the world upside down: he was content that our own man was safely dead, and that the international terrorist had vanished with all the money. This way, neither of them could cause any embarrassment, and that was the main thing. Jesus, we wouldn't want difficult questions in the House, now, would we?

'As you suggested, I contacted Captain Adams at Church Crookham. You were quite correct. Rifleman Bhimbahadur had taken compassionate leave due to a family bereavement. Up in Bradford in Yorkshire apparently. He has relatives there. He returned three days ago, and has applied for a posting back to Hong Kong, again for family reasons.'

'How is he?'

'Adams said he had been very depressed since the suicide of a friend, but he now appeared to be greatly cheered.'

'He would be.'

In carefully chosen words, clearly spoken, Cringle asked: 'Is this something we need to look into?'

I replied without thinking. 'No. Nothing in it for us.' Then I did think about it, and I knew I'd given the right answer.

If Richard hadn't taken his woman, Charles wouldn't have hounded him like that. If Charles hadn't been so afraid of losing her, he wouldn't have set up the charade that led to the Gurkha's death. They couldn't leave each other alone, and in the end it had cost both of them their lives. Like everything that happened between the two brothers, their deaths did contain its own crazy logic.

'Quite sure?'

'Yeah, I'm sure.'

His voice changed. 'By the way, I got your message.'

'Message?'

'Yes.' I recognised the tone he was using: it was his neutral mode. 'What was it now? Something about dabbling in my life, I believe.'

Somewhere there'll be a rule book that says it's a serious offence for the likes of me to threaten the likes of him, and what happens to those who try it.

'I remember. There's something I'd like to say about that, sir.'

'I thought you might.'

'I meant it.'

After a moment's silence, I heard him say: 'From you, Hussy, any other reply would have been a profound disappointment.'

I thought of that as I drove down towards the Downs, and I still wasn't quite sure what to make of it. It was mid-morning. The night frost was still bright in the hedges and the fields, so that the English countryside looked like a woman who'd turned silver without losing her beauty. That reminded me of Anna, and again I felt the empty chasm in my gut.

Caroline was unsaddling a big grey in the yard. I kept well back from the clanging steel hooves and rolling pop eyes, until a stablehand led it away. This time she didn't lead me into the

276

house. Instead, she took me down to the gate and I found myself looking down the road where I'd first seen Winston as we passed in our cars.

'I have had official notification,' she said. Beneath the fresh-air pink, her face was strained and her eyes were tight from not sleeping. 'In Canada, I gather.'

'That's right.'

'Another job for Liz and Phil?' She gave a small painful smile and added: 'Let's hope they appreciate it.'

'Let's.'

She took off her riding hat and shook out her fair hair just as she had that first time. I saw she was nibbling her bottom lip as we both stood there in silence, and I realised then that she was keeping her distance from me.

'Do you remember when I told you that I didn't mind about losing Richard?'

I nodded.

'About always knowing that one day he'd go and how lucky I was to have known him anyway?' She didn't wait for another nod. 'I didn't mean it, you know.' The next sentence she spoke with an ironic twist of the face. 'I was trying to be, well, a good sport about it, I suppose.'

'That's what I thought.'

She looked at me in a thoughtful sort of way. 'Yes, I thought you realised. Would it surprise you to know that I would very much have liked to have killed that other woman?'

'That's how people do feel, I suppose.'

She turned round and looked at the house and the hill behind it, and then shortened her gaze to me. The intimacy between us had been wiped out. Once again, I was someone who knew too much: an embarrassing hangover from other times.

'In the end, I suppose I won.'

I couldn't think what she meant, but she explained it before I asked.

'I mean, officially at least, I am the widow. That's all there is left to fight over.'

The bitterness of her own thoughts was too much for her then, and I saw her eyes swim with tears. Quickly she moved her head, but there was all the old softness in her voice when she spoke again.

'For God's sake, Joe, please go.'

I could hear her heart breaking all the way back to the car.

The second Widow Noble was sitting in the living room of the School House smoking as Stephens, the smoker I'd covered for, showed me in.

'Ah, Mr Hussy the bodyguard,' she said, the minute I stepped into the room.

'I hope you're not . . .'

She dismissed all that with one wave of her hand. 'You need not concern yourself, no one will blame you, I can assure you.'

The room was cold but Veronica didn't seem to feel it. She was wearing a high-necked black dress, whether out of chance or convention I couldn't say, and her hair was still half up on top, half trailing in tails. If anything, she looked better than when I'd last seen her. The hysteria had gone completely, and left her with a weird quality of stillness.

'It was Richard's fault, of course.' Her eyes examined my face for evidence.

'I'm sure that wasn't . . .'

Again she waved my protest down. 'Oh, you'll deny it, all of you. The police told me I'm mistaken, and so did the Ministry of Defence when I telephoned them, but I know perfectly well that that's the truth.'

'I don't think they'd mislead you.'

She raised her eyebrows. Her face was pale but composed. 'What – that some criminal burst into Charles' room and murdered him? Frankly I think that's an insult to my intelligence.'

Frankly, so did I. 'Wasn't the man looking for money or something . . .'

Again she cut in. 'Charles was trying to get Richard out of some scrape or other, we both know that, Mr Hussy. It was bound to happen one day. I told him, I told Charles, but you know what he was like about family loyalty.'

'Yes, I know.'

She hurriedly stubbed out a half-smoked cigarette in an ashtray that was already overflowing. It continued to smoke, but she drew another from a packet and waited while I lit it for her.

'Thank you.' She drew on it deeply and then asked the question I'd been dreading. 'Was that woman there?'

Knowing that Charles had told her, I didn't have much choice. 'Yes.'

'What was she like?' She kept her eyes down, watching the smoke curl up from her cigarette.

'Difficult to say, really.' Impossible to say, when I was talking to Veronica. But again it wasn't really an answer that she wanted.

'The usual barmaid type, I believe,' she said. 'That's what you men like, isn't it?'

'That's the way it usually goes, I dare say.'

'That's by the way. Because, you might be interested to hear, Charles spoke to me the night before he died. He told me the whole thing had been a ghastly mistake and he was coming back to me.'

She lifted her eyes to mine, daring me to deny it. For a moment I thought about the brothers, and the damage they'd done to each other and everyone around them.

I took a deep breath. 'He said as much to me.'

She rose and pushed her new cigarette into the ashtray, and then pulled her shoulders back and faced me. 'So you see, the whole thing was no more than a minor hiccup.'

'The very phrase he used to me,' I said, and I saw the gratitude in her eyes. Well, she needed something to keep her warm on the lonely nights.

When I got back to the garage, at first I couldn't find Jamie anywhere. I looked in the MoT bay and the house before I saw her, on her hands and knees down by the hedge. She scrambled to her feet when she saw me coming and she started to say something, but I waved the long white envelope at her.

'Patrol car just dropped this off,' I said.

She was holding a trowel, and she handed it to me while she opened the envelope that Cringle had left for me to pick up at the airport. I was so scared that she might have a heart attack or something that I never gave the trowel a thought.

Ten years fell from her face. 'Joe,' she shouted, her flat face lighting up with delight. 'Hellfire, you'll never believe it!'

'Believe what?'

'It was a mistake. The shoplifting. Look here, the police say the woman witness now realises she was mistaken . . . no charges will be made . . . sincere apologies.'

She stepped forward and allowed me to give her a big hug. 'Great, Jamie. That's really great. No more worries, eh?'

I looked down and her face was covered in dirty streaks where she was brushing away the tears. Her hands were covered in soil as well as the usual oil.

'Bit early for gardening, isn't it?'

Instantly, she stopped her laughing and crying. 'Oh, Joe,' she said, 'you'll be that upset.' And she pointed at the bank beneath the hedge. Among the grass and debris, I saw a patch of clear, level, fresh black soil.

On a neatly sawn rectangle of plywood, which was jabbed into the earth, I read his name. She'd gone over it several times in ballpoint to make it legible. Charlie.

'He were out like a flash. Straight under a car on the forecourt. Oh, Joe. Don't you worry about shedding a tear. I shed a few myself.'

Charles and Charlie. They'd come into my life together, and they left together. After all I'd seen in those six weeks, you might've thought the death of a hedgehog would hardly matter. But it did, as though all the rest had been just as petty and pointless.

Standing there, arms round each other, we hadn't heard a car slide up to the pumps until a voice called out. 'Is it actually possible to have any service round here?'

'Service? I'll give him bloody service,' Jamie growled. As she set off, she raised her voice. 'Aye, and it's actually possible to get your bloody earhole belted an' all.'